BLIND
PILOT

BY

AMBROSE CLANCY

WILLIAM MORROW AND COMPANY, INC.
New York 1980

Words and music of "I Don't Like Mondays" by Bob Geldorf. © 1979 by Sewer Fire Hits/Zomba Management and Publishers; © 1979 by Zomba Enterprises.

Library of Congress Cataloging in Publication Data

Clancy, Ambrose, 1948-
   Blind pilot.

   I. Title.
PZ4.C5868Bl [PS3553.L237]   813'.54   80-10761
ISBN 0-688-03640-6

Printed in the United States of America

First Edition

1 2 3 4 5 6 7 8 9 10

for
Mary Lydon

The author wishes to acknowledge the generous help given to him by Margaret Catherine Clancy, Helmut Meyer, Maria Guarnaschelli, Elizabeth Regina Clancy, the late Peadar MacGiolla Cearr, and the people of Ireland.

See, blind pilot, what you've done.
You've lost my lady and my son.
If you'd let my ship alone,
I'd have saved my lady on Inishtrahull.
          ANONYMOUS, *The Isle of Ships*

Men of action, when they are without faith,
have never believed in anything but action.
          ALBERT CAMUS, *The Rebel*

IRELAND

IRLANDE   IERLAND   IRLAND   IRLANDA

RATHLIN ISLAND

SCOTLAND

Ballycastle

Derry

DONEGAL

Malinmore

DERRY

ANTRIM

FROM ARDROSSAN
FROM LIVERPOOL

TYRONE

Belfast

DOWN

BENWEE HEAD

FERMANAGH

ARMAGH

LEITRIM

MAYO

SLIGO

MONAGHAN

LOUTH

Dundalk

INISHBOFIN

ROSCOMMON

LONGFORD

CAVAN

IRISH
SEA

SLYNE HEAD

WESTMETH

MEATH

ATLANTIC
OCEAN

GALWAY

The Burin

FROM LIVERPOOL
FROM HOLY HEAD

CLIFFS OF MOHER

Ennistymon

CLARE

OFFALY

Kildare   Naas

KILDARE

DUBLIN

Dublin

Ennis

Portlaoise

Shannon

LAOIS

CARLOW

WICKLOW

Limerick

TIPPERARY

KILKENNY

WEXFORD

LIMERICK

BLASKET ISLANDS

KERRY

WATERFORD

Youghal

FROM FISH GUARD

CORK

Cork

ST. GEORGES CHANNEL

Kinsale

LE HAVRE CHERBOURG

BANTRY BAY

OLD HEAD
OF KINSALE

Daniel Pearala

IRISH SPEAKING AREAS

I

CHAPTER 1

The Raid at Kildare

Phil Coughlin, chief mechanic for Mountjoy Jail, Dublin, was in the long shed teaching James, the new apprentice, the proper method of replacing brake shoes on a lorry. He noticed the boy looking over his shoulder. "A visitor, Mr. Coughlin." Phil turned to see young Raymond Murray walking toward him. "Now, get along with it," Phil said to James and, wiping his hands, went to meet his visitor. "Dull day for a drive, Mr. Murray."

Murray put out his hand in greeting, a trait he had picked up last summer in the States. "Do you have the Fords ready?"

"I do," Phil said.

"Tuned?"

"They are, sir."

"Petrol?"

"And the tires checked and the boy gave 'em a good washing this morning when he came in. They're just outside, will you have a look?"

"No, that's fine."

"You can tell your man he'll have a nice safe ride," the mechanic smiled.

Murray nodded. Cheeky little brat, Phil thought.

"I won't need them until three-thirty, Phil."

"Right you are, Mr. Murray. Half-three it is. I'll make the change on the order."

Murray adjusted his tie at the throat. "You'll bring them round yourself?"

"I will."

Murray turned and walked out of the shed. After telling James he was taking an early lunch, Phil went out into the gray November morning, through the security checks, on his way to a public house in Munster Street where he had his regular lunch, a ham sandwich and a bottle of lemonade, at his regular spot near the fire.

When he finished half his sandwich, Phil went to the rear of the pub where he dialed a telephone number. A man answered, Phil pressed the "A" button and said, "They're movin' him at half-three."

"Half-three."

"Not one, now."

"Right. Half-three."

Phil hung up the phone and went back to his lunch.

At 7 A.M. that morning they were all awake and dressed in the bright, modern kitchen of the house just outside Kinsale, County Cork. It was still night outside with dawn another hour away. Deirdre and Gudrun were well rested but O'Connor had slept only an hour or two. Gudrun prepared a huge meal of thick steaks and fried eggs, brown bread, jam and pots of coffee. The two women ate eagerly, but O'Connor could only manage a few bites of steak and half a piece of toast. Gudrun said, in her gently accented English, "Eat, Terrence. You'll miss it later."

The American lit a cigarette. "I'm not hungry."

"You need it."

Deirdre mopped up egg and juice with a piece of bread. "Let him be. Better not to eat than have it all over yourself." She stuck the bread in her mouth and winked at him. "That right, Terry?"

"I'm jumpy as hell."

"You'll be fine," Gudrun said. "But you should try some food."

"I'll be all right," he said, and left the table. The two women continued to eat in silence.

They set out at nine o'clock. O'Connor drove the Volkswagen van with Deirdre sitting beside him. In the back of the VW was the BSA, and, under a dark green blanket, an M-60, broken down, a belt of cartridges, and three Ingram M-10 machine pistols. Gudrun followed in the Volvo fifteen minutes later.

They drove north to Cork City. The road glistened in the pale light. It had rained all night and now a monotonous wind off the sea blew strong, driving the rain in sheets across the murky green fields. After crawling through the impossible traffic of Cork City, they turned east and drove to Youghal where they met the sea, and headed north again. O'Connor began to feel better. He asked Deirdre to go back and check the BSA. He had changed spark plugs last night and couldn't remember if he'd replaced the old one. She came forward and said, "It's fine. Stop worrying, for Jesus' sake. There's nothing more to think about or do. It's going to work silky smooth."

"Sorry. I'm really okay."

"Sure you are. By evening you'll be a fookin' hero of the Republic." He looked at her and she was smiling when she added, "Or a dead man lying in a dirty street."

"That's something to look forward to."

Deirdre laughed. "The former rather than the latter." They were coming into the colorless town of Dungarvan. The Irish Sea on their right was calm and phosphorescent in the rain. She looked at him as he lit a cigarette. Handsome man. All that pepper and salt hair. And only thirty-one. He drove effortlessly. Last night she'd asked him if he could handle the van. "I can drive anything," he'd said. American. So American. Liam had said Americans were the best drivers in the world because they paid homage to their most recent myth that the car was freedom, love and power. Deirdre wasn't a social scientist. She thought they were good at the wheel because their outlook was pure confidence, and that's all it took to drive a car well. One of her secrets was that she genuinely liked Americans. In the Republican movement this was heresy. Americans were racist imperialists, money-crazed, soulless, hypocritical and emotional children. But she liked them. There was that eternal confidence they all had, and an openness. They didn't seem afraid to look like fools, which was anathema to Europeans.

They were making perfect time on the slick highway. The farms of Kilkenny were green blurs in the gray morning. "Bally-hale," Deirdre said as they approached the town.

"We take a fork north here," O'Connor said.

"Two miles up the road. You can't miss it."

She knew her own country as well as any itinerant. She had been Liam Cleary's aide for four years and most of that time was spent on the road. Liam had loved to travel, and was always off to the backwater towns of Roscommon to speak to a Republican Club, or was setting out from Dublin for a long nightride to Tralee to straighten out a renegade. He even preferred meeting people in cars. It was safer, mobile, and the close quarters, with Deirdre in the back with a shotgun, allowed the meeting a better opportunity for truth to emerge. No more sawed-off, she thought. No longer. The M-10 was a lovely piece of gun. No more blunderbusses that blew up in your hands, no more Jesse James pistols that jammed when you needed them. They now had weapons on par with any army in the world. And all Ireland would know it before the day was out.

"I'll have a cup of coffee," O'Connor said.

"Will you, sir?" Deirdre said, unscrewing the cap of the thermos. "Rashers and fried egg alongside?"

"I'm still not hungry."

"Don't be defensive, now."

He grinned, and sipped coffee. "I'm beginning to like this country."

She said nothing. It was a good idea for her to ride with him. They had decided it would be safer if anyone questioned them to have a brogue in the front seat with an arsenal in the rear. But Deirdre could also see O'Connor winding down, and she was sure he wouldn't have done that with the German. Before she had killed for the first time, an old man who had passed the weapon to her the afternoon of the operation had told her some ancient music hall two-liner, and it had worked. The laughter made her see the world again as a bad joke and not as drama. This was in a house outside of Newry, County Down, the summer of 1972. That evening she called to a major in the Royal Green Jackets who was coming out of a pub in a dark street. She called for a light from across the road, and the major tipped his cap, stepped a bit unsteadily into the street, and came toward her. When he was ten feet away she took a Colt .38 pistol from her coat, let him walk another pace, and shot him twice through the lungs. His face was still smiling when the bullets hit him.

"Carlow Town," Deirdre said. "Bear to your right here, Terry."

The day had softened away from the sea. It was still raining but there was no wind. Traffic was light and most of that was commercial. They drove for another hour and arrived in the village of Ballitoe, County Kildare, without incident. In front of a butcher shop, O'Connor wheeled the van behind a gray Morris Minor and shut the engine. A young man of his age, dressed in work clothes and flat cap, got out of the Morris and walked back. He approached the right side of the van, the driver's side. O'Connor rolled the window down but the man looked past him and spoke to Deirdre. "You're to telephone Cosgrave in Dublin," he said.

"When?"

"Now. Johnny's just after gettin' the call from him."

"Bloody," Deirdre said, looking out the windshield at the empty main road of Ballitoe, lead colored, spare, and light rain drifting. "There's no phone at the cottage?" she asked.

The man shook his head and tugged his cap lower. "There's a box round the corner of the next street," he said, and walked away, crossed the road and went into a pub. When he was inside, Deirdre took her blue waterproof jacket from the floor next to her and got out of the van. She pulled the hood over her head and walked quickly up the road and around the corner. O'Connor could see the man in the front window of the pub, holding a half-pint glass. A lorry tore past and the street was empty again. A few minutes later in the passenger side window he caught sight of the Volvo entering the town. Gudrun drove past without looking at the van, and took the left fork on the north edge of Ballitoe.

Deirdre returned and said, "It's still go. They're taking him out of Dublin two and a half hours later."

"Same setup?"

"It is. Two cars, same route."

"Gudrun's past us," he said, and started the engine. The man in the pub watched them roll out of town, took a sip of stout, and walked over to the bar.

The cottage was just off a farm road near the town of Crosskeys. It was a two-room place surrounded by fields of parsnips and cabbage. Pale smoke rushed from the chimney and then was flattened by the mist and light wind. O'Connor smelled the turf smoke, a thick sweet odor of the earth, reminiscent of marijuana. They parked around the back next to the Volvo. A skinny old man, wearing a black suit that was new when O'Connor was a boy, and a once-white shirt buttoned at the neck, took his hand and said with a toothless smile, "You're welcome."

Behind the old man he saw Gudrun in the doorway of the cottage holding a cup of steaming tea. "How are you, Johnny?" Deirdre called. The old man rubbed his close-cropped stubble gray head and said, "I'm breathin' is the best I can say."

"No trouble?"

"None. Now, come in. There's tea inside." Johnny served them tea and buttered brown bread in the dark shanty. He put on his Wellington boots, grabbed his flat cap and walked out. Gudrun poured another cup of tea. "What kind of problems can we expect?"

"It'll be darker," Deirdre answered. "Dusk. There will be more people about."

"Anything else?"

"Not if we don't get stale."

"Right," Gudrun said. "We move in an hour and a half."

O'Connor stretched out on a broken-down sofa covered with a wool blanket. He shut his eyes and was surprised to find sleep waiting for him. He let it come and slept heavily. There were no dreams.

Raymond Murray, in the office of the assistant warden of the jail, took off his suit coat, loosened his tie, and stretched out on the couch. Mary came in. "Oh," she said. It was the first time she'd seen him without his coat on. So it's not glued to his back, she thought. He'd be a pleasant enough looking young man if he'd smile. He had a good solid head of brown hair, an intelligent face, and was always dressed so elegantly. Important as well. Mr. O'Leary, the assistant warden, told her to take good care of him, he was involved in special government business. She had tried to make him comfortable these past three days, but he was so intense, and snooty. The pressure of his work, she had decided. "I've just made a cup of tea for myself, Mr. Murray. Can I make a coffee for you?"

"Thank you, Mary."

"I haven't disturbed you?"

"You have but it's all right."

Raymond Murray swung his legs from the couch and let his head drop to his hands. He fingered his temples. Up all night for two nights running and the old bastard had given him nothing. What had the old Ulsterman said at four-thirty, here in this office, slumped like a sack of bones in that chair across the desk from him? "I'm not some damn teddy boy you can trick or wear down. I'm not some homesick paddy in London you're used to having your way with. And I've grown quite sick of that face of yours.

I'm afraid we'll have to end these inspiring conversations, Mr. Murray."

"I'm as sick of your face as you are of mine, Joe. But if you won't open up, then we'll have to engage in something more than conversation."

Joseph Walsh's blue eyes, bright with fatigue, stared out of his old face. Murray stared back. "You're the smallest man I've ever seen," Walsh said.

"Very well," Murray said, making a show of moving papers on his desk. "Perhaps a change of scenery will help us."

"That's been on the cards since you lifted me."

"Right," Murray had said, taking a quick sip of coffee, touching his tie, and looking back to Walsh's eyes. "It's Portlaoise for you, Joe. We move this afternoon."

"If shit was music, Murray, you'd be a brass band."

"All right, Tommy," Murray had called, and the guard had entered the office and led Walsh away.

Mary brought the coffee with a biscuit riding the saucer. "You're leaving us today, Mr. Murray, are you?"

He gave her a quick look. "How did you know that?"

"Well—" She was unnerved by his stare. "Well, I don't know, now. One of the girls—"

"Holy Christ on the cross!" he roared, spilling coffee as he stood. "Doesn't anything remain confidential in this hole?"

"I'm sure I don't know."

"I *am* leaving today. Perhaps you'll tell me where I'm going?"

"I'm sure I don't know."

"That's something at least." He caught himself glaring at the young woman with a cup and saucer in his hand. "I beg your pardon, Mary. I shouldn't have shouted."

"I understand, Mr. Murray. The pressure."

"Yes." He turned away and went to the desk.

"I'll leave you be now," Mary said, and left the office. Raymond Murray sipped his coffee, and checked the personnel list for the run to Portlaoise for the third time.

Thomas Fleming.

Age twenty-nine.

Prison officer, Mountjoy, three years.

Married, one child.

Fleming had been appointed by O'Leary, the assistant warden, as the man to personally guard the prisoner. He was efficient, knew Mountjoy well, never complained of overtime or odd hours, was fast on his feet, tough enough to handle disturbances, kept a closed mouth about his job. Murray had been pleased with his work with Walsh. He would ride in the rear of the second vehicle with the prisoner.

Arms: none.

Edward Cooke.

Age thirty-eight.

Prison officer, Mountjoy, sixteen years.

Married, no children.

His work record included a suspension for intoxication while on duty, June 1967. He had been called before the warden on 25 February 1965 and reprimanded for beating an inmate. On 9 January 1965 he had been accused of selling alcohol to inmates. Charges dropped. O'Leary's recommendation: Hard man. Experienced with firearms. He would ride in the front seat of the prisoner's vehicle.

Arms: Pump-action shotgun.

John Tuohy.

Age fifty-four.

Prison chauffeur, Mountjoy, eleven years.

Widower, six children.

Work record: Impeccable. Reliable, responsible. He would drive the prisoner's vehicle.

Arms: none.

John Larrimore.

Age fifty-one.

Irish Special Branch Officer, twenty-two years.

Never married.

Work record: Impeccable. Experienced with firearms. Murray had used Larrimore when they arrested Joseph Walsh last Sunday at dawn, and had been impressed with his skill and style. He looked like a slightly overweight country doctor, or the pastor of a simple parish: balding, bespectacled, with a sense of bemused grace about him. He was a killer. In his early days he made his way by accepting without comment any and all of the truly miserable jobs his superiors asked of him. Now he was known as "the governor," the man who got the job done. He would ride in the rear of the first vehicle.

Arms: .45 Colt pistol, pump-action shotgun.

And, *Brian McMahon*. Murray's personal bodyguard would drive the first vehicle. He was thirty-six, unmarried, a former sergeant major in the British Army until he came home to Ireland and went to work for the Irish Special Branch.

Arms: .38 Smith and Wesson.

I am sick to death of Ireland, Murray thought, tossing the list on the desk and leaning back. When he had cracked Walsh and rounded up the German and the American (it was "when," not "if") he would add one more trophy to his growing collection. It would be a prize. Then he'd take that position in New York offered last summer to direct the security division of Pan American Airlines. The money was phenomenal, and he would be in the States. Instead of dealing with Joe Walsh and ancient history. Life would be new in the States. Even London, where he had several offers, would do fine. Three years ago when the British Special Branch captured six Lebanese attempting to blow down half of London, the British had requested him, Raymond Murray, degrees in political science from Trinity, and psychology from Oxford, lately the boy wonder of the Irish Special Branch, to come over and aid them in interrogating the Arabs. The English were quite impressed with his work, and Raymond began to see that he was the new member in an old club. He had traveled to France soon after and advised the French government when one too many bankers was being murdered in Paris. The Irish government was about to loan him out to the Italians when this new situation came up. His contacts were wide, and his résumé couldn't be better.

Garrett Costello walked in. "Here's the last file on Walsh, Raymond," he said, laying the buff-colored folder on the desk.

"Did you learn anything?"

"It's old newspaper clippings."

"Ah," Murray said, and looked up at his colleague. Costello was a tall man with blond springy hair, a large head, and wire-rimmed glasses. He was a good officer. His handling of the Herrema kidnapping had nearly made him Director of the Special Branch Anti-terrorist Division, but the minister had given the plum to Murray because of his reputation and contacts. Raymond Murray considered Costello a rival. They were different people. Murray saw something soft and romantic in Costello, qualities incompatible with police work. He reviewed books for a literary magazine. He was well liked by all who knew him. A good officer, yes, but no steel to him.

"You travel today?" Costello asked.

"I'll be back on Friday."

"Have a good trip," Costello said and walked out.

The phone buzzed. "Yes."

"The minister, Mr. Murray."

"Put him on."

"Raymond," the minister's voice came on strongly. "Do you have good news for me this morning?"

"Once we get him out of Dublin and into Portlaoise I'm sure we'll get what we want."

"Stubborn old fool," the minister said. "You'll ring me this evening?"

"Yes."

"Prendergast is all over me about the Farrell situation. Should we leave him in Portmarnock?"

"I believe that's the best solution for now," Raymond Murray said, leaning back in his chair. "Once I have my way with Walsh, we can decide what to do. I'm sure Farrell wouldn't mind emigrating to Mexico or some South American country."

"Right. Or we could just throw him back with his own kind," the minister chuckled.

"That would end the affair," Murray said.

"Very neatly. I'll relay this to Prendergast. Have a good journey."

"Thank you, sir."

He set the phone down and picked up his coffee cup. In a little while, only a little while, he wouldn't ever again have to deal with the likes of that dinosaur Walsh. America. Money. Prestige. Celebrity. He finished his coffee and set the cup delicately in the saucer. I'll crack that old man. I'll break him like a stick, tonight, in Portlaoise.

When Phil Coughlin returned to the garage he found James with his head still stuck in the lorry. "No, lad," he said. "You've got it all turned round the wrong way. Here," he said and took the wrench from his hand.

"I don't think I'm suited to be a mechanic," the boy said wearily.

"Rubbish. You've got a strong back and you're not afraid to get your hands dirty. It takes time is all. There, now. Go to work on that."

"Can I take my lunch now, Mr. Coughlin?"

"You finish this job and then you go."

"Yes, sir."

Phil went to his "office" in the rear of the shed. It was just a corner of the garage where he'd put a desk, two chairs, the telephone, and a filing cabinet. He sat down and looked across the stone floor of the shed out to the sullen Dublin day, and thought of Michael, and Liam Cleary, and how he was serving them.

He had been chief mechanic for nine years now, and had worked in this garage a total of sixteen. Living alone had never bothered him; in fact, he enjoyed his own company. He had a nice flat near Phoenix Park, went to the pictures every Monday evening, and enjoyed a rack of snooker now and again. The uncomplicated life appealed to him. He didn't drink, smoke or gamble. There was his work and his faith. The only person he'd ever been close to or loved was his older brother Michael. And he was gone now since Christmas 1969. He saw his sister, who still lived in the old place in Cahirciveen, County Kerry, every summer, and Eileen made the trip to Dublin once a year in the winter. Other than that, since Michael's death, there was no one. Both of his younger brothers had emigrated to Canada the year after he and Michael went to England to find work. He heard from them sporadically, usually at Christmas. There'd be a card from Peter in Toronto, and a full letter from Donald from a place called Flin Flon. Next to him, taped to the filing cabinet, was a snapshot of Donald's two boys, staring blankly, dressed in ice hockey uniforms.

Although Phil proudly said he never regretted a day in his life, he knew it was a lie. In his grief for Michael, which was still strong, he thought of a thousand ways he could have been better to his brother, or appreciated him more fully when he was alive. He regretted taking the one he loved for granted. The years in London were the years he came to know Michael and love him. Being foreigners, two country boys from Kerry in the English capital, had bound them. They had got on quite well, unlike most of the Irish off the boat. Michael got a laborer's position digging track for British Rail out near Gatwick. Phil landed a job in a garage in Chelsea run by a man who had been born in Cahirciveen. They found a flat in the Irish ghetto of Cricklewood where Phil was amazed to see his countrymen carrying on as if the only satisfaction in life was to consume enormous quantities of alcohol, fight, bellow, and go to jail. They seemed to be children finally free of their mothers and so went wild, beginning the party as a celebration of freedom and continuing it, once the initial thrill was gone, out of despair. No wonder, Phil told his brother, the English hate us. No wonder they think we're inferior. But Michael, who was a political man, would argue that it was because of exploitation, class, and all the rest of it. Phil didn't understand politics. He took his politics from the pulpit.

Michael returned to Ireland first after three years. Phil knew he was one of the "lads," as they termed membership in the I.R.A. in London. But it didn't bother Phil. Michael was always true to himself and he had a right to live as he chose. When Phil returned to Ireland he moved in with Michael in the flat near the Phoenix Park, and took his position with Mountjoy Jail. He didn't see much of Michael, but when he did he never questioned him or engaged him in political discussions.

When the North erupted in 1969, Phil knew his brother was part of it. The post of 3 January 1970 brought a letter informing him of his brother's death in the hallway of a tenement located in the Falls Road, Belfast. The letter said Michael was murdered by the Royal Ulster Constabulary, and that he had died valiantly for Ireland. He had requested his brother be notified in the event of his death. The note was signed Liam Cleary. And Phil's grief became a partner to his days.

The following May Phil read in the *Irish Times* that Liam Cleary was to debate at the Mansion House with a member of the government. Phil went along to see him, taking no small risk of jeopardizing his job with Mountjoy. This was a friend of Michael's, Phil thought, as he watched and listened to the broad, ginger-haired, fine-looking man. Phil had never heard anyone more eloquent or passionate, a good man true to himself, who made no show of himself, who spoke what he believed and the devil take anyone who didn't agree. A fine example of what every Irishman should seek to become. And this was Michael's friend. Phil was overcome with pride for his brother. When a good part of the crowd applauded Cleary, and shouted back answers to his rhetorical questions, and cheered him when he was done, Phil stayed silent, out of fear for his job. If anyone noticed him there they'd see him as merely an observer and not a partisan. He left the Mansion House and walked down Dawson Street that bright spring night, and wept for Michael who had died in such a vile fashion, a death without comfort or respect. Overcome with bitterness, surprising himself by breaking down, Phil wept for his brother who had never been cheered. On his way home on the bus he sat alone and thought of Liam Cleary, the finest man you could imagine to be your brother's friend, and wept again, praying for his brother's soul and Liam Cleary's life.

Although Phil never met Cleary, he followed his career closely over the next few years. When Cleary split with the I.R.A., Phil felt as satisfied as if he himself had advised his brother's friend. He's making the best decision of his life, Phil thought. Liam's too good a man to be linked with those thugs. He bought the first issue of the *Irish Patriot*, Cleary's organ for his own political group, the Irish Socialist Party. And every week after he would purchase a copy from a news merchant in Abbey Street, far enough from home, Phil figured, not to warrant suspicion. He read the editorials by Joseph Walsh, editor-in-chief, thinking him an intelligent man with a way with words even if he, Phil, hadn't a clue to what the man was going on about. Every so often Liam Cleary himself would have a piece in the paper. Phil thought he would do better speaking than writing, but he was a man of scholarship, let no one take that from him.

Four months ago, in August, when Liam Cleary was assassinated, Phil felt another brother had died. He went by bus down to Bray that Monday morning for the requiem mass and funeral. He had called in sick to his superior, the first time in sixteen years. It was a grand affair altogether, the funeral. There was a long line of mourners in the hot day, and Liam was carried in a pine box to his grave by six strong lads, all dressed in black from their berets to their boots. After he was in the ground the six young men drew pistols and fired shots into the air. A fitting salute to a great man, Phil approved.

He had noticed a young woman with the first group of mourners, a somber-faced slim thing with dark hair, no more than a girl, really. Was she the daughter? He should at least pay his respects. Phil engaged her as she walked past the cemetery gates toward the cars. "If you'll excuse me, miss."

"Yes," she said, and Phil fell into step beside her.

"I'm—well—" he faltered when he caught her eye. "It's a dark day for Ireland is all I have to say."

"It is that."

"My brother Michael Coughlin was a dear friend of Mr. Cleary's."

"I knew Michael Coughlin."

"Did you now?" Phil said, and was suddenly, with no warning, as quickly as a tear falls across a cheek, drowning in misery.

"I'm glad you've come, Mr. Coughlin."

"He was a great man," Phil said, not quite understanding who he was talking about or what he was saying. The young woman stopped walking and said, "He was, and again, it's good of you to be here."

"Yes," Phil said, letting his eyes drop to the ground and composing himself. "Sorry to take your time, miss. If there's anything I could ever do, I'd do it proudly for the memory of Liam Cleary."

She eyed him carefully before saying, "There is always work to continue, Mr. Coughlin. Will you ring the *Irish Patriot* this week? Ask for me, Deirdre O'Sullivan."

"Deirdre O'Sullivan," he repeated. And here he thought she was the daughter.

She smiled. "You will ring me?"

"I will."

"And keep it to yourself?"

"I will," Phil Coughlin said.

On his way to work the next day, Phil read the report in the *Irish Independent* of the funeral. There were photographs, but he was not in them. What frightened him was the report that the Special Branch had monitored the affair. But nothing was said at the job, and he knew he was safe. That Thursday at tea Phil called the office of the *Irish Patriot*. He was told to go to a flat in Sean McDermot Street that night. There he was greeted by a widow named Mairead who asked him every sort of question imaginable. He was told to return the next night and to keep everything under his hat. The next evening Miss O'Sullivan let him in. She offered him a drink, which he refused, but he took a cup of tea from her. She said the Irish Socialist Party was pleased he was interested in their work, and she was sure that with his position at Mountjoy he would be of help. She said to wait, they would be in touch with him.

Even before he read it in the paper, Miss O'Sullivan called and told him of Joseph Walsh's arrest and internment at Mountjoy. She told him to meet a certain Mr. Cosgrave at an address in Dundrum. And there, in the snug of a workingman's pub, Cosgrave told him to ascertain when the government would move Joseph Walsh out of Mountjoy to the maximum security political prison in Portlaoise, the exact time of day if possible, and the route they'd take. Phil agreed, but added, "Now, I'm not a man of violence, Mr. Cosgrave. I'll have you know that."

"Neither am I."

"I'll take no part in killing."

"There's nothing to worry about. Just this one thing, Phil, and you'll have served your brother and Liam Cleary well."

It wasn't a difficult task. When the order came down on Monday to have two of the new Fords ready at 1 P.M., Wednesday, 4 November, Phil said to his superior, "Well, I can have one of them for you, sir. But Mr. Riordan's taken a fancy to the Fords and likes to have one for his own use. I could have one of the Fiats to go with one of the Fords."

"Two Fords, Phil," his superior said. "This is Special Branch business."

"A celebrity party, is it?"

"I wouldn't know about that. It's old Joe Walsh they're taking away."

He learned the route by first checking the driver's work sheet. Jack Tuohy was scheduled to report on Wednesday at noon and wasn't due back at Mountjoy until Thursday noon. Phil caught Jack when he pulled in on Monday afternoon. "Jack," Phil said. "Do you ever get to County Laois in your travels?"

"I'll be there Wednesday."

"I've got a cousin there, down the country, and I wonder could you—"

Jack held up his hands, "Phil, I'm sorry."

"I was just thinkin', you know."

"They've got me goin' straight through to Portlaoise. One of the boys says it's Joe Walsh we'll be cartin'.'"

"You don't say."

"I do say. We won't have time for your cousin. We'll be takin' the highway straight through. None of your jackin' about down cow paths in the middle of the night. We're goin' straight through and we'll be goin' like blazes."

"Now that's the life."

"Next time, Phil."

"Sure, that's all right, Jack."

I've done my part, Phil thought, alone in the long stone-floored shed. A black form came out of the bare November day toward him. When he was closer, Phil saw it was the boy. "Starting to rain again, Mr. Coughlin."

"You should always remember your family, James," Phil said.

"Sir?" The boy stopped in front of the desk.

"Never go against your family is what I'm tellin' you. They'll be the only ones to care for you, and see you through."

James was confused.

"And when it's all said and done, they're the only ones who'll put you in the ground."

There was silence. Phil was looking through the boy.

"I'll just get at that lorry now, Mr. Coughlin. I think I've got it licked."

"Yes," Phil said.

I've done my part, he thought. And now the others will finish it.

It was Gudrun, her fair face swimming down to him. "Terrence. Time now, Terrence." Johnny was near the fire, smoking. Deirdre was wheeling a baby's pram out the door. She called over her shoulder, "Get the motorcycle out, Terry. Let's go, now."

Johnny brought a plank of lumber and he and O'Connor wheeled the BSA out of the rear of the van. The day was fading. The rain no more than mist now. He kick-started it, let it run for awhile before parking it next to the door of the house. Gudrun set up the M-60 on its tripod on the floor of the van, checking the manual provided by the maker, the Inland Manufacturing Division of General Motors. She tested the swivel of the tripod, sighted it and then connected a belt into the feed plate. She tossed the blanket over the machine gun, checked the Ingram M-10's and called Deirdre and O'Connor over to the van. "All set," she said, handing one of the machine pistols to O'Connor. He put it in his rucksack.

"Is the big shooter ready?" Deirdre asked, looking at the blanket covering the M-60's bulk.

"Yes. Here's your weapon."

Deirdre took it and placed it under the baby blankets in the pram. She and O'Connor lifted the buggy up and into the VW. Gudrun checked her watch. "So. Let's do it."

Johnny tugged at his cap, stepped forward and took Deirdre's hand. "God be with you, girl." She nodded. Johnny took his eyes from Deirdre's face and saw O'Connor standing behind her, his rucksack over his shoulder, and beyond him, Gudrun sitting in the side door of the van. Both were staring at him. "And may God be with you all today," he said quickly.

At quarter after two Tommy Fleming left the guards' common room to fetch Joseph Walsh in the holding cell of B wing. Along the way, through the narrow corridors, he met other officers, who gave a nod or a word of greeting, and inmates, who glanced away when he caught their eye, or stared boldly with contempt. Like all prisons, there was a tropical atmosphere, of living in a cave beneath a warm sea, with the thick air, and moisture sweating the walls, even though it was November and he knew exactly how cold the cells were at night. There were the never ceasing sounds of the jail, which Tommy, after three years, still could not disregard. Noise came through the stone walls as an industrial hum, with the counterpoint of shouts by men drifting down corridors, human voices that Mountjoy distorted; they could be expressions of joy, or disgust, or fear, or pain, you never could connect precisely the sound to the emotion. Poundings of constant construction, a man with a sledge working against a stone floor in the main building coming to Tommy hollow and soft. Cell gates grinding, the ominous boom of an iron door two tiers below. A madman's symphony, Tommy thought. The music of hell.

He had been called to O'Leary's office to see Raymond Murray when he reported in at eight o'clock and was told that he would accompany the prisoner to Portlaoise and return tomorrow. After a mug of tea in the common room he had phoned home to tell

Marilyn the news. She had been disappointed. They had planned a night with her brother. "You go, love," Tommy had said.

"But the baby, Tommy."

"The baby? Take her along, isn't that what we planned?"

"Now I have to change everything. If you'd be there you could care for her and keep her busy, I'd have a bit of freedom from her."

"There's nothing to be done, love."

"Don't 'love' me."

"Do you think I'm enjoying this?"

"Yes."

"You're daft. It's my work."

"Fine work for a healthy young man."

"Marilyn. Let's not have a row over the telephone. I'll see you tomorrow. I'll be free all afternoon."

"I was looking forward to it, Tommy, can you understand that at least?"

"Be a good girl. Give my best to Nick, now."

He met Cooke in the passageway above the mess hall. "Looks like I'm joining the party with you, Tommy," Cooke said. "I've just got to get my weapon checked out."

"Right," Tommy said, passing him, thinking it was a strange time to live in when thugs like that were issued firearms. If I don't get out, as sure as Christmas I'll end up like him, an old man of forty, more criminal looking than the inmates, stony silent, looking at the world the way a gentleman looks at the city dump when the first smell reaches him. Never the kind word, never the smile. A stone jail full of men, is that the place to spend your days? She said last week, when he came home and stared at the telly, that this job had changed him. She saw it long before he did. One of the reasons to see Nick tonight was to ask his advice. He was always full of ideas, full of more humble things as well, but a good man, making his way and enjoying life. I'd work with my hands, work in a shop, anything. Where can I get better pay than this, though? Wife, baby, and another on the way. Only in the trying you get what you want, Tommy Fleming thought, rounding the corner into B wing. I'm not a slave after all, I'm a free man to go where I choose. He who hesitates is lost. Rid myself of this bloody cage. My time is now. Am I to live my life surrounded by misery?

Walsh was sitting on the bench in the holding cell, a prison issue overcoat a size too large draped on him, his manacled hands hanging down between his thighs. "Well," he said, "here's my keeper now."

"Time for a ride, Joe."

"Thank God for that," Walsh said, standing up. "I'm sick of being shunted from one end to the other of this hotel."

They walked side by side through the corridors. An inmate in a canvas and leather straitjacket, his young face dripping with sweat, and a peculiar serenity in his eyes, was being marched toward them by two guards. He began to speak, softly at first, "Hey, Joe, keep 'em workin', hey Joe," and then louder, "We're not alone, Joe, we're never alone." One of his escorts pulled on a belt running around his chest, "Quiet now. No rowdiness now."

"Up the rebels, Joe," he shouted, his eyes still sleepy and calm. They held the young man against the wall and Walsh, passing him, raised his manacled hands, stuck both thumbs up, and then lowered them slowly, completing the gesture as efficiently as a priest blessing a parishioner. "We're with you, Joe. We'll see it through," his voice was an echo in the next passageway.

Tommy guided the old prisoner down the iron stairs. "It doesn't look good to have my supporters in straitjackets," Walsh said, winking at his guard, "but better mad than dead, right, Tommy?"

"Come on," he said sharply.

After handing over his papers to the captain at the front desk of the main building, Tommy led his prisoner down another flight of stairs and out to a small paved courtyard under a sky the color of Mountjoy's walls. The paving stones were slick, darkening in the afternoon, and puddles were forming near the walls. Two green Fords stood gleaming in the light rain. The air was clean and wet on their faces, providing a feeling of unreality, being alone in a suddenly silent place under the sky. "Why two cars? Someone else moving out?"

"It's all for you, Joe," Tommy said. "Come on now, we'll get a good seat." He opened the rear door of the car but Walsh said, "Wouldn't it be all right to stand for awhile?"

"Right," Tommy said, checking his watch. "We're a bit early." He took out cigarettes and put one in his prisoner's mouth. They smoked, cupping the cigarettes against the mist. "Good to be leaving Mountjoy," Walsh said. "Always good to leave Mountjoy."

He breathed deeply, looking at the sky and the filthy walls of the prison. He had been incarcerated here that May in 1972 when the inmates rioted, wrecking everything that was breakable, holding the chief officer and twenty guards hostage. Republicans managed to get to the roof of the jail, shouting that they'd negotiate only with the Prime Minister or they'd butcher their hostages like chickens. Every piece of furniture in the prison was demolished. Heaps of prison uniforms were torched in the exercise yards. Toilets were smashed and plumbing was torn from the walls. They had even destroyed the old gallows, the same contraption that executed Kevin Barry, tearing it down, flailing at it with iron bars like madmen, hooting and cheering as they splintered it, then taking the largest pieces to the roof to throw down on the massed gardai and soldiers surrounding Mountjoy.

When it was over, after the negotiations, the State came down on the rebels hard, transferring 178 prisoners away from their victorious rubble, away from Dublin and its national media, away from the place of revolt where they had given such fierce commitment to their beliefs. The 178 were separated, some going to the Curragh Detention Barracks, others to the maximum security of Portlaoise, a few to St. Patrick's in Dublin, and still others, Walsh included, to the military detention center in Cork. The government was wise to disperse the passion to four new prisons. Eventually, the flame which leapt at Mountjoy was snuffed. At the detention center in Cork, Walsh started again, organizing a protest against the institution, demanding political prisoner status, refusing to wear prison uniforms, using the law, when he could, against itself.

Standing in the reviving Dublin rain, Walsh thought of himself as an eternal prisoner, not only of the State, but of his own ideals. At sixty-seven he had been a professional for nearly fifty years. Fifty years of intrigue, of being followed, hunted and jailed, over and over again. Fifty years of starting over, using the tools of organization, propaganda, assassination, terror. The first lesson he had learned was that the primary objective of the revolutionary is to exist. Without the revolutionary, there can be no revolution. It was not important to exist nobly or successfully, just being there was enough. The revolution was not action, it was an idea that had to be kept alive, presented to one generation, and passed along to the next. It would develop, or it would stay static according to the will and imagination of the revolutionary. Walsh's second lesson had been that all of that boiled down to getting your name in the paper and making the bourgeoisie jump whenever you could. He was satisfied to be alive and protesting the State, but lately a feeling had taken him that he disliked. It was the sense of being a ghost, haunting his enemies rather than being flesh and blood and fighting them.

He took a stroll around the courtyard. Tommy stayed near the wall, close to the door, watching the white-haired man, his thin neck sticking out of the foolish overcoat. "Come on, Joe," he called, flinging the butt away. "Let's take our seats."

Inside the second Ford, Tommy reached over and unlocked the manacles. Walsh rubbed his wrists. "They say steel is good for the arthritis. Couldn't prove it by me."

"It's copper you're thinkin' of," Tommy said, putting the manacles in the deep side pocket of his uniform coat.

"That's it," Walsh said. "I'll write the warden. Insist they only cuff me in copper from now on. How's that, Tommy?"

"He'll be pleased to hear from you, Joe."

Cooke entered the courtyard carrying a pump shotgun. Jack Tuohy was close behind. "Put your hands down low," Tommy said. "Keep 'em together."

"Aye," Walsh said.

Tuohy got behind the wheel and turned the engine over as Cooke sat next to him, leaning his weapon against the dashboard. "Are you set?" he asked, turning his head.

"Waiting for you," Tommy said.

Raymond Murray, dressed in a perfectly tailored trench coat, stepped briskly into the yard and approached the second Ford. Tuohy rolled down his window and Murray asked, "Any problems?"

"None, sir."

Murray glanced into the back seat. "Fleming?"

"All set, sir."

Murray went ahead to the first car. He stopped, touched his tie, checked his watch and stared at the door. Brian McMahon stepped out with John Larrimore. "Let's move it," Murray said, and McMahon got in and started the car. Larrimore, taking his time, got in the back seat, laying his shotgun across his lap. He looked slightly befuddled, a benign gentleman out for a drive. McMahon put in the clutch, and shifted into first. He looked at his boss sitting next to him. "Go," Raymond Murray said.

The convoy passed through the gates and out the North Circular Road, moving fast in the light traffic, across the Liffey and up through Kilmainham. They passed the old prison, once a British jail where the rebels of 1916 were incarcerated and executed. Now it was a museum where on Sundays an old man led foreigners through the decaying building saying, "This is not just an old pile of brick, ladies and gentlemen, but a shrine, a holy place."

McMahon, seeing traffic beginning to block up, swung the first Ford out into the right lane with Jack Tuohy a car length behind. The convoy passed a whole block of stationary cars, and near Davitt Road they saw the reason for the jam. Two country boys on a flat cart hauling scrap iron were trying to calm their wild-eyed prancing horse. McMahon, who knew horses, noted that the big bay was a young one, tired from pulling in the cold day, and outraged at his first sight of Dublin.

McMahon ran the light at Devoy Road with Jack Tuohy right on his tail. The two cars made wide sweeping turns into Davitt Road and ran fast alongside the Grand Canal. "That fellow knows how to handle his machine," Jack Tuohy said, close behind McMahon. He glanced at Cooke sitting next to him, staring straight ahead. Gloomy Gus, Jack decided. He was a man who had no appreciation for life.

There were children playing in the fragile November light next to the canal, which was high, full to its banks, level with the road. It was a desolate stretch, and the houses on the other side of the road, facing the canal, were low squatting places, looking like beggars jungled up at the riverside. The dividing line, the place where Dublin City ended and the country began. Jack Tuohy, who had traveled this road many times, had always seen the children here along the canal. In the summer you could see them swimming, their paper white bodies diving, rolling in the lifeless water. He caught a quick glance at a group of boys knocking a football around. Good ball, he cheered silently. Oh, good ball, shoot high now in close, oh, good goal! Jack was a bluff, self-important man whose only saving grace, his Kate used to tell him, was his admiration, respect, and enjoyment of children. Jack was the type of man you see in Dublin stopping a mother wheeling a pram, with two little ones hanging to her skirt, to bid good day to the missus, coo energetically at the baba, and question the two little ones about their age and interests. A tip of his hat and he was gone on his way, to find himself later in deep philosophical conversation with a sensitive bespectacled boy on the top tier of the bus home. Among his peers, he was forever trying to stand drinks, entertain, and put over the impression he was quite the important man. With children he felt none of these things, but only wonder, awe, a familial connection. He had come from a family of twelve, and although the family was constantly moving from one weary neighborhood to the next, and Dad was looking for work six months of every year, the happiest time of his life had been his childhood. When he became an adult he felt like an immigrant in a new world, and meeting a child was meeting a countryman in the new land. His own children had all got on quite well. There was only Carmel still at home, and she was eighteen and ready to go. The sight of Raymond Murray sitting ramrod straight in the first car made him think of his duty, and put his youngest daughter out of mind. The Naas Road, he told himself as he followed McMahon into the turn.

Traffic thickened when they cleared a town with lorries lumbering through the wet day. McMahon swung out and the convoy swept past four lorries hauling livestock. Both cars just cut back in time into the left lane before an old man in a Toyota, his eyes wide and both hands gripping the wheel, shot past. "Man's a bloody maniac," Cooke said in the front seat of the second Ford.

"He knows what he's doing," Jack Tuohy said, obviously pleased at Cooke's nervousness. "Are you all right, Cooke?"

"Bloody maniac," Cooke said.

In the first car Larrimore spoke lazily to McMahon's eyes in the mirror, "Did you ever drive a fire engine?"

"Is that supposed to be funny?"

"Oh, God, no, Brian. I'm just interested. I was thinkin' only that if you did, you might have forgotten where you are now, and was rushin' to put out a blaze down the road."

"You'll never die in a vehicle with Brian McMahon at the wheel."

Murray, who had been deep in thought, and was still shaken at the sight of the old man hurtling at him, touched his tie and said, "Ease off, McMahon. We have plenty of time."

"Right, sir," the driver said, and checked the mirror to see Larrimore grinning back at him.

Raymond Murray turned back to the view and his interrupted thoughts. What a dreary part of Ireland, he was thinking. Even in summer it was grim country, but in winter it looked like the landscape of a cheap horror film. You expected to come on a black mass just over the next rise, or see a mad dog howling on the far hilltop. But Murray knew there would be nothing so dramatic in this stretch of country. It was just what it seemed: the flat, dead border of the Irish midlands. A skeletal white sun rode in darkening clouds to the west. There would be no evening to a day like this. The light would go out all at once, and a gray afternoon would become a black night.

He had decided to have one more session with Walsh tonight, and then end it. His decision made him breathe the first air of relief and confidence since he had lifted the old bastard. No rough stuff, that wouldn't work against Walsh, but just a simple question and answer, a final catechism exercise, and then he'd leave him in Portlaoise to rot and enjoy his martyrdom. It had been foolish to let the old man under his skin, foolish to engage him. Raymond Murray knew that his success had come by always dealing from strength, and to hook up with Joe Walsh, trying to break him, was fighting on the old man's terrain. Walsh would die first. Why hadn't he seen that simple fact? He would die happily. Murray had the information Farrell had given him. *That* was power. He had the names and descriptions of the German and the American, the list of weapons, and the description of the yacht they'd used to ferry the matériel from Hamburg to Ireland. The first thing he'd done was inform the gardai. *That* was a correct move. But nothing came of it and he had succumbed to impatience, a vice which, when employed, insured defeat. He had lifted Walsh, and tried to break him, letting his vanity disrupt a simple police matter. No, he wouldn't continue this fool's game any longer. He would have the gardai search every bay and inlet of Ireland's jagged coast, looking for the yacht. Every American, every German matching the descriptions would be brought in. He'd crack this one through hard work and not by grandstanding. Then he'd be off to London, or the States, and freedom. There was the whole world waiting for him.

They were moving through the broad main street of Naas, crowded with farmers and their families. Soon the convoy was doing sixty miles an hour on the highway, cutting straight across the Curragh racecourse. A half mile in the distance to the north, across the tabletop course, could be seen the gray grandstand facade, peeking through the mist. Joseph Walsh looked out on the course at the herds of sheep, all branded by dye marks on their rumps, heads down, grazing in the somber day. "Could I have a smoke, Tommy?" he asked his guard.

"Mr. Cooke?" Tommy Fleming asked, clearing it with his superior.

"Right," Cooke said, and Fleming gave him a cigarette and lit it.

Murray is a fox, Walsh thought. All through the interrogation he had refused him cigarettes, knowing he was a chain smoker. When he was first lifted and brought to Mountjoy, Walsh had figured it was a method of ending the war against the Provos. Since Liam Cleary's assassination in August, eight people had died as the Provos and the Irish Socialist Army made war on each other, exclusively in the Republic and almost entirely in Dublin. The government had done nothing to stop it, and Walsh thought their first move was arresting him. He relished that, because it was proof the government didn't know that he had made peace with the Provos the week before. But Murray, even though he asked interminable questions about the I.R.A., was not interested in the grudge match. It was the German and the American he was after. Walsh played with him, and quite enjoyed it for awhile. But Murray was tireless and the game had grown difficult. At Portlaoise it would be worse. There would be more sleepless nights, more bright young men to spell Murray and his questions. And after the questions would come torture. They've got it in their heads that this is some international master plot with a large group of people involved, Walsh thought, dragging the smoke deep into his lungs. That's the way Murray's mind works. It also helps him when he asks his minister for appropriations if he can hint about a huge plot. Doesn't he know that the revolutionary often acts alone or with perhaps two or three others? It's only near the end, in the final phase, when numbers of people come into the picture.

How far they were from that! The war in the North was ten years old, and little had changed. The I.R.A. was split, and the I.S.A., born out of that rupture, was still in its infancy.

The British Army in the North, although obviously losing the terrorist war to the Provisionals, still fought on and were not about to cut their losses and go home. As with Hitler's blitz of London, the Provos' bombs, snipings, and assassinations made the British character more resolute, and not, in any way, war weary. The Republic of Ireland, pressed by three different British governments, and by its own commitment to a non-violent solution to partition, had made it more difficult, year by year, for guerrillas operating above the border to train and find refuge in the South. But the militant Republicans had two things in their favor: time and tradition. They were dedicated and they were indefatigable. They would stay until the last dwelling was leveled by gelignite, they would kill until there was no finger left to pull a trigger. Walsh let his eyes roam across the flatland, at the sheep in the distance looking like gray puffs of fog lingering over the winter green land. Rhetoric, he thought. Oh, God, yes, we have more than enough of that. Michael Doheny had said it more than a hundred years ago: "God knows, if eloquence could free or save a people, we ought to be the freest and safest people on the face of the globe."

Since Liam's death, he had had to change his life. He had to become a soldier again. For years he had been the intellect, the theoretician, the negotiator. Now he was a commander of troops. Troops, he smiled. A handful of true believers, one solid aide-de-camp, an experienced European guerrilla, an American itching for a fight and me, a ghost on his way to the slammer. But they had power beyond rhetoric, in the form of more weapons than eyes to sight them.

Before Murray had lifted him, he had been in the process of forming an alliance with the Provos. Tricky business so soon after they were each at the other's throat. But not impossible. Walsh's and the I.S.A.'s cards were the weapons. The I.S.A. needed soldiers, which the Provos had plenty of, North and South. But the Provos, their press releases notwithstanding, were chronically unable to arm their troops. When Walsh played his hand, hinting at the numbers and quality of the matériel, the Provos fairly drooled. They also knew it would be a propaganda coup for them to have

Joe Walsh and Liam Cleary's army back in the fold. But the alliance would be stalled until he was free and that could be quite awhile.

Murray's a fox, Walsh repeated in his thoughts. Perhaps he *does* know of the alliance. Peter Farrell, the traitor, had his ear. Before he was taken to Mountjoy, the Special Branch and the Army had begun to roll up Provo safe houses, arrest guerrillas, and besides that, Walsh was sure Farrell had told Murray about the shipment from Germany. Had one of the arrested Provos let loose the tale of the proposed alliance? Walsh thought not. They were too good an outfit for that. Their system of cells, whereby four or five guerrillas worked only together, taking orders from one man and knowing no one else in the organization, was, if not foolproof, proven effective. But Murray might have found a link to the top. Mountjoy was just exercise, Walsh thought. A few rounds to limber up and gauge style. They'd come on hard at Portlaoise. No feinting, no parrying, but body punches and head shots.

Half a mile from Kildare town, Jack Tuohy saw in the rearview mirror a man trailing them on a motorcycle. Uncomfortable way to travel, he thought. Must be soaked clear through. He saw he was wearing a helmet and a black slicker. The convoy slowed when it reached the town limits and Jack Tuohy noticed that the black rider maintained his distance. Kildare was quiet with few people on the streets. Brian McMahon checked his watch as they passed the village square, rising slightly to their right, with narrow streets leading off at the north end. Quarter after four. They were making perfect time. The streetlights around the square flickered to life and shone yellow through the pewter light of the failing afternoon. McMahon slowed to let a woman and a boy, both bundled against the chill, hurry across the road. The woman was pulling the boy by one arm, but he was captivated by the sight of his new cowboy boots, purchased just moments before. The boy was compelled to watch every step he took in them. When the two Fords were past, the woman stopped in the middle of the road and, still gripping his arm, wheeled him around in front of her to scold him. The convoy picked up speed, coming in to a slight bend leading out of town. McMahon saw a woman in a blue-hooded waterproof jacket ahead at the side of the road waiting to cross with a pram. He accelerated slightly and Jack Tuohy tailgated the first Ford. They flashed past a Volkswagen van parked on the street, and Tommy Fleming, in the back seat of the second Ford, saw the side door of the VW slide open, revealing in the weak light the black hole of the interior and a glint of metal. McMahon accelerated slightly more nearing the edge of town. He was just shifting his eyes over to glance at the woman with the pram, when sudden movement in the road ahead brought his foot off the accelerator and down with all his weight on the brake. There, ten yards away, rolling easily, directly in their path, was the pram.

The first Ford's back wheels locked and began a fishtail skid on the wet pavement. Jack Tuohy, with his vision flooded by the red tail lights of the first Ford, jumped on his brake with both feet, but he was much too close and slammed into the rear. The few people in the streets of Kildare flinched and turned immediately at the sound of metal ripping metal. O'Connor, passing the boy in the cowboy boots, saw him begin to run toward the accident, while his mother, shouting, took two steps and then froze, her hand to her mouth, hearing the flat popping of small arms.

Raymond Murray was flung through the windshield of the Ford, out over the hood and into the road. He was the first to die. Deirdre O'Sullivan, in one motion, had pushed the pram in the path of the convoy and drawn the M-10 machine pistol from under the blanket. She fired from the hip, swaying her weapon slightly to cover Murray, twisted in pain as the slugs stitched him. The M-60 opened up with its loud authoritative whine from the van. Gudrun sprayed both vehicles, now lumped together, a horn stuck and blaring. The M-60 slugs tore through the car bodies like cardboard, creating cobweb shatters of every piece of glass intact, opening up Jack Tuohy's head as he sat pinned to the steering wheel.

The blast of M-60 fire ceased for a second or two. Deirdre moved in closer and opened up on Tommy Fleming, reeling from the wreck, his right arm splintered, blood gushing from his mouth. Her first shots caught him in the midsection and threw him back against the rear wheel. Deirdre saw O'Connor approaching on the BSA. She ran to the VW, climbed in, and started it up as the M-60 began to fire at McMahon, blind from broken glass, stumbling into the street. He took twelve rounds, all above the waist, and was dead before he fell. Gudrun adjusted the belt of the machine gun and shifted it slightly to fire at Larrimore still in the car.

In the wreck he'd been thrown into the front seat. He was dazed but not injured and was now searching in the wreck for his shotgun. As Gudrun swung the M-60, she let go three rounds before she brought it to bear on Larrimore, and one of these caught the boy in the new cowboy boots as he stood, thirty yards from the ambush, too terrified to move. He was shot directly in the solar plexus, the bullet emerging through his back, opening a hole the size of an adult fist. O'Connor, his M-10 laying on the crossbar of the motorcycle, approached the ambuscade. Gudrun shifted her weapon and caught Larrimore as he poked his head out of the car, searching for the source of the firing. As O'Connor dismounted, Cooke, both legs broken in the accident, his trunk wrenched from the waist nearly all the way around, let loose a blast from his shotgun, shooting blindly at the sky. O'Connor squeezed off six rounds which finished him.

The van's side door slid closed. Deirdre put it in gear, and took the road east out of town. O'Connor pried open the rear door and saw Joseph Walsh on the floor, just coming out of unconsciousness. O'Connor said nothing. He half dragged, half carried the old man out of the wreck. Walsh was spattered with Jack Tuohy's blood. Out of the car he found his legs and was on the back of the BSA. O'Connor mounted the motorcycle, reached behind to pull the old man's arms around his waist, kicked the bike into gear and let out the hand clutch. They took the road west, Joseph Walsh's oversized coat billowing out behind them, his white-haired head hugging O'Connor's back.

From the moment McMahon had seen the eerily abandoned pram, to the moment the motorcycle vanished, leaving the dead amidst glass, twisted metal, and the stuck horn's obscene howl, no more than sixty seconds had elapsed.

The events that occurred at the town of Kildare, on the afternoon of Wednesday, 4 November, later named "the raid at Kildare" by the media, shocked the people and government of the Republic of Ireland. The Republic had been relatively free of political violence since the Civil War ground to a close in 1923. There had been grudge wars between rival guerrilla bands since that time, the most recent being the assassination campaign the Provisionals and Irish Socialist Army waged against each other from mid August through mid October, resulting in the deaths of eight guerrillas. But these arguments between gangs were looked at by the people as an effective way of achieving good riddance to bad rubbish. The raid at Kildare, like the Loyalist car bombings at Dublin and the murder of the British Ambassador in 1976, brought the troubles over the doorstep and into the parlor. The sight of men lying torn to pieces in the street of a quiet rural town was difficult enough to comprehend. But it was the death of the boy, the death of eight-year-old Francis Byrne, that caused the real anger and outrage. Every priest, politician, and newspaper seized the opportunity to eulogize and condemn.

Beyond the sorrow and shock experienced by the people of Ireland was the concern of the governments of the Republic and Great Britain. The ambush had been a rarity for Ireland, North or South, because the Irish revolutionary had, at his best, only been involved in "glorious failures," and at his worst, was simply incompetent. This raid had been well disciplined, quick, vicious, and executed perfectly. It was the first time that ambush logistics used so successfully in Germany and Italy were utilized in Ireland. The weapons were sophisticated. The M-60 machine gun had only been reported in the Republic once, when a woman was arrested attempting to smuggle one into Rosslare via the LeHavre boat.

The names of the weapons, along with the names and descriptions of two of the guerrillas, were broadcast at 9 P.M. the same day on radio and television. The identifications were given to the Irish Government by an informer.

The Irish Socialist Army admitted responsibility for the events at noon the next day. The statement released to the press said the I.S.A. sincerely regretted the death of young Francis Byrne, but this was war, and many more innocents would die before the killing was done. The statement went on to say that Commander Joseph Walsh was indeed alive and well after being sprung from government hands by the three freedom fighters. Commander Walsh was now directing a new offensive against imperialism in the North and the I.S.A. was prepared to take the fight to the enemy. The statement went on to call for the immediate release of political prisoners in the Republic as well as Northern Ireland, the overthrow of the fascist Dail now sitting at Dublin, the immediate withdrawal of British troops from Ulster, and the creation of a united, socialist, thirty-two-county Ireland. Two copies of the release, one in Irish, one in English, were given to the major newspapers in Dublin and Belfast.

There was another person who may be said to have been involved in the events of 4 November. He was an American named Martin Burke, who spent that Wednesday in his rented house overlooking the Atlantic above the village of Moher, County Clare. It is best to see him first, months before that day, fifteen to be exact, in a few private moments with his wife on board the overnight mail boat from Wales to Dun Laoghaire.

Anne and Martin celebrated his fortieth birthday with double Irish whiskeys in the first-class bar in the first hours of the morning. They continued the celebration in the empty dining room with a feast of porridge, eggs, rashers, sausage, tea, toast, and marmalade. Anne asked him how it felt to be forty.

"Old."

"I'll have to get you a shawl and cane pretty soon," she said.

"Old."

Her face softened. "I'm sorry, honey. I didn't mean to be flip."

"I'm sorry, too. Old and grumpy. That's how it feels."

She wouldn't know. At twenty-seven, how could she know? Even at thirty-eight or thirty-nine he hadn't had this feeling. Nostalgic not for times long gone, but for moods and experiences only weeks or days old. And the need to know the precise age of everyone.

"Well, come on, Grumpy," she smiled. "Old Grumpy. Let's walk."

Outside on the deck they saw Ireland looming up bright blue and green out of the soft morning.

II

CHAPTER 2

The Dublin Character

It was in Dublin, on a clear and bright Friday morning in August, where Martin Burke resigned his part in the casual comedy. Grafton Street was busy under puff clouds in a blue sky. Window shoppers jammed the sidewalks from St. Stephen's Green down past Captain America's, MacDonald's, the butcher shops and fish markets, and the boutiques with English rock drifting from behind beaded curtains. Around Switzer's the crowd was two-deep staring at the window display while people took to the narrow street to pass, moving on down to the wrought-iron fences of Trinity where more crowds queued for the double decker buses. Burke stepped from the street into Bewley's with an *Irish Times* rolled under an arm. A high ceiling and dark wood. The elegant smell of fresh ground coffee. Pastry and cakes almost glittering in glass cases, as regal as museum pieces. Down the winding stairs, the sound of dishes and cups and voices filtering up. He walked along the line and stood in front of the coffee urn. An old woman and a young woman stood in their uniforms talking. Arms folded just under their breasts. "You could've done worse," the old one was saying, "than to give him the gate like I was tellin' you."

"That's one easier said than done."

"Sounds like a bad one to me."

"Ah, he's not bad. He's more like a boy. Mischievous, you know."

Burke waited.

The young one turned. A country face, very pretty. "Are you all right?"

"Cup of coffee, please."

"Will that be black or white?"

"White, please."

The old one drew it. "Well, an eighteen-year-old still playin'
the boy is trouble, if you were to ask me."

Burke sat in the corner at a table, back to the wall, facing the
stairs, spread his paper, and sipped. At the next table sat a young
woman who had easily paid £200 to get dressed. On the floor
next to her was a large Bloomingdale's shopping bag sticking into
the aisle. Advertising. Bait for another American. She, too, had
a newspaper and coffee in front of her, but wasn't reading. She
looked about the long room, searching for a countryman, and
Burke gave thanks again that he'd come away.

He read the paper, sipped, looked up from time to time. A
woman carried a tray of cakes and coffee, shouting with the hard
Dublin voice to a friend across the room. She was dressed in a
clinging dress to her calf but slit almost to the hip. Red lipstick.
High-heeled mules with her toes exposed. Brown shadow high on
her cheekbones. Frizzy hennaed hair. Everyone watched as she
tottered by. Burke was impressed. He was hung over and horny
from last night in Madigan's in Donnybrook. An hour ago he had
been lying in bed naked, with an erection, lazy, sipping tea, watching Anne dress. She pulled panty hose over long legs. "Don't let
him take you over, Martin," she said.

"Come here for a minute and I'll let you take me over."

She hooked her bra behind her, her elbows like wings. "He's
a hustler. Be sure you get *your* ideas across right away. You're
much more talented than he is." She zipped her skirt. "Don't let
him bullshit you."

"I'm a big boy. Annie—"

She looked at him with her no-nonsense face, her Irish woman's
face, learned from the cradle, from the nuns, to be used when
speaking to men at particular times. "You know what I mean?"
she asked.

"I know, I know."

She bent and kissed him, gripped his erection and gently tugged
once or twice. "Isn't that pretty."

"Tease."

"I'm rushing, love. I'm already late."

"Where?"

Again her hard, practical face. "You certainly knew last night.
If I'm not mistaken the whole damn pub knew. You had a whole

speech about it. I left when you started repeating yourself."

"Oh, yeah," he smiled. He had sold a story to an Irish tourist magazine and Anne had done the photography. The editor sent the acceptance with a check for £50 and an invitation for Anne to call by to discuss her work. Burke had raged, drunk, shouting that if he was forced to write rubbish then the least they could do was pay him something more than fifty quid. Gloriously drunk, he'd finally understood, he'd said, the true Irish heart which was mean and miserly. A stone cash-register heart, he'd said.

"Oh, you were a grade A lout, my dear," Anne said. She kissed him on the forehead. "I'll see you at eleven-thirty in Stephen's Green. Try not to bring him along. I want the day with you." She looked at her watch. "Goddamn, I'm late." She rushed out, calling, "Half-eleven, Stephen's Green."

"Right," Burke said, but she was already gone.

He took his time with the newspaper while the room filled. He read all the news and columns about Northern Ireland and checked off the ones to be clipped later. Then he read the sports, fashion, book reviews, gardening, chess, and, like all expatriates, took pleasure from reading the temperatures of the day before in cities of his homeland. St. Louis—ninety and cloudy. Los Angeles—eighty-three and sunny. New York—eighty-seven and clear. It was little more than a year now since they had stood on the deck of the mail boat in the Irish Sea. Burke felt he had ended his life as a cliché. No longer the New York character, the bartending poet, the moving-man anarchist, the bookstore clerk novelist, the cab-driving free-lance journalist. In Dublin he was a writer, a reporter with credentials from two Irish-American weeklies, and a stringer for a group of New York suburban papers. Now he was a Dublin character, which carried weight. He was the American bloke, you know, Burke's his name, married to that young beauty, Anne, yes, the dark one, they have a piece now and then in the *Times*, right, the odd piece in *Hibernia*, you've seen her photos, quite accomplished, yes, good people, not American at all really, thought he was Canadian at first meeting, doesn't jabber at you like all the yanks, you've seen him in Nesbitt's, Madigan's, Mulligan's in Poolbeg Street, bearded, burly fellow, likes his Guinness he does, and a drop of Irish to help it along,

friend of Foley's, Mick Mills swears by him, they live on Lansdowne Road, yes, that's the one, good chap, quiet, but not at all
gloomy.

Anne had answered the phone at eight o'clock and nudged him
with the receiver. "It's Terry O'Connor. He's in Dublin."

"What?" Burke's head was packed. Sour smell of stout on his
mustache. "What?"

"Martin, damnit, wake up. It's Terry O'Connor."

Burke took the phone and sat up in bed, his eyes closed.
"Hello?"

"Marty?"

"Terry. Where are you?"

"The Shelbourne Hotel. Can I see you? I've got an idea for
you."

"Anyone staying at the Shelbourne can see me. Where and
when?"

"We could do it here. Anywhere. It's your town, right?"

"How about Bewley's on Grafton Street?" He coughed.
"Downstairs at ten-thirty."

"How do I get there?"

"Ask anybody. How long you staying?"

"Could be quite awhile. Jesus, you sound like death. Hey, see
you at ten-thirty."

Burke handed the phone to Anne who hung it up on the night
table. "He's staying at the Shelbourne?"

"Yeah. Says he's got an idea for me."

"Money," Anne said. "Where did he get that kind of money?"

He was trying to put the knuckles of both thumbs into his eye
sockets. "Oh, Jesus. I'm dying." Up and stumbling to the bathroom with Anne asking questions behind him.

Looking up from David McKittrick's column, Burke saw him
coming down the stairs and into the room. A slight, neat man,
with an athletic sureness of movement. Dressed in jeans, white
shirt and tweed jacket. Thirty-one years old and all his hair gone
gray. He picked Burke out and came over. A quick smile. Burke
stood and they shook hands. "Marty. Hey, man."

"Hello, Terry."

They sat. "Rough night?"

"An Irish night."

"Long time, Marty."

"Yeah. What, two years?"

"How's Annie?"

"She's fine," he said. "In love with Dublin. You want coffee?"

"Sit, Marty. I'll get it. How about you?"

"Yeah."

O'Connor walked to the coffee urn with his loose American stride. The young woman drew two cups, and laughed shyly at something he said. He carried the cups waist high, walking quickly. "You know, in the back of my head I thought Ireland was gonna be like Fordham Road. Thank God."

The kid, Burke thought, is no longer the kid. Ten years ago Burke was tending bar at Eric's on DeKalb Avenue in Brooklyn, living in a small apartment two blocks away and trying to write a novel. Terry O'Connor, a scholarship student of film at Pratt Institute, took his evening meal five nights a week in the back room of the bar. He was at the bar so often talking to Burke that, when the other bartender came in too late one too many times, the owner offered O'Connor the job. For awhile O'Connor, the student, and Burke, the writer, were inseparable. O'Connor shared Burke's view of Irish-Americans which was that they were the most obnoxious group of people walking the planet. He enjoyed Burke's humor, his cynicism, and independence. Burke, on the other hand, had never met a more serious young man than Terry O'Connor. The kid, as Burke called him for awhile, was very Irish that way, with that serious mind, serious outlook, an Irish Jesuit in mufti whose church was radical politics. His idols were Costa-Gavras, Pontecorvo, Buñuel, Godard, Bertolucci. He showed Burke letters he'd written to Buñuel, as eloquent as Joyce's letter to Ibsen, and as choked with hero worship. O'Connor let him see his correspondence with Godard, letters full of politics, questions and answers about the present "situation" in America and Europe, advice on what "road to follow," lists of books. O'Connor wanted to be an artist in those days, an artist, he told Burke, who made films that *moved* people, not emotionally, but politically. "Move them off their asses. Open their eyes to the hypocrisy they swim in and give them characters who free themselves through their own acts and who aren't afraid of struggle." At times Burke saw him as a cold, brilliant younger brother, who would one day put away his bombast. He knew O'Connor was an only child, whose mother died when he was an infant, and who had lived with his father in a tenement in Inwood until he left for Brooklyn and education. Burke enjoyed being a big brother.

After graduation O'Connor got a job at Metromedia in New York as an assistant film editor. He made small films by himself and pursued his other passion—motorcycles. Burke went with him nearly every weekend to motocross races all up and down the East Coast. Terry was an excellent rider who never looked reckless or out of control. He ran steady, had a good seat, and let his bike do the work. Burke enjoyed the races, the drinking, the partying, the long rides to the dirt tracks with the Triumph in its cart behind O'Connor's ancient station wagon. At one motocross in the Pocono Mountains of Pennsylvania, they met Anne Donahoe who was photographing a young woman who was racing that day with the men. For a whole summer they were a threesome, until Burke moved into Anne's apartment on the West Side of Manhattan in the fall. O'Connor was a witness to their wedding three months later.

Three years ago Burke had made a short film with O'Connor about ironworkers. Burke did research, wrote a narrative, and helped with interviewing. He had all kinds of pretensions about film, just like everyone else he talked to. But working every day for three months in close quarters with O'Connor, he saw that the kid was a natural director. Not just for his superb visual sense, his mastery of the technology, his craftsmanship, but more for his genius at organizing even the smallest detail, his serenity in the midst of chaos, and his ability to keep film always pointed in one direction.

The film ran on ETV in New York and received some small acclaim. O'Connor was paid eight hundred dollars and split it evenly with Burke. It didn't cover half the expense. O'Connor said, "So what? It's a business, Marty. We got screwed, so what?" ETV was interested in another film. O'Connor planned an hour documentary on the F.A.L.N. He knew a guy who knew a guy who wouldn't mind some favorable propaganda for the underground group. Burke and O'Connor met with the Puerto Ricans, did research, preliminary interviews, a rough script, and presented it. The proposal made its slow way through the caverns of bureaucracy and half a year later was rejected. O'Connor quit his job cold and went to France, taking up Godard on one of his many invitations. He would sit at the great man's feet, learn, make contacts, rid himself of America. The Europeans also took moto-cross seriously as a sport and O'Connor was eager to see the great Belgian, French and English riders. He could be a bike bum to earn his bread while studying film. Burke hadn't heard a word from him until this morning.

"How'd you find me, Terry?"

"I picked up a copy of the *Herald Tribune* in Cologne and saw the story about the I.R.A. Good piece of work." He took out a pack of cigarettes and offered one. The Gauloises blue in his hand. One butt sticking out with a slight flick from a fresh pack. A Zippo clicked in his other hand. "Thanks," Burke said and sucked in the stale taste. Coughed.

"Really fine piece of work. I called Paris, claimed I was your brother and got your phone and address in Ireland. Guy by the name of Brill talked with me."

"What were you doing in Germany?"

"Long story. I'm into something pretty heavy."

Burke smoked. Sipped coffee through thick Irish cream and decided he'd wait. Counterpunch.

"I need your help, Marty."

"You're not talking about a film?"

"No."

"Any money in it?"

O'Connor laughed and ran a hand through his full gray hair. "You'll never be a rich man. Why don't you accept it?"

"What's the deal, Terry?"

"Smuggling." He tilted his chin and blew smoke straight up. Poker-faced, his eyes even at Burke.

"Dope?"

"Two hundred and fifty Armalite rifles. Sixty M-60 machine guns with belts. Twenty M-10 machine pistols. Ammonium nitrate and gelignite."

"Why?"

"You want in?"

"No. I never even heard what you said."

"Okay," O'Connor said. "Fair enough. You were always a straight shooter."

Burke saw a young man in jeans and a lumberjack shirt sitting

with the Bloomingdale's shopping bag, laughing at her mono-
logue. The room had filled and was even noisier. For some reason
he found he was furious.

"Marty. Drop the pissed-off face."

"You better be careful."

"That's why I got in touch with you."

"You better know what you're doing."

"We need a contact."

"We?"

"One other."

"How're you planning to move it?"

"It's already in Ireland," O'Connor said. "On a forty-five-foot
yacht in Kinsale harbor."

"I never took you for a patriot, Terrence."

"I'm not."

"I took you for a lot more than this. I thought you had more
brains than *this*. Christ's sake. You think *you're* into something
heavy? The people over here'd fix you so quick you'd—"

"Easy, now."

"Tell me why, Terry. What for?"

"For love," O'Connor said. "Is that good enough for you?"

"Give me another butt."

"You have any contact with the Irish Socialist Army?" he
asked, flicking out a cigarette across the table.

"Maybe."

"Marty, look. If you can't help me, say so, okay? And no more
advice. Let's not play with each other."

"Yeah, I know them."

"Guy by the name of Conor Graham?"

"No. Liam Cleary. Head man. I've talked with him a few
times."

"I want to see him."

"Wait a minute. You better tell me your tale."

O'Connor spoke for twenty minutes, interrupting only once
when he got up for more coffee. He spoke chronologically, never
repeating himself. His only movements were with the coffee cup.
He looked directly at the other American who chain-smoked the
foul French cigarettes and listened. Burke thought O'Connor
would make a fine soldier. If bravery were suspension of imagination, then O'Connor would be a lion. He had no imagination.

Only will. Attention to detail. Caution. He was talking about how in France he'd worked as a grip on a Godard film until the project ground down. Described the drifter scene in Paris. The quality of dirt track biking in France. He sits so straight, Burke thought. Straight, but not stiff. Anne, who had never really liked him, once described him as physically beautiful. And it was true. His posture, his litheness, grace in the smallest mannerism, the dramatic gray head, black Irish eyes and pale complexion, a quick smile. "The party was weird," he was saying. "On the Île Saint-Louis. Very weird guy, the host, an Englishman who got off on having dangerous folks in his parlor. Very queer, a lot of bucks. There were Palestinians, Vietnamese, old Black Panthers, English Trots. Of course, it was the quietest party in the world. Nobody talking to each other. Everybody guzzling the free booze. Everybody feeling everybody else out. Weird." There he met Gudrun Böhm, a young German. They spoke about film, drinking Heinekens in the kitchen. She invited him around to her flat. "I thought I'd hit it when I saw her place. Fantastic wealth. A Gauguin on one wall and a Mary Cassatt on the other. It worked fine. Within a week I was living with her," he smiled, almost shyly.

Gudrun was the daughter of a BMW executive who had come from piles of old money. She was a graduate of the Sorbonne in anthropology. What else? Burke thought. She did no work, traveled, collected pictures. It was a perfect cover for her work with the Baader-Meinhoff Group. She financed arms deals, set up safe houses all over Europe. She also recruited. "I enlisted," O'Connor said. "Gudrun had a scheme she cooked up with this Irishman, Conor Graham, in Paris. We used to hang out. Gudrun would buy weapons, we'd deliver them here and the I.S.A., as payment, would provide training and refuge for European guerrillas. Graham looked at it as an historic link, you know, combining two armies into a really potent force." Goddamn, Burke thought. Amateurism. A grand thing ending as a farcical fuck-up.

They purchased the weapons and matériel in Hamburg and loaded it aboard Gudrun's yacht. "Two days later the roof fell in. People lifted. Western Europe turned into a policeman's convention. It got to be very spooky. We're sitting on enough hard evidence to put us away forever, or be shot out of hand. Germany was a circus. We couldn't move and we couldn't stay still. And then Conor walked down the pier to get groceries and we haven't seen him since. I don't know what happened. He might've been lifted or he just might've split. We took the boat up and around to Cuxhaven and sweated it out all over again. Gudrun couldn't get in touch with anyone. I wanted out of Germany. I remembered your piece, I kept it like a fallback. We took off three weeks ago. Out into the North Sea, through the English Channel and around to Kinsale. It was a beautiful trip. I'd never been on a yacht before."

"Just the two of you sailed it?"

"Yeah. We had good weather."

"What about the Irishman? Graham?"

"I don't know. He said he was in Europe cooling out. Robbed a bank in Cologne, pretty as you please. Very neat job. He could've been anybody, though."

"I'll see Liam Cleary, Terry. I'll tell him what you told me."

"Good."

"What's next?"

"Rest. Relax. Breathe. Then I train."

"Here?"

"Yeah. Then I'm going home."

"What more do you want from me?"

"Nothing."

Burke looked away and said, "Why do you trust me?" Turned back to O'Connor's eyes.

"Why shouldn't I? Is there a reason?"

"No."

"You want some lunch?"

"I've got to meet Anne."

"Well, come on," O'Connor said, rising. "We'll all go."

Walking up Grafton Street they didn't speak. Burke took him through Duke Street to get away from the crowd. "Looks like a good town," O'Connor said as they passed Davy Byrnes.

Burke stopped him. "I don't want Anne to know about this, Terry, okay?"

"What? Come on."

"Yeah. Why should she know?"

O'Connor said, "Then I don't want to see her. Not until she knows."

"It's better to keep it between ourselves."

"Okay. Give her my love. We'll be at the Shelbourne for three days. In my name."

"I'll call you."

O'Connor held out his hand. They shook. "Thanks, Marty."

Burke walked slowly back to Grafton and up through the crowd to St. Stephen's Green. In through the gates, the sun gentle in the cloudy sky. He walked west under the trees and then turned south over the bridge. A young woman and three red-headed children leaned on the side of the bridge watching the ducks glide the pond. In the center of the green, on a bench near a flame red bush, he saw Anne sitting, and the sight of her dark hair, her schoolgirl straight posture, head slightly bent to the paperback in her lap, her long tweed skirt and Lord & Taylor boots, gave him a quick revelation of exactly the dimension of fool he was.

CHAPTER 3

Martin and Anne

Burke stayed at the side of the bridge, watching his wife fifty yards away in the open Green. Since they'd met they'd fought the petty wars of children, primitive little battles neither one of them bothered to analyze. "Why do we fight like that?" one would always ask the other during the refuge of making up, but that was as far as the search ever went. He loved her, but most days could only express it through jealousy, criticism, possessiveness and teasing. They were different people, opposite in fact. Their friendship began in bed, when not knowing each other at all they found themselves perfectly compatible in sex. The dollar movies and dinners at Eduardo's on Second Avenue and trips to the zoo that preceded or followed the one great event of their early meetings revealed their habits and manner that each found at first amusing, interesting, and later, with familiarity, became endearing, and even later, altars to worship the loved one. Every time they went to the Central Park Zoo for breakfast Anne would go and stand in front of the cage of mountain goats and weep at the perfection of their family. Mother, father and baby, all exactly the same save father's horns and mother's teats, all bearded and colored exactly the same. And her tears became objects of love for Burke. The way he would smoke non-filtered cigarettes and always light the end with the label had at first seemed unusual to Anne seeing it in his hand and later she was shocked when he did it any other way. Like all lovers, they had made a legend of their life together.

He saw her recross her legs. Pretty and dark. Tall and pretty. She took her sunglasses from her bag, put them on and bent her head again to read. He wouldn't tell her. He'd do the one errand for O'Connor and that would be it. He'd make that clear to

O'Connor. Only this one thing and no more. Only so far and no further. He walked toward Anne.

She looked up over the top of her sunglasses. "How'd it go?" They kissed.

"Great. He sends his love."

She folded her book and put it away. "I'm starving."

"Let's go to Eve's."

"You sound like a man who just found money in the street." She got up and linked her arm in his. "So, tell me. What's his idea?"

"He didn't have one for me," Burke said. They walked through the Green, past the midday bench sitters and shopgirls on the grass having a sandwich. Across the way, near the south wall of the Green, accordion music drifted toward them from the bandstand. A girl was stepdancing on the hard wood as they wandered over.

"I thought you said—"

"No idea, sweetie. He just was in Dublin and wanted to see me."

The girl was young. Her long hair bouncing with the dance. With her arms straight down her sides and her back rigid, she danced only with her legs and feet, stepping lightly, then swinging her legs from the knees and coming down hard on the wood. "What's this?" he asked.

"Bord Fáilte's running lunchtime concerts."

"How'd that go?" He smelled the stale Gauloises on his mustache.

"She won't pay until the story goes to print. That could be next summer."

"Jesus," Burke said, watching the girl jig around the wood, somberfaced, counterpoint to her lively dance and the accordion. Anne, her arm still linked in his, began jigging in one place, laughing. She released herself and stepped all around him. "Martin. Let's be happy today."

They walked arm in arm through the Green and out, past Oisin Kelly's statue of Wolfe Tone near the east wall. Tone stood on blocklike legs in a high frock coat, staring.

Anne went into Joseph O'Reilly's chemist shop on the corner of Merrion Street to buy some cotton balls while Burke waited outside on the busy street. It was one of the corners in Dublin that, if you stayed for an hour, you'd be sure to see somebody you knew. Men and women, in that subtle fashion that at first looked like London but on closer look was all Dublin, passed quickly. Early lunch from the Dail and the government ministries down the street. Burke didn't have to wait an hour because here was Robby Buckley rounding the corner. The big dark Corkman whom he played softball with in the Phoenix Park every Monday afternoon. Robby worked for the Ministry of Finance. After only meeting him twice Burke called him at his office for information about restaurants and accommodation in Cork for a weekend Anne and he had planned. Buckley said he'd get back to him and in the next day's post there was a three-page letter of rooms, restaurants, things to do.

"Mr. Burke, is it?" he greeted, squeezing the American's upper arm like a hurley.

"Mr. Buckley."

"Now, aren't you gettin' good at names."

Burke laughed. "Beautiful day," he said.

"A day you could frame, Martin."

"You're looking well."

"And yourself," Robby said. "Will you play Monday?"

"I'll be there."

"Grand. How's the good lady?"

"Fine. She's just inside."

"They say you and O'Toole were raising twenty kinds of hell in Madigan's last night. Mad-again, Martin?"

"Who's 'they,' Robby?"

"You're the talk of the town. Did you think you could carry on like that and not anyone know about it?"

"It was a good night."

"God, my agéd father told me never to associate with tinkers or journalists and he was a wise man."

"You and your agéd father. My father told me never to associate with flannel-mouthed Irishmen."

Anne came up with her package. "Ah, Anne," Buckley smiled. "God, you're a fair one."

"Hello, Robby."

"Well, I'm off. Rushing today. Take care, both. See you Monday, Martin. Bring the beauty with you this time."

Polite, meaningless words.

She linked with him and they walked.

"He's a treat," she said.

"The original stage Irishman."

"He's not," she said.

They strolled down Baggot Street past Nesbitt's and along a row of tall Georgian houses. A day you could frame. He remembered what Liam had once said. "The incest that is Ireland." Dubliners use gossip like pubs use porter. A staple. You get drunk in a bar one night and the Department of Finance knows about it before tea the next day. Damn fool meeting him in Bewley's. A close little world, Dublin. No wonder people fled the claustrophobia.

At the middle of Baggot Street Bridge they paused and looked west up the narrow canal flowing under the trees. There were tinkers sprawled on the slope near the stone bridge, their faces bright from drink and travel. As they walked off the bridge a boy in a man's sports coat, barefoot, held out a cigar box and rattled the coins at them. Burke dropped a tenpenny piece in the box. "God love ye, sur, I'll say a Hail Mary, sur." They passed a girl wrapped in a red blanket sitting on the pavement with a box in her hand. Burke gave her tenpence. "I'll say a Hail Mary, sur." A big red-faced man played a reel on a busted fiddle further down the street in front of the Quinnsworth supermarket. Two more children sat on the pavement near him, begging. "The whole family's working," Anne said as they passed.

A week ago they had quarreled when Anne refused to give an old female beggar some change on O'Connell Street Bridge. She shook her head and kept walking. The old beggar had called out, "Well, then, missus, would you have some old clothes for a poor woman?" And Anne had turned and shouted, "My old clothes are on my back." Burke had laughed and said she had "a banker's mentality." But Anne didn't think it was funny. When she was a little girl her mother had pointed out a blind beggar they had passed an hour before now reading the newspaper in the Automat and she rarely failed to inform Burke that studies showed panhandlers made $250 a week in New York. Anne thought Burke a spendthrift, and Burke thought she was stingy. He thought most women were tight, acquiring this notion from his days pushing a hack in New York. Those were *his* studies, he'd shouted at her that Dublin day while she strode on ahead, calling him a fool for throwing his money away and a moron for playing macho jackoff for the benefit of strangers on a foreign street.

They made up in a chemist's shop when Burke apologized and bought her bubble bath scented with essence of ivy.

At the corner of Pembroke and Northumberland they stepped into the basement entrance of a Georgian house and entered the foyer. The maître d' came forward quickly. Dinner jacket. Two large white menus. "Will it be two, sir?"

He seated them near the open French doors leading to a walled rose garden. They started with a half bottle of white bordeaux, smoked salmon and brown bread. "What did he want? Isn't this wine a beautiful color?"

"Just to say hello. You said you didn't want to see him."

"How is he?"

"Seems the same. Hooked up with a rich woman in Europe."

"Really? How rich?"

"Loaded, from what he was saying."

"Well, good for him, even if he is a pain in the ass. And good for us," she raised her glass and they clinked. "Let's be happy."

"I love you, Anne."

"Oh, baby. Why when you say that do you always look so sad?"

"Sincere, not sad."

"Jesus, spare me sincerity. I want to be happy. We've been a pair of gloomy gusses lately."

"I love you. I don't care what they say about you."

She laughed. "That's it. More."

"God help me, missus, I do. So. Saints preserve me, I love every inch of you."

They both had a creamy crab bisque and grilled plaice with roasted potatoes and carrots and a full bottle of the white bordeaux.

"We never do anything elegant like this anymore," she said.

"Enjoy it now. Forget about what we never do."

"I will." She sipped the wine. "I never want to go home, Martin."

"Yeah," Burke said. "It's been good."

"And I don't want to go to Clare."

He put his fork down. "When did you decide that?"

"I've been thinking about it all day. I want to stay in Dublin. We'll lose so much work if we go out there."

"We've already paid a month's rent."

"We can get it back. We never signed anything. It took us time to make friends here, understand what we were doing. I don't want to start all over again. I love Dublin and I don't want to leave."

"Don't be a child, Anne."

"Don't be a grandfather."

They sat, staring. "I'm sorry," she said.

"Well, I'm not."

The waiter came and bussed the table. "Let's talk about it later," she said.

"Fine."

"Don't be upset, baby. Please?"

"I'm not."

Eating apple tart and double cream. "We'll save a lot of money moving out there. We'll cut rent in half. We'll have more space. The sea. You were excited."

"Later, okay? I'm sorry I brought it up."

They walked out to Pembroke Road and he crossed the street to the kiosk for a box of cigarettes. When they were home, in the flat, he came up behind Anne and hugged her. She lay her head back and he slipped his hands up to her breasts. "I've missed you."

"Get into bed," she said, going into the bathroom, unzipping her skirt.

Naked, lying on the comforter, Burke looked out the window at the tops of trees, the blue Irish sky. A sea gull cruised by. He heard the air brakes of buses singing a two-note tune somewhere. He lit a cigarette and waited for Anne to finish fitting the diaphragm. Burke hated it. He wouldn't put his mouth on her because of the jelly and he could feel the edge of the plastic and rubber. But Anne refused to take the pill.

He felt logy from wine and food. Burke didn't like sex after a meal, but Anne loved it—especially a restaurant meal. She came in the room naked and stood at the foot of the bed, her hands flat on her thighs. He put the cigarette out and reveled in his good fortune. Permitted to look at such a beautiful woman. She crawled onto the bed, lifted his balls and licked. Then she sucked him, slowly, using her tongue at the tip. She held him firm, rose up and sat down. They both grunted when he entered, and she giggled. She kissed his face, covered him with her hair and rocked steadily and slowly. She whispered in his ear. Burke felt a breeze on his legs. She sat up and he touched her mound lightly and fiddled. She closed her eyes, concentrating, and put both hands on his chest, stiff-armed, leaning hard with all her weight. He put his hands around and rhythmically opened and closed her buttocks.

Sleep. When he wakes the sky has dimmed. Anne is dressed in a loose brown and white robe, carrying a tray of iced coffee.

"Hello," she says, setting a glass next to the bed.

He touches her leg. "I was really out."

"About an hour," Anne says, sitting on the bed.

"Coffee's good."

They sit, silent, sipping.

CHAPTER 4

Conspiracy

After a small meal of macaroni and cheese eaten in front of the TV set, Burke took a long bath, dressed and went into the bedroom. Anne sat in one of the big easy chairs in the living room watching television and knitting. Around her were the books she was currently reading. A biography of Douglas MacArthur, *The Macrobiotic Cookbook*, *Pride And Prejudice* and *The Ginger Man*. She rarely concentrated on one book, but would read a paragraph of one, a chapter of the other. While she knitted she looked up from time to time, watching John Kenneth Galbraith's "The Age of Uncertainty." At one point she looked up and said, "Rubbish. *He's* uncertain, not me," and got up and switched channels to a BBC situation comedy devoted to jokes about homosexuals, women, and the Irish. She muttered at the set and continued to knit.

She had just learned to knit and was making a sweater for Burke out of *báinín* wool. Last night, when she had finished the back, she had held it up to him. It was at least four sizes too big. Burke said it looked like "John Wayne's sweater." She quickly said, "I'll rip it out and start over."

Burke said, "Don't do that. I'll use it as a good old rainy day sweater. I don't care how big it is."

"I'll rip it out. This isn't a joke. I want to make something nice. You're so fucking insensitive, Martin. I'm not making some big dumb-assed sweater for you to throw around." She'd started to cry. "You're so insensitive to my needs."

They'd had an alley fight about it. Anne threatening to finish the sweater for someone else, Burke telling her she was a damn fool for not measuring, Anne saying he was full of shit if he was going to tell *her* how to knit, Burke saying she was an impossible woman, a child, a bitch who didn't feel alive unless she was fighting, and

Anne calling him a pig Irish asshole who was so insensitive he couldn't cry unless he was stupid with drink, and didn't care for her or anything except himself—they had made up. He apologized. Anne ripped the sweater and started again.

He dialed Cleary's number.

"Hello?" A female voice.

"Liam Cleary, please."

"You have the wrong number."

"Tell him it's Martin Burke."

Sitting on the bed watching her knit. Cleary came on. "Martin."

"I've got to see you. Something I think is important for you."

"Do you know the Stillorgan Shopping Center?"

"Yes."

"There's an auto parts shop in the center. I'll be parked there in thirty minutes." And he hung up. Burke looked at the phone.

"I'm going out, sweetie."

She looked up. "Where?"

"Business," he said. "I won't be long. Couple of hours."

"Have fun," she said, counting stitches.

He drove out Northumberland in the Mini. The evening cool and clear, with the late sun giving Dublin a mellow light. Past the Royal Dublin Society. Anne and he had seen the Dublin Horse Show two weeks before. It was all upper crust, quite elegant, all the Irish showing the world they knew how to dress and behave like English aristocrats. That was until Eddie Macken, a tall blond mick with a sweet face from County Longford took an Irish hunter through the course flawlessly, jumping magnificently, riding the big stallion like he was strolling a boulevard, winning the Aga Khan Cup easily for Ireland. Then the crowd reverted to their true nature. They reacted like Irish longshoremen watching some paddy pug beat hell out of an Italian at the Sunnyside Garden for the main event. The R.D.S. rocked with cheers. One of their own had done it. The Irish had little to cheer for and when one of the native sons or daughters rose above the rest, well then, by God, you better get your voice tuned up and ready to yell, it might be a time before you see it again. Anne had taken pictures of Macken that day which she sold to an English magazine. She was in love with handsome Eddie.

Burke hit the dual carriageway and was doing sixty just to keep up with traffic. The Irish drove like they drank. Flamboyantly and carelessly. Full bore. "And always remember the longer you live, the sooner you'll bloody well die." And they killed themselves on the roads. Head on collisions at seventy. Running off country roads into poles. A hopeless people, Burke often thought. Like Puerto Ricans when they drove. No mechanical skill, no clue at all about how to take care of a car, it was all magic, just jump in the buggy and stomp on the throttle, make the world go faster.

He pulled into the shopping center and found the auto parts store. Cleary sat in a mustard-colored VW bug wearing an open-necked white shirt and tweed sports coat, his ginger hair full and wild. Walking to the car he saw someone sitting in the back of the VW. A young woman. He sat next to Cleary. "Hello, Martin," he said, started the car, put it in gear and drove out of the lot, back toward the dual carriageway.

"Deirdre O'Sullivan, Martin Burke," Cleary said, hitting fourth gear.

"Hello, Deirdre," he said, turning. A plain, Dublin urchin's face with huge round eyes, short black hair. In a sweater and jeans. Burke saw a shotgun with both barrels sawed down cradled in her lap.

"Expecting trouble?"

"Always," Cleary said.

He liked Cleary, but they weren't friends. Cleary wasn't the sort of man who had friends. He was a professional. Everything about him told you that here was a hard man, a guerrilla on active duty every waking minute, a combat veteran who, to survive, had stripped his character of every form of social grace, humor and compassion to be competent in his profession. Nothing else mattered to Liam Cleary. His whole life had been spent devoted to the dream. At sixteen he was a gunman in the Irish Republican Army. At twenty-two he was a graduate of Long Kesh Prison where he majored in political writing like Marx's study of "The Irish Problem," the writings of James Connolly, Vladimir Lenin, and Tom Barry. At thirty-five he was a leader of the movement to change the I.R.A. from a solely military stance into the realm of ideas—Marxist-Leninist ideas, attempting to reach out to other revolutionary guerrilla groups outside Ireland. He formed the Irish Socialist Army, a small group, held together only by his experience, reputation and will. Their most dedicated enemy, apart from the British Army, was the Provisional I.R.A. This group solved differences of opinion the same way as Brooklyn loan sharks. And the leaders of the I.R.A. hated Cleary intensely because he had once served with them and was now a traitor to the dream. There had been three assassination attempts on Cleary, all bungled. Liam was blessed, as they said. Years before, in a safe house in Antrim, waiting to move out, his column sat around a table checking weapons when Cleary looked up to see a young soldier mistakenly pulling the pin on a hand grenade and then trying to put it back. In the explosion, two of his men were blown apart, and three others were crippled, but Cleary was knocked unconscious and woke up unhurt.

Besides being a legend for his nine lives, he was also considered one of the most respected Republican spokesmen in Ireland by journalists because of his toughness, intelligence, and his complete lack of rhetoric, romanticism or Irish foolishness. Burke got his phone number from a reporter with Irish television who had been to New York once and had drinks bought for him by Nick Browne and Joe Flaherty one wet night at the Lion's Head. Burke claimed they were colleagues and the TV man had given him names and numbers for information for a trip North. When he called Cleary he identified himself, telling him his great friend from TV had suggested he call. Why? was Cleary's second word of the conversation after hello. Because, Burke said, I'm going North for the first time and want some information about—

Call me when you return, Cleary said, and hung up the phone.

After returning from Belfast, Burke met him one afternoon in the lounge of the Wicklow Hotel. Cleary, drinking club soda like a good cop on duty, listened to Burke make an ass of himself trying to get him to open up. He finally interrupted the American, told him to put his notebook away and listen, and began an hour and forty-five minute lecture about the history of Ireland and the political situation in the North from 1922 to the day before yesterday.

"Northern Ireland is," Cleary said, "and always has been, a place ruled by the gun. The ruling guns are British. And the 'troubles' are colonial troubles. Now, the British people, by and large, wish their troops were home. But they still cling to the idea that the army is in Northern Ireland as a 'peace keeping force.' The average citizen of the United Kingdom believes that the army is there to protect the Catholic from the Protestant. And it's true, for a time, that Catholic women did give tea and toast to British soldiers along the Falls Road. But that was only a moment in the years of war.

"The British Empire, like every empire in history, has worked on the principle of divide and rule. The British planted the six counties with Scottish Presbyterians three hundred years ago, and drove the Irish off their lands. To this day there is a war between settlers and natives. These two classes have been separated by wide cultural, economic and political differences, and the easiest method of maintaining these differences has been to inspire religious hatred. I'll give you an example. Have you ever heard of Jim Larkin?"

"No," Burke said.

"He was a union organizer born in Lancashire of Irish parents. In 1907 he went to Belfast to work with longshoremen, Catholic and Protestant alike. He succeeded in taking them out on strike. It was a remarkable achievement. Catholic and Protestant workers stood together and realized that perhaps culturally and religiously they were estranged, but on one issue they were bound: their common exploitation at the hands of Ulster aristocrats and British industrialists. The workers demanded home rule, separate from Britain, to deal with internal affairs. But the strike was broken by the Protestant ministers, the Orange Order, and the British Press shouting in chorus to the Protestant workers, 'Home Rule is Rome Rule.'

"The whole of Ireland leading up to the first world war was clamoring for home rule. The Protestant people of the North were armed by British interests to fight against this. Randolph Churchill called it 'playing the Orange card.' Over a hundred thousand men were under arms. There was a secret fund started. Waldorf Astor and Rudyard Kipling contributed thirty thousand pounds apiece. The whole House of Lords contributed to it. When the War of Independence started, Ulster stayed unionist. And after the treaty was signed between Britain and the newly created 'Free State' of Ireland, the British instigated the Government of Ireland Act, which established partition, and kept the six counties as part of the United Kingdom." Cleary rattled the cubes of ice in his glass, looked away, and then back to Burke. "The danger to the conservative establishment in Northern Ireland has never been from the insurrection of Catholic Republicans. Rather, it has always been that Protestant Loyalists would see they were descendants of a settler class exploited by the mother country. That Loyalist has to be held to the unionist line if the establishment is to keep power and England keep the North of Ireland. And the most effective way to do this is to nurture ancient prejudices. The Protestant feels under attack from evil forces. He realizes his community is one-fifth the population of the entire island, surrounded on all sides by a religion and a culture he's learned to despise. So he 'stands fast' and gives no surrender.

"The troop level in the North now is fourteen thousand British soldiers, comprising fourteen major units. They believe they are there as a civilizing influence to keep the savage Irish from each other's throats, but in effect, they are preserving the empire. Since the time of Henry the Second the 'Irish problem' has dominated English politics. What they've never realized is that it is not an Irish problem. It's a British problem. And they are the only ones who will solve it by severing their past, taking their losses, and going home for good."

While he spoke, Mick Dowd of the *Evening Herald* came over and he and Cleary spoke in Irish, obviously exchanging pleasantries. Then Mick said to Burke, "He's a tiresome man to interview, Martin. He'll tell you nothing he doesn't want you to hear."

"Journalists," Cleary said, and almost smiled. "The greatest non-job ever devised."

When Mick had gone Burke asked him what they'd said in Irish.

Cleary's gray eyes drilled him. "Why don't you learn the language? What business is it of yours what he said? Normally I don't speak to the press in English. And the lads in the North don't either. But you're a yank, from a trendy New York paper, aren't you? We have to make concessions for such a great personage as yourself, don't we?"

Burke filed his story, which never ran. He didn't learn Irish, but he read three books of Irish history Cleary had recommended. He bothered other reporters for weeks with questions about Irish culture, psychology, economics and day-to-day political matters. Then, before he went North again, he met with Cleary once more at the Wicklow and, like every good student, paraded his knowledge. And like every good teacher, Cleary, sipping his on-duty club soda, began to treat him not as a child, but as an equal. He never insulted Burke, nor was quick, but encouraged, provoked and treated him as a professional.

As Cleary drove the VW along Mount Merrion Avenue, toward the sea, Burke realized that the silence in the car was because he was no longer a journalist. He was a conspirator.

He parks the bug in a small lot off Sandymount Strand facing the sea next to a squat stone tower. The tide is out. There are people out near the waterline half a mile away across the flat rivuleted sand looking like dots in a watercolor landscape. Closer in two dogs scamper across the beach, chasing each other. It is nine o'clock but the melancholy light still lingers in gray clouds over the Irish Sea. A jogger, in a bright blue running suit, runs past.

"You shouldn't do that to such a fine young wife," Cleary says.

"What's that?"

"Go to public houses and get jarred."

Deirdre gives a short barking laugh.

Cleary says, "Shouldn't neglect young women that way, Martin."

Burke thinks: He's testing me, that's it. He's enjoying the spectacle of a virgin losing innocence. Throwing my lot in with a low occupation.

"Since when is my wife a subject for you to talk about?"

Cleary laughs. "Sensitive, is it? Just a bit of banter to pass the time. Well, enough marital advice. What do you want?"

Burke speaks, looking out at the dusk on the beach, beginning by saying he's merely a messenger. Then he tells them of O'Connor, the news from Germany and the rest of his tale. When he finishes Deirdre nudges him, offering cigarettes around. Cleary lights them with a long kitchen match which he extracts and strikes on a slim silver box.

"I'll have to meet our Mr. O'Connor," he says. "How close is he to the woman?"

"I don't know. I'd say they were close. They've been in some scrapes together."

Deirdre, leaning forward, begins speaking in Irish to Cleary, spitting the words at him in the guttural language that sounds so sweet in song but in conversation is like listening to Low Dutch. Cleary responds. Silence.

"Tell Martin in a language he can understand, Dee-Dee."

"They don't want money?" she says, as Burke looks straight ahead at the long shadows on the sand. "Is that what I heard? M-60's, Armalites, and all that blowey gear, and they don't want money?"

"They want what they told me they want."

"We're no bloody diplomats, Liam. We train for one fight, we protect people who struggle for us, not fookin' Germany."

"Aye," Cleary says. "Strange crew, the Germans. And these young ones are stranger still. What country occupies them? I've been doing this all my life. They've been at it for the last fifteen minutes." He pauses, blows smoke from his nostrils. "Palestinians, yes. Moluccans, yes. Even Italians. But Germans?"

Burke thinks: I'm a perfect forty-year-old fool, way over my head, too jumpy for this, a prime jerk, not understanding the turf nor the people. His mind is dead with indecision, not knowing whether to speak or stay silent. His mouth is open and he's saying, "O'Connor's an American."

"Yes, but at least he has ties, roots—"

"No," Burke says. "He doesn't know de Valera from King Billy."

"Neither did you."

"O'Connor's not like me at all."

"Let's walk, Martin. Dee-Dee, you stay."

"No," she says.

"Yes," Cleary says, and they get out. Cleary is walking quickly along the Strand.

"Do you have fags?" he asks.

They stop near the top of stone stairs leading to the beach. Burke gives him a Players and Cleary uses another kitchen match from his silver box. The flame leaps and then is tamed by his cupped hands. Burke thinks: Emphysema must kill more revolutionaries than bullets.

Burke follows Cleary down the stairs to the beach. He has a brisk military step, his shoulders tight and strong in the tweed jacket. They begin walking out toward the sea. The light is falling fast now and the Dubliners are making their way back from the water's edge, looking like refugees with their baskets and blankets and jugs and bottles, herding their children. Looking at them, seeing the pale bodies of a northern climate, the ginger hair, the auburn hair, the glossy black hair, the freckles, the laconic walk of the Irish, the small mouths and snub noses, hearing a boy in a hand-me-down bathing suit say something to his father who's carrying a beach chair, and the mother says, "Now don't be bold, Francis," the softness, the strangeness, Burke thinks, these are my people, I've come from this place, but I'll never be one of them. I'll never really know them.

A stout old woman, the only person between them and the water, with her skirts tucked up, is chasing a mad little terrier across the sand. "Come, Willie," she shouts, and Willie is dodging, scurrying, enthralled with the game. Cleary squats down and whistles and coos and Willie comes and sits between his legs. The old woman thunders up. "God love ye," she pants. She has a piece of rope she ties around Willie's neck. "He's the boy's dog. I give him the odd walk now and then."

Cleary rises and says, "But who's walking who, mother?"

The old woman laughs, and softly God blesses them again before dragging Willie off toward the Strand.

They've come to the water's edge, the sea lapping like a lake, rolling easily, darker than the fading blue sky. Cleary looks back toward the Strand, half a mile away and says, sadly, "It's a fine night for Dublin." Burke looks back with him to the land curling from the south around to the east, with the yellow lights from hundreds of parlor windows dotting the shores of Blackrock, Monkstown, to the gentle lights of Dun Laoghaire harbor and the twinkling light of Dalkey down the coast.

"Do you see Dee-Dee standing there?" Cleary is pointing.

Burke follows his arm but sees nothing. They are now alone on the beach.

"You've got good eyes."

"I just know what I'm looking for."

"Does she always carry that gun?"

Cleary grins. "Most of the time. Awesome thing, the old sawed-off. You've got a weapon you can conceal easily, a hand gun you can't miss with. She's a holy terror, our little Miss O'Sullivan. Good soldier. There are two Brits and an RUC she's responsible for." He squats and grabs a handful of sand. "Are you joining us?"

"No," Burke says, and squats next to him.

"Why are you involved?"

"I'm not, goddamnit. I told you. I'm the delivery boy."

"That won't be good enough for me, Martin."

"I'm trying to help a friend, how's that?"

"Tell him to get a quick plane to the States."

"Yeah. But you don't know my friend."

"I will soon enough." He pauses, the sand slipping from his fingers. "I know this place well. Sometimes I think of this sand as refuge." He shakes his head. His slight smile. "Gone poetic on you, Martin. Indulgence. Which is one more curse of this backward bloody race. Prison did it to me. You'd be amazed what words do to you in jail. They become power, because when you can get a book, or a newspaper, anything with words on it, you're free. Or you think you are." He pauses again. Stares at Burke. "I know this beach very well. I used to come here all the time, the whole summer and autumn after I was ordered to sign out."

"What's that?"

"Signing out? That's what we called it. The order comes to recognize courts, get on good behavior, and they turn you loose. Me and Rocky Ryan, both lads who were doing time. Got word to sign out and we did. Poor Rocky. What a soldier! He was shot to pieces on Capel Street after robbing a pub that June 1950. And will be remembered by most of the Irish as being just a thug, proof that the Republican movement is just a front for criminals and malcontents. But they don't realize, most of them, what prison does to a man. Especially an English prison full of Irish men. God." He shakes his head again, and laughs. "I was in such a daze when they let me go. My orders were to go to Dublin, check in, and then relax and rest for a few months before going back on active service. My father, down in Bray, God keep him, gave me some money every week and I got a little flat on the South Circular Road and just walked around Dublin, stumbling about, and always ended up here. Poor Rocky had no money, and wasn't a man to sit still. He was broken, good and broken. But I disciplined myself. You haven't a clue how odd everything is when you finally walk away from jail. Every little petty forgettable detail of life is a crisis. Paying my rent to the woman of the house was excruciating. Having a drink in a pub, trying to converse with strangers. Crossing a street, my God, it was an adventure. And women. The fashions had all changed and it seemed every woman I saw was a tart. After being caged up with adult men for three years children seemed so delicate, so fragile that I was afraid to be with them. So I came here, and sat on the sand. Looking out at that bleak sea. Just holding on, clinging for dear life. But it's only a strip of sand, isn't it? Bit of beach and the sea. A help to me once. What do you want from me?"

"Nothing, Liam. I'm not asking for a favor. O'Connor is here in a strange country, doesn't know anyone and asked my help. I know you'll give him the best advice he can get."

"I apologize for the remark about your wife."

"Okay."

"Last time we spoke you said you were going out to County Clare. Moher, is it?"

"Yes."

"There's a good man in Ennistymon, just down the road, name of Cyril McGuffin. Mad as a bedbug, but a good man. He'll be a help to you."

"Thanks."

"Did you know, I've never heard of anyone in the Movement named Conor Graham? Your friend might be strolling into a great stupid trap, and he might be dragging me along with him. Mr. Graham could be Special Branch, he could be a rogue Provo, he could be anyone. That's the dicey part. Now, I'm going to ask you a favor." He grabbed more sand. "I want your help with O'Connor. I want you to be with us when we meet, to straighten him out on certain points and—" Cleary stands up quickly, turning back toward the north. Two figures are running toward them. Burke thinks: They're joggers. But then he sees they're dressed in street clothes and running too fast. Dee-Dee shouting. Runs straight toward them shouting something. She lets go one barrel spitting orange and blue. Cleary grabs the American, pulls him to his feet and pushes him toward the Strand, shouting, "Run! Stay low and run!" and takes off along the water's edge. Burke runs ten feet and loses his legs, falls on his face in the cold sand. Dee-Dee passes, her shotgun broken, loading a shell on a dead run. She only looks at Burke for a second. The runners pass and spread out, both in flat caps and sports coats. They're nearly on top of Cleary who is running low, swaying from side to side, when they stop. One kneels and both pistols are far out in front of them, silhouetted against the sea. Two shots, then a third. Cleary staggers, stands up straight and pitches forward as more shots crack. Dee-Dee, still running, is shouting when the gunmen whirl on her. She fires both barrels and jumps out to the sand. They fire a barrage at her, shooting wildly. She loads and fires again. Kneeling now, the sawed-off on her hip, but they're off, running south, digging hard along the sand. Dee-Dee is quick to Liam. She rolls the bunched form over, kneels next to him for a second and runs back toward Burke. "Come on, yank," she's yelling. "Come on, you fool."

He chases her back across the sand.

CHAPTER 5

To the Widow's Room

The summer Martin Burke was nineteen, he and his buddy Tim set out from New York in a raggedy Dodge to explore the country. One midnight, flat broke, and the Dodge thirsty, they found themselves passing through the affluent town of Creve Coeur, Missouri. Tim had a ten-foot length of garden hose he'd packed in the trunk and, with his urging, and a need to keep moving west, Burke entered the life of crime. They backed the Dodge up a long curving driveway next to a Chrysler parked in front of a long low ranchhouse. The Chrysler was brand-new, with chrome gleaming in the Missouri moonlight. After nearly emptying the Chrysler tank and depositing it in the Dodge, Tim and Martin went around the back of the house, and pausing only once at the door, listening for human sounds, walked into the kitchen. They paused again. Silence. No one home or everyone in dreamland. They found their way to the refrigerator and began to load up, giggling at their audacity and the cornucopia they had stumbled upon. Cold chicken, a big ham, jars of pickles, bottles of soda, beer, milk. While Martin hefted the ham out with both hands, Tim was looking for a box to cart their treasure away in. Martin heard him say, "Don't be scared, mam." Turning he saw Tim staring at a woman in a white nightgown standing down the hall in the half light of the dark house. "Don't be," he started again but she let out a holler. She was standing in one spot, frozen except for her vocal chords, raving, shouting the name "Pete" over and over. Martin was out the door running, while Tim was trying to calm her down. Martin ran around the house, but stopped when he heard Tim struggling with someone. Tim was wrestling with a naked man. Curses and shouts, and finally Tim threw him down and they were gunning the Dodge down the drive and away, with Pete's voice shouting at them that he had their number and they'd never get away. They drove through the night, sure that every cop in Missouri was after them, giddy, high on the fugitive's adrenaline rush, feeling more exhilarated by one petty criminal encounter than dozens of good works. Alive to every thought. Alive to the present moment, feeling the present as a tangible thing. Not fleeting, but something that was captured and could be turned over in your hands and studied like a piece of fine glass.

Dee-Dee drove over the Tara Street Bridge, across the Liffey to the north side of Dublin, constantly checking the mirrors, her eyes glittering. Burke felt it again. The tangible present, the string of moments more real than the past, defying the future. His head was clear. He had the animal's total awareness of its body. And he relied on that physical confidence moving into unfamiliar territory. It would be the next day, sitting in front of a fire, listening to a young woman talking, that the thrill of living only in the moment would shatter. He would drop that fine fragile glass and be again splintered, rummaging through jagged pieces of the past, afraid, blind to the future.

One or two kids had seen them running up the stone steps to the Strand and piling into the Volkswagen. Staring, openmouthed as Dee-Dee pulled away quickly into the traffic, going north and then doubling back through the quiet, orderly, Protestant streets of Sandymount, looking for Cleary's murderers. She then decided to make for the north side when they heard the up and down chant of sirens bearing down. She said very little. She thought they were Provisionals. "They've been after him for years. They've tried twice this year and we hit them back for it. Stupid," she said, and then again, "Stupid. Stupid. Stupid. You and your bloody great plan. Who followed you tonight?"

"No one."

"Your great fookin' friend knew."

"No."

"Stupid."

"Why didn't they—"

"Fookin' thugs. They didn't want you. Who cares about your neck? They wanted him. Not me. Not you. Him."

She drove past the Customs House, and out along the North Strand Road. "You'll watch your arse, yank. You'll watch it now or it'll be shot off."

It was finally night in Dublin. They crossed over the Royal

Canal and moved on toward the Annesley Bridge Road and Fairview Park. The Irish were coming out of the park now, walking slowly, and the big barnlike pubs, lit with bright yellow and white lights, were filling with a strong Friday night crowd.

Dee-Dee pulled the bug to the curb, shut the lights off but left the motor running. "I'm scattered," she said, looking straight ahead, both hands on the wheel.

Her plan had been, when they heard the sirens closing on Sandymount, to go to the office of the *Irish Patriot*, the weekly newspaper, the political organ of the I.S.A., and also its cover. No member of the I.S.A. admitted to the government that the army existed. They were just socialists, working in the political sphere, attached to a newspaper. Smoking, staring straight ahead, Deirdre thought out loud, "Liam's dead. The office can't help us."

She didn't feel grief, but she knew she would. She would give herself that. She willed it, to have it. But not now. She was not angry and had no need for revenge. That, too, she would have later. That, she guaranteed herself. Now was a fact, a car, a stranger, a shotgun. Now there was war to think of. Clear action. Re-action, methods, time and terrain.

Burke watched three teddy boys, northside Dublin youths in leather and dungarees, drunk, saunter out of the park and begin roughhousing each other. Pulling hair, slapping, punching, tripping. Headlocks. Women passed by quickly, shooting only one or two glances at the spectacle, that devastating, hard and superior Irish woman's look. Were they the smartest women in the world, Burke wondered, or was it that they just thought they were?

"We'll see your friends," Dee-Dee said, and made a quick perfect U turn. She drove until she spotted a green and beige telephone booth. She pulled over, again shutting the lights and leaving the motor on. "Are you familiar with this?" she said, pulling the sawed-off from under her seat and handing it to him.

"Yeah," he lied.

She broke it down, reached across him and took a box of shells from the glove compartment, rammed two shells home and closed the weapon with a click. The gun felt light as his hand found the wood stock. "Don't hurt yourself, now," she said. "O'Connor's his name. First name?"

"Terry. The Shelbourne."

"If you see anyone—anyone you fancy is up to no good—any

car that stops—don't wait. Open up with that fellah."

Burke watched her in the booth. She made three calls. The first two very brief. The other longer. She looked to Burke like any young Irish woman out on a Friday night in her American outfit of jeans and a sweater, probably a student at Trinity or a teacher, calling a friend. She returned, her eyes not on him, or the car, but on the street, the passing traffic, tossing back her short black hair easily and glancing behind her.

The car in gear, she pulled out and Burke told her to put the lights on, making him feel on top of it, and not just a passenger. He slipped the sawed-off under his seat. "Who'd you call?"

"The gardai. And then your Mr. O'Connor. Had him paged in the dining room. He said they were in the middle of a meal and I said I didn't care if they were in the middle of a great sweaty screwing."

"Why the guards?"

She turned and her eyes were livid. "And leave him lying in the water? Ready to float out to sea?"

"But the sirens—"

"Think, for Jesus' sake! It could have been an ambulance or the guards going for a tea break."

"Were we recognized?"

"No," she said. "Even if we were they won't say a thing to the guards about a madwoman with a shotgun and a man running on the beach."

They drove down O'Connell Street, silent, past Parnell's monument and the Gresham with the blue marquee and doorman dressed in a blue uniform standing at the curb with his hands clasped behind his back. The sidewalks were filled, and the neons from the movie theaters, the Chinese restaurants and shops were flashing green and red.

Something was added to Burke's intoxication, a new thrill synergizing the omnipotent thoughts of the outlaw. Here, on the broad avenue, in Dublin's Friday night parade, a pure, singing rage came to him. Cleary dead. Killed by one of his own. Looking at the Irish strolling by, Burke hated them. Oppressed for centuries by a stronger, wealthier neighboring country, they had, like all victims of oppression, cultivated the values of deceit, cunning, false joy in the presence of strangers, envy, clannishness, bristling donkey-headed pride. And remembered every slight no matter how petty or how long ago. Not only remembered, no! Passed it on, indoctrinating their children, holding the flame of bitterness close, shielding and feeding it, keeping it alive because, if the flame was snuffed, what would they have? What would keep them going? How could they face their children? Their nation? Their past?

The Irish never forget, his old man told him when asked why he had left his home. William Burke had arrived in New York in 1922, at the height of the Civil War, young, strong, quiet, poor, knowing no one. He never talked about his journey or the reason why he left. Only to say, now and again, when he was gentlemanly stewed, or with another mick from the other side, that Ireland, though home and dear and beautiful, was a doomed and damned land, now isn't it so? He left his family to figure it out. He didn't care, he wasn't going to say. And Martin only asked him once. Martin knew. His father taught him the lesson with his silence.

Cleary dead. He had reminded Burke of his father and men from the old neighborhood of 90th Street and Third Avenue, thirty years ago. A certain type of Irishman, who had the sandy hair, the freckled skin, carrying himself well. The type of man who, when not working, would never be caught dead without a clean pressed shirt, the sleeves rolled one turn, just so. The type of man who was more intelligent than his mates, but made no show of it, who seemed at times to be close to boiling over, simmering along, but controlling himself, somehow always at war in some small way with himself.

That was the old man's answer to his son's question—the Irish (or verbatim, "those people") never forget. It was all they had, all they really cherished. Not their gifts, their love of family, not even their religion, but only the memory of what had been done to them and who, among them, was Judas. The Irish hated themselves equally with their enemies, the hatred a product of *divide et impera*, yet one more present from the masters, the Sassanach, the Brit, don't you ever forget, oh God bless England so we pray, whack fol the diddle of the die dol day.

Betrayal, plotting, swift country justice by maiming, blinding, crippling, lynching. Rage and ballads, poetry and loss, imagination, whiskey and priests, death and insanity, death, exile, the wanderer, a rambler, a gambler, a long way from home and if you don't like me then leave me alone. And more death. A heritage of noble causes and ignoble people. Blather, slyness, clever at life, soft smiles to conceal the stone heart, and rage near at hand, easy to find and use, like a tool a good workman always replaces in the same spot, so he won't have to think when he wants it, but just reach out and there it is, ready to go to work.

She parked the bug just west of Kildare Street in the empty cab stand and they stared at the facade of the Shelbourne, the stone nymphs holding electric torches, flanking the entrance. O'Connor appeared on the steps, dressed in a white linen suit. He turned his gray head back toward the hotel and was immediately joined by a young, slim, blond woman, the same height as O'Connor, dressed in a green skirt, high heels and a soft green silk blouse. They stepped to the street after the doorman, whistle in his mouth, beginning his search for a cab. "That's them."

"La di da," Dee-Dee said.

They looked like a lot of foreigners in Dublin. Overdressed, a bit ill at ease, realizing Ireland was not what they ever imagined. An English Ford taxi pulled up, O'Connor tipped the doorman who helped Gudrun in with a flourish.

"Right," Dee-Dee said, and they watched the cab make the turn around Stephen's Green. Dee-Dee followed them around the Green, down through Grafton, across the Liffey and back toward the north side. Then she turned off Gardiner Street into Sean Mac-Dermot and pulled over in front of a dim tenement. "I'm picking them up at Mountjoy Square and bringing them here, I'll let them wait, when I'm sure there's no funny business, and then I'll come on. Second floor of this house," she pointed, "first door at the head of the stairs, knock and say, 'It's time, Mairead.' Got it?"

"Yes."

"Wait for me."

"Right."

"Give me a fag," she said. He put the box in her hand. "Are you with us, Martin?" A cigarette bobbed in her mouth.

"Yes," he said, surprised.

"And why are you with us?"

"I'll see it through."

"Good enough for now."

Burke got out and she said, "Well, cheerio, yank," and drove off.

Alone on the sidewalk. A street light's simple glow. The night was heavy. Damp sidewalk, damp old brick. A priest coming toward him, walking oddly. Up close he has only one arm, the other arm slack, the black sleeve hanging, pinned to the jacket pocket. "Good evening," he says.

"Evening, Father," Burke says softly, quickly, because he can't imitate a brogue.

Burke thinks: What am I doing here? "I'll see it through." God. Not my country, or my cause.

He went into the tenement and began to climb the old stairs, a smell of large families living piled against each other. A radio's insistent cackle. A smell of meat sizzling. Voices, not human, only sounds coming from behind walls. Garbage in the hallways. The floor toilets smelling of disinfectant on top of piss. The supper hour of Dublin.

Reaching the third floor, which is the second floor in this part of the world, a flash of fear comes. Burke thinks: I'm set up. She wants to be rid of me, she accuses me of Liam's death. Those phone calls. She'll do O'Connor and the German, another waits to kill me in this slum. "Mairead, it's time," he said. Nothing. Voices in the stairwell, children coming. Silence, then the children coming closer.

He twisted the handle and stepped into the room, just as a woman reached the door. Both were startled, but Burke more so, flinching, the door opened to the hall, the doorknob in his hand. "Burke?" she said, her eyes wide. A stormy face.

"Yes."

"Come in, come in."

He closed the door and followed her in from a small foyer to a large dim room, crowded with furniture. A Bank of Ireland calendar on the wall, a garish picture of the Sacred Heart, and a cheap print of Sean Keating's "Men of the South." A widow's room, Burke thought, clean, poor, every object a connection, a shrine to the past life, and yet somehow empty. Someone missing. She moved quickly, seating Burke in a plain easy chair next to a bare table. She was big breasted, thick bodied, her colorless hair bound in a bun. When she looked at Burke again, squarely, defiantly, he saw a mustache fringe of dark hairs over her short, set mouth. "Have you eaten? I've got nothing but biscuits."

"Thank you," Burke said, crossing his legs, looking into the bedroom. Neat, orderly. "I'm not hungry, thank you." He reached for his cigarettes out of nervousness, but quickly remembered giving them to Dee-Dee, and felt safe, he wasn't set up. He was accepted, he'd live.

The woman took a kerchief from a drawer of a drum table and bound it around her head, lightly sticking a strand of hair under.

"I've nothing to drink. Only some port wine and whiskey. No beer."

"Whiskey would be lovely."

As she went into the kitchen to fetch it Burke thought of a diary entry he'd made a week after they'd arrived in London. "Must cut 'lovely,' 'fantastic' and 'incredible' from my vocabulary. Use them all the time and hear myself foppish, idiotic."

She returned with a short drinking glass and a full bottle of John Powers Three Swallow. She set both on the table next to him, took a sweater from the sofa and draped it over her shoulders. "I've no ice, if that's the way you take it."

"This is fine," Burke said, pouring the honey booze.

"Then I'm off," she said. "Don't lock up after me."

She stared at Burke. What to say? She seemed to be memorizing his face, then quickly turned and left the flat.

Burke sipped the light, sweet whiskey. Then he emptied the tumbler and poured another. He was at an age where his drinking worried him. He'd often told Anne that, if it hadn't been for her, the four years he'd lived with her, he would be a major league drunkard. Anne, by the way she lived, showed him that it wasn't necessary to drink something every day (which was what he was doing before he met her) and that drinking hard didn't make him more open or imaginative, but merely stupid. Almost everyone he knew in America drank too much. And everyone in Ireland he'd met. Except Cleary. His club soda, the Pioneer's drink. There were times now when he desired, with an urgency intense as lust, to get totally shit-faced drunk. To "crash and burn" as his old man would say, to drown in the warm satisfied balm of booze. He wasn't a violent man, and drinking never took him that way. He got maudlin when he was loaded, and hated it. He wept if he was drunk enough, which was the only time he allowed himself. Part of him knew that drinking was good for him, and part of him saw nothing but catastrophe in it. Anne put it in perspective. He loved her in a moment's time as he sipped the Irish, her youth, her devotion that puzzled and embarrassed him, her body, her humor, but then, whiskey no longer in his brain but in his blood, he thought he loved her because she made him feel he'd live forever if he could be near her.

Burke poured another, set it on the table, stood up and toured the room. No books. Ah, here's the Douay Bible, huge, red-covered, a gold cloth placemark. I'd shoot the pope for a cigarette. They were on the way. He stood in front of the framed, glassed Sacred Heart. He felt fine, meeting O'Connor in this place, meeting his German woman in a place he felt at home in. She was a piece of ass, he thought, remembering her on the steps of the Shelbourne. O'Connor had always been good with women. Attractive, easy with them. There was that secretary at WNET who Burke and O'Connor sat with one August day in a waiting room, waiting to be summoned to see a man who would lay out money. Burke was embarrassed, O'Connor composed. The secretary answered calls, typed, ignored them. She was young, dark, Jewish. Natalie. Very New York, smart as hell, overly made-up, serene. Three days later, Burke called O'Connor and Natalie answered, sleepy and giggly, and put O'Connor on. He could see them in bed, imagined Natalie in all her dark, made-up, Jewish nakedness. Burke made a remark, crude enough, but nothing too bad, and O'Connor passed it by, embarrassing Burke. The boyo had it. When you're hot, you're hot. He went back for his glass and returned to the Sacred Heart.

Jesus with a long cavernous gray face. Long hair to His shoulders, falling apathetically. His breast opened to a bleeding heart, two swords sunk to the hilt, emerging at the bottom with the blades dripping blood. Jesus wept. And He had every reason to.

Am I walking into eternity along Sandymount Strand? I will forge in my pants the uncreated booze of my race. Burke sipped. Did the witch have any cigarettes? I have nothing to smoke, only cigars and hashish. That face would certainly cause Jesus to weep. He took another tour of the flat. She wouldn't smoke, no, and wouldn't hold with them that did. Burke returned to his chair, told himself to drink slowly, think of what would come. He sipped. Ireland sober is Ireland stiff.

Irish whiskey, he thought, was the reason the Irish were in love
with drunkenness. Or was it Guinness? Both soft, sweet, friendly
as a puppy. The stout formidable, noble in its blackness, and easy
on the throat. Mother's milk, and didn't women still drink it when
nursing? If they didn't, they should. Didn't Robby Buckley, the
big dark Corkman, he of the talk, the smile, the clap on the back,
the man of such polite, effortless, meaningless words, wasn't it
Robby himself who related to Burke one soft night when both
were hammered and jarred to their socks in licensed premises that
when Robby was only a wee boy and caught cold his grandma
would put him to bed, propped up with pillows, with good tea
and English chocolate biscuits, and would put a pan of water on
the stove, and when it boiled wouldn't she put a great black
bottle of stout made at Arthur Guinness and Sons of St. James
Gate, Dublin, in the pan and heat it just so and foamily place the
warmed porter in a great glass with a spoon of sugar and have him
drink to help his poor chest and poor throat? Wasn't it soft, and
good and healing? Robby was a man not unfamiliar with the taste
of drink. A good man's failing.

Burke sat. He was making an effort at composing himself when
two men entered the flat. The first was a tall thin man, short
haired, middle aged, followed by a boy in his late teens with a
pale twisted face. Burke stood up and the man came forward
quickly. Smiling, his hand out. "Martin Burke?" he said and took
Burke's hand. A hard, pitted face.

"Yes," Burke said.

He gripped his hand, put his other on Burke's arm near the
elbow and pulled him slightly off balance. The boy wrung Burke's
free arm behind his back and twisted. His other arm was twisted
back painfully and the boy clipped manacles over his wrists, tripped
him and he fell hard to the floor, rolled over and took a kick in
the shoulder.

"That will do, Jimmy," the man said. Burke looked up at the
boy's pitiless, stupid face. Half of his mouth was limp, grotesque,
like a stroke victim's.

The man looked about the room, his eyes falling on the bottle.
"He likes his whiskey. We'll be taking you for a ride now. And
you'll be quiet and respect our wishes or we'll tear you to pieces.
Right, Jimmy?"

"Aye."

Burke looked at the boy. He was still staring down at him. The boy knelt next to him, brought his fish-white face close, his sick mouth dripping. "What are you lookin' at?"

"Where's Dee-Dee?" Burke said. "Dee-Dee O'Sullivan?"

The boy put his thumb in Burke's eye. He twisted his head away from the sudden pain. "Who, now?" the man was asking. "Who?"

The boy pulled Burke to his feet by his hair. He was terrified, panic and pain one. His shoulder was flaming, his eye was sightless, fierce, liquid.

"Look at him starin'. Take a good look, your honor."

Burke continued to stare, trying to compose his face with thoughts of survival, flight. The man was at his side talking soothingly with mockery while the boy frisked him for weapons. Burke felt fear sliding away from him like a boat from a dock, and now that he was on his feet, anger, low and quiet, replacing it. "You will be polite with us, now, Martin, won't you? You will be considerate of us, won't you?"

The boy slid his hand up Burke's thigh and cupped his crotch. He squeezed gently, once, twice, a third time. "I think the bugger's in love with me," the boy said, and his expression was the same, bleak as December. He squeezed hard and pulled the balls toward him. Burke kicked with a short, quick shot and found his ankle. A howl went up. The man was trying to grab Burke's shoulders but he wrenched free and got another kick into the boy's leg. Burke was roaring, furious to free his hands from the cuffs, kicking the boy who was scuttling across the floor, trying to get away. Burke was cursing and spitting, screaming about killing. The man, measuring his blow, stalked him, stepped up lightly and tapped him expertly across the temple with the flat stock of a .45 Colt automatic. Burke was a house coming down. In his fall he twisted his knee badly, and then the boy broke his nose with a kick. He didn't feel these injuries; he was out, feeling nothing real or factual, but only the abstract anguish of unconsciousness.

CHAPTER 6

Wicklow

He came to once, just before they put him in the car, hearing through a gray gauze of pain the man speaking to the boy. "Stop whimpering now like the dog you are. Stop it! Or I'll go to work on you myself." The voice was strange because he was not sure for a moment where he was. An Irish voice, a friend of his father's, coming from the parlor to his bedroom.

Burke couldn't hear the boy's response but felt, before he dipped back into nausea and sleep, a blood thrill that he had inflicted some pain on the monster.

There was a flatness. Cool against his burning face. He was awake, but stayed still and let his body come to him, analyzing what was wrong, what was right. His knee hurt. Legs okay. Crotch fine. Sick in the stomach. Something wrong with the nose, no breath, throbbing. The head was an exposed nerve. Teeth, teeth were there, but his mouth was vile, poisonous glop from whiskey and panic. He opened his eyes and was pleased that he could see with both of them. The back of the man's head, cheaply barbered, the boy sitting next to him. He was crushed against the window, hands cuffed behind and sitting on them, dead, pins and needles. He closed his eyes and fought to think one clear thought.

They won't kill me. Who are they? Monsters. Liam dead. Is it them? No. Yes. No. Remember the beach. Where was Dee-Dee? Set me up. No. Yes. No. She's in trouble herself. No. Open your eyes. See where we are. Moving fast. Going to heave. Hold on. Country, deep night. Where? If they wanted me dead they'd do me in Dublin, yes? No. Yes. Drop me right on the street, or in that witch's parlor. The widow! Yes, the fucking cunt, she knew, yes, yes, she knew these two, but if she did then so did Dee-Dee, the widow! I'll take her head and bounce it on the sidewalk like a coconut, I'll choke her till her fucking tongue turns blue, I'll—

Jimmy swiveled around. "He's up, Laff." The man gave him a quick look. "Sleep well, Martin?" His eyes were back on the road. "Gave us a bit of fright. Carrying on like that. You're not ill, are you?"

Jimmy laughed.

Burke straightened up. When he took his face from the window his head was a mass of aching. Something was broken inside, something was loose. He got off his hands with an effort and sat straight. "That's better," Jimmy said. "You look fresh as flowers now."

"Fuck you," Burke said, and quickly resolved to say nothing more, because words made his nose flare and throb.

"You will, will you? No time for it, yank. You're a dead man already. Sittin' there, you're a dead man."

But Burke didn't hear, he nodded and was taken by something like sleep.

"Time now, Mr. Burke," Laff, the man, was saying.

Standing in front of the car, in a wood. The headlights shining like sharks' eyes. Burke took it in. On my feet. The boy gone. Another man off to the side. "D'ye see this weapon, Martin?" Laff asked, holding the .45 in a beam of light. "See it? It'll paint these trees with your own gray matter. Oh, it'll do a frightful thing to ye. Your own mother wouldn't look at ye afterwards. That is, of course, if ye have a mother. See it, Martin? Does a person like you have a mother? What do ye say?"

A voice from the darkness. "On with it, Lafferty."

"On your knees, now, Martin. We'll hear your confession. On your knees, ah, that's it."

It was a country road, loose gravel. He was kneeling facing away from the headlights. Trees, and a ridge of mountain. There were no thoughts. Anne.

"Did you bring Liam Cleary to Sandymount?"

"No."

"Did you plan Liam Cleary's death?"

"No."

"I want the truth, you idiot!"

Burke hung his head and began to weep. "He was my friend."

"He was not! It's the German's idea, isn't it, Martin? Now, the truth! Now!"

The .45 went off and Burke lost his hearing. He was in a tin can. Echoes. The slap of the slug in the wet earth next to him.

Echoes. He pitched forward. Lafferty brought him back to his knees, dragging him up with the cuffs.

"Truth," he whispered, close behind him. "Truth is life, Martin."

"He was my friend."

"Truth is life, Martin."

"I don't want to die."

Whispering, "Then live. The truth, Martin. Last chance, now."

"I want to go home," Burke sobbed.

"Last chance. Last call for supper. Absolutely the last call for supper."

Burke let his mind go, but kept his body straight, and was quiet as he could be, shivering.

"What, sir?" Lafferty asked.

Silence. Then, "Bring him along. And mind you don't injure him further."

"Yes, sir. It was mostly the boy's doin', sir. He's a bit off. I never would've recommended him, sir, but—"

"Shut your stupid mouth, man, and do as you're told."

A square room with a turf fire burning to keep the damp out. Bare white walls. A table and two chairs. Burke sat massaging his wrists, staring at an old man in a gray sweater. He was white-haired and had high color. A mustache, yellow from tobacco and age. "Where am I?" Burke said.

"County Wicklow. I'm Joseph Walsh."

"I'm a newspaperman. I was delivering a message and had—"

"I know, I know," said Walsh in a soft voice. He had the delightful accent of Ulster. A marriage of the burr and the brogue. "Tell me what happened, Mr. Burke. From the beginning, if you will."

Burke told him all, like a man confessing, not hearing himself. Walsh interrupted several times with questions. When Burke finished, Walsh stood up and opened the door. "We'll talk again. This way, Mr. Burke."

When Burke turned and limped toward the door, O'Connor came in with Lafferty behind him. O'Connor's white suit was filthy. The two friends went out to each other with their eyes, but said nothing. Lafferty closed the door and led Burke through a hallway and out to a screened porch, lit here and there with paraffin lamps. Burke sat in a chaise lounge, a cheap beach chair. Lafferty left him and Mairead, the widow, came with a bowl of warm water and a sponge. She began to wipe his face. "You poor man. You poor brave man."

"Where am I?"

"You're in headquarters, now, and you're quite safe. Ah, look what they've done to you."

"There's something wrong with my nose."

Mairead laughed. "Not a thing wrong with your nose, pet. A bit out of place. Tender."

"I thought he was going to shoot me."

"There now. At least you're clean. Any good doctor will make you new. I'll bring you tea." She got up, an expression of clear pride on her face. "Oh," she remembered, "do you smoke? I'm to give you these." She put a pack of Sweet Aftons and a box of matches in his hands. "Now, I'll fetch tea for you."

Burke lit a cigarette and the smoke was a drug, easing him, connecting him to his life. His hands felt novocained. He stared out at the dark moonless night. There was much activity for awhile. One flat pistol shot which made him jump. Men coming and going, all armed. Cars starting in the still night.

After giving him a large cup of light sweet tea, Mairead said to rest and she'd be back to check on him. The tea and cigarettes were like a feast. For the first time since Lafferty and Jimmy had strolled into his life, he felt safe and could think halfway clearly.

"Hello, yank. You're lookin' a bit under it," Dee-Dee said, looking down at him. He hadn't heard her come out. She dragged a straight-back chair up close to him and straddled it, her arms hanging loose across the back. Her sawed-off lay in her lap. "The nose is lovely."

She was smiling. Her plain urchin's face.

Burke laughed. "Jesus, I thought I'd never see you again."

"Pining away for me, were you? That it?"

"Why'd you leave me? Why'd you set me up?"

"Do you want more tea? Or something better?"

"Yes."

"Hold on."

She came back with a bottle of Jameson's and splashed some in his cup. She had a jelly glass for herself. Burke drank greedily, not tasting it. And then another. Dee-Dee lit a cigarette for him. "Can you travel? You're not that bad, are you?"

"I'm fine," Burke said. "My knee's fucked up. My nose is busted. I'm fine."

"Well, there's nothing more to be done. You're all right and the rest will take care of itself. You'll be snug at home in a few hours. Listen to Walsh, do you hear?"

"What?"

"Listen to Walsh, and to no one else. He's your man. Keep your eyes open."

A young man came to the door; Deirdre nodded at him and left the porch. The young fellow stayed, staring at Burke. He was dressed in a dark suit, his tie loose at the throat. In the weak light Burke could see that the man was handsome, with a smooth, pale face, long dark-blond hair, tall and thin, with broad shoulders. Staring. "Take a picture," Burke said, "it lasts longer."

"Easy, Mr. Burke."

"Have we met?"

"My name's John Boland, Mr. Burke. I'm a member of the staff."

Burke became silent, and looked away. A woman was standing to the side of his chair. It was the German. She brought a lamp closer. Her face was shining, beautiful in the soft shifting light. There was a swelling bruise on one cheek and her fine blouse was ripped around the throat. "I'm Gudrun Böhm, Martin."

"Yes."

"Are you injured badly?"

"I'm okay."

She sat on the chair with him. John Boland, at the door, was still staring, but now he was looking at Gudrun, at her bruise, at the scrape on one knee, her blouse torn open, revealing her throat.

"Interrogation. Rather mild interrogation. We're safe now. We're holding a lot of power."

"Not me. I'm going home. Fuck it, I'm out."

She smiled. "Terrence was right about you."

"Then that's the only thing he's ever been right about. This isn't a fucking game."

"Old ideas."

"Not me. I don't like getting beat up and the shit scared out of me."

"Just remember," Gudrun said, then paused because Burke was looking away. "Martin? Martin, listen to me."

He looked at her, furious at her cool bruised presence.

"Just remember who hurt you. The individuals. Remember the specifics. Your time will come." She looked over to young Boland at the door.

"I've had enough craziness." Burke looked up from her face to the door. Boland was gone.

"Tough guy," she said, smiling. "Humphrey Bogart? John Wayne? Can I have a drink?"

He passed her the teacup. "Then leave me alone."

She sipped. "You're a baby. You're new to this. But you *are* in it. Mr. Walsh, he won't let you go, yes? Liam Cleary, would he let you go?"

Burke staggered up and off the porch, found his balance in the dark hallway and stopped. Lafferty was ten feet away, standing in a doorway, the light framing him. Burke went back to the porch and paced, while Gudrun sat and studied him. Dee-Dee came with a message that Walsh wanted her and they both left him alone. Burke's head cleared. The whiskey had helped and he took no more of it. He was hungry, but turned down offers of food because the hunger helped him think.

Lafferty came to the door of the porch, leaned against the door-jamb, and said, "You have an appointment with Joe Walsh."

Burke followed him. Lafferty knocked on the door and then opened it. The white room, gleaming. Burke stepped in and Lafferty closed the door behind him. Burke heard him walking away down the hall.

Walsh was sitting at the table, smoking a cigarette. "Sit, Mr. Burke." Walsh reminded him of a certain type of priest he had known when he was a boy. An intellectual, Jesuit, perhaps the head of philosophy at Fordham or St. Peter's, fragile, private, with no sentimentality or pious ways.

"The boy has been punished," Walsh said. "About ten minutes ago."

Burke was confused.

"The boy," Walsh said. "He was knee-capped ten minutes ago."

"It wasn't necessary," Burke said, and suddenly remembered his face.

"Mr. Burke," Walsh said. "We are a guerrilla army. We don't have the luxury of a fair judicial system. We don't have the luxury of a compassionate penal system. Our punishment is crude, it's barbarous, but it is necessary. Full stop. Our only consideration is that justice be swift. I'm telling you about Jimmy to let you know that the I.S.A. does not condone thuggery and sadism."

Burke looked into the fire.

"I'm not a military man," Walsh said. "But now I have to become one. I'm a newspaperman, like yourself. A propagandist. Liam was our general. It's my responsibility to take charge of the army."

"Good luck," Burke said.

"Liam must have trusted you. So I trust you."

"Mr. Walsh, you can trust me all you want, but I've got to tell you again. I'm an American. I got mixed up in this against my better judgment. This isn't my country and this isn't my cause. I'll only bring more trouble to myself and to you."

"I rather doubt that. What did O'Connor tell you about Conor Graham?"

Burke looked at him. Blue eyes, white hair thin on his pink skull. It doesn't make any difference, he told himself. He didn't even hear what I just said. "He told me they met him in Paris, he robbed a bank—and he, he was a member of the I.S.A."

"Yes," Walsh said, and blew smoke out of his thin nose. "The fact is that this man is Peter Farrell, of Dublin, a former Provisional I.R.A. officer who is now an informer."

"What's that got to do with me?"

"Your life is endangered and I thought you might want to know the facts."

Burke crossed his legs. Walsh went on, "A fortnight ago a team of German and British agents arrested Farrell at Port La Gelene on the Riviera. He was taken to the high security prison, Les Baumets in Marseilles. The British want him for securing arms deals, for breaking prison at the Crumlin Road Jail in 1971 and for the killing of an RUC man. The Federal German Police want him for a bombing at the British army base at München-Gladbach and for eight other bomb attacks at Rhine army bases carried out with European guerrillas. We believe he has become an informer. He allegedly escaped from Les Baumets ten days after he was arrested. And one doesn't 'escape' from that place, as any Breton Republican can tell you. He was set free, and he is probably here in Ireland now, looking for O'Connor and the German. I believe that the British Special Branch and the Irish Special Branch are doing the same."

"So they're looking for me?"

"They might," Joseph Walsh said, taking the cigarette from his mouth and smiling, "have already found you. Those are the facts. I want you to be in touch with Deirdre O'Sullivan, to stay close. I also *don't* want you to stay in touch with O'Connor or the German. You can't help there. We will protect you. We'll do our best to help you. You must know that there is going to be a war against Provisionals in Dublin commencing today. I believe they killed Liam. Not the Special Branch. You were a coincidence. You and O'Connor and the German. The Provos have to be hit for this. And they also have to be hit if I'm to hold this army together. Are you married?"

"Yes."

"Then I'd advise you to keep yourself and your family aware of everything."

"We're going out to Clare soon."

"Excellent idea."

Walsh stood up and Burke rose to shake his hand.

"Luck," Joseph Walsh said.

"You too," Burke said.

Lafferty escorted him back to the porch, silent and stony. He was alone for awhile and then O'Connor came out in his ruined suit, sat across from him, and the two friends said nothing for awhile. Watching Burke sitting very still, burly, bearded, chain smoking, his face set and disciplined, O'Connor felt a touch of regret that he had involved him. He knew it had been Burke's choice, but the sight of the lumpy, swelling nose in the middle of his friend's face made O'Connor feel that from here on in he was responsible for Burke. He would take care of him.

"I'm wiped out," O'Connor finally said, rubbing his face.

"What's going on, Terry?"

"Our deal's going down right now. Gudrun's talking with

Walsh. From what I could understand, he's only been involved in the political side. But now with Cleary—that must've been really something."

"Yeah," Burke said. "It was really something."

"This whole group is coming apart. Seems without Cleary there's no center."

"I'm not in the mood for your half-assed political analysis. I want out of here."

"Yeah." He paused. "Think they'll let you?"

"Yeah, I think they will."

"Who gave you the nose?"

"None of your business."

"Right."

They sat for awhile in silence. Lafferty came to fetch O'Connor, and Burke sat on the porch watching the false dawn creep in, showing the hills and trees in black relief against the dishwater sky. With full morning he could see the house was set in a wooded hollow. There was a creek running off to the right. The Wicklow country looked very old and beautiful. A lost place. Explorers would come over the hill any minute and see it all for the first time.

Mairead brought tea again. She went about the porch, blowing out the paraffin lamps, one by one. When she left, Burke stood up and stretched. He touched his nose once, flexed his knee. Dee-Dee came and said, if he was ready, she would drive him back up to Dublin. "Walk to the car straight and don't look back. Follow me. Make it quick but don't be hurrying. Got it?"

"Yeah."

She was worried. Burke didn't care. He was alive, he'd lived through the night. There was joy inside him that he kept like a jewel in a private safe. There would be time to go to it and marvel at his fortune.

Dee-Dee started the car. She handed the sawed-off to Burke. "Don't hesitate," she said. "Even if you can't hit a barn it'll make enough fookin' noise."

They took a curling farm road up out of the hollow past green fields where sheep grazed. The sun was bright in a high blue sky. The country summer green under dew. A boy on a tractor came toward them and Dee-Dee pulled to the side to let him pass. "Eyes open, yank," she said looking in the rearview mirror. The boy passed on the lumbering tractor and gave the thumbs up. Dee-Dee nodded once at him and gunned the car away, shifting at the top of each gear. Within half an hour they were driving through Dublin's sleepy Saturday morning.

She dropped him on a side street near Herbert Park in Ballsbridge because Burke said he wanted to walk. When the VW was gone he was alone with the morning, and remembered the old neighborhood of home on summer Saturday mornings, coming up from the stale night of the subway after hours of taverns and conversation, feeling full, crowded with the night, alive to a new day, a cocksure boy going home. He walked along Wellington Road with the Georgian townhouses set back from the street by thirty yards or so of green lawn. The parked cars seemed asleep. There were the sounds of doves murmuring in the trees and the occasional yowl and indignant screech of gulls cruising in the high whitewashed sky. Burke saw a cat solemnly cross the street and vanish through an iron fence. At Pembroke Road he looked north and saw the purple Dublin Mountains in the distance under the pearl sky. You're really getting to be an old man, he told himself, but he didn't feel old.

CHAPTER 7

All Souls

The day after Liam Cleary's funeral in Bray, Joseph Walsh met with ten officers of the Irish Socialist Army at the Wicklow farmhouse. At the meeting he informed them that he was assuming the position of chief of staff. The first order of business was that army personnel in the Dublin area were to billet away from their homes and be prepared for active service. Next, Walsh said that Deirdre O'Sullivan was his adjutant and any order from her in the future could be taken as an order from the chief of staff. They were to reorganize their own columns along the I.R.A. system of cells numbering five men apiece. They would begin an attack on Provo personnel and could expect retaliation. Walsh had learned through old Official I.R.A. sources who the assassins of Liam Cleary were. They were the Provo hit team of Lawrence Canny, Belfast, and Thomas Strahan, also of Belfast, and were now back in Northern Ireland. Walsh told his officers they would leave the hit team alone; they were too far afield, and on their own ground. The I.S.A.'s retaliation would begin with a Provo officer in Dublin on Friday night. He then said that Deirdre O'Sullivan would be in touch, shook all their hands and adjourned the meeting. He asked one of the officers, Paul Cosgrave, to stay behind for a moment. A man named Phil Coughlin, a mechanic at Mountjoy, had expressed interest in their work. He seemed to be all right, but would Cosgrave put him under surveillance for a fortnight to make sure he wasn't a plant? Deirdre would have his address. And keep a very low profile, he's a virgin and we don't want him spooked if he's real. Would Cosgrave do it? He was sure he would handle it with subtlety. And only for a fortnight. He also ordered Cosgrave to set up a bank robbery team and hit three banks for funds within a week.

No member of the I.S.A. except Deirdre O'Sullivan saw the

new chief of staff again, or even knew where he was, until he was arrested three months later.

Friday 12 August. George Crowley, O/C of the Dublin 3rd Battalion, Provisional I.R.A., was having an evening of cards with his mother and brother Bobby, quartermaster of the unit, at their mother's home in Dundrum. It was a ritual the two brothers had started once the old man had died to cheer their mother, and soon found they enjoyed the get-togethers, drinking a bit of Guinness, having some cake along with the gin rummy. At nine-fifteen Mrs. Crowley was in the kitchen getting a bottle of stout for George when a knock came at the front door. "I'll get it, boys," she said and went out to the foyer, opened the door and there were two men dressed in dark suits. A mustard-colored Volkswagen with a woman behind the wheel idled at the curb. The street was quiet. The August evening's sun was just at the turn of brightness. It had been a fine hot day and now the sky had turned soft. She told the gardai later that she could not identify the two men, but that was a lie. She would take their faces to her grave. One was a man of about forty, with a hard face pitted with acne scars on his cheeks and nose. He had black hair cut short, as if it had been done quickly, not for style, but to keep it away from his face. His companion was a younger man, in his late twenties, tall, thin, handsome, with long muddy blond hair.

"Yes?" Mrs. Crowley asked.

"George Crowley, please."

"Who should I say—?"

"It's Army business, missus."

"Yes, I see."

She went back into the living room. "George. Two men on business."

George looked at his brother across the table. "Now don't stack that deck." He got up from the table, taking his cards with him.

"You can't even trust your own brother? You're a bad man, Crowley."

"Trust no one, Bobby, me boy. *Especially* your own brother over a game of rummy."

On his way to the door his mother said, "You're entitled to one night free, now, George."

"Only a minute," he said. "And watch that son of yours in there."

George Crowley saw his own death in the form of two men in

black suits with cheap neckties holding a .38 Cobra Special and a .45 Colt. Frozen in one spot, he didn't see their faces, only their weapons. Holding the ten cards of his rummy hand fanned out to stop the bullets, his mouth open to say something, he took three rounds from the Colt and a fourth from the .38. He was lifted slightly off his feet and fell dead against the hall table, knocking over a votive light and a small china statue of the Virgin.

As the sound exploded in the foyer Mrs. Crowley screamed and ran for the door. Bobby Crowley was up and running for the back door to escape to a pistol hidden in the coal shed. The older man brushed Mrs. Crowley aside as she knelt next to her son and walked into the living room while the other cut up the driveway toward the rear of the house. He got to the backyard in time to see Bobby Crowley enter the coal shed, leaving the door open. Resting his .38 on a slot of the fence, he waited until Bobby turned around and squeezed off one round which hit Bobby through the left breast pocket of his white shirt and dropped him back into the darkness onto a heap of coal. Running back up the driveway and over to the VW he heard the wailing of Mrs. Crowley piercing out through the open door into the evening. Doors were opening all up and down the hushed street. The man got in the back seat. John Boland, age twenty-seven, who previously had worked only as a party organizer. For months he had pestered Liam Cleary to put him on active service. The night Cleary was murdered he was ordered to the Wicklow farmhouse, and interrogated the German woman with Lafferty. He was on his way, he had thought. At the moment, sitting in the back of the car, brushing his blond hair away with his hand, he was wondering why he had ever desired to be a soldier.

"Where's Lafferty?" Deirdre asked from behind the wheel.

"The house," Boland said breathlessly. "In the house. I got the brother in the yard. Christ, let's move."

"Ten seconds," she said.

"Fuck him, let's move."

The screams from the house ceased.

In the hallway Lafferty observed the mother holding her bleeding son. The red votive light lay on its side, still burning. Broken china and scattered playing cards. She was staring up, a macabre grin on her face, whispering, "Murderer. You'll howl in hell for this."

Lafferty slipped the .45 in his belt and buttoned his jacket over it. His whole body felt liquid, as if he were in a warm bath. "You tell 'em this is for Liam Cleary, right, missus? Paid in full, hey?"

"You'll roast, you devil."

"And there's another receipt for you in the yard."

Lafferty walked out of the house, closed the door and strolled over to the VW. He looked around the neighborhood once before getting in the back. Deirdre put the car in gear and drove off at speed.

Wednesday 17 August. Edward Fagan, age thirty-one, a member of the Irish Socialist Party and frequent contributor to the newspaper, the *Irish Patriot*, a baker by trade, was found on the third green of the Milltown Golf Course off Churchtown Road, handcuffed and dead with a bullet fired at close range through the back of his head. A piece of paper was found pinned to his back reading: "Traitor executed by the I.R.A."

Sunday 3 September. Hugh Hegarty, age forty-four, officer in the Provisional I.R.A., was sitting in his car in Terenure, waiting for his wife Margaret who was visiting her aunt. He didn't notice the young man in jeans and a sweater until he was next to the car. "Hello, Hugh," the young man said, laying a pistol with a taped butt through the vent window and firing it into Hegarty's face. He shot the slumped figure once more as it lay on the seat, dropped the pistol into the car and calmly walked away.

Monday 4 September. The editorial office of the *Irish Patriot* in Fairview, a two-story building, was demolished by a gelignite bomb at 11:05 P.M. The entire structure was trashed, and windows all over the neighborhood were blown in. There was one death. Sineád MacGiolla, twenty-five years old, was in the rear of the building typing up her weekly column in Irish when the device went off. The next day the Republican Information Service released a notice saying the act of sabotage was carried out by the I.R.A. against the "black propaganda machine." The statement went on to say it was also in retaliation for the murder of officer Hugh Hegarty.

Tuesday 28 September. Kevin Powers, nineteen, unemployed, a "runner" or messenger for the Provisional I.R.A., was walking along Upper Stephen Street on his way to meet a girl in St. Stephen's Green. It was five-thirty of a clear cool evening. At the corner of Drury Street two men in dark suits stopped him, one asking for a match. As he reached in his pocket one man went behind him and stuck a revolver in his ribs. The man facing him held onto his wrist and said, "There now, laddie buck, we're goin' to take you over to that blue Renault and go for a ride. No trouble now."

As they began to walk Kevin broke free and ran down Drury Street with the two men chasing. He tripped over a shopping basket left in the street in front of the Market Arcade, a skylighted shopping gallery running from Drury Street through to George's Street. He scrambled up and ran into the deserted gallery. The light fell delicately from the glass roof into the shadows of the arcade. There were shops of household goods, a greengrocer, boutiques, all locked and shuttered. Kevin paused once, trying to decide whether to attempt finding refuge in one of the shops or making it to George's Street. The two men came charging into the arcade and stopped, twenty feet away, weapons drawn. They each took three or four steps away from each other, and one of them motioned with his pistol to come forward. Kevin turned and ran toward the weak light of George's Street. He was hit in the buttocks and spine by .45 Colt slugs. Lying face down on the stone floor, he was killed by a .45 slug through the back of his head fired at point-blank range.

Lafferty slipped the .45 in his belt and buttoned his jacket over it. Boland had already left the arcade. Lafferty strolled out the George's Street end and walked to a safe house in Essex Street. When he arrived Boland said, "What in God's name is on your leg there?"

Lafferty looked down to see some kind of gray and white slop spattered on the pant leg of his cheap black suit.

Monday 11 October. Patrick Muldoon, fifty-seven, mechanic, former member of the Irish Socialist Party, presently holding a card of the Communist Party of Ireland, was killed by a shotgun blast as he walked out of his home in Ringsend on his way to work in a garage in Irishtown.

Saturday 16 October. At 10:30 A.M. the 7A bus from Sallynoggin to Eden Quay was stopping to take on more passengers at the corner of Alma Road in Monkstown. It was the old style of bus with an open door at the rear, and was packed with people either late for work or going in for a day's shopping. The conductor was on the upper level taking fares when the commotion started. Two men with drawn pistols were escorting an old gentleman through the silent bus toward the rear. The elderly man, dressed in a three-piece gray suit and a red tie, made no protest, but looked calm and vague. Passengers with stunned faces made way for the trio. The driver turned from his seat and watched the procession. Later, along with other witnesses, he would tell the press he had assumed the two armed men were plainclothes gardai or Special Branch men.

On the rear platform one of the armed men gave the old man a kick in the back, shoving him out into the road where he fell on all fours. Some passengers moaned. A few men rose from their seats, outraged at such a display, and one or two were even making their way toward the rear to give assistance. The packed upper level looked down at the scene. The two men shot the old man three times as he knelt. The bus lurched away from the scene as the two gunmen fled down to Trafalgar Lane. They were picked up in a gray Fiat at Seapoint Avenue which took the coast road south toward Wicklow.

The man killed was Donal Grennan, age seventy-four, a former I.R.A. officer and a legend in the Republican movement. He was no longer active in the I.R.A. but gave his name and reputation to the Provisionals and had recently written an article condemning the I.S.A.'s assassination campaign. His death finally brought the grudge war to an end. The next day, Tuesday 12 October, a newspaperman with the *Irish Press* relayed a message from an officer of the Provisionals to an officer of the I.S.A. asking for a cease-fire and negotiations. The offer was rejected. The I.S.A.'s response was that Chief of Staff Joseph Walsh would entertain negotiations only with Chief of Staff Higgins of the Provisionals. Within twenty-four hours the word came through saying the terms were acceptable, but the chief was in Northern Ireland at the moment and would not be available until near the end of the month. A temporary cease-fire was called on both sides until November 1.

It was Friday 30 October, one day before All Hallow's Eve, and Mrs. Mooney's shop was decorated in orange and black ribbon, paper jack-o'-lanterns, and silhouettes of witches riding brooms. A big orange and black bin set near the cash register overflowed with plastic bags of boiled sweets. Mrs. Mooney had left the door of her shop open when she came downstairs after her tea at five o'clock. Even though it was a wet cold day she would rather wear her wool sweater and have the shop a bit chilly than deny herself the sounds of Dublin coming home from work, the lights of traffic and streetlamps playing across her doorstep. It was better for business, she told herself, to have an open door to the street. Besides the chill, there were other disadvantages, but she would put up with them, too. People would step in, pretend interest in the rack of magazines while keeping an eye out for the bus, and then dash out without buying so much as tuppence worth of goods. And there was that blasted public house dog from next door, nosing in, shaking his beery fur over her paperback book display. She was coming out after him from around the counter for the second time in ten minutes, ready to give him a well-placed kick instead of shooing him with her hands, when the gentleman in the fedora stepped in. She gave him a smile and he touched the felt brim. "Nasty day," he said.

"Desperate," Mrs. Mooney said.

The dog slipped by her and was heading for the toys and stationery at the rear of the shop. "I'll shoot that dog," she said over her shoulder as she went after him. "I swear I'll shoot him. Now go on, get out, get out," she told him, waving her hands as the dog trotted placidly past the gentleman and out to the sidewalk where he turned, sat down, and stared back into the shop through the rain. "Did you ever see a more noble beast?" Mrs. Mooney said, folding her arms under her breasts. "Doesn't know night from noon, sun from rain. Intoxicated most of the day." She put in quickly in a lower voice, "The publican next door gives him stout, isn't it dreadful?"

"He looks happy enough," the gentleman said.

"Oh, but that's a terrible thing to do to a poor animal. And letting him run loose like that, it's a desperate thing to do."

Three girls came in, their hair wet and stringy, happily disheveled in their school uniforms now after being released from a long day of sitting straight and still under the eyes of nuns. They crowded around the candy display and Mrs. Mooney went behind the counter to serve them, thinking that in her day a young girl wouldn't be caught dead with her blouse out of her skirt or her knee socks congregating about the ankles. "They're all for sale, now, girls," she said, watching the gentleman as he walked over to the magazines.

Just as some men can't pass a hardware store without stopping in to browse, and others feel a gravitational pull from bookstores, so Frank Higgins was drawn to newsagents' shops or any place where the goods were brightly colored, cheaply made and designed to soothe boredom. When he had a few moments alone, which was rare for a man in his position, he could be found in places like Mrs. Mooney's. If he had to meet someone, which was what he was doing today, he would pick a place like this. A copy of *Ireland of the Welcomes*, the magazine of the tourist board, was in his hands. He flipped through, his mind grateful for the opportunity to think of nothing for a change.

Frank's father had been a butcher in a village in County Meath, a luckless and bitter man who insisted his only child work with him from age six on in the shop. He gave young Frank regular hours with tea and dinner breaks and at every opportunity Frank escaped from the shop with its smells of fresh blood to cross the road and spend time in Mr. Harmon's sweet shop. There it was clean and bright, with smells of peppermint and chocolate, and a whole wall of magazines easy on the eye. A place of refuge. He didn't even mind the embarrassment of losing track of time and having his father rap on the window, standing in the street in his bloody apron, pointing to his watch.

Mrs. Mooney was busy as people popped in for a copy of the *Evening Press* or *Herald*. She thought both papers rags suitable only for stuffing your shoes after a walk in the rain. But she almost always sold them out, so she had no right to complain about the quality. The *Herald* would go quickly today. The headline, in vulgar-sized type, read: MAN FOUND DEAD IN TV KILL-ING. The story concerned a bachelor in Donegal who electrocuted himself attempting to rewire his television set. Imagine. Who in their right mind would care a bit about some daft man destroying himself out of sheer stupidity? No one. But "TV Killing," that could mean anything. Mrs. Mooney was wise to the snares of cheap journalism. There was the summer afternoon when the headline was: KERRY MAN CAPTURES SON OF SAM. Referring to that maniac in New York. The Kerry man was some fellow born in Tralee whose family had moved to America when he was two years old. He, it seemed, when you read the story, gave the Son of Sam a parking ticket which led to his arrest.

The *Press* was doing brisk business as well. I.S.A. LINKED TO BUS MURDER. That gave her a smile. How, exactly, does one go about murdering a bus? Good English didn't concern the hacks on the *Press*. Oh, no, just feed the people another cold supper of violence. Dreadful. A man shot dead in front of all those people. A human being's death becoming a sideshow attraction. They shouldn't print stories about these mentally deranged people, because that's what they were, they belonged in asylums every one of them, running about with guns, thinking it was still 1920, ready to "die for Ireland," not one of them ready to "live for Ireland." They should be locked away and forced to do a day's work. Desperate. She noticed the gentleman in the fedora looking through *Ireland of the Welcomes*. This nonsense would hurt the tourist trade. Keep decent Irishmen and Irishwomen from making a living. The petrol shortage was hurting it already but now with this—well, we'll be stuck with ourselves. *Sinn Fein*, Ourselves Alone, we'll see how we can put food on the table by "ourselves alone." Bus Murders and TV Killings. Have to laugh, really. She saw the gentleman checking his watch. Would he buy anything? Probably not. Oh, let him browse. He's meeting someone and it's better he wait here than sit in a smoky public house. Fine figure of a man. Sharp featured, the sign of intelligence. High color and freckles, the sign of health. Beautiful hat, doesn't it give him a style? Mrs. Mooney remembered the days when everyone wore a hat, men and women alike. It was a sure sign of a person's lack of concern for his appearance if he didn't wear a hat then. Or outright destitution. Let him browse. He might return and buy.

A teenage boy came in and headed for the magazines. He took one down devoted to hot rods. Chewing his gum deliberately, he shifted his weight from leg to leg, oblivious of the man in the fedora next to him, staring at pictures of chrome exhaust pipes with the attention of a scholar. Higgins observed him. Look at him. Sloppy bugger. Careless pup in his bolero pants and high-heeled boots. Banana-boat shirt. Only thing he regrets is he wasn't born a nigger. Hair combed in butter. Just when you get used to their hair long and flowing, they start greasing it up. Punks, they're called, and the shoe fits. Life'd catch him up. Rootless. Thinks Elvis Presley a great social thinker. Wanker. Look at him, will you.

Higgins checked his watch again and went back to *Ireland of the Welcomes*. But his thoughts were jarred at the sight of the hot rod punk and he held the magazine and thought again of

Walsh. What a fine speech he'd given at Bodenstown twelve years ago. Talking about tourism he'd said, "Tourism as an industry? What product does this industry produce?" Clear thinker, old Joe. "What work do the workers in this industry perform?" Persuade him to drop all the commie cowflop and what a man to have as a press officer. "An industry rife with opportunism and graft. Workers becoming grease to oil the capitalist machine." No, mustn't insult him with press officer. Give him a batallion? No. God, no. Send him to the States? Yes. Keep him in Dublin? Every reporter worships him. Or make peace and let things cool and kill him? He might be of use, the old bastard. Oh, what a speaker. What a brain.

Frank Higgins, chief of staff of the Provisional Irish Republican Army, the most wanted man in the British Isles, replaced the magazine on the rack and wandered to the rear of the store where the greeting card display stood under furled orange and black paper hung from the ceiling. "On Your Birthday, Mother." "To My Loving Wife." "Here's To You, Grandad." The last time he'd seen Joe Walsh was in January 1972 at a press conference here in Dublin. Walsh and Higgins along with three other men had just escaped from H.M.S. *Mountain*, the prison ship anchored along the Belfast docks, and had made their way south to inform the world they'd escaped "the horror of British justice."

Higgins, then adjutant to Chief of Staff Seán MacStiofáin, had been lifted in Derry City that Christmas Day 1971. He was brought to Magilligan Internment Camp where he underwent "interrogation." First he was interviewed by a group of British officers connected to the SAS, the Special Air Service. He was taken from hut to hut of the sprawling concentration camp, the wet wind of December howling like a lunatic all day long. He was treated very cordially by the British officers, but after a day of being shunted back and forth to the same huts over and over, to hear the same pleasantly phrased questions, without food or drink or sleep, the insistent cordiality became torture. On the second day he was given a meal of black tea and cold stew and the merry-go-round began again, except they removed his shoes. When he asked why, they told him it was for security, but the real reason, Frank knew, was to humiliate him. During the next twenty-four hours Frank realized he had nothing to lose, so he stoked the flame of his anger and let it out on his captors. The officers all remained civil, polite, courteous. Near midnight they told him he was to receive a uniform and then they'd take him to the "music room." His uniform was a pair of long johns three sizes too large, a woman's sweater, much too small, and a hood over his head. He was then run by two guards all over the camp, down along corridors, bouncing off walls, falling to the floor, taking kicks and an unending stream of verbal abuse, thrown out into the yard, dragged up, set running again, trying to hold up his absurd trousers with bleeding fingers, beat with batons in the shins, kneecaps, kidneys and shoulders, and finally, after hours (or minutes, pain makes mockery of time), he was brought into a hut, told to sit on the floor, his hood was removed and he was questioned once more by an SAS major in the most solicitous, quiet, mannerly manner. When he refused to answer, he was asked if he enjoyed music and before he could answer was hooded and run into a stifling room, told to spread his legs wide, lean forward and grip the wall with his palms. There was a low monotonous noise, the sound of a buzzsaw two rooms away, which never altered its pitch or volume, but just droned on and on. His pants around his ankles and legs quivering with fatigue were bad enough, but it was his head that became his real enemy. His head encased in the hood, suffocating on his own breath, his head splitting, the sound burrowing like a worm into overripe fruit. Every now and again, with no schedule of regularity, he would be questioned, and called an imbecile, a moron, a child molester, retarded, a cocksucker, a dog. Then there would be silence and the "music" would tunnel into his brain again. He would drift, a migraine his only companion. His guard would creep up close behind and crash two garbage can lids together inches from his head. When he collapsed he was allowed to sleep on the floor only two or three minutes, just long enough to pass through the door to sleep, but not long enough to close it behind him. Awake, he was put in his position, and left with the music.

Finally he was allowed to sleep for an hour before being issued a prison uniform and handcuffed in a line with six other men, Walsh included. They were hooded and told they were going for a helicopter ride. They were frog marched to the chopper and taken up. They were questioned again and told if they weren't cooperative they all would be thrown from the chopper. When they refused to answer, the man at the center of the chain was kicked out of the helicopter with the rest being dragged with him, to fall four feet into a wet field. They were dragged back into the helicopter, their hoods removed to show them that now they were truly flying high above the checkerboard farms of Ulster. Then hooded again.

Their guards discussed in working-class English accents whether they should drop them out of the helicopter for real. The micks below could use some fertilizer for their fields. What they had here was better than horseshit, but only a little better. Two men on the chain became hysterical and a third was beginning to succumb. Higgins knew that hysteria was as contagious as sea sickness. Soon, he thought, we'll all be jabbering like terrified children. Frank was merely drifting again but Walsh exercised leadership, shouting orders at the babbling men, and then soothing them.

They were flown to Belfast, and as they were setting to land their hoods were removed so they could "see their new home." They were landing on a dock near H.M.S. *Mountain*. Frank thought they were bound for England, but the *Mountain* didn't travel. It was a prison ship, cramped, overcrowded, with the prison at the stern, the soldiers' quarters amidships and the exercise "yard" on the bow surrounded by ten-foot-high barbed wire. British soldiers observed the ship from the bridge. It was said to be escape proof. Higgins and Walsh were, after two hours on board, ready to test the idea, and immediately began to study the tides around the ship.

They enlisted three other men and after a week were ready to move. A fret saw was used to cut the bars of a porthole on the sea side. The five men smeared butter from the mess hall over their bodies to protect against the chill of the water, smeared shoe polish on top of that, and slipped out and down the side. The water was near freezing and strewn with barbed wire. They were all shredded by the barbs but somehow managed to make the five-hundred-yard swim in single file in twenty minutes. Once on shore, a lorry was hijacked and driven to the Republican Markets area of the city. Two cars from there took them into the Republic before the staff of the *Mountain* knew they were gone.

Higgins had thought then that there could be a link back between the I.R.A. wings because of the escape. But Joe Walsh came on again with his commie line, and the escape meant nothing. He knew then that the Official and Provisional wings of the I.R.A.

would never realign, would never be at peace. And when Joe
Walsh joined Liam Cleary and other Officials not long afterwards
to form the I.S.A., he knew they were potentially as dangerous
an enemy as Loyalist Protestants and British soldiers. Seán Mac-
Stiofáin, the chief of staff, had agreed, and the Provisionals had
gone after Liam Cleary, leaving Walsh alone because he seemed
to have retired and was only working at propaganda. When Mac-
Stiofáin was removed from leadership, and Higgins stepped in, he
had pursued Cleary, and finally run him to ground. He had miscalculated that Joe Walsh still had some fight in him, or that the
little beast, Deirdre O'Sullivan, could become such a shrewd
leader. Frank had miscalculated the strength of the I.S.A., which
had had a cease-fire until he had forced them out to battle by
killing their general. Once Cleary was gone, Frank had always
said, that tiny rabble of commies would vanish into smoke. But
he was wrong. Their rage at Cleary's death had strengthened them.
Why hadn't he remembered old Joe in the helicopter, leading
men out of panic and shock and helping them to restore their sense
of dignity? He had miscalculated, yes. But he had learned a lesson.

He looked up from the airmail stationery rack to see the pro-
prietress staring at him. Best not to be noticed, best to buy something. He walked toward her, picking up a bag of boiled sweets
in yellow and black plastic on his way. "Forty-four," Mrs. Mooney
said.

Higgins handed her a pound. "Thank you," she said, handing
him his change.

"Is the new *Hibernia* in?"

"Yes. Just there," she pointed.

Higgins nodded and went over to the magazines. He looked
through the window just as Rúairí parked the Rover across the
street. It wasn't his father looking for him this evening, but there
was someone waiting, and again he was wanted to return to the
business of blood. Higgins saw Rúairí check his watch and look
over at the shop. Higgins checked his watch. Three minutes late,
the bugger. Was anyone ever *early* in Ireland?

On his way out Higgins nodded once to Mrs. Mooney, crossed
the street and sat next to Rúairí. "You're late, I.O."

"Bloody traffic, Chief."

"Traffic? Did I say anything about traffic?"

"No, sir."

"You're late."

Rúairí looked away. "Yes, sir."

Higgins looked back to the shop, a bright orderly place off the wet street. He took off the fedora and tossed it in the back seat without looking.

"Where to, sir?"

"Do you know Lucan?"

"Yes, sir."

"Drive slow now, we've plenty of time."

Rúairí moved the Rover out into traffic as Higgins opened the bag of sweets and popped one in his mouth. He held out the bag to Rúairí. The young man took one and said with a grin, "Trick or treat, Chief?"

"Aye," Higgins said, staring dead ahead, sucking the sweet.

The village of Lucan lies nine miles due west of Dublin on the River Liffey. Driving straight out of the city, past the Phoenix Park and on through the suburban communities oozing away from Dublin, you will come down a hill on the highway with Lucan on your right, the church's spire standing gracefully amid a cluster of new and plain houses. Through the town you come to a wide, gently arched bridge. Here you can see the Liffey, not sluggish and dull as it is in the city, not the "iffy Liffey" that plods by the Guinness Brewery at St. James Gate and is never its true color once it's past, but a simple country river. Here it is fast moving, coming out of a bend flanked by green trees and pouring out over a "weir," or group of rapids. Some of the weir is man-made, and some of the miniature falls were made by nature. The water streams silver in one spot; next to it the river boils over haphazard rock, becoming white froth ribboned brown from the clay of the river bed. Below the weir, trees stand stunted in the river, overly lush, overly green, and the banks are green rushes, soft as the sound of the rushing Liffey which fills the air, constantly whispering.

From the bridge you will see a row of attached two-story houses standing alone across the river, twenty in all, built of red brick, each with its own small gate and garden in front and view of the Liffey. The terrace of houses was built in the last part of the nineteenth century to house the workers of a woolen mill further east downriver. They are bright well-kept homes, and the people who live here are good neighbors who have lived together for years. You will find none of the litter that has become a part of every town and city in Ireland, no sign at all of the careless and slipshod way of living that characterizes modern Irish life and has made Dublin, a city of distinctive architecture, lovely parks and sea views, the dirtiest capital in Europe. The people who live along Weirview keep their gardens tidy, their walkways swept, their lives as ordered as the flowers in the windowboxes. It is rare that people move out, but at times another baby or death forces them away from Lucan. Last July, Mr. Joe Bryant, a young electrician, and his wife Geraldine brought their newest son (they had three others, aged one, three and four) home from the hospital to Number 19 Weirview, the second to last house along the row. They soon found that they needed more space and Joe decided to rent his house and move to a larger place in Palmerstown. He put an advert in the *Irish Independent* and the same day showed the house to a young woman, Miss Helen O'Donnell, a short, slight young Dubliner with closecut black hair, a secretary in the city who wanted to live in Lucan for the benefit of her father who was not well and could enjoy the river and the greenery of the country. It was done quickly. Miss O'Donnell paid her rent promptly every month, and Joe Bryant had no cause to believe anything but what she had told him. Months later, after Miss O'Donnell and her father had had to move suddenly (an operation in England for the father followed by a long rest cure in a drier, warmer climate), Joe saw a picture of Miss O'Donnell in the newspaper, saying she was someone else entirely, a known and wanted killer and terrorist. You could've knocked him down with a feather. Made him wonder, these people could be anybody, now couldn't they, they could be all around you and how would you ever know? The father, a kindly and gracious man of about seventy, turned out to be no one less than Joseph Walsh, leader of the Irish Socialist Army. From the way they had carried on that autumn he was far from sickly. Drier and warmer climate, indeed! Made you wonder. Bloody people should stay up North. Having professional killers in his family's old house. Thank God the neighbors knew nothing. When Joe asked in an offhand way about them, they all said they practically never saw the two of them. The father never stirred from the house, and the daughter, away most of the day, used the back entrance and kept to herself, never stopping to chat, but ducking her head, waving and walking by. A shy little thing, well, give her time, she'd come around. It had given Geraldine a shock, though. Women felt that way more than men, Joe knew. A man coming home to a burglarized house will feel anger while a woman will feel frightened, violated. Must be that they feel safe at home and the evidence that someone has been in their house makes them feel there is no place safe for them. Tell the truth, Joe got a kind of thrill knowing Joseph Walsh and Deirdre O'Sullivan had lived at old 19 Weirview. He knew they were criminals, damned misguided fools fighting for something that was all settled years ago, stirring up trouble and sorrow for dead causes, but still, it was something, wasn't it? There was the thought of telling the boys when they were a bit older. It was the kind of story boys enjoy. "Now, when you were all little fellahs, who do you think was livin' in the old place in Lucan?" He could see their eyes lighting up.

Deirdre parked the Renault around beside the last house on the row, shut the lights and looked to see if any of the neighbors were about. No one. She took her large canvas bag which held the sawed-off and placed the bread, ham, cheese and milk around it, with the two evening papers on top. The shotgun was arranged so she could get it out quickly.

"TV Killing." What in hell was that? She took the keys from the ignition and looked out again. No one. Grotty weather. Half-four and raining again through darkness. Did Joe have sense to remember a fire tonight? Old fool would ramble around the place for days, never feeling the cold at all. Locking the car door she missed again Liam's yellow Volkswagen. A good car, always perfectly tuned. But it would have been advertising an attack on you to keep it. It had been sold in Galway and she was given this boxy rattletrap. It ran, not well, but it ran. That was the best could be said for it.

Deirdre walked quickly along the path behind Number 20 and down the wooden steps into the walled, paved yard of Number 19. The rain fell at an angle across the light coming from the back room. It fell soft and cold turning the slate roof to ink. She knocked once at the French doors and immediately the heavy woolen curtain was pulled away and Walsh let her in. He was dressed in shiny black pants and a green sweater which he never changed. "Do you have the papers?" he asked as she went past him into the large main room.

"I do," she said, setting the bag on the table in the center of the room, taking the sawed-off and putting it on the sofa. She moved towards the bare fireplace. "God's sake, Joe," she said, laying the turf in, "do you ever think of heat? And put on a light. You must have snake's blood."

"TV Killing?" Walsh murmured, holding open the *Herald*. "What in—"

"We got a headline in the other one," Deirdre said, lighting the firelighter and shoveling coal around the turf. "There," she stood up and took the bag of groceries into the kitchen. "Tea and a sandwich?"

"Yes," Walsh said, still standing in the dark room, reading.

"Turn on a fookin' light, Joe," Deirdre called, plugging in the electric kettle. "Jesus, you'll be blind as well as frozen. Go sit by the fire there."

"Yes," Walsh said, still standing, reading.

As she was setting the tray he came in and stood watching her. "There's whiskey, isn't there?"

"Paddy. Will you have one?"

"No, the tea's the thing for me now. Just that Higgins likes a glass."

She took the tray over to the fire, now burning high, the coal throwing heat out into the dark room. The tray went on the hearth and they drew two straight-back chairs up to it. Deirdre switched on a light near the window, and the dark damp cave she had entered minutes before was now a place of warmth and life. How could he stand it? she wondered, pouring him a cup as he stared into the fire. It was as if he were doing penance, yes, an old priest full of the misery and squalid little secrets of the confessional, who near the end of his days is attacked by doubt.

"There's whiskey, isn't there?"

"I just said there was."

"Good. He takes a glass now and then."

"Have another sandwich there."

"Yes," Walsh said. "Thank you, Deirdre."

Before Liam's murder she had not known him well. But he seemed very different then. A man with intelligence breaking out of him and capturing you, a good sense of humor to go with his sense of seriousness, a man who liked his food and a jar now and then. She remembered a meal she and Liam and he had at the Royal Howth Hotel and how urbane and cultivated he was in the candle-lit room, speaking humorously of how the French made such a fuss about wine. He then took five full minutes to study the wine list, looking up to ask them what they'd prefer and receiving a big laugh from Liam, and joining in himself, going on about how the Ulsterman and the Frenchman were really one and the same. Since Liam's death he had been absentminded, a man with a fierce inner life which he constantly seemed to be observing, who cared nothing for food, never drank, slept four or five hours in the early morning, and was silent most of the day, living in the back room with a table, chair and bed, surrounded by newspapers which he studied like a cryptographer searching for a clue, receiving intelligence. He dealt with no one in the I.S.A. except Deirdre. But he ran the Army through her dictatorially. Since August every killing had been planned and ordered by him. Every reprimand or accolade to one of his troops was made by him through her. Every statement to the press was written by him in his cell at the back of the house.

She thought she'd cheer him up. "It's been a good two months, Joe. We've never been so strong."

Walsh set his teacup down and looked at her. "Good? Have you gone daft, girl?"

"We'll have a say in the Republican movement finally. All in two months' time. We've got strength."

"Nonsense. Three of our own dead. Not counting Liam. What have I done but shoot in the back five people?"

"But Higgins. The Provos are coming to *us*. We've forced them to come to *us*."

"Higgins? The man is a bastard to his boots. You can't trust him as far as you can throw a chimney by the smoke. And he's the man we negotiate with."

"But you said the weapons."

"Aye. We'll see how that one attracts him. But what then? We go North and shoot Brits together?"

"Yes," Deirdre said.

Walsh stared at her. "You'd like that, wouldn't you?"

"Fookin' right I'd like it."

"More death for our Deirdre."

"British death."

"Killing Brits won't turn this island into a just place."

He turned away to the fire. She drank tea, watching as he lit a cigarette, the only habit he'd kept since Liam's death, but now he smoked three times as many. "Killing Brits is the least of our problems," he said to the fire, and then turned to her. "Don't you see that?"

"No," she picked up the tray and went into the kitchen. She was banging the cups and plates into the sink. "No, I don't see it at all," she said, coming to the door. "We'll drive the English out of Ireland, and *then* we'll worry about a 'just place.' "

"Don't give me a speech, Deirdre. Jesus, I don't need rhetoric from you."

"Yes, sir."

"Come over here and we'll go over the operation. He'll be here in an hour or so."

When she was seated he said, "I was angry at your word 'good' before. A 'good' two months. Years ago I thought killing was good. Now, I don't. But I'd say it was a 'successful' two months. How's that? And largely due to your work. We are strong. We are moving. But I don't know where, and that's a terrifying thought." He paused and then continued in a soft voice, "I don't know where."

"North," Deirdre said, just as softly.

"I'm not thinking of geography."

"Any way you think of it, Joe. Politically, morally, it's got to be North."

He smiled. "Maybe so. Now, let's go over it again."

After they discussed the meeting, with Deirdre poking the fire, Walsh asked, "Did they seem restless down there?"

"The German was," she said. "We'll have to make a decision quickly. She wants to move and get in on the action. She couldn't understand why we wouldn't take delivery sooner."

"And how's O'Connor?"

"He seemed very peaceful about the whole thing. He just follows orders."

"Good. You'll go down Monday if Higgins is interested to bring back samples for him."

"Right."

"Anything more?"

"One thing, Joe. Change your clothes, will you?"

Walsh laughed. "I thought I looked very proletarian."

"You look like a beggar, if you have to know."

"Yes, I'll change for Mr. Higgins," he said, getting up and going to the stairs. In his room at the rear of the house, changing his clothes, Walsh stopped and laughed again, enjoying the sound. Deirdre had been correct. They *had* accomplished something real. The Provisionals would talk, and he could horsetrade with them, get his people involved with them, and gradually change their movement from within, give it a Marxist ideology, and eventually control it. The Provos had no ideology now to speak of, only diaphanous theory. But what a military organization, what fighters! They had remained alive fighting a modern army for ten years. To weld ideas onto that machine, that would be his goal, that would be his direction. To give the fighter a voice and an intellect. And, if successful, the old Official I.R.A. of which he was once a member could be brought into the fold. Three separate guerrilla armies becoming one.

In 1969, when the Civil Rights Movement in the North was being batoned on every street corner, and with sectarian riots every night, the I.R.A., at its *Ard Fheis,* split between the "politicals" and the "militarists." The former, or Official I.R.A., believed what Mao Tse-tung had written forty years before: ". . . the Party commands the gun, and the gun must never be allowed to command the Party." The militarists were anti-Marxist, totally nationalistic, and called for the arming of the people in the North. The Officials made a motion for strict control of weapons. The militarists walked out, forming the Provisional I.R.A. Walsh had been present, one of the leaders, along with Liam Cleary, of the Officials. He had watched the Army split, knowing what Lenin knew, that the faction that disrupts, will not compromise, and eventually demands a split, is always in the strongest position. He could never join the Provos with their complete lack of social ideas or program, their elitist stance, their adventurism which was inevitably fascistic. Walsh let MacStiofáin and Twomey and O'Connell and Higgins walk away in '69, taking half the Army with them including most of the Northern units. He'd let them fight their fight and had remained in the Official I.R.A. as a staff officer working in the North, watching the organization crumble and the Provos strengthen. It had not been a total loss, however. He and Cleary became closer, and made plans to form a new Party and a new Army. His escape along with Higgins from H.M.S. *Mountain* gave him publicity and on that momentum they announced a week later the formation of the Irish Socialist Army with its militant guerrilla activity ruled by the Party and its ideas. Then they began the long laboring years of organization, working in the shadow of the Provos. But now there was an opportunity that must be seized. Vladimir Ilyich again: "The wind always blows from the far left." Walsh had set his life's course on that wind and now it was taking him home, where power waited and where true revolutionary war could be fought.

Walsh put on a clean white shirt and a black crew-neck sweater. He checked himself in the mirror and went across the hall to the master bedroom overlooking the weir. The bedroom was plain and clean. Deirdre's room, when she was here two or three nights a week. The bed made with a *báinín* cover. Books on the windowsill. What was she reading? *Barbary Shore*, Norman Mailer. How the young loved Mailer. He held the paperback in his hands. He'd never read it. He had great respect for Mailer's reportage and essays but could never understand his fiction. A powerful writer. A writer who knew how to use his senses and instinct, who wrote with his nose rather than his education. Next to *Barbary Shore* was *Anarchism: Concept and Praxis* by Daniel Guerin. Never heard of him. More than likely Daniel had never fired a metaphor in anger. *Man's Fate*, André Malraux. Strange man. He had met him once, in 1938 in Andalusia, where Walsh had gone as a war correspondent for the *Irish Independent*. He had interviewed the Frenchman at a small airfield and Malraux had refused to answer his questions until he first corrected Walsh's French. A cold ego-blinded man. It was like talking to someone behind glass. And there was his own book wedged between the American's and the Frenchman's, *The Private Revolution*, by Joseph Walsh. He picked it up and held it like a piece of crystal. She had his book. He hadn't seen a copy in years. Printed in 1961, the story of the "border campaign" of the mid fifties and how the people of Ulster had failed to support the I.R.A. It had been that campaign and this book that had turned him away from the militarists. The last two chapters called for a rethinking of tactics in the Republican movement with an emphasis on socialist political work on the ground in the working-class quarters of Ireland. The book had brought many people to this view, Liam Cleary among others. The book now was heresy, and Liam Cleary had died for embracing the ideas in it. Liam Cleary, Eddie Fagan, Sineád Mac-Giolla, Paddy Muldoon, all had died because of these ideas. And Donal Grennan, his old comrade-at-arms, one of the bravest men he had ever known, he too, Walsh thought, died because of these ideas. And I ordered his death. I killed him. An old man shouldn't be involved in violence, there was something obscene in that. Violence was sexual, Walsh knew, as every soldier knows. But murdering his own countrymen, an old man and a boy of nine-teen included, held no pleasure for Walsh. It confused him, and for a man like Walsh, cloudy thinking was worse than torture. Mao Tse-tung had never felt any confusion, or had he? Certainly not in his perception of what revolution was about. Walsh had used his definition often to soothe friends who came to him with doubts concerning the purpose of their struggle. "A revolution is not a dinner party, or writing an essay, or painting a picture, or doing embroidery: . . . A revolution is an insurrection, an act of violence by which one class overthrows another." Well said. But too well said. Revolution was religion along with insurrection. And like all religions it was cast in dogma, run by a hierarchy which was insulated, self-perpetuating, canonizing whom it chose and branding as heretics whom it wished. Revolution was a maze of contradiction, interminable convolutions of theory, astrology made concrete by sophisticated weapons. Revolution was thuggery justified. Revolution was setting fire to department stores. Revolu-tion was slaughtering an old man and a boy of nineteen.

"Are we ready, Joe?" Deirdre asked from the door.

"Yes, yes," Walsh said, turning to see her standing in the dark hall. "I was miles away."

"You should turn that light out and come away from the win-dow."

"Right." He replaced his book on the windowsill. "Where did you ever find this ancient thing?"

"It's a great book," Deirdre said.

"Oh, I wouldn't say that."

"You shouldn't put it down, Joe. It's a great book."

"Quotations from Chairman Joe," Walsh said softly.

"What?"

"Nothing. Now," Walsh turned out the light and became a shadow near the window, "everything set downstairs?"

"It is," Deirdre said from the darkness. "I've put the table near the fire and the whiskey's on the sideboard."

"Then we wait."

Deirdre went into the back bedroom. Walsh heard her bringing a chair over to the window looking out on the backyard. The sound of metal on wood. Her shotgun placed on the windowsill. Walsh sat in the dark looking out on the river. It was high this evening. Revolution was waiting. Drizzling rain died silently in the black running Liffey. A vigil without prayer.

They waited an hour in the dark house. Deirdre was just checking her watch again when she heard Walsh say from the other room, "They're here."

"How many?"

"Looks like two. In a gray Rover."

She heard him passing the room and walking down the stairs as she moved her chair to the side of the window. It was open just a crack, just enough room for the barrels of her shotgun. They came around the side of the house, Higgins walking first with Rúairí watching his back, and came down into the yard and over to the French doors under her window. She heard them knock, and Walsh opening the door.

"Hello, Frank," Walsh said when they were in the living room. "Can I take your hat?"

"Thank you, Joe," Higgins replied. The same air of politeness two estranged brothers might show when meeting in a lawyer's office to discuss the estate of a dead parent. "Do you know Rúairí MacCurtain, our I.O. for Dublin?"

"No, we've never met. Rúairí," he greeted, smiling. "I didn't realize that intelligence officers in the I.R.A. were so young these days."

"They're generally not, but Rúairí's work demanded the position."

"Ah, I see," Walsh said, still looking at the young man. He had a short military mustache and a piece of sandy hair had fallen over his forehead, making him at first seem like a schoolboy until Walsh noticed his green eyes staring arrogantly, as if he used them not just to see, but as weapons. "Were you appointed I.O. before August or just recently?"

Rúairí remained stone faced, and looked to Higgins, warming his hands at the coal fire. "I've nothing to say to you."

"I'd wager it was a recent appointment," Walsh said. "You can take a seat there, Mr. MacCurtain," he pointed to a bench near the doorway to the kitchen. When he was seated Walsh called, "Deirdre? Could you come down for a minute? Leave your weapon there."

Higgins turned from the fire and clasped his hands behind his back. Deirdre walked down and into the room. "Deirdre O'Sullivan, Vice Chief of Staff, I.S.A., this is Frank Higgins, Chief of Staff, Provisional I.R.A. And Rúairí MacCurtain, Intelligence Officer for Dublin."

She nodded once, and checked the room. Had he locked the back doors? Were they armed? Higgins walked over to her. "Vice Chief?" he smiled. "We're both in a youth movement, Joe. I've looked forward to meeting you. *Without* your sawed-off. You don't look half as bad as they told me you did."

She turned away from his smiling face and said, "Anything else, Chief?"

"No, you can resume your position."

When she was gone Walsh turned on the overhead light directly above the table. It was bare except for an ashtray. Higgins went for the chair which faced Rúairí across the room, but Walsh stopped him and said, "Sorry, Francis, if you don't mind. I'd rather keep an eye on your man over there."

"Certainly, Joe," he sat down and lay one freckled hand over another out on the table. Walsh took out a box of cigarettes and offered one to Higgins, who refused. He lit a cigarette and tossed the match into the fire.

"Will you end it, now?" Higgins asked.

"Yes," Walsh said.

That is how they finished it. Three months of hunting and being hunted, eight deaths, all resolved with a five-word question and a one-word answer.

"Will you have a drink to seal it?"

"I will," Higgins said.

Walsh went to the sideboard and brought back the bottle of

Paddy and two crystal glasses. They held their drinks up.

"*Sláinte*," Walsh toasted.

"*Bás in Éirinn*," Higgins said, and drank. Death in Ireland.

"Why are you suing so soon, Frank?"

"I'm not suing a blessed thing. It's to your advantage we have peace."

"Now, I wouldn't be so sure about that. You asked for a cease fire. *You* asked for negotiations, not us. We were ready and able to carry on."

"It's to our benefit we stop squabbling with you. We have much more at stake than you do. We have a war to fight."

"So did Liam Cleary," Walsh said, and took another sip of whiskey.

"I didn't order his death."

"Who did? Your infant I.O. over there?"

"Liam took his chances, Joe, he made his bed—"

"You started this 'squabbling.' And now you want to end it. Fair enough. But your first communiqué mentioned negotiations. Well, I'm all ears, Frank. Here, have another drop."

Higgins swished the whiskey around in his glass and looked into the hissing coal fire. He took his time before turning back to Walsh. "I'll give you peace."

"Keep it."

"Let me ask you—what do *you* want?"

"Nothing more and nothing less than power in the Republican movement."

Higgins took his time again, moving his glass from side to side in front of him. "We'll give you assurances of peace and then you can say any bloody thing you please."

"We want alliance."

Higgins laughed. "With whom? The I.R.A. or the Russians? You're too far gone on that commie stuff for us, Joe. We're socialists, yes. But Ireland for the Irish, not the Russians or Cubans or feck-all else."

"You sound just like the Englishman."

Higgins drank. "Who?"

"John Stephenson. Or should I say Seán MacStiofáin. That's the way he wants to be called in Ireland, isn't it? The smartest thing you ever did was to put him to pasture."

"He's a better man than you or me."

"He's a right fucking eejit."

"A man who is on hunger strike for—"

"Get away, Frank. Hunger strike? It didn't take him long before he was laying into the sausages."

"What I say, I say for the I.R.A. They're my words, not his."

"Grand. Those Russians you're going on about, they're not too bad that you won't buy matériel from them."

"Aye," Higgins smiled. "We'll buy their guns but not their party line."

"How much do you pay, Frank, for a new Armalite these days? When you can find one for sale."

"Is that your concern?"

Walsh tossed his cigarette in the fire and watched blue flame envelop it, splitting the paper, the brown tobacco bursting with smoke. "Two hundred quid a rifle? And another twenty quid a rifle to get it into the North? Are my figures close?"

"What are you getting at?"

"The I.S.A. now, this minute, have two hundred and fifty Armalites, here, in Ireland," Walsh said, tapping one finger on the hardwood table and delighting in Rúairí, across the room in shadow, shifting his weight.

Higgins drained his glass. "Give us a drop more, Joe."

"Takes the chill away, doesn't it?" Walsh said, splashing Paddy into the cut glass.

"Ah, it does that."

"And what're the thieves in Amsterdam asking for a certain American-made machine gun, the one they used to mow down all those Vietnamese?"

"The M-60?"

"The same."

"How many do you have?"

"Sixty of them. Belts, tripods, the lot."

"What do you plan to do with all those shooters, Joe? You could make your fortune."

"We've also got twenty wee machine pistols. The Ingram M-10. Ever heard of that one?"

"I've heard of it."

"It's a wonder of a gun, Frank. Small, light, and will shoot all day and half the night if you want. We've also got some plastic and ammonium nitrate, if you're interested."

"I am interested. But why should I believe you?"

"You don't have to believe me. Arrange a meeting with your quartermaster general and one of my people and we'll show them to you."

"Done," Higgins said, rapping the glass on the wood in front of him. "How much do you want for the Armalites?"

"*Tada.*" Nothing.

"And the M-60's?"

"*Tada.*"

Higgins never took his eyes off Walsh. He calmly laced his fingers together.

"Come on, Frank, you can't beat the price."

"Tell me what you want, Joe."

"Alliance."

"There must be conditions."

"Certainly."

Higgins took the bag of boiled sweets from his jacket pocket and popped one in his mouth. "We have fifty active service units now, Joe. All men who are disciplined by our own line. You'd have to abide by that."

"The I.S.A. has its own politics."

"Politics!" Higgins drank with disgust, the ball of sugar sticking out of his cheek. He quoted, "All politics leads to war, and that is its only value."

"Clausewitz," Walsh said softly.

"That's right. And that's my belief."

"Have you heard his three aspects of war? The first is that the operations of reason belong to the government. If we agree on an alliance, that could be you, or Sinn Fein, or whoever writes the press releases. I'll guarantee that the I.S.A. political line will not emerge through to the public. The second aspect is that free spiritual activity belongs to the commanders. You must guarantee that to us. I, and my staff, must be free to believe what we believe. We can fight together, but we don't have to agree politically."

"It could be done. What's the third aspect?"

"That hatred belongs to the people."

The two men stared at each other across the table. Higgins nodded, and said, "Wise old bird, wasn't he?"

Walsh shrugged.

"This will take time, Joe. I'll have to sound out the Movement. But I think it could be done. When can we see the weapons?"

"As soon as you want. Communicate with us the same way."

"Good. One more for the road, Joe? Jesus, we could've used a bit of this coming off the *Mountain*."

Walsh smiled. "If we'd had it, I never would've gone swimming, that's for sure."

Higgins laughed. "You know, with the kind of matériel you're talking about, we could take London, you know that? Jesus, we could take London."

"What do you know about the present whereabouts of Peter Farrell?"

Higgins' smile melted away. "He's not part of this stew you're serving me, is he?"

"No," Walsh said. "But I think he's here in Ireland keeping company with the Special Branch."

"Rúairí," Higgins turned. "What is this about?"

"Peter Farrell is not a member of the Army. He hasn't been since 1971."

"I know that," Walsh said. "And I know he's been involved in some action in Europe with European guerrillas, that he was arrested recently by British and German agents at Port La Gelene, and was released from Les Baumets. He's been passing himself off as Conor Graham, a member of the I.S.A., which he is not."

"Your intelligence is good," Rúairí said from across the room.

"Thank you. You better take another look at the Bretons, Frank. They're beginning to like us more than you people."

"Is that where you got it?" Rúairí asked.

"From them, and others. Tell me about Farrell."

A piece of coal fell through the grate. Walsh waited and then said, "Well, will you tell me? Is he still working for you?"

"Rúairí, go ahead."

"He is not. Farrell was burned out in '71. The man's a head case. We got rid of him, pensioned him off to France, and severed all ties. The last time we had contact he was making a deal in Amsterdam for arms. He didn't ask us, just went ahead. We sent a man over to tell him to stop. We understand, like you, that he has been involved in some bombing in Germany, but he has nothing to do with us. As for passing himself off as an I.S.A. man,

well, again, he's not all there mentally. That's the only explana-
tion I can give. If he's informing now, he won't damage us. He's
been out of it too long."

"You've lost some cover, haven't you?"

"A few safe houses, one small operation," Rúairí said. "It was
out of carelessness. We'd let them go too long and we knew some
old hand was singing, we just didn't know who."

"Now you know," Walsh said. "I suggest, Frank, after we
finalize this alliance, or rather I should say *if* we finalize, that we
get together and track down Mr. Farrell if he's in Ireland, and
put an end to his song."

"Fine," Higgins said. "It was something that should have been
done years ago."

When they were gone, and Deirdre had checked them leaving
the yard, with Higgins walking looser and lighter than when he
had entered, she went downstairs to find Walsh sitting at the
table, smoking. "I think we've done it," he said.

"He accepted?"

"Near enough. We'll see. He's a man I normally wouldn't touch
with a barge pole, but he seemed genuine tonight."

"Holy Christ, Joe, you've done it," Deirdre said.

"Almost. Tonight we move to a new billet. And Monday you
get the samples. Our next meeting with them should be away from
Dublin. Some place where we can breathe. Maybe Crenshaw's
home in the Burren. The Provos still have good contact with
him."

"Who?"

"Robert Crenshaw. You've heard of the mother?"

"Sure. But she's been dead ten years."

"Her son isn't. And he's a big supporter of the I.R.A. It's a
wonderful old house," Walsh said. "I'll give you a course in how
to behave in an aristocrat's home before we go out there. Let's
move now, no celebrating yet."

The next night, Halloween, Walsh and Deirdre met with the
newspaperman from the *Irish Press* in the blue Renault parked on
Fosters Avenue near University College. The newspaperman had
been under surveillance commencing that morning by two Special
Branch officers. When the reporter left the car and walked away
the detectives let him go and tailed the Renault to a house in
Rathmines. When they saw Walsh get out of the car, walk into

the house, and the Renault drive away, they radioed for instructions. They were told to keep the house under surveillance and tail Walsh if he left, but not to interfere with him. The next morning at dawn, 1 November, the Feast of All Saints, Raymond Murray, Director of the Special Branch Anti-Terrorist Division, along with John Larrimore and Brian McMahon, broke into the house and arrested Joseph Walsh. He was charged with Section 30 of the Offenses Against the State Act, was held in custody that morning, and in the afternoon was brought before a Special Court. There were three judges but no jury, and only one piece of testimony was given, by Raymond Murray, explaining that he believed Joseph Walsh was a member of an illegal organization. This is all that is required for conviction in the Republic of Ireland under the Offenses Against the State Act. A senior police official merely has to inform the court of his belief. The court found Walsh guilty and he was immediately taken to Mountjoy Jail. Fingerprinted, issued prison clothes, and led to the administrative wing where Tommy Fleming took charge of him.

By the time he was seated in a shabby room at a wooden desk, it was nearly 6 P.M. Fleming brought the old man the evening meal on a partitioned tin tray. Chicken pie, carrots, potatoes, coffee and pudding. Walsh ate as his young guard stood across the room. He spoke to him about the last time he'd been in "Joy," and when that story was done he began another. Long ago, in the thirties, during his first internment, he had overcome the intrinsic loathing that the inmate feels for the prison guard. Walsh rejected that hatred for being the baggage of the common criminal, which he was not. He was a prisoner because of his beliefs, and would never stoop to the old "con-screw" cock fighting. When they had issued him his prison clothes, he had not protested. Time would tell. If he was thrown into the general population in the uniform, he would raise hell. If he was segregated or quartered with other political prisoners, he could protest the uniform quietly, or continue to wear it. "So," Walsh said, sipping the cold coffee, "I'm to be questioned, I suppose. That right, Tommy?"

The young man said nothing.

"Are you afraid to speak?"

"We have an order against fraternizing."

"Don't fraternize then. We'll just talk."

Tommy smiled. "You're a chatty man. It's like you're on a trip to the sea instead of prison. You've finished?"

"I have," Walsh said as Tommy picked up the tray. "That wasn't all bad."

"It's the officers' tray. You'll have the inmates' tray in the mornin'."

"Ah. First day softening. Would you have a cigarette, Tommy?"

"My orders are not to give any to you."

"Whose order?"

"Orders," the young man said, and carried the tray out.

A tall man, dressed in light brown slacks and a black crew-necked sweater came in carrying a buff-colored folder and sat across from him. He had a halo of blond hair frenetically kinked. His eyes were soft behind wire-rimmed glasses. The prison psychiatrist? Walsh wondered. Do they think I've slipped my moorings? Certainly this one can't be Special Branch. Walsh noted a redness around his nostrils. "Sorry," the man said, and blew his nose. "Garrett Costello, Mr. Walsh," he touched his nose with the handkerchief one more time before putting it away. "I'm with the Special Branch."

"You're not."

Garrett smiled. "I have some questions."

"So have I."

"Mine first, though."

"Certainly, Mr. Costello."

Garrett looked down at the folder. "How long have you been in contact with Gudrun Böhm and Terrence O'Connor?"

"Who's that again?"

"There's no need," Garrett said. "It will be just that much more difficult for you if you won't cooperate."

Tommy Fleming came in and stood behind the prisoner.

"Could I have a cigarette?"

"Fleming, get a packet of cigarettes. And a cup of tea for me. Black."

"Yes, sir."

Garrett blew his nose again.

"What are you doing for it?" Walsh asked.

"Sorry?"

"The cold. Or is it flu?"

"A cold. I'm doing nothing for it."

"Waiting it out? That's the best method. Live with it."

"Terrence O'Connor. Gudrun Böhm," Garrett said.

"I've never heard the names. I knew a Teddy O'Connor, years ago. Dead now, I think, yes, I'm sure of it."

Garrett remained detached, and asked his questions. His cold insulated him from the old man and the whole situation. It was Raymond Murray's case, after all; Garrett knew nothing about it. That was the method his superior employed. Work alone. Don't delegate. Pit officer against officer. Divide and rule.

Murray had briefed Garrett this morning about Walsh, the German and the American, giving him a list of questions that would run an hour. Murray had then gone to "the white house" in Portmarnock, a place where informers were debriefed and protected, and others, Garrett was sure, were imprisoned and persuaded to inform. Murray was up to something out there. But let him be. Garrett had his cold, his wall, his detachment, his concentration on self. His only ambitions were to get home, have a hot lemonade, and sleep for days.

He had joined the Special Branch directly out of University College, Dublin, sixteen years ago, not thinking of police work as a profession but as security. He wanted to write, but supporting a wife and himself by hustling editors seemed ridiculous. The recruiter promised a good salary, full benefits, early pension, and the chance to do something for his country. The last did not appeal to him in the beginning. It took years before he truly saw his duty.

"This difference of opinion you've been having with the Provisionals—it ended quite abruptly, didn't it?"

"That's lovely," Walsh said, "difference of opinion. Jesus, you're a thick man."

"Did you deal with them?"

"We don't 'deal,' Mr. Costello."

Garrett went on to his next series of questions. Only an hour, he thought, and then I'm home. The kids will be there, Nuala will put me in bed, nurse me. Comfort, sleep. Instead of this place. Garrett despised the prison. Mountjoy was defeat, a monument to the reality of police work. Justice, humanism, order were not to be considered. Only brick and iron, seething cages of hatred, swarming with pain, humiliation, brutality. To be a progressive policeman was to go to work each day with futility as your partner, and to cut your losses when you were through, day in and day out.

The old man was giving him a history lesson now in response to each question. Garrett listened. He knew the old Ulsterman by reputation only. Murray had warned him, "He'll impress you. Try not to show it." Too true. Joseph Walsh was impressive. Speaking about duty and history. He wouldn't engage him.

Garrett, dwelling on his streaming nose, his dry ticklish throat, headache and burning eyes, knew something of duty and history. The satisfaction Garrett took from his job was that he saw himself not as a judge, but as a guardian of the people of his country, and his duty was to fight "Green Republicanism," as he described it, because it was tyranny, pure and simple, a minority imposing its will on the majority. He knew the history of his country as well as any other Irish person. The Irish people were haunted and hounded by their history. But Garrett had a different view from most. He thought the great Easter Rising of 1916 a useless waste of life, orchestrated by crackpots, led by Pearse, the chief lunatic, who was now an uncanonized saint. They were going to put him on a postage stamp! All you had to do, Garrett thought, was read Pearse's writings, go beyond the gallant "Ireland unfree shall never be at peace" rigmarole and read his jabberings about fresh blood washing Ireland, blood sacrifices, blood love, to see how seriously deranged he was. And the people of Ireland at the time had not risen to it. Not at all, although certain Irish history books would have you believe differently. It was only through British stupidity, transforming the organizers of the rising into martyrs by hanging them, that moved the people away from Britain. A shame, Garrett thought. He was Irish, and had no love for England, but it was a shame, all in all, that Ireland had broken from Britain. A shame for both countries, in the end. Britain's industry and Ireland's soul, that would have been a match. If ever the two islands could have come together, finally, and thrown their differences into the sea, how much death would have been overcome, what tides of hatred would have been tamed. Ireland at war would forever be unfree. Ireland drowning in hate would float on until its lungs burst.

Raymond Murray entered, dressed in a pinstripe suit and soft blue tie. His shirt had a short London-style collar and was the color of bone. "How are we getting on, Garrett?"

"Mr. Walsh has been discussing history."

"Yes," Murray said, staring at the old man as he took off his jacket. "You get home, Garrett, and tend that cold. Thanks for breaking the ice."

Picking up his folder from the desk, Garrett noticed how the atmosphere in the room had been changed by Murray's entrance. Tommy Fleming, standing behind the prisoner, had been attentive, interested, a man listening to a play on a radio in the next room. Now he was standing stiffly, his face blank, staring at the wall across from him. Walsh, who had been speaking as a professor to a doubting student in the pub after class, gesturing with his cigarette, organizing his argument, was now still, looking at the ashtray, his face resigned.

Murray draped his jacket over the back of the chair. Garrett stood for a moment at the table. "Anything else, Raymond?"

"Not a thing," he said, sitting down. "Take the day tomorrow."

"Grand."

As he turned away he heard Murray say, "Get rid of those cigarettes, Fleming."

As he closed the door behind him he heard, "I'm not interested in history, Joe, but the present, right now."

CHAPTER 8

The Fort without Walls

O'Connor woke alone. The digital clock winked at him—7:47. Once awake, O'Connor was up and out of bed and walking quickly to the bathroom. Years before, as a sophomore at Fordham, he had read a Zen story where the master tells the pupil, "Upon retiring, sleep as if you had entered your last sleep. Upon awakening, leave your bed behind you instantly as if you had cast away a pair of old shoes." Following this advice had been difficult in the beginning. But even as a little boy, he felt most himself when wrestling with discipline. Now, after years of instantly shedding his sleep, he did it without thinking. It was part of him. Gudrun, the first morning they woke together in Paris, laughed and asked him where the fire was. "It's just the way I get up," O'Connor had said.

He took a long shower in the bright tile and chrome bathroom, starting with very hot water and gradually working down to totally cold. His last dream was still with him. There was a long gray landscape. O'Connor was walking alone. The road dipped down and ran next to a stream of clear water. He saw smooth stones artfully placed in the bed of the stream. Across the stream there was one tree with leafy boughs sharp against the gray sky. Some people were gathered in a circle, and others were edging closer, trying to look over heads to see what was at the center. O'Connor walked across a steeply arched wooden footbridge and came closer. The man directly in front of him was the long-haired American traveler he'd met a week ago in town. He turned away and O'Connor was part of the circle looking at a nun in a white habit sitting on a pile of firewood. Her face, framed in starched white cloth, was somehow familiar. She lit a match and tossed it behind her. Flames shot up. O'Connor felt the heat on his face. "Sister," he shouted. "Sister, isn't it hot in there?"

She looked directly at him, eye to eye, and said, "Only a fool would be concerned with a matter like that."

He toweled himself and didn't think of the dream again. He was eager for the day. While he was shaving he saw Gudrun in the mirror enter the bedroom and look about for something. She was dressed in a sweater and white shorts. Her exercise clothes. Every morning she did half an hour's worth of yoga. "Terrence," she said, still searching.

"Yeah," O'Connor said, working the razor between his chin and lower lip. "Your journal's in the kitchen, on the counter by the onions."

She came and leaned in the doorway, watching him shave. She smiled when she caught his eye. "You're sometimes too smart for your own good."

"You were reading it last night standing up against the counter. And now it's time to work on it." He looked at her in the mirror and used the razor as a pointer. "Elementary, my dear Watson."

"Pardon?" her smile faded. O'Connor loved that expression, learned from the Scot who tutored her in her father's house when she was a girl. A clipped British word in her sensual German voice. He also loved to see her face grow suddenly serious and guarded when she didn't understand something. It was one of the few times Gudrun looked less than confident.

"Sherlock Holmes. His assistant was Watson."

"Oh, I see," she said.

"Ellafitzgerald, my dear. That's Lennon. Lennon of Liverpool, not Lenin of Mother Russia."

"You're a happy little one this morning," she said. "What makes you so happy?"

"Why, you, my *streusel*," he said, putting the razor away and quickly embracing her. "The nearness of you," he whispered, close to her face.

"Brush your teeth, Terrence," she said, and pushed him away.

He dressed in a flannel shirt, jeans and high-topped, rubber-soled hiking boots. He drew the brown curtains to have a look at the morning. The sky was a mess of gray, the sun a lopsided child's drawing. Kinsale Harbor in the distance the color of concrete. O'Connor took his rucksack from the closet and sat on the bed. He took out the Ingram M-10. Black with a light blue clip of .380 ammunition stuck in the metal butt. A machine pistol, no larger than a .45, capable of firing a thousand rounds a minute. O'Connor folded a sweater around it and placed it in his bag. He made the bed and looked about the room. Ready.

In the living room Gudrun sat curled up on the long brown velour couch. She was comfortable in this rich house. Like all who are born wealthy, she was natural in any home—at peace in a palace, an interested visitor in a shack. O'Connor, a poor man's son, had never been at ease anywhere. In opulent surroundings he was either stunned that people actually *lived* there, or took the peasant's attitude that it was all somehow sinful. The homes of the poor made him remember the dark and dirt of the Inwood tenement where he grew up, and he always wanted to flee the air of failure, embarrassed not by the poor, but by his own embattled emotions which swung like a pendulum between the adult's learned respect of the simple life and the child's hatred of the shanty smell.

She wrote in her journal, bound in a plum-colored folder. Every day, usually in the morning, she recorded her thoughts. It was a discipline she enjoyed, feeling that self-criticism was best when written down. Any competent guerrilla would never keep a diary. But she excused herself by never mentioning names, plans, or locations. The journal had become dearer to her since they'd come to Ireland because it was the only time she used German.

She'd been up since six-thirty, and was pleased to be awake before Terrence. After her exercises she had tea, toast, and a boiled egg and had looked at yesterday's paper. On the fashion page she'd been shocked to see a photograph of a model who looked like her mother. The cold mannequin's face, the haughty stare, released a memory of that day the winter she was fifteen. Her father picking her up, a snowy afternoon, at the boarding school in the country outside Cologne, taking her out of class, home in his gray BMW with the walnut paneling, to go shopping with Irmgard, the family *Haustochter*, for a suitable mourning dress. She had known something was wrong. People just didn't die of pneumonia, especially if they hadn't been ill with something else, and especially not if they had her father's money. When she was a child she'd thought only poor people died of illness. Rich people could buy doctors and hospitals and drugs. It was sad, but rich people had to die in car crashes, or be hit by a bus crossing a street. There was still a trace of that feeling with her at her mother's grave, and added to her suspicion was her father's face which was not grieving, but embarrassed. When she was nineteen she had forced it out of Irmgard, who only told her part of the story, the rest, the *Haustochter* said, would have to come from her father. When Gudrun confronted him, he told her calmly, in detail, as if he were speaking about a neighbor or a business associate's wife. Her mother had been ill for years, had finally succeeded in her fourth suicide attempt by taking a hot bath and slashing her wrists with his straight razor. The reason he had lied to Gudrun was to spare her mental anguish. Had he ever planned to tell her? she demanded. Yes, he replied vaguely, eventually he would have told her. When he thought she could handle it.

She had never told anyone about it. Once she had spoken to Conor about suicide, her fascination with the act, but never about her mother. Conor, she cursed him. Traitor, liar, weak. There was a day fishing with him on the Seine, one lovely August afternoon in deserted Paris, long before she'd met Terrence, and that afternoon she'd loved him. Fishing with the old men of Paris, he'd been her bright, handsome, wild Irish boy, speaking French like a native, telling jokes, bubbling, passionate as the heat that hung over the city. They always spoke French with each other, until Terrence arrived, when she put an end to it. The notes Conor would write her, full of joking, turn of phrase, love, had amazed her because she knew that writing a foreign language was the most difficult part of mastering it. She could speak French and English fluently, could appreciate literature in both languages, but writing either one of them was a chore. Conor, though, seemed at times more French than Irish.

She washed the dish and cup from her breakfast and dried them. He led me here. He's provided me with one more terminal to wait for one more train.

It had begun for Gudrun twelve years ago, on a warm June night in Berlin, where she had come up from Heidelberg with a group of her classmates to protest the Federal German Republic's reception of the Shah of Iran and the Empress Farah. As she stood on the elegant Bismarckstrasse that evening across from the Opera House in a crowd of hundreds of students, waiting to cat-call at the Shah and Empress when they pulled up to attend a performance of *The Magic Flute*, Gudrun Böhm was an eighteen-year-old girl, with no real sense of politics, philosophy, or life. She was bright, pretty, and had that curious 1960s emotional quality found in many young people in Europe and America, what the Germans call *Leidensneid*, an envy of suffering. The poor blacks of America seemed to live life more fully because of their oppression. The Cuban veterans of their revolution were more attractive than the plain bourgeois men of dying Europe. Gudrun, like many others, wanted to reject her parents' affluence and values, and live life as a battle and not as a holiday. She had joined a pacifist group at university, and had marched in protests against nuclear weapons, had distributed leaflets condemning American involvement in South America and Vietnam, a country which she would have had difficulty locating on a map at the time. When the call had come to protest in Berlin against the fascist Shah, she had signed on for the ride. She'd always loved Berlin. After the protest there were so many glittering cafes to go to and talk the night away.

But something was wrong. She had never seen so many policemen in one place at one time, and they were violent, clubbing people who strayed across the lines. She understood now why they were called "bulls." There seemed to be no control over them. They charged blindly, this way and that. It was frightening to see the pleasure they took in their work. The glow of floodlights, flashbulbs erupting, sounds of jeers, chants, wood on bone, firecrackers, made it seem not quite real, as if it all were a stage, or a movie set, or a dream gone wrong and rushing toward nightmare. The swinging swaying mob, of which she was a part and could not escape, terrified her. She was a slight girl. It would crush her. Her head could be broken as easily as the eggs people were throwing from behind her, sailing luminously through the television lights, spattering bright yellow and semen-colored on the dark street, dripping from the visors of the faceless riot police, and when they charged she was swept along in panic to keep her balance, relieved finally to feel the crowd around her scattering, giving her running room, but then horrified to see that now she was separated, and the police could pick her out to club. Two of them had a long-haired boy cornered against a shop front. One policeman raised his baton up and back, the club pointing straight down to the street behind him, before he flashed it up, over, and across the boy's skull.

Gudrun followed a crowd into narrow Krummestrasse, racing

through the unbelievable noise, feeling that perhaps she would make it. Her head wouldn't be swept up with the eggshells. The police turned on the water cannon. A girl next to her caught the blast full in the chest and was shot back, skidding across the pavement like a piece of paper in a swollen gutter. Gudrun kept running, following a group of boys, and slowed when they did. Cars were parked across the street blocking the exit. The police rushed behind them. The tall apartment buildings looked down into the narrow street. No escape. Rubber truncheons flew into them, and Gudrun backed against the wall, as the street filled with police. She begged, her arms covering her head, and the police showed mercy. One of them told her to straighten up. She did and saw a man in civilian clothes fire a pistol at a young fellow with close-cropped black hair. And watched him fall dead to the street.

The man killed by the plainclothes policeman was one Benno Ohnesorg, twenty-six, attending the first and last demonstration of his life. At the marathon student meetings on the following days, Gudrun saw the way others looked at her. She was a veteran. She had seen the State revealed, and was changed, overnight, from a member of *Schilli*, or German "radical chic," into a dedicated, uncompromising revolutionary. When Ulrike Meinhoff, the columnist of *Konkret*, called for the use of violence four years later, Gudrun was already ahead of her, having trained under George Habbash in Jordan. She secured permission for Andreas Baader, Ulrike Meinhoff, and others to go to the camp.

But over the years, as a leading member of the Red Army Faction, supplying arms, recruiting, planting bombs at British and American Army bases in Germany, Gudrun had begun to move from anarchy, and the tactics of random violence, arson, kidnapping, and other terror to force the State to reveal its face, into a search for a genuine revolution. She had grown to hate Baader and the clique around him. He was childish, stupid, sadistic. An adventurer, nothing more. He had been a spark and nothing more.

She still worked, mainly from Paris, but only in setting up and maintaining safe houses. She spent weeks in her flat looking down on the river, reading, filling notebooks with her thoughts. The R.A.F., since Meinhoff's suicide by hanging at Stammheim Prison in 1975, was finished as a political force, she believed. It had never been anything but a group of radicals with no direction, no constituency, no ideas; but with Meinhoff alive, Gudrun had thought, there was the *potential* to become something powerful. She made no excuses for herself or the group in her journals. It had just been the wrong tack. The whole experience must not be condemned, but studied and used. It had been only an expression of anger, and the revolutionary couldn't afford anger. Tactics, and the correct fight, the fight you could win, that was what she wanted. Western Europe would never wake up, at least not in her lifetime, no matter how many banks or embassies you trashed or how many business-men you murdered.

Those months after Ulrike Meinhoff's suicide, when Gudrun sat in the window seat hour after hour, watching the Seine cut through Paris, disgusted with herself, disgusted with the schoolboy revolution she was a part of, she had written in her journal, describing herself as Lenin in Zurich, surrounded by intrigue, trusting no one, frightened that failure was as certain as death, knowing there was a revolution out there somewhere, but not possessing the means to go to it. Meeting Conor Graham had taken her from her window seat for good. At home that evening, she had written in her journal, "I have met a man today who will change my life. He is not aware of it, but he will change my life. My sealed train has arrived, and Conor Graham is the Finland Station." Romantic claptrap, to be sure, but that was the way she felt about the hand-some Irishman. Now, after his betrayal, and finding that Ireland was not Russia of 1917, she still believed that she had been right to come. Working with someone like Joseph Walsh was worth Conor's betrayal. She still could not call him Peter. He would always be Conor. He was probably, this minute, waking up in a chic flat, having his coffee and croissants brought by some woman who will love him even after he's betrayed her.

She read over her last paragraph and heard Terrence enter the room.

"What's the lesson for the day?" O'Connor asked with a smile.

She finished a sentence, looked up and said, "Only that actual combat is the only way to learn to fight well. It's the only way to know who will fight and who will not."

"I'm ready," O'Connor said.

"You're ready? For what?"

"You said I was good."

"A good marksman may be a coward under fire."

"I'm ready, Gudrun. You don't have to worry about me."

"Good," she said. "You're not going today?"

"Sure," he said, on his way to the kitchen. "Perfect day for a ride."

"You'll be soaked to the skin," she said, already back to her journal.

He made coffee for the thermos and two sandwiches of Swiss cheese and mustard. He put them in his bag and tossed in two apples. Back in the living room she said, "She'll be here at five."

"I'll be back by then. Any more news?"

"Nothing. The radio is hopeless."

"I'm going."

"Don't be foolish," she said. "This close to an operation, maybe you should stay inside and not—"

Standing with his rucksack on his shoulder, like a schoolboy, he interrupted her, but held his anger. "I'll be back by five."

"Check the boat, then."

"The boat's fine."

"Check it," Gudrun said.

"Right."

"Bring some wine for tonight."

"Right."

O'Connor walked down the hallway and into the garage. Next to the BSA was the gray and black Porsche 10-speed. O'Connor checked the tires, rigged the bag on his shoulders, and lifted the garage door up over his head. A drizzle of rain through the mist. He leaned the bike against the door and went back to fetch his slicker off the handle bars of the BSA. In the rear of the garage, behind the Volvo, stacked against the wall to the ceiling and covered in canvas were the crates of ammunition, the new Arma-lites, the M-60 machine guns. The ammonium nitrate and gelignite were in the basement. The night after they rented the house they had stored all of it, going from the boat to the house in a van he'd leased in Cork City. It had taken two trips.

O'Connor cycled up the driveway to the road, turning once to look back at the house. It was set below the road in a shelter of trees on a shelf above a sharp descent to a green valley of farms. The valley rolled softly to Kinsale Harbor. A sprawling modern structure, it was the summer home of an English architect, Mr. J.M.J. Southely, who had put an advert in the *Cork Herald Examiner* and was only too pleased to rent to Mr. Paul Harrison of New

York, filmmaker, and his Swiss-born wife, Marthe, also involved in film, who had sailed from France on their own yacht to Kinsale and wanted a good house to winter in Ireland while Mr. Harrison worked on a film script. Stable, courteous, well-to-do young people. Mr. Southely was most helpful, telling the young couple various places to eat and drink in the surrounding area, and charging them £250 per month rental. O'Connor paid him two months' rent in cash. Since then he'd drawn checks from his account at the Allied Irish Bank in Cork. The money was Gudrun's, transferred from a Munich bank. Mr. Southely didn't know, and, O'Connor thought, coasting through the mist, he wouldn't care whose money he received. O'Connor had run into a few English people in and around Kinsale, all wealthy, all discreet. Money was money, the English in Kinsale believed, and it was best to keep one's profile low in Ireland, oh do enjoy it, have a bit of fun and live well, but don't lord it about the place, and the money, well it mattered little, really, whether it *was* your wife's, or your dear old granddad's who took it from the labor of West Africans. Rather stupid to ask a person who has money in his hand where he got it. One's own business, really. Money was money.

Alone on the road, the morning coming at him soft and gray, he braked down easily, concentrating on the wet pavement, cycling easily through the tight S curve, gliding through the last turn, taking it wide and then flashing down again between the trees where other homes like Mr. Southely's sat half hidden, closed up for Ireland's off season.

He knew the road well. He had traveled it nearly every day for two months, cycling for the exercise, and to see the country, but also to get away from Gudrun, who had been bad company since they'd come to Ireland. Since the night in Wicklow she had felt alien here, and didn't go out much, or have contact with anyone because, she said, she could be spotted. Originally, with the flight to Ireland and the expectation of a fight here, she had been very much alive. But after leaving Wicklow that August morning, things had turned sour. Walsh had said the I.S.A. didn't want the weapons right away. He had told her about Conor Graham/Peter Farrell and she grew even more wary of Ireland and the Irish. Like other European guerrillas, she'd always respected the long-term, no-compromise battle the Irish fought. But now the reality, especially the reality of betrayal, drove her inward, and she cultivated an already severe caution about people.

They had come back to Cork and had waited. They read newspaper accounts of the I.S.A.'s war on the Provos. Gudrun had railed at him about the futility and ignorance of wasting revolutionaries. Then Deirdre O'Sullivan came two weeks ago. She came for just an evening with word from Walsh to sit tight. Soon they would be able to take shipment. There was to be a new offensive in the North. Walsh was now making a truce with the Provos. There might even be an alliance, because the Provos were desperate for matériel. They had the manpower and organization the I.S.A. lacked. If they could join—it was all up in the air. And then three days ago, Sunday at dawn, Joseph Walsh was arrested in Dublin. Deirdre called and told them she knew when Walsh was to be brought to Portlaoise Prison from Mountjoy Jail and the route the convoy would take. She and Gudrun began a plan to spring him. Deirdre was coming this evening. Tomorrow was the day.

Now that an operation was coming up, Gudrun had become less austere to him. They had even made love last night, on the velour couch in the living room. It was the first time in a month. Gudrun went about it mechanically, realizing perhaps, O'Connor thought, that an orgasm and another body were necessary to blow out her tension, make her more flexible and physical for the operation. It had also been good for him, but not as a training exercise. O'Connor needed her body, he needed her gracefulness, because it was then, and only then, locked into her, skin against skin, that he allowed himself softness and healing. He took no comfort in anything else in life. He had never developed a sense of love in anything except the physical act of sex with a woman. He needed the warmth of compassion that women gave him, and he pursued it with the dedication of a poet searching for an image to connect perfectly with others already made.

O'Connor had never concerned himself whether he loved Gudrun or not. He was excited by her, and that was enough. She had shown him a method of acting, and O'Connor realized in a cold moment of satori that it was through action that he'd finally be released from the flabby life of the intellectual, the inward anger of the artist, and the knowledge that there could be no compromise made with a world foul in its institutions. She had given him a commission to fight, to live life as a patriot only to himself and what he knew was moral, to realize the power of silence, exile, cunning, and automatic weapons. And she had given him herself without sentiment or strings attached. He could care less whether he loved her or not.

O'Connor cruised through the town of Kinsale, still asleep in its off-season resort town aimlessness. He took a narrow street curving up into the old part of town, giving the milkman a wave as he passed. At the post office the girl greeted him with a shy smile, soft day, Mr. Harrison, no mail today. He bought a bar of chocolate. Are you on the bicycle today, Mr. Harrison? Wet day for a ride. The radio says we'll get some sun later. If you believe them. So. Cheerio, Mr. Harrison.

He rode by the pub where he'd met the American traveler a week ago, and a fragment of last night's dream filled him for a moment before fading entirely. It was a simple pub patronized by the pint men of the town, laborers from the marina, crew members off the boats. A good place in the early afternoon to sit near the turf fire and sip a pint with a newspaper before the place filled. He was doing just that on a windy day of cold sun, reading in the *Irish Independent* of a Provisional I.R.A. officer's death while sitting in a car in Terenure, Dublin. A young man of O'Connor's generation came in wearing a red and black poncho, jeans and a watch cap. He was big and blond with long hair and a beard. He set his shoulder bag and bedroll next to the door, nodded once to O'Connor, and headed for the bar, rubbing his hands. European, O'Connor thought, hitchhiking Ireland. Danish by the color of him. Not Irish. Certainly no Irishman would wear a bright blanket for a coat. Only tinkers wore red in rural Ireland. But he was wrong. The man was American. He came straight to O'Connor's table and said, after setting his pint on the table, "Hi, I'm Dave Jessup." It wasn't just his flat accent; only Americans told you their names in greeting.

He was surprised to find O'Connor a countryman. They talked about Ireland. "I've hitched all over Europe," Jessup said, "and never had better luck than this country. People really go out of their way to help a traveling man."

"If you're a foreigner," O'Connor said. "Irish traveling people don't fare too well."

"Oh, yeah, yeah. Tinkers, huh? I've heard about them. But I got off the ferry up there at Rosslare and it's been easy as hell since I hit this country. Hey, would you like some cheese? It's okay to eat in here, isn't it?"

He went to his bag and brought a small wheel of cheddar to the table and cut it with an evil-looking pocketknife. Long, black handled, with a wide brightly honed blade. A pigsticker, O'Connor remembered. The man caught him looking at it. "My only weapon," Jessup said, clicking it closed, "except my good looks."

"You think you need it?" O'Connor smiled.

"Sure," Jessup said. "A man alone can always use protection. This blade scared the shit out of a punk in Liverpool who was bothering me. And I thought Liverpool was supposed to be a tough town. Scared the shit right out of him. I bet he's still running. You sound like a New Yorker."

"You've got a good ear."

"Now, that's what I call a *really* tough town. What're you doin' over here?"

O'Connor gave him the fiction. Script writing, wife, etc.

"Well, it's better to be here than there. You want another pint of stout? I'm buyin'."

He watched him standing at the bar. He didn't like him. There was that American trait of failing to take yourself seriously. Grown men acting like boys of eighteen. He was obviously educated, obviously came from a solid bourgeois family. Thirty years old. And yet he was traveling like a boy scout. His hair, hanging limp to his shoulders from the watch cap, struck O'Connor as slovenly, denoting a character of no depth, no reflection, no commitment.

The cheese was light colored and sharp. O'Connor thanked him for the pint and commented on the cheese. "Yeah. I smuggled it in from England. I hear the cheese is great over here, too."

"You heard wrong."

"No shit? I thought this was a big dairy country."

"It is, but they don't know how to make cheese. Great fishing all around the island but no commercial fishing industry. The Japanese come from the other side of the world in canning ships but the Irish still are just two men in a rowboat."

"But it seems they've got a good thing goin'."

O'Connor offered him a cigarette which he declined. "What do you mean, 'a good thing?'"

The other American put a piece of cheese in his mouth, and noted O'Connor's cold, composed stare.

"Well, the easiness, the—the—"

"Ireland being the last peasant country in the British Isles? The only peasant country in Europe except Spain? Something like that?"

"Hey, man. Did I say something? I'm sorry. But you seem to be on my case in a big way here and—"

"You don't know what you're talking about. That's all."

"Fair enough, Paul. I'm just passing through and you live here. I was just shooting the shit with you."

"Read a newspaper."

"Gave it up," he smiled. "Nothing but bullshit and pictures. You've been here—"

"I've been away for a year."

"Well," he took a sip of stout. "This stuff is sure good. I'm safe in saying that, right?"

O'Connor eased off. "Yeah. It's beautiful stuff."

He was cutting cheese again. "You know, Paul. It's gotten really weird at home. I'm from Waukegan, just outside Chicago. And, I mean, it's gotten *weird*. I passed through New York and, Jesus, what a strange place. Like the last days are upon us, you know? Crime and paranoia. And the rest of the country just—just slap-happy. Look at TV. Man, the whole country just slaphappy. You know what I'm saying?"

O'Connor had had enough. He drained his pint, adding more fuel to his anger by hurrying his drink. "Yeah, I know. Look, have a great time. Maybe we'll run into each other."

"Sure." He lowered his voice. "If you're going my way, I've got a joint we can split. Nice stuff."

O'Connor was standing, putting his arms in his coat. "I don't use marijuana anymore."

"Why?"

"I grew up."

The other American tipped his pint toward him. "Take care, then."

"You, too," O'Connor nodded, then walked out of the pub, got on his bike and pedaled away on the empty road.

If O'Connor had been right in his first perception, that the young fellow in the red poncho who walked into the sleepy pub *had* been Danish, he would have welcomed his company. Long hair, fuzzy thinking, dope smoking and all. It was not just that he was an American, either. If he had been ten years older or ten years younger, O'Connor would have enjoyed passing the time with him. It was because he was of his own generation that O'Connor was rude, and angry. He saw his generation as a failure. They had settled for meaningless work that paid them bread and circuses, cars and jogging shoes, marijuana, and subscriptions to magazines and museums. Their promise had been to fight a battle against an imperialist war. They didn't end the war. Nixon ended the draft, and O'Connor's generation settled. They had never cared. They had never cared about the military-industrial complex, racism, or the rights of working people. Every social movement had been taken over by public relations mercenaries before they were out of their infancy. The anti-war movement, the black power movement, women's liberation. It all went into the maw of the tube, and was used to sell cars and cigarettes. People who shut down universities later joined the "Dodge Rebellion" and women who asserted their identity bought cigarettes that told them, "You've come a long way, baby." "The generation that changed the world" had done nothing that lasted or mattered. Politicians grew their hair longer and talked of love and peace. Stockbrokers smoked pot and wore blue jeans around the house. Everybody got fat and voted Democratic. Everybody laid back and believed the words of popular songs. Go for the big money, read a novel about devil worship, "party," ride a raft down a river on the weekend, go skiing, see a flick, watch the tube, get high, lock your door, learn about wines, tone your body, get your head shrunk. Vietnam? Chile? Cuba? Ireland? The South Bronx? Fred Hampton? Bernardine Dohrn? Mark Rudd? (He's selling insurance, isn't he?) Abbie Hoffman? (Selling dope, right? Framed? Oh yeah? Really?) Rap Brown? (Doing time, isn't he? Oh yeah?) Rennie Davis? (Fried his brain. Oh yeah? Found God in India, didn't he? Freaked out. Oh yeah?) Eldridge Cleaver? (Found God in Paris. No shit?) And O'Connor was left betrayed, with disheveled memories. He made films for no money, read, ran motocross, and felt himself dying, waiting, rotting. Once he had become a radical because of the poverty and injustice he saw in his country. Now he went deeper into radicalism after witnessing the great mindless oppressive affluence of America. But he was a radical without issues or community, forever yearning for the good old days. All he had was slogans. When he was researching the F.A.L.N. in New York he knew he had to end the sham. He would get out of America and save his life.

Being a foreigner had opened his eyes. The stranger could taste life, could *see*. To be a stranger was not lonely or odd to O'Connor. To be a stranger was to be alive. To be part of his generation in America in the 1970s was to be not only dead but dead without an epitaph. A cheating little soul. Europe had drawn him because of film and motocross. Both avocations had always let him exist in details, strategy and personal will. One was intellectual and collaborative. The other was physical, mechanical and solitary. He had given up both like he gave up sleep every morning. Old shoes. In Europe, through Gudrun (and if it hadn't been her it would have been someone else, he told himself), he had put all of himself in a tradition that had always drawn him but had been elusive because, as he saw it, he had never been truly awakened.

The American 1960s of protest, youthful righteousness, and eventual, inevitable betrayal, had brought O'Connor to a country road in Ireland with a sophisticated weapon in his bag. He was thinking of a line from a book he had read on another solitary morning nearly ten years before. He was on the A train going home to Inwood from his job slinging papers from the back of a *Daily News* truck. The book was by Ernesto Guevara and the line was: "I was born in Argentina, I fought in Cuba, and I began to be a revolutionary in Guatemala." O'Connor had copied it into a notebook, but had forgotten it until this day.

He passed a group of children hurrying through the rain to school. He waved. I can fight here, he thought. I can fight in Ireland. Now I can fight anywhere.

At the marina O'Connor left his bike near the petrol shed, slung his bag over his shoulder, and walked out on the wood dock between the boats. The smell of gasoline and salt. The gentle slap of water on waterlogged wood. Wind in the riggings. The rain falling harder. A whispering of the harbor receiving the shower. There was not a soul on the docks nor, from what he could see, on any of the boats. At the far end, safely tethered between a bulky cabin cruiser and a private big game fisherman, lay *Die Freiheit*. Forty-five feet of tough American elm, white with a green stripe near the waterline. Eleven tons with a dry bow, wide decks and a two-masted rig. Made in 1936 in Bermuda, it had had three owners before Gudrun's father bought it for her in 1965 as a graduation present. O'Connor stepped aboard, *Die Freiheit* swayed under him, and he lost his footing on the slick deck. He fell hard, and got up smiling, remembering Gudrun, that first night at sea, telling him, "She doesn't know you so she'll kick you overboard if you're not careful." O'Connor found his balance and stepped gingerly in his hiking boots.

He checked the doghouse door. It hadn't been tampered with so he toured the decks and then went below. He had a cup of coffee from the thermos and lit a Woodbine, his first of the day. Blowing gray smoke rings through the gray light of the galley, his boots propped on the stove, rocking, listening to the sounds of the yacht. He remembered the first night on board, running toward the open sea, working hard under Gudrun's command. The coffee they drank all night long, the thrill of learning something new, the pleasure of practicing a physical skill. And the first dawn, some-where in the North Sea, realizing with a tinge of panic, Jesus, you can die out here. *I* can die out here. That day had been bright, calm and cloudless with a good breeze as they ran southwest past Brussels toward the English Channel. Gudrun made a thick vegetable soup from the canned goods, they drank chablis, and sunbathed under a warm sky. Near sunset Gudrun taught him to use the Ingram M-10. O'Connor caught on quickly and was a natural shot. They tossed bottles and cans overboard and shot for two hours. They talked about purpose, discipline, caution, and trust. She told him he must not be an adventurer, which curbed the joy that pumped through him. He must be as aware of what he was doing and why he was doing it as a lion tamer. One mistake, one bow to the crowd, and the beasts would turn.

That night Gudrun taught him the stars. He had never seen stars that way, as order, signposts, compass. They had large cognacs in coffee cups and talked of Ireland. O'Connor told her stories his father had told him. He talked about Marty to her, and how both had been bound by their hatred of Irish-Americans. The lout, the lawyer, the priest, the cop. She spoke very little and O'Connor finally took the cue. They sailed west through the theatrical night, making good time, drinking coffee, silent, locked into the moment.

Near him on the bench was a small red rubber ball. Nearly the same as the "spaldeen" they used in stickball games when he was a kid. Gudrun used them to strengthen her hands and arms. She was slight, and delicate looking, but O'Connor knew how strong she was. Once in the flat in Paris they had wrestled playfully, but it had turned serious. She gave him a persistent, intelligent fight for awhile, and he was impressed by the power in her hands, arms and legs. O'Connor fought back with effort, enjoying the battle, and began to throw her off balance and pin her. Gudrun then took the fight into the alley, pulling his hair, clawing at his balls and slamming her open palm against his ear. O'Connor called a halt, shocked by the killer in her, but admiring it.

He gripped the ball, squeezing, remembering days in the spacious gloom of the flat. The secrets she shared with him, the sex, and the meals, and the education. The freedom he felt, not just as an idea, but real freedom, the opportunity to take his life anywhere he wanted. He got to know Conor Graham, the Irishman whom Gudrun had met in Régis Debray's flat in Paris. She told him about George Habbash, the head of the Popular Front for the Liberation of Palestine, and the expert training she, Ulrike Meinhoff and Andreas Baader had received in Jordan. She told him how nearly every nationality in Europe was at the camp. Basques, and Bretons, Italians, Corsicans, Irish and Greeks. She told him of operations she'd been involved in where teams of Palestinians fought with Italians, and how the next step was a truly united struggle. He sat in with Graham and Gudrun discussing Ireland, and admired his wit and toughness. The great plan. The great synergism of two armies. The idea of going to Ireland to train and fight with professionals made O'Connor fall in line behind them both. He remembered one evening when they had gone out, leaving him alone in the flat. They'd come in late and gone into Graham's room. O'Connor heard smothered laughter. He went down the dark hall and stood near the door of the room. He listened to them fucking. Gudrun had been dazed by the knowledge of who Graham really was. She said she had never had any reservations about him. But O'Connor, sneaking down the hallway with intimate sounds in his ears, had known, even for a moment, that Graham was dangerous.

He had been an attractive, easy man to be with, always with a tale to tell. There was money around him, and he had a tendency to flash it. When O'Connor first got to know him, Graham was making a fortune in the illegal arms markets of Amsterdam, but spent it as soon as it was earned. Not long before they set sail for

Ireland without him, the three of them had been in Cologne, where Gudrun was trying to make contact with the diaspora of the old Baader-Meinhoff group. O'Connor and Graham spent a day alone, cruising the city. After lunch, driving down a busy street, Graham had said, "Pull in here, Terry." O'Connor wheeled in front of a bank and Graham said he'd be right out. Five minutes later Graham came running to the car, his hands full of D-marks. "No gun, no bag, just balls," Graham had said.

"No brains either," O'Connor had said, terrified as he drove away.

There in the yacht, in the thin light, full of memory, O'Connor saw himself with a startling third-person sight. It wasn't quite like "astral projection" that mystics spoke of, he was not looking down from a height at himself, it was more like he was sitting beside himself. He was very still, relishing the moment like a lover who has ceased moving, knowing a quiver will detonate the climax. His mind was as clear as mountain air. He saw himself. The ball rolled out of his palm and O'Connor saw it drop to the deck, bounce once and roll away. The moment passed.

He put the thermos back in his bag. Climbed out of the boat and was back to the day with the feeling of leaving a theater, surprised at the sights and sounds of a forgotten reality, and thrilled by the time passing without him.

He fell into a strong rhythm with the bike. There were ten miles to travel and the road was something to beat. Through the farm country of Cork. Bog country. A man and a boy herding six weary mud-spattered bullocks. Dark hills in the distance. Occasionally a tractor came at him slowly and he and the driver exchanged a nod of greeting, the custom in Ireland to anyone you meet on the road. At a wide clearing near a creek he passed an itinerant band. Blue smoke evaporating in the mist. Battered caravans, strong horses grazing behind the camp. Children with faces both depraved and innocent, and women whose faces and postures spoke the language of the eternally poor. Ten or so men were jungled up near a long fire, passing a bottle. O'Connor waved but they just stared.

A wind came up and the heavy clouds began to move to the southwest. It stopped raining, turned colder, and the day grew cleaner. He was making good time. Through villages coming awake with farmers in town after mass. A girl dreaming in the door of a dry goods shop, her arms folded under her full breasts, auburn hair straight and shining, rosewater complexion, staring into the road, lost in herself.

Back in the country, coasting down a hill under all that sky, O'Connor thought he had never imagined a place of greater beauty. It was not the beauty he'd always heard about and connected with his American notion of natural beauty: something *real*, something you could look at, a mountain, a river, a desert. Ireland's beauty affects you, if you understand it, inside. It touches the other part of you, the ancient part where you live alone, a stranger. A green island washed by sea wind, where beauty is not something dwelled on, but allowed privacy to retain its mystery. O'Connor worked up a hill. Off to his right two brown donkeys lowered their big handsome heads to graze in a green field. Beyond them, far away, a patch of glistening sea. They looked up together at him, watching him with dark steady eyes as wise as wisdom itself. Ireland was not a country. Ireland was a dream.

O'Connor was alone with the fort for two hours. He had to walk the bike up from the road across a cabbage field to reach the old place. He didn't know how old it was, and never tried to find out who had built it. There wasn't much to it, low bushes and weeds growing through crumbling blocks of stone, set on a hill above a drowsy valley. He'd heard once that Ireland was an archaeologist's delight, not just for the wealth of sites, but more for the fact that most lay undisturbed, allowed to rot without signposts or study. O'Connor enjoyed the place as a cell open to the sky, a place to picnic, to pass the time. A fort without walls where he was safe, while at the same time completely exposed.

He wiped the bike dry and took his bag up onto a block of white stone. The wind was powerful, driving the high cumulus like white sheets on a line. He took his sweater out and put it on. Fondled the M-10 for a moment and put it back. The cheese sandwiches and coffee were delicious in the clear air. He wished he'd brought a book, and remembered Marty in his ramshackle Brooklyn apartment years ago giving him Steinbeck's *In Dubious Battle*, telling him how he hated to lend books, it was like making a loan without collateral. O'Connor had told him he'd respect the book and Marty had said he was sure he would but just in case—and had taken the book and written on the title page: "Martin Burke's book. You take, I break, your nose."

Marty. The last time he'd seen him was in Dublin that Saturday morning in August. Gudrun had been sleeping in the hotel, but O'Connor was too charged to let sleep in. So he showered, changed into jeans and a clean shirt, and took a taxi over to Lansdowne Road. He told himself he was going to see if Marty was all right but the real reason he went was to try to say something about their friendship, something that had never been said before.

He rang the bell of the pleasantly seedy Georgian townhouse, and turned to look back at the neighborhood from the stoop. He heard footsteps in the hall and saw Anne through the glass panels coming toward him. O'Connor had forgotten how beautiful she was. She opened the thick door and stared. "Hello, Anne."

"You shouldn't have come, Terry."

"How is he?"

"He's going to have his nose set in a little while. You shouldn't have come. Haven't you done enough?"

"I didn't twist his arm."

She gave a defiant laugh. "Someone did. Twisted his arm and damn near killed him."

"Could I come in?"

"Why? Do you have more plans for him to take over the world?"

"Please, Annie. I won't stay long."

She turned her back and walked away. O'Connor closed the door and followed her up the stairs and into the flat. When she entered he heard Burke say, "Who was it?" And saw him sitting in an easy chair, bare chested, his shoes and socks off and a glass of whiskey in his hand. "How goes the Republic?" he asked him.

A fire burning in the small Georgian fireplace. Anne's pictures on the wall, books, an Oriental rug. Anne stood and poked the turf. "Long night," O'Connor said.

Burke was grinning. He lifted the glass to his battered face. "How're you feeling?" O'Connor asked, sitting on the couch across from him.

"You should see the other guy," Burke said, and tilted his glass toward him. "Drink?"

"I don't want him here," Anne said, her back to both of them.

"How about some tea? Did you eat?"

"I'll take a drink."

Anne turned and threw the poker down on the tile floor in front of the fireplace. It bounced away, ringing, and was silenced by the rug. She glared at Burke. "I live here, too."

"Get him a glass."

"I will not," she said, her eyes unfocused with tears. "Are you going to sit and get drunk like—like—" she stuttered, caught herself, and raised her chin. "You're a fucking imbecile, Martin." She went to the kitchen, and returned with two glasses. Burke poured them large shots, then raised his glass and said, "Friends." Anne laughed, but O'Connor caught his eye and toasted solemnly. And that was it. Whatever he had wanted to say was impossible for him, so it was left with a gesture Burke probably missed. All O'Connor had was a toast given by his friend, a toast that might have been sarcastic. Burke was half-drunk, grinning like the imbecile Anne had called him. The despair O'Connor felt was the history of their friendship, two men who never really knew each other, who never could speak, but only follow a ritual and give a gesture now and then. Irishmen had a lock on this relationship. At best their love for one another was expressed as camaraderie, and at worst it was silent, guilty and bare.

Burke decided that O'Connor would take him to the hospital and then later fetch the car with him. While he was taking a bath and changing, O'Connor was left with Anne in the quiet, sunny room. She sat on a footstool and stared at the fire, with both hands around the glass between her knees. O'Connor sipped his whiskey, watching her. She had never liked him, and he wondered if she had liked any of Marty's friends. He had always been polite to her, even formal when they saw each other. Perhaps that's why, he told himself. If he had shown more humor, had been easier, she would have liked him. "Anne," he said, but she didn't move. "It was his decision."

"I know."

"If they hadn't got Cleary, it wouldn't have happened."

She looked at him.

"I'm sorry," O'Connor said.

"Yeah. Terry, can I ask you something? Will you leave him alone, now? We're going away soon. I want to go home, but he won't listen. We're going to the West soon, though. We'll be away from it. Will you leave him alone? Even your being here scares me."

"Yes," he lied.

"I'm so frightened. His face—" she drank. "He looks at it like a football game or some damn thing. Showing off your injuries after the game to your girlfriend."

"He's a good man," O'Connor said, and the look she gave him told him he had no right to say that.

"Don't let him drink. Bring him right home."

"Right."

"Please," she said, looking at the fire.

They took a taxi to the hospital. The emergency room doctor was a small, brown Indian man, very cheerful. He asked Burke what had happened. "You should see the other guy," Marty told him, and the doctor thought that was very funny. After he had set the nose he told Burke, "I think now, Mr. Burke, less drinking will suit you and your nose better. If half the men who showed up here on Saturday morning drank less on Friday night, they would be in a much better condition."

"Then you'd be lookin' for work, Doc," Burke said, and the doctor again laughed, shaking his head at such wit.

They took another taxi out to the shopping center. They had the driver park far enough away from the Mini, and they watched the car for ten minutes. The lot was filled with Saturday shoppers. Finally, Burke said, "Let's try it," and got out. O'Connor told the driver to wait. Burke slid behind the wheel and started it while O'Connor looked about the lot. "Okay?" O'Connor said. "You want me to drive?"

"No, I'm all right. We're going to Moher in about a week, Terry. That's just General Delivery, Moher, if you want to get in touch."

"We're going to Cork tonight."

Burke reached his hand out. They shook. "Take care," Burke said.

"You too, Marty."

Burke drove out of the lot. O'Connor walked over to the cab and got in the back seat. "The Shelbourne," he said.

O'Connor finished the apples and coffee and meditated on the treeless landscape of the valley. The day was passing. He was ready to go. The ride back to Kinsale was difficult in the approaching gloom of evening. It had turned colder. Venus to the east was ice at the horizon. He pedaled hard, reminding himself to take a hot bath as soon as he got in. He wanted no stiffness tomorrow. When he reached Kinsale near five o'clock it was already night. He stopped at The Spaniard and had a small whiskey in the warmth of the pub. Then he remembered and bought a cheap bottle of Valpolicella. "Valpolicella," the publican said with a smile, "makes your teeth yella."

O'Connor laughed.

"Will you have one more, Mr. Harrison?"

"Thanks, Jimmy, but I'm late already."

At the house, coasting down to the garage, a brief sensation passed over him. It was a feeling similar to *déjà vu*. He opened the garage door. A VW van was parked next to the Volvo. Deirdre was here.

He admired the van. Exactly as ordered. Nondescript color. A sliding door along one side. "Good girl," he said aloud. On his way into the house, just as his hand found the doorknob, the feeling crept over him again. He paused. All he remembered were broken images of a dream. A footbridge. A nun's face. But his day had been a thief and stolen the rest. The feeling slipped from him like water. He opened the door and walked into the warm house. He heard women's voices in the kitchen.

III

CHAPTER 9

The Speed of the Day

The van's side door slid closed. Deirdre put it in gear, and took the road east out of town. The van was stifling. Cordite fumes stung her eyes and nose. She looked in the side mirror and saw O'Connor steadying Walsh, as the old man slumped against him and then mounted the motorcycle with the careless confidence of a sleepwalker. The stuck car horn wailed through the streets of Kildare.

The mother carried her son, his head hanging down, swaying from side to side, his new boots dangling. She was walking out in the middle of the road in a half circle, her eyes closed. Deirdre pushed the van into third and shot past the *pietà*, turning on the windshield wipers and the lights. She glanced back at Gudrun, sitting on the floor next to the M-60 now covered by the green blanket. The German sat, white-faced, staring. Deirdre turned back to the road and said, "Come on, now. I need you up here."

"Is he dead?"

"They're all dead. Or soon will be."

"The boy?"

"He's finished. Come on, now."

Gudrun came forward and sat next to Deirdre. She was exhausted. And could not shake the sight of the boy lying in the street. "What was he doing there?"

"Stop it!" Deirdre said. "Now, stop it right there. We weren't lucky, is all. Everything else went perfectly. Walsh is free. That's what we came to do and we did it. You did your job and we were unlucky, that's all. Let's just pray your boyfriend finds the cottage now."

"Yes," Gudrun said. "We were unlucky."

The empty road ahead ran out of town past houses full of yellow light. Lighting up time. Out of town the fields were invisible in the sudden velvet night of rural Ireland. The world had slipped away. Two headlights pushed ahead, and in the van the two women stared, as though they were waiting for a sign, the gray glow of the speedometer resting on their hands and faces.

Deirdre took the road east for five miles and then slanted off on a farm road which meandered its way south to the village of Nurney. There they took another unlighted dirt road going northwest toward Crosskeys. Heavy hedges rose high on either side of the road, and Deirdre drove slowly, avoiding ruts and deep puddles. When they came on a stretch of blacktop, Deirdre pushed the van up to fifty. Coming around a bend the headlights picked out a dog only thirty feet away, eyes dazzled, crouching, frozen in the road. She wrenched the wheel and they went into the ditch. Gudrun fell heavily on her and the M-60 banged up against the side of the van.

The engine continued running. Gudrun saw Deirdre's hand, shaking, turn off the ignition and the headlights. They were immersed in darkness, and heard only the airy sound of light rain falling on the fields all around them. Gudrun felt the Irishwoman's breast moving heavily under her.

"Are you hurt?" Gudrun asked, untangling herself.

"No," Deirdre said. "I'm all right. I should have run over the fooker."

"Wait a minute before we go. We have time."

Deirdre got out of the van, and went to the ditch on the other side of the road. At first there were only dry heaves and then, with the speed and tension of vomiting, up came her big breakfast of steak and eggs. When she finished she felt lightheaded and flushed. She came back, climbed in, and began to rock the van back and forth between reverse and first gear, cursing the machine, "Come on, you hoor." Finally the rear wheels caught and the van lumbered and staggered out of the ditch. "We'll be fine now," Deirdre said.

"I've never seen such darkness."

"I've seen it worse than this," Deirdre said, driving slowly. "And when the wind is blowing, Jesus, it's like the bowels of hell."

"We're all right now, huh, Deirdre?"

"Yeah," she said, fatigue settling warmly all through her. "We're all right now."

Gudrun checked her watch when they saw a single light

somewhere far away out of the emptiness. Gradually she could make out the form of Johnny's cottage with the chimney standing tall. The headlights caught the chrome of the Volvo parked next to the shanty. "They should be here in ten minutes," she said.

"Careful, now," Deirdre said, reaching down and pulling up her M-10. Her voice sounded tinny, like a bad telephone connection.

"There's no one," Gudrun said, as Deirdre rolled the van up, pulled out the emergency brake, shut the engine and let her weapon down to the floor.

Johnny opened the door and the weak light of the fire inside glowed red through the night. When Deirdre stepped out her legs gave way and she fell heavily to the ground. "Jesus, Mary and Joseph," the old man said. "Are ye injured?"

"I'm all right, Johnny," she said as he helped her up.

"You'll lie down inside," he told her, taking her arm and guiding her into the house as Gudrun broke down the machine gun and stored it in the trunk of the Volvo. Inside she sat next to the fire while Johnny brought a glass of clear liquid to Deirdre sitting on the dilapidated couch with her legs up. "Drink it slow, now."

Deirdre took a sip. "Christ, you could run a tractor on this."

Johnny grinned, showing his bare gums. "Hard work the fightin', girl?"

"Hard work," she said.

Johnny turned to Gudrun. "Would you have a taste of the poteen?"

"No, thank you. There was no trouble here?"

"There was none. Quiet all day. A drop wouldn't harm ye, ye know."

She ran her hand back through her blond hair, the fire reflecting red on her fair face. "I'm fine," she said.

Just west of town with the speedometer bouncing around fifty, O'Connor leaned the bike into a narrow road cutting south. Walsh pressed himself to the American's back, a wind all around him, the motorcycle whining through its gears between his legs. He didn't know how long he could stand the piercing pain in his lower back. Closing his eyes, he laid his face closer to the wet slicker, and hugged the young man harder.

The BSA was running fine and O'Connor concentrated on driving. At times pieces of memory flashed through him, threatening to stay, but he pushed them out. The wild look of the man he had shot. There had been something wrong with him, his upper body turned the wrong way, trying to level the shotgun, the blood all over him, fear lighting his eyes. He pushed the bike hard through the darkness, searching for the cowpath that would take them cross-country to the cottage. The bike flashed through puddles and dipped through turns, O'Connor balancing with his boot, winding it out, getting all he could from his machine. It was not necessary to run so fast. They had plenty of time and no one pursued them. It was just that if he had to concentrate on the road and the BSA he could have his mind free of images. Such fear in his eyes. Even after taking six slugs, already dead, such fear in his eyes. The old man was shouting something. O'Connor slowed the bike and heard him. "I've got to stop."

O'Connor braked down and stopped the bike in the middle of the road. Walsh struggled to get off, and when O'Connor helped him he saw the pain in his face. "Am I hit?" Walsh asked. "I can't tell. There's no blood."

O'Connor blindly felt the old man's back. "No, you're all right."

While Walsh walked around, O'Connor pissed at the side of the road. His mouth had never been so dry. "Where are we going?" the old man asked, standing next to him.

"Kinsale."

"Maybe you, but not me. Not on that bloody thing."

"Not on the bike. We're rendezvousing at the old man's place outside Crosskeys. They'll drive you down from there."

"What old man?"

"Johnny. We better move, now."

The old man groaned as he sat on the buddy seat. O'Connor drove slowly, and half a mile up the road came to the gated cowpath. The American gripped the BSA hard and pushed it through the open field. They were splashed and spattered by mud and manure. He nearly lost the bike twice, the rear wheel swinging out from them, the field suddenly dropping away and the bike falling into thick ruts full of water. It was half an hour's worth of blind soggy work before they came out into the cabbage field next to Johnny's cottage and rode up to the back door.

When Johnny and O'Connor helped Walsh into the room Deirdre got up quickly from the couch. They laid him out and Deirdre said to Johnny, "Poteen."

"Do you have a smoke?" Walsh asked, looking up at Deirdre and Gudrun.

Deirdre lit a cigarette and put it in his mouth. "Where are you hurt?"

"The back. Ah, Jesus. I must've wrenched it."

O'Connor took off his slicker covered in wet shit, went outside and laid it over the BSA. Gudrun followed him out. She watched him fiddling with something in the engine, and then smoothing the slicker over and tucking it around the motorcycle. He walked back slowly to her, his gray hair dark, tousled with sweat, his face composed and shining with rainwater. They stood under the eaves, side by side, and looked out at the night. It was pouring rain now, and the wind was up.

"How are you?" she asked.

"Good, good. How about you?"

"Fine. We move in twenty minutes."

"Yeah. Wild fuckin' night."

"The bowels of hell, Deirdre called it."

"How's she makin' it?"

"A little shaky, but she's fine now. She's hard. Those were her countrymen in that street. You're sure you want to drive the bike?"

"Yeah," O'Connor said. "I can outrun anything on it."

"I don't mean that. The weather."

"Fuck it, I'm used to it."

Johnny brought him a tin cup of clear liquid. "There you are, lad," and went back inside. O'Connor, thinking it was water, drank it off. The moonshine burned straight through him. He could taste it in his nose and his eyes were watering. "What the hell—" he coughed.

"I killed that boy," Gudrun said.

O'Connor was laughing. "What the hell is this?" He whistled slowly.

"I killed that boy."

"Yeah, I heard you the first time."

"So. I just wanted to say it to you. Because I'm not going to speak of it again. I killed him. It was a mistake."

O'Connor put his hand to her cheek and left it there, turning her face toward him. She raised her eyes and looked at him. "Terrence," she said softly, "it was a mistake."

He drew a finger across her cheekbone. She began to speak but he put his hand over her mouth, came close to her ear and whispered, "It's done."

Garrett Costello was at home with his family, nursing his cold when the call from the minister came through informing him of the raid at Kildare. By 6 P.M. he was interviewing the mother of Francis Byrne, and other townspeople who had witnessed the attack. An hour later, after walking the main street of the village back and forth several times, he had perceived the logistics and called the minister in Dublin. The minister said he would release the details to the press, radio, and television. The minister had Raymond Murray's file in front of him, he said, and he would name Gudrun Böhm and Terrence O'Connor. Garrett was ordered back to Dublin to take charge of the case.

Gudrun and O'Connor helped Walsh into the front seat of the Volvo. He sat rigidly, his face set, a cigarette burning low between his fingers, the huge prison overcoat wrapped about him. Gudrun collected the M-10's and put them in the trunk. When she finished, O'Connor said, "I'm going to wait here awhile. Maybe the wind will let up."

"No more than thirty minutes."

"Right."

Deirdre climbed into the van without a word, started it up and drove off. Gudrun turned to Johnny standing in the doorway. "Thank you, Johnny, for all your help."

"It was nothing. Let me say goodbye to himself there." He went to the passenger side and reached his hand in. "How's the old back then?"

"Gameball, John."

"That's the idea. It's grand to see you free, Joseph. You weren't made to live in one of their jails."

"Thanks for your help, John. Is there anything you need? The party will send you a few pounds."

"Not a thing. You tell that girl to drive it slow."

"And you'll keep a closed mouth, now. For your benefit, not mine."

"No worry on that score, Joseph. We're not too old yet, are we now?"

"Never. Stay well, John."

"Aye," the old man said, and walked over to the door near O'Connor. Gudrun got in and drove off. They watched the red tail lights winking at them across the fields. "The finest man in Ireland, there," the old man said. They went inside and O'Connor said, "Do you have anything to eat? Tea and bread or—"

"Rashers and potatoes is all I have. And a bit of cabbage. Will that suit ye?"

While the old man fried the rashers he spoke to O'Connor in the next room at the fire. O'Connor was only half listening. Part of him was back in Kildare approaching on the bike. The glass in the street. "You're from the United States of America, I'd say."

"New York."

"New York. By Christ, if there's one regret I have it's that I never went out to the United States of America to see it for myself. A country where freedom rings and there's true democracy, not like poor Ireland and the criminals who run her. Are you Irish?"

"Irish-American." The boy lying twisted, a hand flung out as if to beckon him. Where?

"You're Irish, all right. You don't have to tack the American on the end of it." He brought a plate with him, heaped with mashed potatoes, thick country bacon, and cabbage. "You're American by voice but I could see Ireland in your face. There now, lay into that, young man." Deirdre running to the van, her blue waterproof, her weapon held in one hand.

"You're not eating?" O'Connor asked.

"I'm not. I don't take much pleasure in food these days. But I'll watch you eat. That, I'll enjoy."

O'Connor dug in. He hadn't eaten all day, and had to warn himself to eat slowly. "The blond girl, now what nationality would she be?"

"German."

"German. Aye, there's many of us in Germany. France as well. One of Napoleon's generals was Irish, did ye know that?" O'Con-

nor listened and ate the old man's food, watching him as he put-
tered around his pathetic shack, bringing the clear plastic jug of
moonshine and sitting down gingerly near the fire, going on
about Irish men and women who had found fame in foreign parts.
Chewing the lovely spiced rashers, he thought there were no more
smug people in the world. The French were humble compared to
the Irish. Why? Why were they so sure that they were the finest,
smartest, kindest? Their mythical past, full of royalty and honor.
His own father told him he was descended from kings, as every
Irishman was. And that when the English were still living in caves
the Irish were by God teaching in universities.

"Were there many killed?"

"What?" O'Connor looked up, a fork full of buttery potatoes
halfway to his mouth.

"Were there many killed today?"

"Six." He wouldn't tell him about the boy. Beckoning him.

"Have a drop?"

"No, Johnny, thank you."

"Ah, have a bit," he said, already pouring some. "You'll be
leaving soon and wished you had it."

"Thanks. This is some booze."

"A bit raw, I'll have to agree. *Sláinte*, lad, and to the great country of your birth."

They drank.

"Six dead. I'd say that was a fair amount of killing. I've done
some in my own time, you know. Not six. Not half of that. But
the ones I did, I'll say, they wanted killing, the bastards. Still, it's
a tragedy to kill your own. Brother murderin' brother, wouldn't
you agree?"

"I agree."

"They'll think twice, though, before they'll try and put the
chains to Joseph Walsh again, the motherless bastards."

What was wrong with his body? It was twisted, trying to get
at me with his shotgun. The eyes so afraid! The van's side door
slid closed.

He was ready. The old man told him to stay, the wind was still
strong, but O'Connor begged off and thanked him for his hospitality.
"It was nothing. All I'm good for now is waterin' the horses."

"You take care, Johnny."

"God bless."

After a brief meeting with the minister back in Dublin, Garrett settled in with Murray's files. The excitement of being thrown into the middle of the case soon wore off as he read his dead colleague's reports. Some of Raymond Murray's coldness and efficiency came to him, and he castigated himself for not taking more interest in the case when he had interviewed Joseph Walsh last Sunday. It was true that Murray had kept him in the dark, but he should have pressed him to open up about the case.

There were detailed reports about Peter Farrell, the informer who was kept in the "white house" in Portmarnock. Garrett called Portmarnock to let the guards know he was taking over, and would see Farrell within the next few days. He then called a meeting of Special Branch officers and informed them that he was assuming Murray's position. Every garda station in the Republic would receive a description of the American and the German immediately.

A few miles north of Timahoe, on a dirt road near a stream, Deirdre pulled the van up into a field and parked it. She went over the whole van with a cloth, wiping away prints, before walking back to a spot behind the hedges. After awhile her eyes became accustomed to the night and she could make out the tired little river next to her with a row of small trees running along both banks, looking like an honor guard standing to attention in the dark. The rain had let up but the wind, coming from the east, blew cold. It had been a good day. Ireland would know now that they were serious. There'd be no need now to show samples to the Provos. They could read about it in the papers. But there had been too much death. They hadn't realized the car wreck would be so effective, incapacitating their prey so completely. And the boy. How could they have foreseen the boy? If the convoy had come out on schedule he wouldn't have been there, standing in the road. If. It was a good operation, though. The German and O'Connor had been splendid. The only thing wrong with the operation was that it had worked too well. Walsh had given her one or two fierce looks when he was lying on the couch. The look a parent gives a child when something displeases him in front of strangers. Disapproving, full of menace, just wait till I get you home. Maybe it was the pain.

She caught sight of headlights on the road coming south. It had seemed to be a good idea to check the weapons in after the first phase of the operation, but now she wished she had the M-10. If they were Irish Army or Special Branch they'd shoot her out here, forget a trial. Shot while escaping. With a weapon she could at least fight. The Volvo pulled up and Deirdre got in the back seat.

Gudrun drove south to Carlow Town and picked up the main highway to Cork. There was silence until they left Carlow, when Walsh said, "Deirdre, give me a report on this operation."

She told him quickly.

"Who ordered it?"

"I did. It was Gudrun's logistics."

"Why?"

"To free you. We can't go on without you, Chief."

"This is going to bring a blizzard of shit down on us, did you think of that?"

"We did. But we had to free you. Not just to lead us, but because of the Lucan meeting."

"Do you know anything about that?" he asked Gudrun.

"Nothing."

"We'll talk when we get to Kinsale, Deirdre."

"Yes, sir."

"It's a safe house, Gudrun? You're sure of that?"

"It's safe. But I think we should move in a week or two. I have experience with safe houses. They don't remain safe more than a few months."

"Excellent idea. We'll move within the week."

But they moved sooner than that. Once in the house in Kinsale, Gudrun made coffee and Walsh sat down stiffly on the velour couch. "Have a bath, Joe," Deirdre said. "A hot bath's the thing."

"I will. I'll watch the news first."

At nine o'clock, sipping coffee, they all watched Don Cockburn come on with the RTE evening news. Behind the newsreader was a large photograph of Joseph Walsh taken in 1954. "That your confirmation picture, Joe?" Deirdre said, grinning. "The town of Kildare was turned into a charnel house late this afternoon as three members of the Irish Socialist Army, the small, extreme left-wing gang, attacked a convoy of two cars, one of which was carrying the I.S.A. leader, Joseph Walsh, to imprisonment at Portlaoise." The picture changed to film of the scene. Gardai milling about in the dark street, the bizarre sheen of portable lights glaring on the two lumped vehicles, bodies covered in blankets in the road, a pump-action shotgun resting in the gutter, the townspeople looking on, ghosts in the wet night. "Seven people died in the raid, including a bystander, young Francis Byrne, aged eight years. Joseph Walsh was seen leaving the scene on the back of a motorcycle. The attack began at approximately 4:20 and took only a minute or two to complete. The vicious attack by the gang was well planned and powerful assault weapons, rarely seen in the Republic, were used, including the American-made M-60 machine gun and the Ingram M-10 machine pistol."

"So soon," Gudrun said. "How did they know the weapons so soon?"

"The dead who, gardai say, never had a chance, are: Raymond Murray, the chief of the anti-terrorist section of the Special Branch; Thomas Fleming, a prison officer, married and the father of one child; Edward Cooke, another prison officer; John Tuohy, one of the drivers, a widower who leaves six children; John Larrimore, a Special Branch officer; and Brian McMahon, another Special Branch officer who leaves a wife and three children. The six men will be buried in Dublin on Saturday, and young Francis Byrne will be buried in Kildare on Saturday.

"The murderers have been identified as—"

"What?" Deirdre shouted.

"Quiet!" Walsh said.

"A German national, Gudrun Böhm, age thirty; and a citizen of the United States, Terrence O'Connor, age thirty-one." Behind Cockburn a police sketch gave a facsimile of Gudrun's and O'Connor's faces. "The third member of the gang was another woman, believed to be Irish, but gardai at the scene have refused to say anything more. The Taoiseach, learning of the news, called a press conference at Leinster House and said—"

"Only the three of us," Deirdre said, staring at the floor, counting in her head. "And Johnny knew, and one other."

"It's Farrell," Walsh said to Gudrun. "Murray, the chief there, he knew all about you and O'Connor. *And* about the weapons. *And* about the yacht. All the way down here I was hoping the information died with him. Either he kept wonderful files or Farrell's still in custody in Ireland, singing away."

Gudrun got up and turned off the set. "*Gottverfluchter Scheiss-*

kerl!" she cursed, and saw two Irish faces staring at her, astonished. She turned away from them and went on, "*Man sollte ihn in die Fresse hauen bis ihm die Kacke wegbleibt.*"

Walsh eased himself back, inch by inch into the couch, his teeth gritted. "We must move tonight."

"Yes," Gudrun said.

"That boat of yours."

"Yes. But the weapons are here. In the garage."

"Then we'll move them back and take the boat around to Dingle."

"Dingle?" Deirdre asked, draining her coffee. "Why?"

"Why not? It's better than here."

"How are we going to move all that stuff?"

"That's your problem. But get it done. Now, where's the bathroom?"

"I'll go to Dublin tonight," Deirdre said.

"You will not. The boat will carry all of us, won't it, Gudrun?"

"Yes," she said, standing near the curtained window, her back to the other two.

"But I can't go," Deirdre said.

"It's an order."

"I can't swim, Joe."

He laughed. "Now, a hot bath. We'll meet again when O'Connor arrives. Give me a hand, Dee-Dee."

She helped Walsh up and walked with him to the bathroom. "Do you think anything's broken?"

"No. A long sea cruise and I'll be fine. Run it hot, now. And close the door," he said, taking off his cheap prison clothes, stained here and there with dark brown circles of dried blood.

Deirdre began to leave, but he said, "Stay. You've seen a man's body, I trust."

She sat on the toilet and watched him as he slipped painfully into the steaming tub. He had a strong upper body, the torso of a man twenty years younger, but his legs were old, skinny and pale. His penis hung dark, uncircumcised, a brown sausage on a bed of curls. He caught her looking at him. "How do I look?"

"You're no Adonis, but you'll do. Do you want me to rub the back?"

"I didn't ask you here for nursing. Turn that water off." Walsh lay back, and breathed in the steam. "I don't know what to do with you, Deirdre. How could you be so foolish?"

She got up and wiped the steamed mirror with her hand. Looked at her face, haloed by white, distorted by moisture, the features flimsy, a foreign face swimming up to her from a cloudy pond.

"Three of those men were unarmed, for God's sake. Did you have to kill all of them? *Any* of them?"

"We didn't have time to ask them if—"

"Time? Jesus Christ, woman! That's the only thing we have. It's the only thing any revolutionary has."

"You're free, Joe. I can't run this army. We're nothing without you."

"They weren't going to kill me in Portlaoise. I could've run things from there." He pointed a finger at her and then splashed his fist down into the water. "And no one, *no one* is indispensable. Fullstop. Is that correct?"

"Yes," she said, turning to him.

"Did you inform other personnel about this operation?"

"No, only to tell them to be on their toes, and find new billets as of yesterday."

"If you ever go over my head again, you're through."

"Yes."

"Finished. Now, go out there and give some orders. I'm in command here, and you are my aide. The German and the American are our soldiers, they're to take orders, and not to give them. This is *our* struggle."

"I commanded this operation, Joe."

"Well, it was a bloody botch from the time you dreamed it up until this moment."

"Yes, sir."

"What would Liam have thought of this? Six injured men killed in cold blood—and a boy slaughtered? What would he have thought?"

The mention of Liam's name infuriated her. "How do you come off so fookin' pure?" she exploded. "What about that kid Kevin Powers in the Market Arcade? What about Donal Grennan, hey?"

"You fool," Walsh said slowly. "Can't you see the difference?"

"No, I can't. It was a good operation, Joe."

"You settle down, now. I don't want any hotheads tonight. I just want to make it clear to you. As long as I'm breathing, I'm commanding. In prison or out, I'm commanding."

"Yes, sir."

"Go on out and figure how to move the matériel. And then write a statement about today. Admit responsibility, regret the death of the boy. When you're finished show it to me. And cool down."

"I'm cool."

"You're a good soldier, Dee-Dee. The best I have. That's why when you make mistakes it's so hard on all of us."

"Yes, sir."

"We must *think* now, think even as we run. When we get back to Dublin, after we know the weapons are moved and safe, after things have quieted down a little, I want you to call an army council, and hold them together. I'll begin work with the Provisionals and organize a meeting, somewhere away from Dublin. I'll suggest Robert Crenshaw's home in the Burren. Now, go on, let's think, not only act from here on."

Walsh lay back, the liquid heat beginning to heal him. It was not only his back, every joint in his body ached. I was in Dublin this morning, he thought. A hundred years ago, looking at Raymond Murray's ambitious face. Tommy Fleming, poor Tommy, what had the news said? Married and one child. God be good to him. A brutish prison cell this morning, and a hot bath in this plush house in Kinsale tonight. Where tomorrow?

"I can get a truck," O'Connor said, standing in the kitchen in his slicker, his helmet hanging down in his hand. He had just come in, and Gudrun and Deirdre had told him of the news, and the order from Walsh to move. Gudrun handed him a cup of coffee. "Where?" she asked, going back to packing tinned goods and tools in a large carton.

"Just down the road. A green pickup."

"Then get it," Walsh said, walking into the kitchen, dressed in a pair of O'Connor's corduroy trousers and a white shirt, the press statement Deirdre had written in his hand.

"How're you feeling?" O'Connor asked.

"Get the pickup and we'll load up and move."

"Yes, sir."

Walsh walked out. "What's with him?" O'Connor asked.

"Nothing's with him," Deirdre said quickly. "You've got your orders. I'll go with you."

Outside the rain had died and the wind, still blowing from the east, had eased into a breeze, bringing them fresh smells of the open sea. O'Connor drove the Volvo for a mile or so before pulling up between two stone pillars and into the grounds of an estate, the long country house dark, standing solidly against the black sky. "The guy who lives here is away in England now. I've had a few drinks with him." They drove to a garage set in a grove of trees. O'Connor left the lights of the Volvo pointed at the doors, opened them up and walked in. A cat ran past him, making him jump. Deirdre giggled. "Jesus," the American whispered.

"Some protection," she said. "A bloody cat. Someone should tell him about Alsatians." She opened the door of the truck and looked at the dashboard. "Shite," she cursed.

"What?"

"There's no keys."

"That's all right," O'Connor said, opening the hood. "I'll hot wire it."

"You'll what?"

"Get up there and put it in neutral. When I tell you, pump the gas."

A few minutes later he said, "Okay, goose it." The pickup coughed once and then bucked and roared to life. O'Connor slammed the hood down and came around. "Keep pumping."

"You're a regular genius."

He smiled. "The product of a misspent youth. Take the Volvo and follow me."

When they were back on the road, O'Connor turned toward the town, away from the house. Deirdre followed, thinking he was going to check on the boat. But he drove instead into a carpark behind a large pub just north of town. "Slattery's" blinked at them in blue neon. She pulled beside the pickup. O'Connor was already standing outside the truck. "What do you think you're doing?"

"Come on in, I'll buy you a jar."

"You're mad. Let's go, Terry."

"Come on. One pint."

"Do you *want* to be arrested? Is that it?"

"I'm Paul Harrison around here. Rich American filmmaker. Hail fellow well met. Come on."

She got out of the Volvo. "You're mad."

"No. Thirsty. They've got good Guinness here."

When they reached the door she said, "They've got a police sketch of you. It was on the television."

"Did it look like me?"

"A little."

"See, there you are."

They walked into the big lounge of the pub, carpeted in purple and black. The room smelled of beer and bodies. Smoke hung like a fogbank just above the heads of the drinkers, who sat around the small tables, and crowded on the lime-green banquette running the length of three walls of the room. Deirdre found a spot near the ladies' room at a small table littered with heaped ashtrays, stained coasters and pint glasses with stout and ale froth clinging to the lips. She sat down and checked the room. People had looked up at them when they entered but quickly went back to their conversations. Middle-aged men and women, a few young people, a pram holding a sleeping baby parked by a table where a woman rocked it back and forth with one hand, and sipped from a half-pint glass with the other. Deirdre watched O'Connor standing at the bar between two seated men. Madman. Was he showing off? I should've given him orders. And let it stand at that. He could obey or not. Good to be away from Joe for awhile, though. Is that what the yank felt, too? To be away from the German? We'll be together on that bloody deathtrap of a boat for awhile, maybe it's the best thing. If he's recognized, then what? But he won't be, she told herself. A man in the corner, thoroughly jarred, dressed in an old suit, a tie knotted the size of a penny, and with a face plain and raw, began singing "The Butcher Boy." His clear voice ran through the buzz of voices in the room.

In Dublin City where I did dwell
A butcher's boy I loved right well
He courted me my life away
But now with me he will not stay.

The barman topped up the two pints and set them before O'Connor. He turned to the other barman passing behind him. "Is that old Mike singin' again?"

"Singin'? Wailing is more like it. Jesus, he sounds like he'll drop a calf any minute." The stout foamed brown, rushing to the top, turning black through the glass and the high creamy collar grew as he watched. "Ninety-four pence, Mr. Harrison."

O'Connor handed him a five-pound note.

The barman took it and said, "Well, you finally brought the missus by."

"What?"

The barman nodded his head toward Deirdre across the room.

"Oh, no, that's my cousin down from Dublin."

"Your cousin, is it? What's the missus up to?"

"Something on TV she wants to watch."

He brought him the four pounds six pence change. "The television was full of all that shootin' up in Kildare today. Hell of a thing, the boy and all. And those other lads."

"Hell of a thing," O'Connor said, reaching for the pints.

"Now, if Mike there disturbs you, there's nothin' to do but throw some water on him. That'll put out his fire."

He carried the pints waist high through the room. No one looked at him.

I wish I wish, I wish in vain
I wish I was a maid again
A maid again I ne'er will be
Till cherries grow on an ivy tree.

He set the glasses on the table and sat next to her on the banquette. "You should dye that hair," she said. "It's like wearing a sign around your neck. Does she have any hair color at the house?"

"How about I shave it off? They love Kojak in Ireland." He picked up his pint and toasted, "Happy days."

They sat and looked out at the room. All the way down on the ride south, O'Connor had looked forward to this. He had thought of stopping somewhere along the way, of watching the news in a pub, with his secret inside him, alone among strangers. But then he thought leaving the bike outside a roadside pub would be too dangerous, so he had decided on this place when he got home. When Gudrun told him they had his name and a rough description, it hadn't deterred him. On the contrary, it added spice, a kick on top of the high he felt on leaving the old man in Crosskeys. When he was running moto's one summer in North Carolina, he began hanging out with a group of riders, mostly Southerners,

who introduced him to what they called "truck driver medicine."
For three months he lived on it. The pills were quality pharma-
ceuticals, pure Benzedrine and buffered Dexedrine. Coffee was
the crank, as they said, the crank to keep the speed pumping, and
they drank pots of it all day and night. That was what this pint
and sitting in this room was, a crank to keep the speed of the day.
He never wanted it to wear off and float down to the crash. That
was why he had stopped taking benny and dex, the self-hating
silent crashes were too much to bear, they demanded that you
honestly see yourself. The crash stole your body away and left
you alone, with nothing and no one except lucid consciousness
that couldn't be turned off by sleep or conversation or anything.
Numb, hopeless, chained to a mirror, staring at a face that is
first familiar but then, after a time, becomes a stranger, and later,
grotesque. And words, repeated endlessly down a gamut of your
own making being beat naked of sense. If he could keep cranking,
then those images that came to him in front of Johnny's fire would
remain just that—fleeting, transient, and could be kept from finding a home within him.

Mike took a deep breath for his last verse, picked up his quarter-
full glass of ale and held it high out in front of him, closed his eyes
and sang out:

Oh make my grave large, wide and deep
Put a marble stone at my head and feet
And in the middle a turtle-dove
That the world may know, I died for love.

There was some applause, and an old man called for Mike to
sing another. He allowed he would, if he had something more to
lubricate his voice box. And was bought another pint.

"Any happy Irish songs?" O'Connor asked.

"Oh, yes," she said. "Haven't you ever heard of the happy
Irish? Singers and dancers, laughing and enjoying life, lazy, a
bit like children, you know, but oh, can they sing. So musical.
The niggers of the British Isles. Haven't you ever heard of them?"

He drank. "I'm sorry."

"What for? I've nothing against you." She drank, and then
looked at him. He was watching her, an expression of concentration on his face, as if he were trying to understand a foreign lan-

guage, trying to pick out a familiar sound in the rush of words. His dark eyes looked powerfully out of his face, making the other features merely parts of a mask, leaving only the eyes alive, the only sign that there was humanity there. Deirdre looked away, feeling somehow ashamed.

"What's wrong?"

"Nothing. It's been a long day."

"Are you tired?"

She looked at him again. It was the same. Black eyes trapped, looking at her from a long way off. "No," she said, "but I will be."

"It went like clockwork today, didn't it?"

"Yeah," she said. "It was a good operation."

"When something goes perfectly, when everything fits, don't you feel like—like you could live forever?"

She drank and chanced another look. His face had eased, and what had been happening had passed. "No," she said. "An ambush doesn't make me feel a bit like I'll live forever. And I don't want to talk with you ever again about today."

"Sure."

"Now, come on, Terry. We're both a bit crazy after today. Let's go back and go to work. Finish your pint and let's move."

"Right." He took a swallow of stout and they left as Mike began to sing another slow, lilting ballad.

A sharp easterly wind. *Die Freiheit* slipped away on the midnight tide. Gudrun piloted out of the mooring under power, and down the deep river to the sea. The lighthouse high on the Old Head of Kinsale the only light in a quiet watery world.

They met up with daylight south of Cape Clear running due west, keeping land in sight to starboard, cruising under full sail around the tip of Ireland. The day rose up dull at first, with heavy gray cloud cover, turning the sea to lead. At noon the day changed, with gentle light whitening the tall sails of *Die Freiheit*. Blue sky and mountainous clouds over the changing colors of the sea. Aquamarine, then deep green with blue channels, now black as the sun sailed through clouds. Gudrun checked the chart on the table in the cockpit. They had tacked north by northwest around Mizen Head and now were moving across the wide mouth of Bantry Bay. Ahead, floating just off the bowsprit on the horizon was the point of a knife blade named Dursney Head on the chart.

She went on deck and saw Deirdre, her face as white as the mainsail. Short black hair blowing straight back, gripping the tiller at the stern, staring into the wake. "Don't look at the water. It'll make you sicker."

She looked up. "I couldn't be any sicker."

"I'll get you a cognac. That might help."

"A little dry land would help a lot more."

Gudrun looked up toward the bow and saw O'Connor, his jeans rolled up, barefoot, clicking the winch to adjust the jib sheet. "How are you, Terrence?"

He looked back. "Steady as she goes, Admiral."

Back below decks she made tea and took a cup into the forward cabin, where Walsh swung lightly in a hammock, surrounded by crates of weapons. "Have some tea."

"Thank you," he said, getting up on his elbows and moving back in the hammock to a sitting position. "There's no sugar," she said, leaning against a beam.

"This is fine," he sipped, licking his white mustache. "How's your crew?"

"Deirdre stopped vomiting. I don't think she likes the sea."

"It's panic more than motion sickness, I'd say."

She smiled. "How're you feeling?"

"Better. I had a good sleep. We've got a good day for it."

"Perfect. Keep your fingers crossed."

"I'll be up in awhile to lend you a hand."

"We won't need you. Can I ask why we're going to Dingle?"

"Well, there's some islands off the coast there where we could go. From there, I don't know. I just thought it was best to move."

"So there's no decision after that?"

He looked at her clear, beautiful face. "No. We can find some help there on one of the islands."

"Which one?"

"Make for the Great Blasket. How long will it be?"

"At this rate sometime around midnight."

"Good. This is a wondeful boat by the feel of her."

"Not too conspicuous, I hope."

Walsh laughed. "The Irish Navy is four fellahs with water wings. We won't have to worry about that."

"But other vessels," Gudrun said. "Fishing boats, other yachts."

"Not in November, I wouldn't think. We could go all the way to Ulster if we wanted."

"Do we want to?"

"The Blaskets will do for now."

"And then?"

"Maybe," he said. "It might be the best way to get our cargo where it'll do the most good."

"You know, I was checking the chart. Scotland is very close to Ulster. I never realized how close."

"Yes?"

"Once we've delivered this, we could set up a supply route for more through Scotland."

"Scotland is Britain. How would all those Presbyterians feel about it?"

"My father has property in Scotland."

"He does?"

"Yes," she said. "I was there only once, it's a big house with some land. Secluded. He used it for hunting. And for his mistresses. I was taught English by a Scot. The summer I was ten, I went with my father to Scotland, and to keep me out of the way he had this Scot teach me English. When the summer was over my father brought him back with us to Germany to continue my studies."

"He was an excellent teacher," Walsh said.

"I was thinking perhaps we could use the place. My father would give it to me if I asked."

"I'll consider it, Gudrun. But I don't think so. The Scots might think it strange to have a crowd of Irishmen running around in a hunting lodge."

She smiled. "It was just a thought."

Walsh was somehow touched by her, seeing a little girl far from home in a big house learning a foreign language. When she had mentioned her father's mistresses, she had shrugged, making it sound like an afterthought to conceal the pain, and end any discussion about it. "And your father gave you this yacht, as well?"

"As well as what?"

"As well as your English lessons."

"Yes. Oh, yes, my father gave me many things."

"Why are you here, Gudrun?"

The question stopped her. Walsh put the cup to his lips, and waited for her to answer.

"I thought you wanted tea."

"Why are you in Ireland?"

"To fight. To express myself. To act."

"But why here? Why Ireland?"

"Why anywhere, Mr. Walsh?"

Walsh continued to stare. "Tell me, please."

"Because of Conor, or Peter Farrell," she said, his name causing her face to tighten and she cursed him, *"Der Hurenkerl.* Can I make a suggestion? We find that bastard and put his eyes out."

"Yes," Walsh said, "but he can't harm us anymore than he has. It would be a waste of time at this point. Besides Farrell, though, why are you here?"

"Because of your struggle. Because it's a real struggle, and not a leaderless, powerless combination of nothing which the Red Army Faction is waging."

"It sounds like you've thought that sentence out before."

She smiled. "I have. I admire your tradition of revolution, the protracted struggle, the professionalism."

"And our tradition of failure? What of that? Our tradition of betrayal? Of bitterness and agony as a way of life? Has any of that attracted you?"

"No. Your perseverance *through* failure has attracted me."

"You could kill a British soldier?"

"Yes. I killed yesterday. And I've killed before. I'm here to help, to be a part of anything you want me to."

"Your arrangement with Farrell called for payment of these arms to be in refuge for Europeans. Is that still part of the deal?"

"I'm a long way from France and Peter Farrell. The arms are yours. I just want to work with you. Later we can discuss my comrades in Europe."

"Good. You'd be an asset in any army, Gudrun."

She nodded. "I'm going to get Deirdre some cognac. Do you want one?"

"No, thank you. I'm dying for a smoke, though."

"Not down here."

"Aye," Walsh said wearily. "What about above?"

"Later," she smiled. "If you're careful."

She brought a cup of cognac and two large wheatmeal biscuits up to Deirdre, sitting next to O'Connor manning the tiller. "Have some of this. Take it slowly."

Deirdre ducked her head to drink, the biscuits in her lap and both hands around the cup like a child at her milk. "Is it better to eat or not?" she asked.

"Are you hungry?" O'Connor asked.

"Yeah."

"Then it's better."

"I could be in Dublin right now," she said miserably. "How long before we get off this thing?"

"Tonight," Gudrun said.

All afternoon *Die Freiheit* reached northwest, plowing happily, the shoulders of the bright bow breaking the waves. Walsh came up for awhile and sat next to O'Connor while Deirdre went below and tried to sleep in the hammock. "Is your man still in Clare?" Walsh asked.

"Marty? Yeah," O'Connor said, drinking soup from a cup. "I called him from Kinsale just before we left."

Walsh shook his head slowly. "Did it occur to you to tell anyone?"

"I was going to tonight, I was busy moving—"

"Terry, don't have any more initiative. What did you tell him?"

"I asked him if he was with us. He said he was."

Walsh looked to starboard at the mellow afternoon light resting on the green shore of Kerry. "We'll lay up on the Blaskets and then go north. Will he want to see us?"

"I don't know. He helped us once. And he said yes last night."

"Clare might be the place for awhile."

They were quiet. The soft flapping of the mainsheet spilling wind, the creaking of lines, the rattle of chain, and the rush of water made their silence deeper.

Tomás had seen the two lights of the boat sailing under his hill and stopping. The night was windy and cold, and he had just gone out to the turf pile for more fuel for tomorrow's fire when he caught sight of the lights. Above him a quarter moon curved in a black sky. It was just before midnight. He told Eithne, who was on her way to bed, that he was going down for a look.

"*Bí cúramach*," Eithne said.

It was unusual to see a boat this time of year. In the summer, yes, but in November the sea around the island was left to itself. It was a lonely life on the island. There was only one other family. But Tomás loved the island because it was home, and home had always been lonely. He and Eithne had been married only a year, and for the first six months lived with Tomás' mother, until she had died. Eithne, a town girl from Dunquin, had at first been desperately lonely, but now, after a year, the chores, the sheep, the sea and sky, the power of being outside looking in, had eased her ache, and Tomás was a good man. Soon there would be children.

He walked across the meadow to the wooden gate in the stone fence, and down the dirt road to the slope above the sand beach, a carpet of bluish-white in the darkness. The two lights blinked and rolled in the sea, and a large white sail, merely a shadow in the moonlight, was slipping down a tall mast. Tomás went down to the beach, and waited. Twenty minutes later a dinghy nosed onto the sand, and four figures stepped into the surf and pulled it up. Tomás walked to the water's edge and greeted them in Irish, welcoming them to the island, and was pleased to hear a white-haired man answer. He had a student's accent, it was obvious he had never lived in a *Gaeltacht*. The man said his friends and he were in trouble and needed a safe place for the night. At first he thought they had boat troubles but the three young people with the old man didn't look like they were on a pleasure cruise. He asked them what kind of trouble, specifically.

Deirdre and O'Connor helped Gudrun drag the dinghy further up the beach, past the high-tide line, and then the three went back and stood behind Walsh, talking with the young man.

"What's he saying?" O'Connor asked Deirdre.

"He's asking for help. He said we're in trouble. We're Republicans."

Tomás asked them if there were more of them out on the boat. The old man answered no, and Tomás said they were welcome to what he and his wife had. He led them up the beach to the road and on up across the field to his house. Gudrun looked back, down to the sea breaking on the beach, and the outline of *Die Freiheit*, far away below, swinging at anchor.

Tomás called for Eithne when they were all inside the front room of the small, clean, orderly cottage.

"*Dia dhuit*," she greeted, fear in her eyes.

"*Go méidigh Dia do stor*," Walsh said. "You speak English?"

"We do," Tomás said.

"My name is Joseph Walsh."

The young couple looked at him, unbelieving. "I'm Tomás O'Ceallaigh." Eithne turned away and went into the other room of the cottage.

"This is Deirdre O'Sullivan—"

"*Dia dhuit*," she said.

"And Terry O'Connor from the United States, and Gudrun Böhm from Germany."

Tomás nodded and went to squat near the fire. He turned his back and said, "Please sit."

Walsh drew a straight-backed chair up next to him. The others sat at the bare wooden table. "You've heard of us?" Walsh asked.

"I have. We heard it on the wireless this morning. You're a long way from home, Mr. Walsh."

"Ireland's my home."

"And mine. I'm a farmer. I'm not a man of violence."

"All we want is to rest for a day or two."

"Eithne," he called, and she came into the room and started to make tea.

"*An féidir liom cabhrú?*" Deirdre asked, getting up from the table. The young woman looked at her for a moment before turning to the cupboard and handing her cups and saucers. "*Go raibh míle maith agat*," Deirdre said. Eithne, her face set and sad, shook her head and put water on to boil.

"I won't turn you out," Tomás said to Walsh. "You can sleep here in this room tonight."

"Thank you."

"It's nothing," the young farmer said. "I'd have to put the devil himself up if he came to my door looking for shelter."

"Am I a devil, then? I'm a soldier of the Republic."

"I was taught the devil assumes many shapes in order to have his way with men."

Eithne looked up. The wind in the chimney sounded like a seashell held to the ear. Walsh waited until Tomás looked at him.

"I'm a man of no property. I have no apologies for you, and if the price of your hospitality is to be insulted, then it's far too much, Tomás."

He nodded, but didn't look at Walsh. "I believe in the Republic, but I won't kill for it. And I won't insult you anymore."

They had tea in silence, and then Eithne brought blankets into the room, heaped turf onto the fire, and went with Tomás to the back room and closed the door. They were all exhausted from their sleepless night and the long hours on the sea. Soon they were all asleep on the floor in blankets near the fire. Except Walsh, who couldn't sleep. His back had flared up again, and the conversation with the young farmer had unsettled him. He went outside, taking the straight-backed chair with him and sat wrapped in the blanket, looking out over the sea. The lights of the mainland were white sparks twinkling from a long way off.

The times had changed. The struggle had continued on into a new age, and had been changed. Only a few years ago he could have come to Kerry and lived underground as a hero. Now he was called a devil. The attack at Kildare was necessary. Deirdre had been right. There was no time for a gentleman's war. And there never had been. Only time for slaughter, for madness to shake mad Ireland awake. As these thoughts formed he knew they were nonsense. Shake Ireland? Better to shake a mountain. A devil, he called me. Once I could swim like a fish in the sea of my own people. Now I terrify country housewives and take insults from young men.

The wind was playful around Walsh, tearing at the blanket and then tucking it around him, bringing smells of salt and heather, and a distant sound of waves. The moon hid in clouds, and the stars seemed tired, weak and old in the indifferent sky. The night was endless, and Walsh waited through it, in mourning for something that was still alive. Away from here, he thought. And north to home, to Ulster, where the outlaw is Everyman, and the savage is understood.

CHAPTER 10

Disreputable Friends

When Maeve arrived at two o'clock she called to Anne from the hall that she was home, went into the large kitchen and began to prepare lunch. She unwrapped the quiche she'd purchased in a Baggot Street delicatessen, and started to make the tuna salad. Anne, lying in bed, heard her busily setting down packages, opening the refrigerator, chatting with the dog, and calling, "Have you been out?"

"No," Anne said, stepping into her jeans, embarrassed by being caught in bed. Since she'd arrived at Maeve's flat she had slept twelve to fourteen hours a day. She put on her white blouse embroidered at the neck in blue and red. There was a spot just near the hem in front. Last night's wine. She started to take off the blouse but halfway to the closet decided she didn't care. A quick look in the circular mirror displeased her. Brushing at her hair with her hands, staring into her own eyes. They were sleep-bombed. Her face looked blotchy.

"It's a glorious day," Maeve was calling as Anne stepped barefoot into the kitchen. "More like May than November," she said loudly, turning from the counter to see Anne sitting at the butcher block table. Maeve laughed. "Why am I shouting?"

"Don't ask me," Anne said.

"Are you hungry?" she asked, as Wellington, the English sheepdog, leaped up on her. Maeve pushed him away. "Not you, you dirty beast."

"I guess," Anne said, stretching her arms, shaking out the sleep.

"Here," Maeve said, setting a slice of quiche on a plate in front of her. "Start on this."

"Umm," Anne murmured, eating. Lately food held no interest for her until she took the first bite, then she couldn't get enough. Maeve brought tea and poured large cups as winter sunlight filled the room, flooding sharply through the high windows and falling on the two women at the table. There was a disorganized grace about the meal, as with everything connected to Maeve, with the paper bags and wrappings still on the table, her keys and newspaper lying where she'd tossed them, and a big mixing bowl in which Maeve, between bites, was stirring up the tuna salad. The light fell from the room slightly. Anne watched her friend. Always busy, pretty, talking about her day, feeding Wellington pieces of quiche. Anne began to cry, staring straight ahead, afraid to put her hands to her eyes. Maeve handed her a dishcloth and Anne put her face in it, smelling a clean laundered fragrance with a *soupçon* of fish.

"Bad dreams again?" Maeve asked.

"No," Anne said into the dishcloth. A lie. She had dreamed of her mother, grandmother and sister dressing her in a red crinolined formal gown in the living room of the house in Moher. When Anne raised her arms over her head, they all saw that she hadn't shaved under her arms. Her grandmother's face, turning away, flinching with disgust.

Anne shivered. Took her face from the dishcloth and rubbed her eyes. She wouldn't tell Maeve about the dream. The first two nights here, she had been plagued with dreams of brutality, violence and blood. When she told Maeve, she sensed that her friend was not interested, or else somehow afraid, somehow not wanting to hear.

Maeve dusted the tuna with paprika and handed Anne a wooden spoon, pushing the bowl toward her. She got up saying, "Oh, my pineapple potato salad, I almost forgot," opening the refrigerator and bringing back another bowl. Anne looked in the bowl, eating tuna from the spoon. "You've got to be kidding."

"Kidding?" Maeve said in mock outrage. "You mean you've never had it?" She took a taste, chewed thoughtfully, and looked back at Anne's grinning face. Waving her wooden spoon slightly, she said, "Exceptional. Superior. The quintessence of Irish cuisine. Haphazard, contradictory, and insane."

Anne laughed. "May I?"

"By all means, missus."

Anne licked her spoon clean and dipped into the bowl. She tried just a bit, and then dug in for more, taking out a pineapple chunk and plopping it in her mouth after she withdrew the spoon. "It's great."

"Of course it's great," Maeve said, drinking a large draught of tea and pushing the sheepdog down. "Get away, you great woolly thing."

"How did you find it?" Anne asked, eating greedily.

"Letters to the column. I was reviewing a whole slew of cookbooks and at the end of the piece I asked for recipes, saying I'd print the tastiest and most interesting. Jesus, you wouldn't believe some of them. I must show them to you. Remind me. Most of the responses were from men, isn't that interesting? All these dotty men, creating the most vile dishes. Ham roll and whipped cream—"

"Oh, come on."

"No, the truth. I'll show you the letters. Onion and apple pie."

They were both laughing. "Guinness and wine coolers."

"Stop."

"Angel food cake topped with cabbage and pieces of sausage baked in."

When they were just giggling, Maeve said, "You can laugh, my girl, but who knows? Perhaps banana and mayonnaise sandwiches are tastier than they sound," which sent Anne off again. "The only one I tried was pineapple potato salad."

"It's fabulous," Anne said, tilting the bowl, scraping at the sides to get the last of it.

"Is good, isn't it?" Maeve said, looking at Anne, happy as a child home from school with a cold.

They were eating gooseberry tart with cream when Anne said, "You've been so good to me, Maeve."

"Now, stop it."

"No, really. You're such a good friend."

Maeve was embarrassed. "You're no trouble a'tall so please stop saying things like that. It's fun having you here and you're to stay as long as you want."

"He called this morning," Anne said and set her teacup down. "Around ten, I think. We talked for a minute and then I went back to sleep."

"You don't have to talk with him. Do you know that?"

"I think he was drunk. He was saying something about Halloween candy."

"Did it upset you?"

"No," Anne said. "Yes. I guess it did. I keep thinking."

"If you ask me," Maeve said, petting Wellington's massive head as he sat next to her chair, "you're doing the best thing. It's only been a week."

"Ten days."

"Ten days. Let him come to you, Anne."

"It's awful," she said softly.

"He knows that."

"But I can't live with him. I keep thinking that, if I love him, I should stay with him. And then I remember the last three months. I hated what he was doing with himself."

"Give it time."

"You've been so good to—"

"Now," Maeve interrupted, rising and taking bowls to the sink, "don't start informing me of the quality of my character again."

They did the dishes and straightened the kitchen. "What should I wear tonight?" Anne asked.

"Oh, jeans, I think. Jeffrey said this morning it was going to be outside, rain, shine, or freezing. Take your shawl."

"Maybe I'll stay here," Anne said, vaguely.

Maeve put the teapot on a shelf in the cupboard, standing on tiptoes. "You will not. Jeffrey said this morning he was happy you're coming. You'll be the only American and he said he needed your advice on the barbe—"

"Barbecue."

"That word always makes me think of pillage and rape. It'll be fun, Anne."

"Okay," she said.

When Maeve went into the small room off the kitchen to work, Anne sat at the bare table watching Wellington snap at dust particles floating in the thin light. What to do? She yawned. If I go back to that bed, I'll never get up. Funny, the more you sleep, the more exhausted you are. She heard the rapid fire of Maeve at her typewriter. Anne stood up and put the collar and leash around Wellington's thick neck. "Maeve?"

"Yes?"

"Sorry, but I'm taking himself for a walk. Do we need anything?"

"Nothing. Have a good time."

Anne put on her "English tourist shoes" as she described them to Martin when she'd bought them in London, took a paperback off the night table, and walked down the stairs out to the bright

Dublin day with Wellington joyously tangling the leash around her legs, pulling hard, nose to the ground.

At Northumberland and Lansdowne two blond girls dressed in the green uniforms of the bank up the street stopped and petted the sheepdog.

"Isn't he a queer old fellow."

"So playful!"

"What's his name?"

Anne was looking down Lansdowne Road, at the postman making the delivery to Number 20, where she and Martin had lived. "What's his name?" The wild young woman who had lived in the flat below them was out on the stoop, taking her mail, flirting with the postman. Every weekend she had thrown noisy parties, blowouts that ran from dinner to breakfast. Martin had called her "Crazy Daisy" even though her name was Bridget, and in time they referred to her as "C.D." The postman tipped his cap and C.D. went inside.

Anne turned back to two young faces staring at her, a trace of fear in their eyes. "I'm sorry. I wasn't listening."

The two girls walked away, exchanging short glances with each other. Anne pulled on Wellington's leash. They think I'm a loony. The Irish are only afraid of two things, her mother had told her: tuberculosis and insanity. Cirrhosis of the liver and wife beating were completely understandable but if you had a bit of a cough or were depressed for a few days then they ignored you or made out that everything was fine, just fine. Terrified to confront it. And mental illness was more contagious than t.b., the Irish believed. Anne's anger shook the last tinge of lethargy from her.

Herbert Park was nearly deserted when she and Wellington arrived. She walked under a wide arbor of vines naked of blossoms, and came to the bowling green, bordered on four sides by clipped hedge. Last summer she and Martin would come after dinner to the park two or three evenings a week to watch the elderly people bowling black woods across the green lawn. Neither of them understood the game, but that wasn't the point. It was the joy of being in the tender evening of another age, where there was quiet, and people civilized by tamed, ordered nature, where nothing was required of you except that you take your ease. The parks of New York City required you to have ear plugs against portable boom boxes, eyes that could pick out dog shit ten yards away while disregarding the other filth all around you, and a fierce expression on your face to ward off hawkers of narcotics or thugs looking for an easy assault and battery.

She had lived in New York City all her life, and so any city was comprehensible to her. But Dublin had her heart from the first morning she had arrived. Will I live here the rest of my life? she wondered. Where else? Leaving Dublin for Clare, rocky, empty Clare, had been leaving a loved one to participate in an arranged marriage. I'll never live *there* again, Anne thought. And I'll never live in New York again. She caught herself thinking of living alone. Is it really, truly, over?

At the duck pond she had to scold Wellington for chasing the cocky little mallards off the grass and trying to leap in the water after them. He finally calmed down and Anne led him to a bench, tied him up and sat down. She took the novel from her back pocket and began to read. It was one of her pleasures, reading in a park. She thought of reading in Stephen's Green last summer, remembered the book, the weather, even what she'd been wearing. That was the day she'd met Martin and gone to Eve's. That was the day it all started, or ended if she thought of it that way. She laid the book in her lap. It's not ended. I'll give him time, I'll let him come to me like Maeve said. He will come. He will.

A man walking a dachshund strolled over. He was tall, dressed in a soft tweed jacket and trousers. His face was full and round, and his thinning hair was blond, kinky, an Afro untended, springing away from the top of his head and around his ears. Anne had never seen hair like it on a man in Ireland. "Poor hair," her mother would have described it. His wire-rimmed glasses gave a note of seriousness to his comical head, and also spotlighted his eyes, which were not comical at all, but kind and curious, intelligent, with something private there, something sad. Anne thought he was very attractive, all in all. Martin's age or thereabouts. The type of man who the older he got the more he grew into his looks.

Wellington strained at his leash to play, crouching down to get even with the dachshund, putting his nose on the ground with his rear end sticking straight up, wagging with fun. The dachshund stood haughtily, ignoring Wellington, not about to play the fool.

"He's a beauty," the man said. "Is he a he?"

"Last time I looked," Anne said.

The man smiled. "They're such happy dogs. They never grow up, it seems."

"I think crazy is the word."

He smiled again. "May I?"

"Of course," Anne said.

The man sat down at the other end of the bench. "It's lovely weather today."

"More like May than November," Anne said, smiling, thinking of how she would describe him to Maeve when she got back.

"You're American?"

"Yes."

"On holidays?"

"No, I live here."

"Do you?" he said, taking out a bar of Cadbury chocolate and offering her a piece. She shook her head. "Oh, have some," he smiled. Anne broke off a piece and thanked him. He broke off a small piece and held it out to the dachshund. "There you go, Fritz." Fritz smelled it at length and licked it once before eating it thoughtfully.

"Would, em—what's his name care for some?"

"Wellington will eat anything."

"Here you are, old man," and he tossed a small piece which Wellington swallowed immediately. "The ducks are usually up here on the grass this time of day," he said. "Ducks are abnormally fond of chocolate. Did you know that?"

Anne laughed.

"Well, at least Herbert Park ducks. Fritz here is terrified of them. Aren't you, Fritz?"

"Wellington isn't scared of anything. Except mops or brooms. When you start to use them he hides under the bed."

"Fearless Wellington," the man said. "More chocolate?"

"No, thank you."

They sat and watched the ducks gliding close to the edge of the pond, keeping their distance.

"This is such a beautiful place," Anne said.

"I like it," he said. "I'm here nearly every day. Walking Fritz. In the summer my wife and I play tennis here. The courts are quite good for public use."

"It's wonderful in the summer," Anne said, feeling somehow

discontented, somehow foolish. Talking with a stranger so easily was something she'd forgotten. Another city experience that in Clare had been impossible. Clare, she thought. The insane wind, the brutal isolation, the coldness and strangeness of the country people, and Martin slowly burying his personality from her, staring into his roaring fires, drinking heavily with a long sad face, staying out all night with that fool McGuffin, coming home drunk, until she was shocked one day to discover that this man she loved was a person she didn't know and didn't want to know. He hadn't changed, he'd disappeared and left an imposter in his place.

The man was talking. "He's given me such pleasure. I identify with his characters so much. For a long time I thought I was Scobie."

"Who?" Anne asked.

"Scobie."

He was smiling at her.

"I'm sorry, I—"

"The hero of the novel you're reading," he said, pointing to her lap.

"Oh," Anne said, glancing down at her book. She blushed. And then laughed. "I'm sorry. I was miles away."

He nodded. A good face, she thought. "Well, it's a perfect day for daydreaming. You shouldn't be sorry." He stood up. "Wellington, old man, it's been a pleasure. It was good of you to share your bench. I enjoyed talking with you."

"Bye-bye," Anne said.

He walked away toward the tennis courts, Fritz stepping daintily at his side. Why had she blushed? Anne reprimanded herself. Because he was a man and I'm supposed to cling to his every word? Men. But he was very nice. At least he wouldn't have you committed for not being all there 100 percent of the time. Yes, very nice. Men *and* women. That was it. That was the reason for blushes, and everything else.

She thought of Maeve. I've got to stop being this stupid teary woman around her, being a cliché. I've cried enough, goddamn it. Ten days of weeping, the tears coming from nowhere and leaving as quickly as they came. Enough, Anne said to herself.

Wellington was trying to hop onto the bench with her, choking himself with the effort. Anne brushed the hair from his weak eyes.

She untied him and led him away from the pond. I'm too full of myself, she thought. Carrying on like a war widow. It's not my problem, it's his. Either he solves it or he doesn't. I won't grieve about something I can't control.

She thought of the party tonight and resolved to have fun. If people ask where Martin is, I'll tell them in Clare and nothing more. What do I care what they think? A seagull swooped low over the grass and Wellington charged it, leaping with all four feet off the ground. The gull was only a white speck in the high sky, but Wellington continued to charge and leap. Anne ran with him, her dark hair streaming behind her. She was hungry. She'd make pastry for Maeve and herself for tea.

When Maeve and Anne arrived at Jeffrey Norris's house in Ballinteer at five o'clock, the party was already in full swing and out of control. Maeve parked the car down the road and they walked on a gravel path toward the large old house looming up, with Japanese lanterns lighting the facade and flickering all through the garden. It was dark and chilly. They heard many voices. Just as they reached the entrance to the sprawling terraced garden, a stout woman in an evening dress stepped out of the shadows and said to Anne, taking her by the arm, "What are we going to do with him?" She pointed at a young man lying in a flower bed dressed in a pinstripe suit, wide awake, an expression of bliss on his face.

"He really has had too much to drink," the woman said, looking at the young man.

"I would leave him be," Maeve said, guiding Anne away.

"I think *she's* had too much," Anne said as they stepped up off the path and into the garden.

"That's Ada Norris," Maeve said. "Jeffrey's wife."

"Really?"

"And she's not drunk. That's just the way she is."

They had arrived just in time to be herded together with thirty or so others into a circle around Jeffrey Norris who began a speech. He was tall and thin, a man of fit middle age with long brown hair. He thanked everyone for coming and for their support of the *Irish Review of Books*, a slick monthly he published and edited. He described the early days of the review in biblical terms, "a voice crying out in the wilderness," "escaping the land of illiterate bondage," "building a new Jerusalem of Irish letters," etc. Anne saw two or three journalists she knew in the crowd. She glanced into the next section of garden where a few people stood around holding drinks near a large fire pit where sausages and hamburgers sizzled on a wide grate. Jeffrey Norris called for the prizes and one of his daughters came forward bearing a silver tray where medals in velvet boxes were stacked. She was applauded by the group after Jeffrey introduced her. He then gave out the gold medals with checks of £250 to authors, publishers, and editors. They each had an acceptance speech.

Someone tapped Anne on the shoulder. She turned and it was Stephen Foley, a young reporter for the *Irish Times*. "Stephen," she whispered.

"Has he been speaking long?"

"About half an hour."

"Oh, Jesus," Stephen said, edging up next to her and taking out his notebook. "I'm covering it for the paper." He listened for awhile, taking shorthand notes, and then stopped and whispered to Anne, "What in Christ's name is he going on about?" He looked at his notes and read aloud: " 'Pillar of salt,' 'The ark of decent prose composition in a sea of trash,' did he just say that?"

Anne was amused, looking into his earnest reporter's face. It was a profession that compelled them to be irresponsible and adolescent when not working, but when on the job they were more serious than politicians at a communion breakfast. "He's raving," Stephen whispered. "I can't file this shit."

Anne laughed, louder than she intended, and Jeffrey Norris paused, somewhere between the twelve apostles and the raising of Lazarus, and said, "Thank you, dear. At least there is one amongst us who appreciates satire of a high level."

"More, Jeffrey," someone said.

"Have no fear, my children, there is much more." Someone handed him a drink. "Where was I? Oh, yes, Lazarus, come forth!"

"Come on," Stephen said, leading Anne away. "I'll get a statement from him later when he's really jarred."

They walked through an opening of the tall hedges where people were gathered around a long table. "What will you drink?" Stephen asked, stepping up to the table.

"Wine," Anne said. Stephen poured her a glass and took a small whiskey for himself. "Here's hoping," he toasted. Ken Grayson, actor, theater critic, and short story writer, came over with a bottle of stout in his hand. "You're beautiful in this light," he said to her. " 'Lo, Stephen."

"Your man is having a religious experience over there."

"Yes," Ken said, seriously. "He's a latent lunatic. I've maintained it for years. You know his fondness for automobiles? Last summer he rang me to come look at a vintage Rolls he was buying from an old man in Blackrock, so I went along. It *was* a beautiful car. Your man was all set to fork over a thousand quid to the old gombeen man when I said let's have a look under the bonnet. When we opened it up there was nothing there. Nothing! We were looking straight through to the ground, our shoe tops staring at us."

"Did you get a prize?" Stephen asked.

"No," Ken said. "Not a penny. Not a medal. Not a chain."

"Would you know who did? I'm covering it for the paper."

"Do your own legwork, Foley, you lazy man." And then to Anne, "Are you with someone?"

"I'm here with Maeve."

"Maeve? Oh, good, I'll see her. You'll be here awhile?"

"Yes," Anne said, and Ken walked away, taking a short pull on his bottle of stout.

"Man's as bad as a wino," Stephen said. "Worse. Any self-respecting wino uses a glass when one's available."

"I think he's charming."

"Charming? Did you know—" and here Stephen went into a gossipy story about an aspect of Ken's sex life.

"Like I said," Anne answered. "Charming."

"Oh, that's right. I nearly forgot. Americans are mesmerized by sexual eccentrics."

Anne laughed. "You're standing in the middle of this party and telling *me* about eccentrics? You should catch a literary party in the States."

"What's it like?"

"I shot one once in Westhampton. That's a summer community in New York. Everyone standing around being intelligent and literary. It'd put you to sleep."

"I'd get the story filed, though," Stephen said. "There's Ada. I'll get the quotes from her. Mrs. Norris?" he called. Ada Norris came over. "Stephen. Just the fellow I wanted to see. Did you notice the young man in the flower bed on your way in? He's a colleague of yours, I believe. Poor man, he's quite drunk and the ground is so cold. I haven't a clue about what to do with him."

"Oh, he'll be all right. Mrs. Norris," Stephen began, pulling out his notebook, "could you give me some information—"

At the fire a short man in a long white apron handed her a sausage on a roll. She walked over to where Robby Buckley was relating a story to three other men. Robby winked at her and went on, exaggerating his already thick Cork accent. "So, here is Kate and Bridey standin' in the village square, lookin' at a cart of freshly picked carrots. Bridey says to Kate, You know, Kate, that one carrot just there puts me in mind of himself.

"Oh, God, Kate replies. Sure, it's not the size of it.

"No, Bridey says. I wouldn't say it was the size of it.

"It couldn't be the shape of it, God forbid, that puts you in mind of himself.

"No, says Bridey, I'd say it was more the dirt of it."

One man listening to the story nearly collapsed. He spilled his drink, went into a coughing fit and tottered dangerously close to the fire. Finally, he very delicately sat down on the ground. "The dirt of it," Robby was roaring, and the seated man pounded on the ground with his fist.

"Who is that infidel?" Jeffrey Norris asked, standing next to Anne. "A pantheist? A worshiper of the humble earth? How are you, Anne? I'm so glad you've come."

"It was a wonderful speech, Jeffrey."

"Did you think so? I thought it was fine. Are you enjoying yourself? Enough to eat?"

"Hot dogs are great."

"Hot dogs. Oh, yes, hot dogs!" he laughed. "Come, let me get you more wine."

"No, this will do."

"Maeve says you'll be up for awhile. Would you like a job?"

"Doing what?"

"Come and see me next week. I can organize some portrait work for you. Next month's cover is Denis Johnston. Does that interest you?"

"Yes, I'd love it."

"Ring me tomorrow and remind me of what I've just said, will you?"

"Yes," she said and Jeffrey strolled over to the seated man.

Maeve came by, holding a glass of whiskey. "Are you cold? I'm freezing. Let's go inside. That bloody Grayson thinks he's in love with me."

They stepped out of the garden and into the kitchen. People sat on the counters, crowded into the pantry, and stood around the table where bottles of beer, stout, whiskey and wine were placed, not going to waste. Cigarette smoke fogged the room. Maeve went into the dining room while Anne listened to Stephen Foley and two other reporters talking, all holding glasses waist high.

"Why in hell they haven't been rounded up is the question. You might be able to hide yourself, but a forty-five-foot yacht?"

"They say Joe Walsh is already here, back in Dublin."

"Rubbish. Who's 'they'? Our man tried to get in touch with the I.S.A. but all his sources have gone to ground. Vanished."

"Bloody horrible state of affairs. Americans and Germans playing cowboys and Indians."

"What's the difference? It's all madness. It's no less horrible if only Irish were involved."

"And three of those men were unarmed."

"Plus the boy."

Anne tried to edge her way past but Stephen stopped her. "We're just talking about that dirty business in Kildare."

"It's awful," she said. "Excuse me, Stephen."

She went into the dining room where more people were drinking. The noise of voices. She looked for Maeve. She had to get out. Ken Grayson came up to her. "Need company?"

"Leave me alone," Anne said, turning away toward the hall.

In the hallway a young man with a sweating, drunken face stopped her. "You're the American."

Anne felt her legs weakening. "I was in the States last summer. What'd you think of Neil Young? I saw a concert in L.A."

Anne went towards the bathroom where there was a queue of four people. The door opened and a tall man in tweed with a halo of kinky blond hair came out. Anne was weeping. "Hello, again," he said, and took her arm. "Here, let's get out of this." Anne saw faces that appeared disembodied, staring. He led her into Jeffrey's study, a wide high-ceilinged room full of books jammed in the long bookcases, bound by twine in stacks on the floor, lying open on the desk. The man sat her on the couch. "There," he said. "Feel better?"

"Thank you, yes." It was very quiet.

"Can I get you something? Brandy?"

"I think a whiskey," Anne said.

"Right. Now, stay put."

When he was gone Anne closed her eyes. She had telephoned Martin that night after she and Maeve watched film of the wrecked cars and bodies covered by blankets in the main road of Kildare. She knew even before the name Terrence O'Connor was announced. Maeve had been furious, as she was when confronted by any kind of violence, especially political violence. Anne had said very little and Maeve stopped talking and put on music. Anne said she'd like to walk to clear her head, alone. She telephoned Martin collect in Moher from a booth in Baggot Street.

"I didn't know," Martin said, stunned, when she told him. He sounded like he was drunk, or had just awakened.

"It was just on TV."

"I didn't know. You're sure?"

"I'm sure. Thank God. I thought you were—"

"They mentioned his name?"

"Yes."

"Good God. How many dead?"

"I don't know. I'm telling you now, Martin, if he gets in touch with you, you should have him arrested."

"Are you all right? You sound kind of shaky."

"Of course I'm fucking shaky. What do you expect?"

"Take care of yourself, baby."

"I will," Anne said, and hung up.

Jeffrey Norris came into the study with the man in tweed behind him carrying a glass of whiskey. They sat on either side of her. "How are you, dear?" Jeffrey asked.

"I'm all right," she managed a smile.

"Here, have some of this."

She took one sip and handed it back. "I really don't need it."

Jeffrey took her hand and patted it.

"I think I want to go, Jeffrey."

"Of course. You came with Maeve? I'll fetch her."

When they were alone the man said, "I'm glad you're feeling better. You're sure you won't have some more?"

"No."

"My name is Garrett Costello."

"Anne Burke. You've been very kind, Mr. Costello."

"Garrett. Lucky I found you. My daughter's name is Anne."

"Oh. Are you a writer?" Anne said, embarrassed, trying to make conversation.

"No, I work for the government. I reviewed the new de Valera biography for Jeffrey last issue."

"Oh, yes. I read the review. It was very good."

"No, it wasn't. You're really all right?" His eyes were concerned, parental.

"Yes, thank you."

"I'll leave you be. My wife must think I deserted her."

When they were back in the flat Anne lay down on the bed and insisted Maeve return to the party. "Did Jeffrey mention a cover portrait to you?" Maeve asked, bringing Anne a ginger ale in a tall iced glass.

"Yes."

"Sounds exciting."

"I don't think I'll do it," Anne said.

"Well, don't decide too quickly. You're sure you don't want me to stay?"

"Please, Maeve."

"Wellington will keep you company. I won't be late." When she was gone Anne lay very still, her eyes closed. She pulled the blanket over her. And sleep, a disreputable friend, but still a friend, comforted her.

CHAPTER 11

The Meeting of the Waters

At nine o'clock he puts on his pea coat and goes out for the paper. The wind is steady and strong along the road next to the sea. Burke looks back and sees his chimney smoke being battered. Down the road he meets a girl walking, bucking the uphill wind. From under her hood she gives a smile. The two town dogs crouch next to each other in the doorway of a pub, only their noses sticking out to the wind. Burke takes his usual route along the concrete strand running past the seafront. Huge breakers pound the wall. The sound is layered; below there is a dull roar and above a furious, irrational whistle. Thick surf, the top whipped fine as cream, vaults the wall and falls heavily on the strand. The sea is white and green running high from the horizon all the way in.

Burke cuts up the lane between the seafront houses with the wind at his back pushing him along. He smells a sharp thin odor. Wood smoke along the alley. Rounds the corner onto the main street and ducks into the post office. The small room is packed with men. Flat caps and hard faces. One or two nod, the rest stare. He sees the priest at the far end of the room, near the newspaper table, smoking, holding the *Irish Independent* open. Saturday morning mass over, down to the post office to talk about this, that, and the other thing.

"Wild this morning," the priest greets him. He's a tall, fat man.

"Yes," Burke says.

"And how's the writing on a wild morning?" he offers Burke a Benson and Hedges. Lights it with a gold lighter.

"Slow, Father."

A farmer with black hair combed straight back says, "I knew you'd be a writer. I knew. I was tellin' James just the other day. Wasn't I?"

James, standing in shit-covered rubber boots, grinning, says,

"You were *thinkin'* your man a writer. You weren't sayin' any definite word about the matter in my recollection." And the rest begin their sing-song talk where they'd left it when Burke, the stranger, had opened the door.

The priest says, "I'm reading here about the flooding. This is a dangerous time of year. Galway, under water. Sligo as well. The wind left me sleepless last night."

"You weren't the only one, Father."

"Yes? How's the missus?"

"She's fine."

"We don't see much of you about."

"We're not churchgoers, Father."

James says, "Is that your Austin taxi I see parked on the road? The black fellah?"

"That's a friend's," Burke says. "You know him. Cyril McGuffin. I've got a Mini."

"Fine automobile, the Mini. Terrible on the tire rubber, I understand. Did you know it was an Italian designed the Mini?"

"Is that right?" Burke says, and notes his sly smile. Yes, they all knew McGuffin. And they all knew he was his friend. He had been shit-faced drunk with him in pubs in this town where these men drank. Is the farmer letting the priest know he is a friend of the heathen McGuffin? Burke smiles at him, the stupid, narrow little bastard, probably been sucking up and snitching to priests all his life.

"That's right. An Italian designed it."

An old woman with a clear beautiful face and wide eyes limps from the back room and goes behind the counter of newspapers. The postmistress. "Mr. Burke," she says. "You'll be wantin' an *Irish Times*."

"Morning," Burke says.

"Fierce day. I have a *Times* of London that your man over in Lahinch neglected to take away yesterday. You'll be wantin' that."

"Could you get me some Old Holborn, too, Mrs. Ryan?"

"Aye."

She folds the papers and places the brown and white pouch on top. "Will that do you? Matches? Rollin' papers?"

"That's fine."

As he pays her the priest says, "Now, I wasn't speaking only of churchgoing, Martin. You should bring the missus and yourself to the rectory for a glass of wine some evening. *In vino veritas,* you know. An exchange of ideas."

"Thank you," and, aware that every ear in the room is listening, says, "She's in Dublin with friends now, but as soon as she's back, we'll come by."

"Dublin, is it? She's weary so soon of country life?"

"She's just there for a few days, Father."

The postmistress says, "And here's your mail, Mr. Burke. You'll take it now. Sean's not been seen this morning and I don't know when it'd be delivered up to you."

He takes his leave with nods and smiles and is out into the day again. Down the main street trots a herd of cattle. Bug-eyed, barrel-bodied, saliva swinging from their mouths in the wind, bawling. The drover is a boy with a curved stick, working with a dog.

Yes, Anne had been weary of "country life," you fat, useless— he sounded like his old man. All yes, Father, no, Father, how's your health, Father, when you're with them, but as soon as you're away it's mocking and hatred. That first day in early September, driving the Mini across the country from Dublin and arriving at Moher at five o'clock, rainy and gray, he'd gone into the parlor of a bed and breakfast house along the strand looking for the man who had the keys to the house on the hill, while Anne waited in the car, and had met the priest sitting with the old woman of the house in front of the fire in the gloomy room. The man with the keys was out, will you have a cup of tea, he's sure to return soon, and this is Father Rooney. "What is it you'll be doing here, Martin?" he'd asked. Burke pegged him as a closet whiskey-priest, or simply a madman in a black suit and Roman collar. His quick brilliant smile, one leg crossed over another, teacup balancing on a knee and a black shoe bouncing to some private rhythm. "I'm a writer, Father."

"A writer? That's the life, it is. What sort of writing is it that you do, Martin?"

"I'm a journalist."

"Ah," he'd said, and then, something that Burke could never figure out or forget, coming so smoothly and quickly in the con- versation, the priest had said, smiling, "And do you have a motor scooter to travel about on?" Burke had laughed. The priest stared, smiling. Mad. Lost in a country parish, lost in an old woman's dim parlor, full of inner music.

In the alley walking towards the strand Burke checks his mail. A blue airmail envelope from Anne's mother in New York. An envelope from the *Village Voice*. And a plain envelope addressed to him, postmarked Dunquin, County Kerry. He puts them into the inside pocket of his pea coat and walks up the strand against the heavy southwest wind. Walking up the hill to his house is a struggle. A tractor rolls towards him down the road and the man sitting it gives him the thumb up. When he reaches the house he's breathless. He makes tea and toasts bread, and carries it on a tray to the front room and sits in front of his fire. The letter from Kerry goes on the right of the mantle and the *Voice* letter on the left. Burke is "squeezing." A gambler holding his bet for as long as he can, not reading the race results until he's home and comfortable. Finally, after finishing the pot of tea, he opens the letter from the *Voice*, and looks first at an enclosed check for one hundred dollars.

Marty,

Got the piece and it's a good one, but you already know
that. It won't run now, and I can't guarantee when it will.
So, accept this paltry kill fee. It's the best I can do. The paper
is full of election news, and rock and roll, but you already
know that too. I'll hold it and push it but it's tough to sell.
Weinstein isn't interested in Ireland unless it's written by
people named Hamill or Breslin. But I'll see what I can do.
Keep plugging. It's a fine piece.

Love to Anne. Hope you're enjoying yourselves.
The house sounds beautiful.

Best,
Rob

He pockets the check, tosses the letter into the fire, and opens the other letter.

Marty—

Leaving today. All packed. You will see us, you make
contact. Four of us will arrive in one or two days.
Watch.   Love, T.

Damn him. Damn his soul. Cryptic hard guy. Tough man. "Love, T." Heavy dude. Burke knows why they are coming to him. The whole country is looking for them, and with their baggage it is easier to travel by sea than the suddenly well-patrolled roads of Ireland. And here they have a friend with a house on the west coast in a village you'd have to set fire to to wake up. O'Connor had called around eleven Wednesday night, an hour after Anne's call. He had asked one thing after Burke interrupted him to say the phone was a party line. "Can we count on you?"

"Count on me for what?"

"Marty, we're moving right now. Understand? Can I count on you?"

"Yes," Burke said.

"Okay," O'Connor said. "I'll write you. I'll send it today, or tomorrow. You'll get it Saturday," and he had rung off.

Burke's first thought had been to run. I'll go to Dublin, I'll get Anne, I'll say she had been right, I'll say I'll change for her, rid ourselves of this evil country. But even as he was formulating these plans, he knew he would stay and wait. The seven dead at Kildare, which Anne had told him about on the phone Wednesday night, and which leapt out at him in the next day's newspaper, had affected him in a curious way. The horror, the blood, the senseless death, seemed to be a part of his own ramshackle life, and perhaps the only thing that was real anymore. To run would be to leave scores unsettled. These rationalities came when he was drunk.

He could do with a drink now. He takes an ashtray and flushes the butts down the toilet in the bathroom. Anne had always been amused by his neatness. She was the opposite, letting a room dissolve quickly into chaos. He'd envied her ability to spend a long Sunday in a room full of newspapers, dirty dishes, clothes. And because he envied her he'd fought with her.

They had bickered for weeks before she'd left. Hit and run. Brief engagement, retreat and surprise. Anne had loved Dublin, the large flat in Ballsbridge with high ceilings and fireplaces, the new friends she'd met, the conversation, the pubs, the city itself, the recognition she had begun to receive as a photographer. Here in Moher, there was no one except her one friend in town whom she never invited around to the house. Burke knew why. She was ashamed of him, his morning boozing, his coldness and silence.

No one but farmers and pubs that were never cleaned and served as hardware stores or bakeries. The sea and sky were prisons to her. She had hated the feeling of being looked at as a stranger the minute she walked out the door. She had hated the sound of the wind, moaning, shrieking around the house, living in a crystal glass someone was constantly flicking with a finger. She had hated the cold. Cold hands, cold feet. Wrapped in sweaters, they couldn't quite remember the last time they'd made love.

Their first fight had been about McGuffin. They had met him together the second day they had settled in when they drove to Ennistymon, the lovely town on the River Cullenagh, for lunch at the Falls Hotel. There Burke was told by a man at the bar, when he asked him where he could find timber for fuel, that there was a man not far away who sold good seasoned wood. After lunch they followed his directions up above the town to a long low house overlooking the falls of the Cullenagh. Next to the house was an open shed hung with gray rabbit and shiny auburn fox pelts. A shy woman with an English accent answered the door, and right behind her came this huge redheaded madman, tearing a napkin from his chin, wiping his mouth, all smiles and hundred mile an hour talk. When he told them his name, "Cyril McGuffin at your service," Burke felt something go inside him, remembering Liam Cleary on the beach at Sandymount recommending him to this man. McGuffin gave them a drink, which Burke threw down and McGuffin topped up, joking, manic, constantly moving. He loaded up the Mini with timber, gave them freshly caught fish, and promised to deliver more timber tomorrow. He showed them his car, the London taxi, genuine except for a cane chair he'd set next to the driver's seat replacing the meter. And all the while, the Englishwoman, whom McGuffin never introduced, looked on, shy and sad, never smiling, but watching.

McGuffin told them both to come back later after he'd finished a day's work, and driving home, with three glasses of whiskey in him, Burke said what a great character he was.

"Don't go back, Martin."

"Why not? I thought he was great."

"He's the craziest man I've ever seen. And not in a funny way, either. Did you see that woman? She looked like a slave, never speaking."

"Well, I won't turn down his hospitality. I thought he was fun."

"If you want to drink, stay home and drink there. Don't go back."

And that had decided it. He did go back after an ear-splitting row with Anne, and McGuffin took him down to Doolin that night, the village where the best traditional music in Ireland is played. Later, back at McGuffin's, Burke told him about Liam Cleary, and how he was with him the evening he died, and how he spoke of McGuffin. It had bound them. McGuffin had not seen Cleary for ten years, not since the day he had given up the I.R.A. and come home to Clare. McGuffin said he loved Cleary, and was pleased he had spoken of him on the day he died.

They were inseparable after that. The only time Burke felt any connection to life or joy was in McGuffin's company. He spent many days and nights away from Anne, sleeping at the house above the river. Being with Anne made him feel embarrassed for some reason.

They were eating breakfast in the dining room when it had finally broken. She spoke to him calmly for fifteen minutes. They were quiet, drinking tea, listening to Irish radio playing music dead for ten years everywhere else.

When she finished he was looking away from her into the empty fireplace. In the kitchen the refrigerator groaned and settled.

"What can I do?" she asked.

"Take the car and go to Dublin. Stay with Maeve. Go today."

"I feel so—ridiculous. I'm your wife," and the last word was spit at him.

He had started to speak but she interrupted him.

"No. No, don't lie to me. You *want* me to tell you you're a goddamned fool. Absurd. Ridiculous. Don't think I'm impressed." She poured tea. "Another cup?"

"No."

"You're cruel, Martin. And you think you're kind, but you're cruel. I've had it. I'm going to Dublin but not because you want wifey out of the way so you can play. I'm going because I don't want to be with you."

"Fine," he'd said. "Fine."

"Why are you so secretive? You're like a little boy playing with himself in the bathroom, always—"

"Now, stop it."

"Pretense," she said. "Secrets. Lies. Ask you a question and pray for a straight answer."

"What do you want from me?"

"Honesty, for Christ's sake. Involvement. Who are we? Two animals sharing a hole in the ground? Oh, God," she was shouting, both hands on the table, "I hate that face. Charm me. Humor me. Cruelty and lies—" She got up and threw the teapot into the fireplace. The sound seemed to calm her, breaking her rage. She said with a soft voice, looking at the broken china in the empty fireplace, "You have no idea what I want from you," and went to the bedroom and began to pack.

Burke walked into the kitchen. Ran cold water over his hands and wrists. Then he went into the bedroom. On the fourposter was a suitcase. Anne was at the closet, her back to him. He put his arms around her and she went still. He whispered, "Annie."

"Don't."

"You don't know who I am. I don't know who you are."

"Don't, Martin. Please."

"Can't we share a hole in the ground awhile longer, Annie? I need time."

"I'm going away. You can call me. I can't be here with you now. I can't take it anymore. Now, let me go."

She turned around.

"Soon," he said.

"You use me," she said.

"I need you."

"To use," she said. "To have a place. That's what I am. A place to you."

"You're my love, Annie. Let me be for awhile. Talking about it—help me."

Her eyes were soft, but far from tears, which surprised and hurt him. She wouldn't melt. "Oh, goddamn you, Martin. You're such a foolish man." She finished packing and called Maeve in Dublin. He told her to drive safely and she left without a word, or even a look at him.

Burke takes the airmail letter from Anne's mother and holds it, staring into the fire. It was Saturday, what would they do today? McGuffin had said he and Neena would be by early. He looks at the letter and wonders, burn it or read it? Replacing it on the mantle, he thinks, no, neither. I'll respect her.

Eleven-fifteen by the clock. Only two old jossers at the bar this time of morning. The bartender Fergus across the room showing Neena, looking very nice today in black slacks and a white sweater, the framed pictures of Clare hurlers from years past. The whole place, the two old pint men, Neena and Fergus, merely background to his thoughts of orbits. All a matter of balance, really. Burke took another swallow of the soft brown ale. Orbits, looping parabolas of your life. How perfect and easy a way to live, happily swinging along, orderly, fixed. But how dangerous if the balance of your orbit is tipped. Then chaos, blind fate as your compass, disintegration. Only one touch, just a tip in the right spot spins the whole thing out of kilter. He took another swallow of Smithwicks, and tasted the word kilter along with the ale. Kilter. Kill-ter. Nice word. Where did it come from? Kilter.

"And that's Jimmy Murphy, there," the young man pointed at a big country boy in shorts, staring sadly from the wall. "He used to drink in this pub."

Neena said, "Is that right?" She could care less. When she had come over to the bar for another bitter lemon, the silence and emptiness of the place, and the barman's odd smile, had forced her into conversation, so she had asked about the pictures on the wall. "That there is one of the best goal keepers in Ireland." She looked back at the American sitting in the corner, staring into space behind his pint. Strange man. Cherishes his sadness like a teenager. Like me. Neena Middlemiss was furious with herself. Thirty-seven and she was still without an anchor, looking at a bunch of foolish pictures. She had left London, where she was born and raised, to visit relatives in Clare last May. It had seemed so perfect, leaving the city, taking a fortnight holiday from Harrods, to spend time in Ireland, which she had heard was so beautiful. The relatives, whom she had never met, were an aunt and an uncle living on a chicken farm just west of Ennistymon. They were both silent, stupid people, their home as filthy as the chicken houses. Depressed, feeling cheated, she had gone to a *coeli* dance in Ennistymon for a bit of life and fun one bright spring night, and there met Cyril, big and bluff and a laugh that made you laugh along. He made love to her that night in his clean, fresh-smelling

house near the River Cullenagh and she cooked him breakfast the
next day. She had attached herself to him, going fishing and hunting, helping him when he cut timber. Two weeks later she knew
she'd never return to England. She would be with Cyril. And the
spring went on into summer. She thought he was getting tired of
her now, but it was hard to tell. Such a complex man. Laughing
and joking one moment and shouting at her the next. Making sweet
love to her in the morning and insulting her in front of strangers
in the afternoon. Where could she go if he no longer wanted her?
Back to London, back to loveless London, and live alone?

"You're a bit of a high-flyer, aren't you, now?" the young bartender was saying.

"What's that?" Neena said in her quick, high London voice.

"I say you're a bit of a high-flyer," he was grinning that odd
grin, and Neena now knew what it was about.

"A high-flyer?"

"You like a bit of fun, I'd say."

"Yes," she said. "But never with a half-wit culchie like you."

"Culchie," he laughed, looking her over slowly, lingering on her
legs in tight slacks, on her breasts, her neck, her mouth. "I'll show
you what a culchie can do."

Neena turned away, livid and ashamed at the same time, and
went over to Burke. "I have to leave."

"McGuffin said he'd be right back."

"Will you please come with me?"

"Sit down and have a drink, Neena. He'll be right back."

"Please come with me. Please."

Burke drained his pint and got up. "See you, Fergus," he called.

"Right, Martin. Don't fall off her," he said grinning.

"Right," Burke said, following Neena storming out the door.
What was he talking about? Fall off? They stood outside the pub
in the main street of Newmarket, a fine rain filtering down. It was
a barren little town. Burke couldn't for a moment quite remember
what they were doing here. Oh yes, McGuffin had gone to make a
deal with some man. He was forever making deals. And then he'd
gone to Alf Hogan's, Turf Accountant, down the street to see how
the horse had run. "What's the matter, Miss Middlemiss?"

"That bastard made a pass at me."

"Fergus?"

"Did you see any other sex maniacs in there?"

"This country," Burke said, "either drives lust out of you or makes you obsessive about it. There's no middle ground." The last swallow of ale had set him up nicely, driving the headache and towel mouth of hangover away. He rolled his weight to the balls of his feet and then back. Middleground, Middlemiss.

"Oh, Martin," she said. "He really did."

Burke looked at her, standing in the street next to him, gentle and afraid. "I'm sorry, Neena."

"This is a dreadful place," she said. "I can see why your wife couldn't stick it."

"It wasn't the place," Burke said.

Up the street they saw McGuffin, big and broad, his red hair like a sign advertising his presence, walking in his curious forward-leaning bristling way. He was waving something in his hand. When he got closer they saw it was a wad of purple ten-pound notes. "We won," Burke said to Neena as the redhead approached.

McGuffin spread them out, fan-shaped, in front of them. Burke counted. Seven. Neena looked away. "Did I tell you?" McGuffin asked. "Did I tell you?"

"You're a genius."

"And when Arsenal comes through tonight, we'll be a hundred quid richer." Whenever Burke had been with McGuffin it was always "we."

"How many goals did you give?"

"Only four. What's the matter, Neena? You don't like money any more?"

"Four?" Burke was astonished. "You're as crazy as you look, McGuffin. Four goals."

"Ah, they'll whip 'em by six. Ride a hot streak, my son. Tell me, Neena, what's wrong?" And then to Martin. "Have you ever seen a sadder woman? She looks like she lost her last friend. What is it, pet?"

"That bastard made a pass at me. The barman, Fergus. For all you care."

McGuffin took her by the shoulders, and shook her gently so she would look at him. When he caught her eye he said, "Are you all right, Neena dear? You're all right?"

"It just—" she said, and shook her head. "It just made me angry. It's nothing, really."

"Well, we'll see about that. Be back in a second, Martin. Meet you inside," and he put his arm around her and led her across the road to the black taxi. Burke heard her say, "Can't we go home, Cyril?"

"It's home we're goin', pet. I'll just straighten the lad out. Won't be a minute."

Burke went inside and sat at the bar next to the two old men. They were the nearest thing to asleep over their pints. Fergus came up. "Another of the same, Martin?"

"Yes. What'd you say to her?"

"Ah, nothin'," the young man said. He set the ale in front of him, wiping the spillage on the wood away with a cloth. "Just a bit of sport."

Burke took a long drink. "Is that sport in this place, Fergus? Insulting decent women?"

"Decent? She's McGuffin's whore, isn't she?"

"She's a friend of mine," Burke said, and drank deeply again. McGuffin walked in, a smile on his face, rubbing his red head, leaning forward, seemingly embarrassed and up to no good at the same time, the friendliness of the charmer, the snake smartness of the conman. He went over to the two old-timers and clapped them on the back. "How are ye, lads?"

They nodded in unison. One smiled. The other was looking for the door. "Will you have one with me?" McGuffin boomed.

"Aye," the smiling man said.

"There, Fergus," McGuffin said, looking at the barman for the first time. "Two pints for these good lads. A whiskey for me. Make it a Jameson. A large one. A large whiskey for the yank, here. And draw him another Smithwicks to help wash it down."

"The horses were good to you, Cyril?" Fergus said setting to work.

"It's not luck with me, Fergus. It's a science."

"God bless ye," one of the old men said, lifting his pint.

"You'd do the same for me, I'm sure," McGuffin said. "Now you'll drink it in good health."

Fergus put two glasses of whiskey in front of them, and then went to draw another ale for Burke. "That'll be three pounds one pence."

McGuffin held out a ten-pound note. Just as Fergus reached for it, he pulled it back and said, as an afterthought. "What will you have, Fergus?"

"Nothing, thank you, Cyril."

"Oh, you must have something. Have something, Fergus."

"I'll have a glass."

"That's it."

Fergus took the ten and drew a glass of stout. While he waited for the stout to settle, he made change. Burke thought he saw his hand shake over the till. He brought his glass and the change over. "Well, thanks, Cyril. To luck."

"To luck," one of the old men said.

"To luck," McGuffin said. "An appropriate toast. Seeing how yours just ran out."

Fergus sipped at his glass, looking at McGuffin's suddenly furious face. Two young farmers walked in, both giving the Irish nod, a turning of the head toward the right shoulder, and were answered by the two old silent fellows at the end of the bar. Fergus went to serve them. "What're you trying to prove?" Burke asked.

"He wants a lesson taught him."

"Come on. We'll withdraw our patronage."

"That too," McGuffin said, and called Fergus over. When he was before him, McGuffin reached over and grabbed the barman by the collar. He then yanked him onto the bar, took a handful of his trousers with his other hand, dragged him cleanly across the bar and stood him up next to him. "I'll need an apology from you, Fergus. Give me an apology now, like a good man."

"For what?"

"You fucking well know for what."

"I'm sorry," Fergus said, still shaken, still not quite believing he was on the wrong side of the bar. "Tell her I'm sorry."

"Good man, Fergus. Now, can I give you a lift back over?"

The two young men were laughing loudly at the end of the bar. And one of the old men joined in.

McGuffin drained his glass. "Drink up, Martin. We have a day and a night ahead of us."

Walking across the road to the black taxi, Burke felt as light on his feet as if he were escaping gravity. Neena sat in the cane chair next to the driver's seat. Burke climbed in the back seat. "Your honor still stands, Miss Middlemiss."

McGuffin put the taxi in gear and drove off, saying "Well now, how would you fancy luncheon at the Old Ground? Neena, would that suit you?"

"Cyril, I'm not dressed."

"You look lovely. Doesn't she, Martin? Doesn't she look lovely, now?"

"Lovely," Burke said, looking out the window at the high sky of Clare, soft as a piece of old satin. They were driving on a road lined by stone fences separating the farms into small pens of land, crisscrossing the winter-green earth wet with night mist that still clung here and there in the small hollows and valleys. They passed an old woman at the side of the road in front of her simple house, wrapped in a dirty sweater, her hair wild and blowing, pulling turf blocks off a pile and tossing them into a wheelbarrow, looking up as they passed. Full fat magpies, long tailed, white breasted, chattering on a stone fence, and then taking flight, fluttering clumsily at first, and then banking away.

In the old market town of Ennis they parked near the river and walked through crowds of farmers in for a Saturday of selling and buying. Neena and Burke followed McGuffin, who strode on ahead, his broad shoulders rolling like a sailor's, greeting people he knew, acting as if the Saturday market were his and his alone. The vegetable stalls lined the street, and beyond them were open-backed trucks selling shoes and shirts, boots and trousers, belts and socks. McGuffin led them further on and they stood overhearing the sale of livestock, the men and women dressed in gray and black and brown, pursuing a ritual as old and as important as the mass.

"He's a fine pig. You can see that yourself."

"Well, I have me doubts, now."

"You can have what you bloody well like. But you won't cast aspersions on my pig here."

Horses and donkeys stood powerful, patient in the drizzle. Men pulled back their forelegs, patted their flanks and checked their teeth, while handsome mongrel dogs, fur shining, trotted by. Children held onto parents' hands, farm ragamuffins grateful for another Saturday in Ennis. The pubs were full and friendly with their doors open to the narrow streets. As they walked past the town square two severe-looking men in old shiny suits stood selling religious paraphernalia from two card tables under the tall statue of Daniel O'Connell, the Liberator. A Legion of Mary banner held by one of the men gave them license to sell the holy cards of dreamy-eyed saints holding up hands punctured and bleeding, and rosary beads made of mother-of-pearl, blessed beeswax candles, missals and bibles, black little books with red paper edges that held the secret, the mystery, the way, the truth and the light for the hard people of the West. The Liberator stood in his stone clothes high above, never looking down, but eternally out over the rain and rock of Clare.

Narrow O'Connell Street leading off the square, lined with shops all with the distinctive Irish facade of a long bright panel of letters standing out solidly above the doors and windows. On their way up the narrow street Burke saw two tinker women dressed in multi-colored blankets, both pregnant with windburned faces walking on the other side of the street, haughty and alone among people dressed in dark colors. Foreigners in their own land, with faces that seemed to say that they understood why towns must be cool to those who have banded together and run away, leaving others to hold the fort.

Near an alleyway McGuffin stopped them and pointed. Up the alley a white-haired priest had just walked out of the back door of a public house and was mounting his bicycle. He pedaled blissfully toward them. "Soft day, Father," McGuffin greeted.

"Thanks be to God," the old priest said.

"And his holy mother the pope," McGuffin said. Neena poked him. The old priest nodded, and then looked back, not quite sure of what he had heard.

"Never let a day pass," McGuffin grinned, "without a bit of blasphemy."

They followed McGuffin up a flight of stairs just off the narrow street into a crowded pub and had hot whiskeys at his insistence, the glasses steaming smells of clove and lemon. "An apéritif before our feed," he said. Neena sipped and seemed to melt back in her seat. For such an attractive woman, Burke thought, she relishes the role of the mouse. McGuffin waved to a big fellow wearing bright red suspenders over a blue work shirt, and he sauntered by. "Will you have a drink, Paddy?"

The man had the heavy features and perpetually innocent expression of the slow-witted. "I'm drinkin' with that crowd over there, Cyril."

"Well, tell me, where've you been hiding yourself then?"

"I was in the jail."

"The jail, Paddy. What jail is that?"

"It was the Limerick jail, this past month."

"Good God, man. What did you do?" Burke was rolling a cigarette from his pouch of Old Holborn, but McGuffin's constant poking underneath the table made him stop and listen.

"Ah," Paddy said, embarrassed. "It was really nothin'. They had me in for assault. I had a few jars, you know, just a few and then a bit of a punch-up outside the pub, you know. A Dublin man, he was. And we were havin' the punch-up, can't remember what for, and I give your man's leg a kick with my boot and the leg broke. It was just the one kick broke it. The guards collected me the next mornin', you know. At the mother's."

"That's a hell of a thing," McGuffin said. "One month for a bit of a fight."

"It wasn't the fightin', you see, it was on account of his leg breakin'." He lowered his voice, leaned forward, and said very seriously, "Sure the leg must've been rotten, Cyril, to give way like that, with only the one kick. He went over like a dead tree in the wind."

Burke saw McGuffin disciplining his face against laughter. "You think it was that then? The leg wasn't bona fide?"

"It must've been rotten. It took nothin' to break it."

"Well, it's good to see you here, Paddy. That old jail isn't the place for you."

"That's the truth. I better be gettin' back, it's my round."

After Paddy had sauntered away, McGuffin exploded with laughter and Neena and Burke joined in. He had a strange laugh, the kind people hearing from across a room will join without knowing why. It began as a low chortle which escalated madly to startling whoops and shouts. "A rotten leg! Jesus, isn't he something? What does he think we're made of? Sap and wood?" And he raised another booming laugh to the ceiling. Although McGuffin was a Clareman, and had lived in the county most of his forty-four years, he looked at its people the way an anthropologist studies a primitive tribe, with inexhaustible curiosity and wonder, with great reservations concerning their morals, and with humor at their odd ways. He was known and liked all up and down Clare as a man who could do a good day's work in four or more trades, a man to fish with, or hunt hare, or clear a wood for timber, a man not unfamiliar with the taste of drink. On top of that, he was known to be a bit of a wild man. He didn't practice his religion, and was living in sin with the Englishwoman. But his neighbors saw him as a case of a poor thing but our own, and not a bad sort all in all.

Burke drank off his hot whiskey, which had cooled, in one gulp and went to the toilet. McGuffin called to him if he'd have another and Burke nodded his head. Neena sat back deeper and looked sadder at the prospect of more broken promises and yet another barroom afternoon. The toilet was a square room with a gutter running around the base of the tiled walls. Burke stood, alone in the room, and looked above the yellow wall to an open window looking out on the shingled roofs of Ennis under the slate sky. White clouds blowing through veils of rain and a smell of livestock on the wind mixing with the urine tang of the toilet. Funny, Burke thought, the smell of urine was the same as the butcher shops out here. How Anne had hated the butcher shops. The meat unrefrigerated, lying in brown lumps. The filth, the flies thick, buzzing around the puddles of blood. He jiggled the last drops off and zipped up, lost in intoxicated memory of that day, Wednesday, when Anne had called from Dublin about the raid, and later, Terry had called from Kinsale to tell him they were on their way.

McGuffin had driven him home that Wednesday morning. He told Burke, who was still drunk from the night before, that he had to fish at least one day in seven, but that he might see him later that night. Burke made a fire and went at a full bottle of Paddy, listening to the radio, reading the paper, staring into the fire which he never let merely burn; it had to roar, the flames leaping wildly, the whole fireplace raving mad with natural ferocity so he could see in it a forest fire, the death of a witch, a whole city burning.

He hadn't eaten anything since the afternoon before and was on his way to the kitchen when in the dining room he saw the bowl of candy Anne had bought a week before she had gone. He remembered her saying that they should buy it now so they wouldn't forget and be left with nothing when the children came trick or treating on Halloween. Not one child had come by that night, and the sight of the brightly wrapped unwanted candy seemed to mock the gentleness of his wife, who had lived with him in the cruel silent west these months, forever fighting to maintain a sense of gaiety and softness. The bully had triumphed.

A boy came into the toilet and looked up at the burly man standing in one place, staring out the window. The man's clothes didn't look like he'd changed them in a week and his hair was uncombed and wild. Brown bushy beard matted with something wet at the chin. The boy went and stood at the gutter as far away as he could from the man. He unzipped his pants and watched his thin trickle hit the wall and flatten, sliding down into the gutter. He kept one eye on the bearded man.

"Hiya, champ," Burke said when he finally noticed the boy, moving effortlessly from memory to a reverie of the present moment.

The bearded man's strange accent and phrase convinced the boy he was mental and he hurried to zip himself.

"In town for the market? It's a good day for the race."

The boy took a step for the door but couldn't resist asking, "What race?"

"Why, the human race," he said smiling. The boy had never seen anyone with eyes so red. They must be burning out of his head. He left quickly.

Burke reached in his pocket and brought out rolling papers and tobacco. He had originally taken to it to save money, or rather to convince Anne he was trying to save money, but soon found he enjoyed the ritual. An editor at *Newsday* years ago told him when he was first starting to work as a reporter that anyone who could blow perfect smoke rings was merely telling you he was a person who was lazy and had time on his hands. Rolling cigarettes was the same, Burke knew, it was a way to pass the time. As he was licking the paper and carefully smoothing the cylinder a short man dressed in dungarees and Wellington boots walked in giving Burke the nod, his ear almost touching his shoulder. He turned his back and urinated. A quick shiver when he finished. Burke lit the cigarette and the man came over and said, "Could I share that?" holding out a cigarette.

"There you go," Burke said.

The man inhaled deeply and coughed. "Good for the chest," he smiled, and walked out.

Maybe he would just stay in here for awhile. What better crossroads to see the world pass? The world of men coming by nature's demand for relief and comfort. What better place to meet your brothers, shoot the breeze, pass the time? A place perfectly suited to observe the members of your species. Men's room attendants knew more about human beings than psychiatrists. Hail the silent observer, the knower of secrets, the lavatory philosopher, servant of the toilet, who knows all and tells nothing, here at the meeting of the waters, reading the streams of bodily wastes as a seer reads entrails. Hail the one who lives in private places which are called public. All hail the one who stands at the terminal of our guts.

He turned and looked out the window, his present tense reverie angering him for a reason he couldn't understand, and thought of Wednesday night. He had gone to bed around eight-thirty, falling down and away to dreamless sleep as soon as his head found the pillow. And woke up around ten to the phone ringing. It was Anne, calling from Dublin, telling him about Terry, and Kildare. When he hung up the phone he made a fire, a big one with coal and timber, and had a glass of whiskey. Not long after that, Terry's call had come through from Kinsale. McGuffin came by and they drove down to Doolin in his black taxi to hear a late night fiddle and whistle session. They drank pints with the musicians until three and then drove back up the coast road to Moher and had a long talk back at Burke's about the raid at Kildare over the remaining Paddy, and when that was done, two bottles of warm sweet white wine. Burke told McGuffin about Terry's call.

The next day he woke at one in the afternoon on the couch in the front room of his house, all the windows open to a miraculous, sunny day. The wind toyed with the billowing curtains, the sounds of the waves echoed through the room, and looking up from the couch out the window he saw a gull hanging like a kite in a blue sky. The gatelegged table, the basket of turf, Anne's rocking chair covered with a Donegal blanket, the frame of the circular mirror over the fireplace, the television set, everything in the room seemed to be touched with stillness and radiance in the peace of a summer day in November. He thought of Terry's call again. And remembered saying yes.

He toasted bread and searched the house for a drink. He went to the pub for a pint and then hitchhiked to Ennistymon, two miles away, to McGuffin's place where he waited with Neena until the big man came in from fishing. They walked outside, leaving Neena, and McGuffin told him, "I'm with you, Martin. Don't worry, now."

"You're with me? What in hell does that mean?"

"Anything you want it to. But I'm in on this. It seems I was in on it since the day Liam Cleary was killed, doesn't it, now? Let's get a drink, and we'll figure when the boat will arrive, and what we'll do. Come on, now. A drink's the man we want."

McGuffin put his hand gently on Burke's shoulder and said, softly, "Martin, are you all right?"

Burke turned to his friend, his face concerned, questioning. They were standing together at the tiled wall, the gutter below. "Yeah. I'm all right. Yeah."

"I thought you were in a bloody coma or something, standin' starin' out the window. Neena thought you fell in."

"I was—I was just—I was—"

"Come on, man. A good feed is what you want. A little food. You can't live on fermented juices alone."

"Yes, thanks, Cyril. You're my friend, aren't you?"

McGuffin looked at him squarely. "I am and will forever be. Mother of Christ, you're hammered." He took his arm. "This way, Martin. A good meal's the thing." McGuffin led him through the noise and the bodies of the pub down the stairs and out to the gray street and the tender fall of rain. Neena took his other arm and looked searchingly into his face. Burke nodded and smiled.

Burke cast the long pole side arm. The line ran out from the spinning reel chasing the hook and wooden float in a perfect arc over the brown water, plopping just where he wanted, off the main stream at the center of the river. He watched the wooden float spin this way and that, catching a slight whirlpool before running with the flow downriver to his left. The day had changed to a breezy clear late afternoon. Two birds flew from the trees across from him and he watched their flight mirrored in the river, the sky and water one. He reeled in slowly to his spot on the bank in the rushes, just at a curve of high ground, surrounded by the brown and green fields of Clare.

Lunch in Ennis, which had begun so well, had not been a success. He had returned to something like sanity by the time they had walked into the Old Ground. It was a good hotel, with the lobby bright, the brass gleaming, and softened by the warm colors of the furniture and walls. A wood fire burned merrily in the fireplace and two well-dressed elderly women sat near it having tea poured for them from a silver pot. "We're not dressed," Neena whispered.

"Are we naked?" McGuffin asked in a loud voice, leading the way to the dining room down a narrow corridor lined in dark polished wood, setting off the expansive brightness of the dining room. It was a room of tall windows, bouquets of fresh flowers and linen. When they were seated they collected one or two stares from other diners. Neena looked in place in the room in her sweater and slacks, her hair neatly combed. But she stared with an embarrassed expression at her china plate and large napkin artfully flowering from her wine glass. Burke was rolling a cigarette over his plate, hands curled together gray and lifeless, the fingertips nicotine yellow. McGuffin, his red hair looking like he had just awakened a moment before, was signaling wildly to the waitress across the room. A group of three young couples at a round table near them had gone tomb quiet, all staring at McGuffin's waving arm. He smiled at them. "What do you have to do to get a drink in this place?" he asked the nearest to him, a young, exquisitely made-up woman.

"Cyril, please," Neena said quietly to her plate.

"*Pardon?*" the woman asked. "My Anglish ees not very—"

"*Êtes-vous française?*" McGuffin asked.

"*Oui.*"

"*En vacances?*"

"*Oui. Nous venons d'arriver de Shannon.*"

"*Bienvenus en l'Irlande!*" McGuffin said, getting up, holding her eyes with his, taking her hand and brushing his lips once on the back. Still lightly cupping her hand, he addressed the whole table, "*J'espère que vous ferez un bon séjour dans notre petit coin du monde.*"

He then chatted with them amiably while Burke and Neena watched, astonished. The waitress had arrived and McGuffin excused himself with a flourish. "We'll have some bread right away," he said, sitting down, "and the soup du jour for that hungry lookin' fellow there, and a bottle of red wine. You pick it for us, dear."

"I'll send the wine steward over."

"No need," McGuffin said. "A bottle of Ste. Emilion, tell him. Something good."

"Where did you learn French, Cyril?" Neena asked, her face bright, impressed.

"I'm not some bog man, am I? I know a thing or two. A little *español*, as well. Enough to get by, at least. Enough to keep me out of jail."

The waitress set rolls of bread in a basket on the table. "Eat some of that, Martin. It'll work wonders. Sop up all that bad booze."

"Where, Cyril?" Neena asked. "Where'd you learn it?"

"In Brittany," he said, tearing a hunk of bread apart. "Nineteen fifty-eight. I was workin' there nine months as a janitor. Didn't I ever tell you that? Bloke who owned a restaurant came here in '57. He was a Breton. They're Celtic people, did you know that? Well, your man came here the summer of '57 and I got to know him, drinkin', fishin', and he said if I ever wanted a job to come see him. And so I did. Swept out his bar and restaurant for all that time. Learned to eat, to speak the language, drink wine, and detest the French race, all at the same time." He turned to the six people and waved delicately with his hand, a signal from the baron to carry on.

The meal, which McGuffin ordered for them, checking with the French table to inquire about the quality of the dishes, was superb. Everyone was very taken with the savage redheaded Irishman with the immaculate manner, even the waitress, who looked at him as if he were a national treasure. While they were selecting pastries from the trolley and having the coffee poured, one of the young Frenchmen had brandy sent over. And before they left they all stood around the table and chatted a bit more, before wishing them all *bonne chance*.

Burke had sobered and felt good except for a headache of sizable proportions. He had only had one glass of wine, and decided to pass on the brandy. Throughout the meal, the more sober he became, the more he began to understand, not precisely because of his headache, but in a general way, the dark side of McGuffin. Burke had seen it perhaps three times in the three months he'd known him, the most recent being the flaying of Fergus just hours ago in Newmarket. He was a cruel man underneath, and the startling thing about his cruelty, which never came often or lasted very long, was the enjoyment he took in it. As Burke went from the vegetable soup to the coq au vin, he thought that McGuffin wanted to be taken on his terms alone, and whenever he was forced to become something he was not, he reacted childishly, and inflicted his confusion on people around him. With the mousse Burke saw that being misunderstood was not what turned his friend cruel, but that he had no clear understanding of himself, and his sadism was triggered by situations where he had to adapt to a new role. McGuffin was a hundred people. He would have made a splendid actor, not only because he could assume a new role like changing clothes, but because he knew the new person fully, deep down, as well as he knew his own face. Or the face the mirror gave him. When Fergus had insulted Neena, Burke thought McGuffin would just have a word with him, or tell the owner, and never drink there again. Instead he had given his barroom cowboy performance. And for those few moments, good-hearted McGuffin was gone and in his place was a cold bullyboy. The theatrics with the French were the opposite of wild Cyril, the Clare madman. But he definitely was the intelligent, charmingly eccentric man of the world that the French saw. And it was after he had taken that role, that he became a bully again, with Neena. Burke wondered, if he *was* a hundred people, why had he chosen Cyril, the man of small towns and late nights, unstructured, living life as loosely as possible? Because it was a role that let him live with a minimum of self-disgust? Because it was the easiest life? Or the most difficult?

The cruelty started early on when he interrupted Neena, who was feeling proud and enjoying herself, talking about a French restaurant in London. He broke in saying, "Who gives a fuck?" And then started a conversation with Burke about soccer. Burke was shocked and soon was asking Neena about the restaurant. But McGuffin wouldn't let up and launched a lecture on the depravity of the English race. Neena remained quiet, looking down, eating delicately. McGuffin asked her if what he'd said wasn't true, that her country was a corrupt, bloodstained, insane land. She still looked down and McGuffin looked from her to Burke and winked.

"No, I wouldn't say that, Cyril. England is my home and—"

"Home! Bloody mental asylum is more like it."

"I'm not going to argue with you."

"Did you know," McGuffin asked Burke, "that the English are pure contradiction? Or else they're pure logic. The people who developed the most versatile language are the same people who developed the best fighting dogs. The people who developed an all-encompassing code of justice also put to the sword every country they ever visited."

"Is Ireland so much better?" Neena asked, her anger rising.

"We're all only people. Just men and women going on about our lives. Why hate one another?"

McGuffin wiped béarnaise sauce from his lip and threw his napkin down. "Jesus, spare me words of peace from a Brit."

"Don't call me that, Cyril, please."

"It's what you are, isn't it?"

"It's derogatory and you know it."

He laughed. "What other way to address the people who raped my country? And who still are here, holding the six counties by force of arms. And who do everything they can to fuck the economy of the Republic. 'Ireland was Ireland when England was a pup. And Ireland will still be Ireland when England's time is up.' The sons of bitches. What should I call them? Sir? Madame?"

"We're only people—" she started, tears filming her eyes.

"People? Christ, woman, what's sacred about people? That's what the hangman says: 'I'm just a man like the rest. Doing my job.' I won't have England defended in my presence."

Burke went to the men's room. The delight McGuffin was taking in Neena's tears was too much to endure. Passing through the lobby he heard the sound of a radio coming from the gift shop, where a young man was showing two elderly people a display of lace. The radio was giving a live report from Dublin, the announcer speaking in hushed tones, describing the ceremony, presided over by the Primate of All Ireland, at the graves of the six men who had died at Kildare. He washed his face and hands, smoothed his hair, and went back.

Neena gave Burke a half smile, trying to be brave. "You know, Martin, this is a very fine Englishwoman here. She's perfect in every way but one. Her feet, Jesus, her feet smell something awful. I tell her to wash them but she won't listen."

Burke said to his smiling face, "Why don't you can it?"

"What's that?"

"Hasn't she had enough insults for one day? You made her cry, embarrassed her, isn't that enough?"

"Mother of God," McGuffin said. "Now I'm getting manners from an alcoholic." He stared at Burke. There was nothing in his eyes. Then he turned to the French table to inquire about the pastries.

When they left the restaurant, after McGuffin had over-tipped the waitress and sought out the wine steward to give him a five-pound note, and were back on the streets of Ennis, he began to grow back to himself. He put his arm around Neena, who shrugged him away, but finally she let him embrace her. "There Neena, dear, don't look so sad. See, the sun's startin' to shine. Just for you. Only for little Neena."

In the black taxi, with Neena sitting in the cane chair next to him, McGuffin said to her, "Let's take the lad fishing. What do you say, pet? You're up for some fishing, aren't you, Martin?"

"I wouldn't mind."

"Grand. We'll let Martin fish and we'll soak up some of this sun. Get the benefit. How's that?"

"Yes," Neena said. "Do you never apologize, Cyril?" Burke watched his profile, turned toward her. "Apologize? For what, love?"

Burke reeled in, wondering if he really knew what to apologize for, if he really was aware of what he'd done. All the way on the drive to the river he had been himself, soothing them, kind, making jokes as the day opened up to sun and cloud. McGuffin stopped the taxi off the coast road and they all got out to look at the view. Clare was shining. Below them the sea was wider than the world, coming in softly to boil around the rocks of Spanish Point, where a galleon from the Armada of 1588 had crashed. Behind them the town of Miltown Malbay lay a mile or more away across the fields, the church spire standing tall, twice the height of any other structure. Just there, the town of the bad bay, under the sky, in the middle of fields. To the north, near where they stood, on a rise of land over the sea, a big stone house abandoned long ago squatted with twelve windows blindly staring. On the other side of the road stern-faced cows leaned their heads on the rock fence and watched.

While McGuffin was telling Neena about the Armada, Burke left them to walk up the road to look at the monument. He had passed it many times but had never had a close look. Set in carved stone just off the road was the large iron plaque, going green around the edges, showing in relief a man standing dressed in a beret, trench coat, sturdy shoes and leggings, with a rifle slung across his shoulder and a bandolier across his breast, holding a

pistol in one hand and his other hand outstretched, one finger point-
ing up. Below the figure were words. THIS MEMORIAL HAS
BEEN ERECTED BY THE OFFICERS AND MEN OF THE
4TH BATTALION MID CLARE BRIGADE TO COMMEM-
ORATE THE GALLANT STAND MADE AT THIS SPOT
AGAINST THE FORCES OF BRITISH OPPRESSION ON
THE 22ND DAY OF SEPTEMBER 1920 AND TO HONOUR
THE MEMORY OF COMRADES WHO PAID THE SU-
PREME SACRIFICE DURING THE PERIOD 1917–1923.

The wind blew soft, as Burke read, bringing a chill from the
sea. An old man in Moher had told him the story of this place
when Burke had asked him about the monument. Three men had
waited in ambush here that day and attacked a car, killing three
British officers. The following night the Black and Tans retaliated
by burning down the town of Moher. For nights after that the
whole town slept in the fields. Any man the Tans caught was
beaten and jailed. Burke looked back up to the fierce iron man,
alone with his words.

They turned onto a farm road and stopped. McGuffin got the
pole out of the trunk for Burke, joined it together and gave him
a garden spade to dig for worms. He said he and Neena would
leave him to fish in peace. They were taking a blanket and going
up river "to get the benefit."

An hour's worth of fishing and not a nibble. Burke watched
a crowd of bugs circling lazily over the river. Were they just
born, fooled into thinking it was summer? Would they die when
the short day ended and November returned with the night? He
reeled in slowly, jigging the pole slightly, and cast back out
through the insect cloud. He thought of the lunch again, and the
masks of McGuffin. France, and the I.R.A., and how many other
identities? Suddenly he thought of the man O'Connor had told
him about that first morning in Bewley's over coffee. Conor Graham, the Irishman living in Paris. And that night in Wicklow,
Joseph Walsh telling him the same man was really Peter Farrell,
an informer. The similarity of France and the I.R.A. and the
twin identities shocked Burke, standing on the bank. Could Mc-
Guffin be trusted? It was the first time since O'Connor's call that
Burke had thought about any of them. He hadn't been sober long
enough to really think about it. They were coming, coming here

to Clare. Cleary had trusted McGuffin. So would he. Who else was there, really?

The sun was resting in high pink clouds to the west. Already there was a bite to the wind feathering the surface of the river. Burke reeled in for the last time, set free the worms and started to walk back upriver and toward the black taxi, his head full of details about the arrival. Off to his right, on a grassy bank above the river, partially hidden by the trees, he saw something white, moving. The last time he'd fished here there was a family of wild swans cruising the river. He crept closer and from behind a tree he saw Neena and McGuffin lying on the blanket near the running river. McGuffin was lying back, his forearm over his eyes, his pants down around his knees, and Neena lying curled, facing away from him, her arm curved around his belly, half-sitting half-reclining, her head bobbing over his erection. Burke felt blood quickening him. McGuffin took his arm from his eyes and placed both hands on her head. His face seemed in concentrated pain as she took her mouth away and let one hand roll his balls in her palm, her other hand scratching through his red pubic hair. She stroked him once or twice. McGuffin said something and Burke saw Neena smile, and turn back to him, stroking, wetting her thumb with her tongue and running it lightly across the tip. She turned and took all of him in her mouth again, rapidly bobbing up and down. McGuffin, his eyes still closed, bucked his hips up and she gagged, took him from her mouth and began to lick.

Burke crept away, up through the field to the taxi, feeling full of light and life. He crawled up on the roof of the taxi, and lay down, his head resting on the broken roof light, looking at pink and purple clouds stationary above him. The sight of Neena bent to her secret work thrilled him. It was the first time in a long time that he had felt anything like it.

Die Freiheit arrived near 1 A.M., Sunday. McGuffin and Burke had left Neena and McGuffin's place at around ten and had gone to Burke's house to watch "Match of the Day" on television. Arsenal was winning by five goals at half-time and McGuffin was already counting his money. They had pint bottles of Guinness brought from the pub, but Burke had only had one and was slowly nursing the second. At the start of play in the second half McGuffin was bemoaning the fact that Liam Brady, Frank Stapelton and David O'Leary, all Irishmen, were forced to play for an English squad because of the fabulous salaries they offered. Burke decided he'd tease him. "It's an English game, after all, Cyril. Why don't you watch Gaelic football?"

"Gaelic football?" McGuffin asked, his eyes still on the set, watching Brady bringing the ball up through the Nottingham Forest defense. Brady, the kid from Dublin, the Irish International, the best soccer player at midfield in the world when he was healthy, shredding the defense elegantly now, playing give and go with O'Leary. "That's not sport. That's like watching some kids' game in the street where they make up the rules as they go along. This, this—" he pointed, then went quiet as Brady sidestepped a defender to the left of the goal, drew the keeper out, and nonchalantly lifted the ball over him across the goal mouth where Stapelton charged and headed it into the open net. McGuffin jumped straight up out of his chair bellowing, knocking his glass of stout across the room. He did a quick dance and then stopped to watch the replay, kissing the set when Brady once again lifted the cross to Stapelton.

Burke went to the window. The wide bay lay calm under the clear night. Up the coast to his right the lights of Liscannor stretched in a thin line and above the town the headlights of a single car winked along the coast road. He looked out at the bay again. Orion stood straddling his piece of sky, the three stars of his belt outlining the waist of the hunter. Burke saw two rolling lights moving from the south into the open mouth of the bay. Clearing Spanish Point and moving north. "They're here," he said, surprising himself with his calmness.

"What'd you say?"

"They're here. That's the yacht."

McGuffin joined him at the window. "Might be. Let's get a look from the glasses." Burke followed him out through the house to the back door where the black taxi stood. McGuffin got a pair of field glasses from under the front seat and they went around to the front of the house, to the hill of deep grass, thick and soft as carpet, above the sea. McGuffin took the glasses out and handed the case to Burke. He squinted and focused. "Have a look," he said, handing the binoculars over. Burke focused on the black sea, the waves clawing slowly like a cat at play, and then saw the tall mast and sail and the long low line of the yacht. At the bow light he saw a standing figure. He took his eyes away from the glasses and watched with McGuffin as *Die Freiheit* proceeded slowly, royally into the empty bay. "Let's go," McGuffin said.

Burke sat in the cane chair. McGuffin turned the engine over and brought out two pistols wrapped in greasy cloth from under the seat. He handed one to Burke. "That lad is a .38 Smith and Wesson Police Special. Bought in Liverpool in 1956. And this is his twin here. Two great Irish patriots, Mr. Smith and Mr. Wesson."

"They look mean enough," Burke said, staring at the black bulk of gun in the dark.

"Oh," McGuffin said, shifting into reverse, looking over his shoulder and backing out to the road, "these lads will hear your case."

All the way down the hill to Moher, Burke watched the lights moving in the bay. He saw McGuffin sneaking glances as well. Outside the town they took the curving coast road north, past the golf links next to the sea, and out the road through the marsh land of the bay where black pools stood stagnant in black rushes. Across the water, like a dream, the lights and dark form stopped moving.

At the small dock at Liscannor, McGuffin shut the engine of the black taxi and Burke followed him over to a shed where outboard motors stood clamped in a row, the shafts and propellers resting in fresh water. He lifted his Mercury 20-horsepower motor out and Burke followed him down the pier to his eleven-foot-long rowboat. He stood the motor up and stopped walking, looking out. "I hope they're patient and don't signal. Give me a hand here, Martin."

Burke helped him into the boat with the motor and listened to him explaining how to run it as he clamped it to the stern. "Now, you'll come back here and I'll pilot them down the coast. Do you know the old big house on the hill past the Point?"

"Yeah."

"You'll drive the taxi down there. There's a deep stream just south of the house. We should be able to fit her in there nice and snug. How big is she, did you say?"

"I think forty–fifty feet."

"Well, I'll get 'em down there and you be waiting. Now, let's see these friends of yours."

How quickly he had changed, Burke thought. He had explained everything calmly and thoroughly. He was excited, Burke knew, but he didn't show it.

Burke cast off and pushed away from the dock with an oar. McGuffin pulled at the Mercury and on the third pull it stuttered and caught. He idled down, swung the boat around and they motored out into the calm bay. The breeze was cold and Burke turned up the collar of his pea coat, feeling through the heavy wool the weight of the pistol. *Die Freiheit* crept closer. Twenty yards away they could make out the white hull swinging away at anchor, and figures on the deck. McGuffin circled *Die Freiheit* slowly and cut the engine, letting the boat ride softly into the yacht. A line was thrown and McGuffin secured the boat before scrambling up and then reaching down to give Burke a hand.

"Welcome aboard, Martin," Gudrun said holding him by the elbow as he found his feet on the slick wood. Her hair blew gently from her face, her smile a beacon in the darkness. O'Connor came forward and put his arms around Burke. It was an embarrassing moment. Burke had his hand out to shake, and O'Connor's embrace caught him off guard. "Marty," he said. "Goddamn, it's good to see you." McGuffin stood, hands on hips, looking about the deck. Deirdre sat on the furled sail. "Hello, yank," she said.

"Dee-Dee."

"That's not you, Cyril."

"It is," McGuffin said grinning. "It's been a long time, Deirdre."

Walsh came up, walking stiffly. "Thank you for being here, Mr. Burke. Will you introduce us?" he motioned toward McGuffin.

"He's a friend of mine, Cyril McGuffin."

"He's all right, Chief," Deirdre said from her perch. "He's one of us. He served with Liam."

"What does he know?" Walsh asked Burke.

"What I do."

"Welcome, Cyril."

"It's me should welcome you, Mr. Walsh."

"I suggest we move," Gudrun said. She turned to McGuffin. "Do you know these waters?"

"As well as any man in Ireland. You're the skipper here?"

"My name is Gudrun Böhm."

He shook her hand, and held it a moment longer than necessary. "McGuffin at your service, Captain."

"Let's take a look at the charts," she said, turning away. "Mr. Walsh, will you join us?" They went to the lighted cockpit and stood around the chart table, Gudrun questioning and McGuffin answering.

Burke sat next to Deirdre. "How was the trip?"

"Bloody awful. I can't swim, you know. This is the closest to suicide I've ever been."

Burke began to roll a cigarette. O'Connor said, "Hey, no smoking here, man. There's enough shit down below to put us in orbit for good."

There was an odd sense of quiet about them, Burke thought. A sense of solidarity between the two of them that made them cool and shy of outsiders. He looked out across the water to the thin line of lights marking Liscannor, and moved his view south to the one streetlight of Moher. Above that, just a spot of light, a weak star in the sky, was the light from the front room of his house. O'Connor had said orbit. Why did that stick? Did I read that word today, or dream it last night? O'Connor and Deirdre seemed content with the silence, but Burke was uneasy. "See that light just there?"

"Yeah," O'Connor said.

"That's my place."

"How far," Deirdre asked, "is it away from the sea?"

"It's right on it."

"Shite," she said.

O'Connor laughed. "You won't let on that you started to like it these last few days, will you?"

"I've hated every blessed minute of it."

"She's a great sailor, Marty. Is that really your place? It looks like you finally got rich."

"Only forty quid a month," he said, looking out.

"No shit? How's Anne like it?"

"She hated it. She's gone, Terry. Back to Dublin."

O'Connor touched his arm. "I'm sorry."

Burke shrugged, and continued to look out. "Yeah." Deirdre looked over to the cockpit. Walsh was talking to both of them. "Christ," she said, "Napoleon crossed the Alps with less planning."

"What is the plan?" Burke asked.

Deirdre got up and went near the side. She turned back. "We'll find a place tonight to hide this boat and then we'll all stay with you for the night. Joe and I will get transport and go to Dublin tomorrow. Terry and Gudrun will stay with you."

Burke nodded. "Isn't that kind of dangerous? Going to Dublin now?"

"Dangerous? Yes. I'd say it was dangerous. But we have to contact the Provisionals and finalize the alliance. We'll get in touch with them in Dublin and then meet them out here, somewhere in the Burren." Deirdre was set to say more but she looked at O'Connor sitting, staring out at the water, and saw his eyes looking out of a mask, concentrating, the same way he had looked in Slattery's pub the night after the raid. He was a prisoner looking through the bars of a cell, unknowable, alone.

She went to the cockpit and joined the group. Burke sat with O'Connor in the uneasy silence that Terry didn't seem to mind.

"Did some killing in Kildare, huh, Terry? How does it feel?"

O'Connor continued to look out. "That's past, Marty. That's all over and done."

"I guess there will be some more killing, huh?"

"We didn't bring this stuff all the way up here for the hell of it."

"Did it ever cross your mind that this isn't your fight? Sometimes I can't get over how far from home I am. Or even where home is any more."

"This is my fight. And you're part of it now. Don't ask those kinds of questions any more about home or reasons. These people aren't a debating society, Marty. They have a lot at stake, and you're just a body to them. A soldier. Okay?"

"Okay," Burke said. The deck rolled easily with the waves, running under them and away, toward the dark shore. He looked over to the cockpit where McGuffin was speaking, pointing to the chart, while the others looked on.

CHAPTER 12

Le Chat Perdu

While I was exercising this morning I thought there was something not quite right with me. And it's because of the cat, something to do with the cat. He was a nice one, a big black tom, strutting about the place, good company he was, soft purring machine, and the swish of tail. Why did they take him away? Why am I writing this? They'll see it, I know, but do I care? I might even give it to them. It's something to do. Mexico will be as good a place as any to come to the end. Do they speak French there, any of them, I wonder? Maximilian, no, he was a German, wasn't he? The French Foreign Legion were there, weren't they? For what?

We're off to Dublin in the green in the green
With our bayonets glittering in the sun
And we're off to join the I.R.A.
To the rattle of a Thompson gun.

Dublin, you've taken my youth, my manhood, my end, and now my cat. Dub-a-lin. Dublin, dirty and dear. My head won't let me be, there's such nonsense running through me, de fiddle de dee, through me. Think of France. And Paris. I learned the language in no time the first time I came. Suffering Jesus, what a headache I've got. A real blinder. This writing helps me a little, but when I take the pen from the page—Christ! it's bad this time. Maybe Spanish will be easy, too. I have an easy time with languages. Time. No time, first time, last time, all aboard! End time.

I don't know how it will end. That's not true. I know how it will end, I don't know where it will end, and what I fear is that it will end here, in Ireland, a country I fought for nearly all my life and now I hate. Perhaps I always hated it. Just reading these

228

lines I'm amazed at how I lie, even with this—this what? Journal? Confession? Apologia? I've built my life on lies. They're stronger brick than truth. Why do I say "it will end" when what I'm talking about is my life, my death. They're out there, somewhere in cruel Ireland, waiting to kill me. It's part of the game, part of the deal, and me, who wanted to share in the history of my country, to play a role, have found one, finally, the role of traitor. And what a fine historical part to play! The English couldn't have held Ireland for the centuries they did without people like me. Lord Edward Fitzgerald, Tone, Bold Robert Emmet, the darlin' of Erin, they all were betrayed. I lay down my life for the Emerald Isle. Yes, I join quite a club, I take my place, not where I thought I'd end up, but I have mattered, after all, in the end. This is nonsense, again. Traitor to what? Traitor to thugs, hounds who love blood? Like I love it?

Traitor, informer, you know how you meet your end, your destiny. From the first thought, not even act, but thought, you buy your end. How the game is played. A dead cock doesn't crow, fal di die doe. I'm not crowing. I'm playing the game, but I don't want to stop bullets here in Ireland, Jesus no, make it France. But they won't let me go there. Costello says something about Mexico. A hot place. An Irishman goes mad in hot climates, that I know.

> So I gave up my boyhood
> To drill and to train
> To play my own part in
> The Patriot Game.

More rubbish.

I know it's Sunday. I don't count days here or ask my keepers. And exactly how long I've been here, I don't know. Quite awhile. Gaol is nothing new to me. Even a strange one like this, where I'm the only prisoner. But this is not prison, they tell me, no, they're keeping me under lock and key for my protection. Do you believe it? The isolation, though. I must admit it is getting to me. That's why with the cat gone it's that much worse. But I read and I exercise twice a day, and do some writing like this. And I wait.

They don't give me newspapers. Why? But I know it's Sunday.

It has the feel of Sunday, the lonely feel of the Sabbath, when all you can do is have a lie-on, a bit of a fry, the papers after mass. Gudrun loved that, when I introduced the Irish Sunday lie-on to her, and the sausage and fried egg and grilled tomato with the papers. They don't have any of the big Sunday papers in France, so I used to go to that kiosk in St.-Germain-des-Pres and get the Times *and the* Observer *and bring them back to the flat, and lay around with her half the day. Gudrun. She once loved me, I think. I wonder if they got her yet. If I could just once more see her naked, have one more sexy Sunday, see that sharp little face shudder in orgasm, her legs white around my waist and the two of us staring in the mirror next to the bed, staring at our pornography, a performance. Raising her leg to see me moving in and out thick and hard in and out reaching down touching me as I move in and out moving the newspapers in the rumpled sheets off the bed for a better view and reaching down touching me as I move in and out her face detached clinical wetting her lips letting her mouth feel the pleasure but keeping her eyes wide open aware, a greedy kitten. And me looking from her mirrored face to my face and always being startled at the sight of that other man there looking at him the way you do a man in a dirty movie, what's his name? what did he have for breakfast? that man there fucking the good-looking blonde, who is he anyway?*

This nonsense! It's because they've taken the cat from me. Why? Although this prison is the best I've ever spent time in, with two rooms all to myself at the back of the house, and good food, and any books I want, and privacy, and it's clean, it's the cruelest. I think I'm not quite right anymore. I think something has changed in me. The bastards. They've had me for months, it must be months now, when will they let me go to my end? Months. First Les Baumets where the deal was struck, then the Brits took me to that place in Essex, and then shipped me here, and that little shit Murray. Haven't seen him in awhile. I wonder, did they sack him? Costello, the new one, I hate worse than Murray. Not true. Costello, with his Jew hair, kinky blond Jew hair. Oh he's a sharp one, make no mistake, he's a tricky one. Why did they take the cat? There's something behind all this.

Think of France, of Paris! Why did I have a need to betray, I wonder? And it was a need. I think it had something to do with O'Connor, the American. And Gudrun, certainly. Telling Murray

*about her, describing her, betraying her, it was all so odd! It was
sexual. I could feel myself flushing, growing as I told. Think of
Paris! I could have lived there, could have gone into business there,
made some money, but I couldn't, Jesus, I couldn't stay out of it,
could I? And also, what else was there left for me to do, but betray? If I refused to answer, who would benefit? Not the I.R.A.
I'd been away too long. Gudrun and O'Connor would benefit if
I hadn't talked, surely. But I didn't care anymore. I was with her
if I betrayed her, does that make sense? Sense! There's no place for
sense anymore.*

*And now as I lie here
My body all holes
I think of those traitors
Who bartered and sold.*

*When I broke gaol at Crumlin Road they told me to take a rest,
go to France again, retire. They gave me money and threw me out.
The I.R.A. I Ran Away. But they told me to go. To rest. And
when I had that arms deal set up in Amsterdam and told them we
could get it cheap, their man came and said, We? Ah, no, Petey.
You're not a member of the club anymore. Stay out of it. We
won't protect you anymore. And what was I to do? It was my
whole life, going down the drain. They didn't want me anymore.
But it all changed. MacStiofáin gone, and anyone from Dublin was
looked at as a poet and not a fighter, no it was all the Northern
Command, you couldn't move in the Army unless you had the
Ulster accent. Why go on? Because I loved it. You can't betray
something you don't love. Is that true? I didn't betray anything at
first, though. In fact, when I was drawn back to it all, I never said
I was I.R.A. No, I said I was I.S.A., just a slight change of alphabet
soup, but an enormous change. I couldn't betray the old outfit, no,
if they had drummed me out, I'd stay out. And anyway, the Europeans all liked the I.S.A. better because it was "political," not solely
nationalistic. Jesus, it makes you want to puke. But how easy it is
to learn all the right political expressions. How easy. And they all
loved the Irishman, all the French and Germans. Loved me as much
as the Arabs, even more because I had a sense of humor. And also,
no white person can really love an Arab after all, or vice versa.
But they loved me, because they were all amateurs then, playing at*

*revolution, blowing up department stores, striking a blow for—
what? The silly little sods had no idea. They just loved the* idea
*of revolution, while I love revolution because it is something I am
good at. How they loved me, Conor (which is what I called myself), who had done time in English gaols, had fought the forces
of imperialism all my life, not with hot words, my friend, but cold
lead, and was a trained bad man. I couldn't stay away.*

*I remember the day I met her. It was Régis Debray's apartment
on the Île de la Cité. Régis had come back to Paris after serving his
time in South America and I used to see him from time to time.
Régis was a good skin. He knew what prison walls felt like, doing
three years in a Bolivian gaol. He didn't regret it, though, and like
all ex-cons he came back with the hard discipline prison gives you,
that sureness and calmness that, if you make the most of it, prison
gives you. A good skin, like I said. Mad though, chasing after Major
Guevara and his band of louts and cornerboys, the only "soldiers"
he could find at the end. At least that's the way I see it. Régis paid
for his thrills, to be sure, looking for Guevara like a pilgrim
searching for a piece of the true cross. He'd gone a bit sour on
the major by the time he hit Paris, but still worshiped him. All
in all, Ché was a good one, I suppose. Yes, a good soldier but a
jackass of an officer, trying to organize a group of thickheaded
peasants who didn't want him. But a good soldier. Perhaps he was
just looking for his end. He found it, is the one thing sure.*

*Anyway, Régis was good company. A beautiful flat there near
the Palais de Justice. There was always good crack around Régis.
And that day we were talking about guns. Régis was always wanting pistols. I think they were just for himself, but he would always say, I have a friend who needs a side arm, can you help?
Could I help! In those days, if you wanted a gun, I was the man.
It was easy to work Paris and Hamburg and Amsterdam for arms.
Easy for me because I had served as a guerrilla all my life and
understood to live you have only one flag: caution. I could size
someone up quickly, I was always discreet, and knew from my
experience as quartermaster in Derry in 1970 that for results always have cash on hand. That's the way these swine like to
operate, and who can blame them? If you pay up front they remember you. If you don't have the money, they remember you,
too, and you become fish chowder in Marseilles. Where—? oh,
Gudrun.*

Proud little bitch, she was. She was there one day and Régis said, My friend needs an etc.

I quoted a price and told him I'd have it in a week.

Gudrun said, I can get it for half that, tomorrow.

Debray laughed, I remember. Well, Conor, what do you say to that?

And I said, It's the trend, Régis. The supermarket is running the shopkeeper out of business. It's German efficiency taking over the world.

And she laughed at that. I saw her again at Régis' place and we talked. I could see the admiration in her eyes when I told her my tale. Was I just trying to fuck her? Was that it? No, there was something else, besides her beauty, or better, within her beauty, something naturally wild, the intelligence and killing power of a leopard.

I'm back now to this drivel. I was interrupted by one of my keepers. There's always two in the house, they take shifts. This one, Sullivan, a big lad from Kerry, I think, by the sound of him, brought my grub. Is it Sunday, Sully? I asked him.

Saturday, he said, setting the tray down. Porridge and eggs and tea. Good food in this gaol. Have I said that?

He looked at these notes. A letter home, Peter?

I ignored him. Why don't you let me go to mass? I said. This is still a Catholic country, isn't it?

Mass? And you excommunicated?

Who says I'm excommunicated?

He smiled his Kerry smile, the worthless fucks, they think that all wit and humor hails from Skibbereen. Stupid farmers, the lot. It must be rough, Sully, I said, having to eat real food now you're in the city. I'll wager you miss the old spuds and cabbage and other fine shit you're used to.

Do you want any new books, Peter?

I want a bible, I said.

A bible, Sully says, and writes it down in his notebook. Don't let it go cold, he says, and leaves me. He's gone and I forgot to ask for paracetamol. A good hypo of morphine straight into the top of my head is what I need. Or a bullet just behind the ear. Ah, that'd do it. Click, click. Boom. All gone. The end.

I didn't ask him about the cat. Whenever I do they ignore me or make a joke. What a fine cat he was, too. Good company.

Perhaps they're trying psychological torture. Idiots, I've been worked on by experts, the British Fucking Army, and they don't come any better than that.

Mexico. That's what the Jew Costello told me the last time I saw him. Mexico. It's death. Death for me.

I walked away, just walked away on that dock at Hamburg and left them there. Because after all of it, the planning, the idea to run the guns into Ireland, and link with the I.S.A., I just couldn't go through with it, I couldn't bear, finally, seeing Ireland again. And here I am. I don't know how they found me. I went to the door of the hotel in Port La Gelene, thinking it was the maid. I was living well, I still had the money from the bank job in Cologne (how O'Connor was impressed by that!). I opened the door and there was this Englishman sticking a bloody pistol in my ear. I was in England before he removed it. And then here, to holy Ireland. God, don't let me die in Ireland. Please, not here.

And now I think of those bombings I did in Germany. What for? A blow against British imperialism? God, no. It was just to be working again. Doing what you're good at, impressing the Germans and the French. That's all. A "glorious failure" is what I am.

No more he'll hear the seagull cry
O'er the murmuring Shannon tide,
For he fell beneath the Northern sky,
Brave Hanlon at his side.

Informing on the American, O'Connor, I wished I hadn't done that. But I did and the hell with him. I liked him, though. A good one, cold as the eyes of a bishop, he was. He must've reminded me of myself when I was younger, learning the trade. Quiet, studious, ready to fight. Like all Americans, or the Irish-Americans, he wanted to get to Ireland, to see it, to feel it under his feet. I gave him the usual seventy-five varieties of horseshit about the place, like every Irishman in a foreign land, slobbering on about dear Erin, the sunsets and rainbows, salmon jumping through the mist, dark Rosaleen and Cathlin ni Houlihan, the four green fields and all the rest of the flapjaw too ra loo ra loo ra. He ate it up with a spoon until one night we were in a little dive in Montparnasse, a place where you could hear the Breton lads playing the bagpipes, and I was drunk, going on about the pubs of Dublin, cursing the English race, and he said, Goddamn, Conor. (I was Conor then, am I Peter now?) Goddamn, Conor, the yank says, you sound just like Third Avenue to me.

What? says I.

That shit you're running past me will buy you a drink in New York, but not here.

Had to laugh, really. Terry was all right. Taught me to ride a motorcycle. Ah, that's the way to capture the fluff, the girls go wild over you on a motorcycle. I went with him that summer to Belgium for a race. The three of us went. I knew Terry was into Gudrun, but I was never jealous. Gudrun was the kind of woman I just wanted to be around, and I knew she'd drop me if I pulled any rank. Anyway Terry ran the race and got wiped out. Finished fiftieth or some bloody thing. After the race I said, What happened, boy?

He says, I'll be back. Just being on the track with these riders taught me a lot.

Like I said, always learning, always watching. To hell with him, trust no one, he should have known that. But that was a good summer, à trois.

I've just checked this room, the one I use to exercise and read and write and found no trace of the cat. Then I went into the other room, the one I sleep in, and there's no trace of him. There's something quite wrong, but what? I think I know, it's like a name on the tip of your tongue that you can't quite remember. The cat. I think he's gone. The cat is dead. Long life to him. The Death of the Cat. What is cat in Spanish? Gato? Something like that. If my head would stop its pounding.

Sullivan just came and left again. He brought the bible. There you are, Peter, he says.

It's not the King James version, is it? says I, turning the book in my hands.

Like you said, this is a Catholic country. You're going to see Mr. Costello this evening.

The Jew again.

Why do you call him that? Sully says, grinning as wide as a turf bog.

Because that's what he is.

He is not and you know it.

I know some things, Sully. I know you've taken my cat.

Will you stop about the cat, Peter? he says, innocent as the dawn.

I just stared at him. The big farmer. Finally, I said, Can I have some aspirin, Sully?

The head again, is it?

Like someone drivin' nails into my skull.

I'll get some for you. You might try turning out the lights and lying down. Give yourself a break from the writing there.

Don't tell me how to live.

Right. Aspirin on the way. And he left me.

The aspirin hasn't helped. It hurts so much I can't remember feeling good. And these pages haven't helped either. Sully was right about that. I'll end this. If I could only end other things as easily. But they'll do it for me, out there in cruel Ireland, waiting, the rules must be followed, they'll help me out there. Why do I write this, this epitaph? I'll give this to the Jew tonight. See what he says. It might amuse him.

Finis.

As the minister was walking in the fairway up to his ball, gauging the distance to the eighteenth hole, he saw Garrett Costello standing just to the side of the green, holding a briefcase, his suit coat flapping behind him. Strange man, the minister thought. Efficient, though. A leader. Could do with a haircut. Or have it straightened. But a good man. Easier to handle than Murray. Refuses to have a bodyguard. The minister wasn't too proud to have a bodyguard. He had three, in fact. His caddy this morning, as usual, was carrying a pump shotgun in the golf bag. And two other men, dressed in bright golf clothes, keeping a distance of twenty yards, were also armed.

He had had a good round. Sunday morning when he teed off at seven he had the course to himself. Now at nine he could see other golfers in the neighboring fairways. A cold, dull day for golf. If he could reach the green with a two iron. But was that enough club? He'd never had any accuracy with the fairway woods. But it was good to use them. "I'll take the three wood, Michael."

"Three wood it is, sir," the young man said, slipping off the tasseled wool sock on the wood, which the minister's wife had knitted, and handing him the club by the shaft. The caddy, who was the minister's personal guard and servant, had never been on a golf course before his job with the minister. But since coming into his employ he'd bought a set of used clubs and was out every chance he got at the public course. A fine game, he thought, the sport of gentlemen. He'd love to have a go with the old man some day. But that would have to be later, after he left this position. His job was to protect the man, not shoot golf with him. And besides, he wasn't quite good enough to take him on now. The minister said, "Ah, to hell with it. Give me the two iron there, Mike."

"Is that enough club, sir?"

"Well, it'll have to be." He set himself, wiggled his hips and swung quickly and cleanly through the ball, driving it up, white against the gray clouds, falling in a soft curve, dropping away onto the lip of the green, rolling forward and stopping.

"Well played, sir," Michael said.

"That's the club," the minister said, walking to the green. The two other men followed, keeping their distance.

Garrett watched the group approach, wondering why golfers chose such strangely colored clothes. The minister came up the rise of the green, Michael beside him carrying the bulky red leather bag. The other two guards came up, one walking past him, nodding and going into the clubhouse, looking side to side and up at the roof. "Morning, Garrett," the minister called across the green. Garrett waved, but said nothing. Didn't golfers prefer quiet? "Now, Michael, tend that flag if you will because I'm going to drop it right dead center." Michael handed him the putter and waited for the other guard to mind the golf bag. They all watched, silent, as the minister took his time, squatting down behind the ball, holding his club out in front of him as a sight, and then stepping up. He took two practice swings, addressed the ball, and stroked it. They all followed the ball, skimming across the green. Michael pulled the pin and the ball rimmed around the cup and shot back a foot in the opposite direction. The minister was bent sideways, still trying to coax the ball in with his body. "Hard luck, sir," Michael said. The minister stepped up and holed it one-handed. He handed the putter to Michael and came striding across the green. "Garrett, good of you to come."

"Minister."

They walked along the path of hard rubber matting to the porch of the clubhouse, which was also floored in rubber matting.

A group of men were putting on golf spikes. A middle-aged man, dressed in lime-colored clothes from his shoes to his hat, caught the minister's eye. "Oh, hello, Bob," the minister said, going over to him.

"Shoot well, minister?"

"Not at all bad. But I could shoot this course in my sleep. You're with Maurice today?"

"Yes. I'm hoping one day soon to be able to come on my own and not as a guest."

"Right," the minister said shortly. "Oh, excuse me. Garrett Costello, Bob Fitzwilliam."

They nodded.

"Were you playing, Garrett?"

"No," he said, holding his briefcase with both hands in front of him. He hated people who used his Christian name the first sentence they spoke to him. Something vulgar about it, an invasion of privacy. American influence.

"No," the minister was saying. "Garrett is a policeman, Bob. He doesn't find the time for play. That it, Garrett?"

"Not when I work for you, sir." They both gave laughs totally devoid of amusement. Another hate: being charming, or going through the motions of being charming. Charm as ritual. He was doing a lot more of that lately with this new position.

"If you could put in a word for me at the next meeting," Bob said. "Just a word from you would—"

"Well, now," the minister interrupted, "no politicking on Sunday, Bob, that's my motto." He grabbed a good handful of his lime-colored arm, and added softly, "I'll have to check the list over, though. Maurice is sponsoring you?"

"He is."

"Well, we'll see. Have a good round."

As the minister led Garrett in through the high-ceilinged main room, he whispered, "That's Bob Fitzwilliam of Aer Lingus. The chairman."

Garrett nodded.

"What I like about this club," the minister went on in the same conspiratorial tone, "is no matter how much bloody money you have you still have to queue like everyone else to get in. Here now, I've reserved the card room for our chat."

It was a wide dark room, oak paneled, crowded with solid tables

bordered in leather and covered in green felt. Garrett put his briefcase on the table and took a seat where the minister motioned. The
chair was covered in soft brown leather. There was a warm smell
of liquor and wood smoke about the room. The minister took his
cap off, tossed it on the table, and ran a hand over his bald head.
Garrett noted his deep tan, and remembered some gossip about him.
A house in Spain, on the sea, with a Spanish mistress. "Will you
have something, Garrett? I can get you a drink here. A g and t?
Whiskey?"

"Cup of tea, if you have it."

"Oh, we do, we do! Anything you want. Good man. If you'd
wanted a drink I'd have to sack you on the spot," he laughed.
Again it was humorless, like coughing. "Ah, here's the man."
Michael entered and brought a large tumbler of whiskey and set
it before the minister. "And a pot of tea for Mr. Costello, Mike."

"Pot of tea," and he walked out.

He ran his finger around the rim of the Waterford glass. "I never
enjoy whiskey as much as after a good round. Or a bad one, for
that matter."

"Which was it this morning?"

"Oh, three over par. Do you play? I'm sorry if—"

"No, I've never played," Garrett said. "I wouldn't know which
end of the club to use."

"Well, the one with the wrapping around the end, the grip, that's
what you hold."

Garrett stared at him, and then smiled. The minister laughed
again. "My wife read a cookbook once that began, 'If you're the
type of person who can't boil water, this is the first lesson. Put
water in a pot and place it over heat. When the water is agitated,
you've boiled it.' I thought that quite good."

"Yes," Garrett said. "Quite good."

"Here's your tea, now." Michael set a pot of tea and a cup and
saucer on the table.

"Oh, get the man some milk and sugar, Mike, for God's sake."

"Sorry, sir."

"This is fine," Garrett said. "I take it black."

"You're sure?"

"Yes, thank you."

"We won't be disturbed, Michael?"

"No, sir."

The minister waited until he had gone before lifting his glass and toasting. "*Sláinte*, Garrett."

Garrett toasted with his teacup. "*Sláinte*," and took a sip. Wasn't that bad luck? he thought. Or was it only toasting with water? The minister set the crystal glass on the table. "By God, there's nothing like it to drive away the bad taste of Saturday night from you. Now, right to the business at hand. I want to settle this bloody Farrell situation straight away."

Garrett opened his briefcase, "Yes, sir, I've—"

"Did you talk to the Mexican embassy, see Ramirez?"

"I did. There's no problem there."

"Fine. We'll take his passport, set up the pension for him and get him to hell out of here in a week's time."

"Yes, sir," Garrett said. "I have some questions about it, however. I saw him just last evening. He's been writing."

"Writing? Writing whom?"

Garrett pulled the sheets of paper from his case. "Not letter writing, it's—well, I think you should have a look. Do you read French?"

"No," the minister said sourly, and took another sip.

"He wrote it in longhand in French and gave it to me yesterday. I had it translated and typed. It's a rather loose translation, I was told. He peppered it with Irishisms. Here, if you'll read this, minister." He handed the stapled sheets across the table. The minister took out his glasses and began to read. He flipped the first page over and scanned the second. Then he tossed the pages on the table. "Jesus Christ, man," he said, putting away his glasses. "I have better things to do of a Sunday morning than read nonsense like that. The man's an eejit."

"I wouldn't say that. Did you read the part about the cat?"

"Yes. What of it?"

"He never had a cat, sir. Never."

"Well, what of it?"

Garrett sat back. "He's ill. To the point of being suicidal, I believe. He's asked to see a priest and attend mass."

"Out of the question. Absolutely out of the question. He's an eejit or he's playing games with himself, that's all."

"In the illegal arms markets in Paris and Amsterdam, Farrell was known as *le Chat*. That's French for 'the Cat.'"

The minister took a sip of whiskey and waved his hand at the last phrase. The alcohol gave his mouth the look of disgust. "Garrett. The man is either playing a game with you or he does have a slate loose. He's suicidal, what of it? It would solve our problem, I would think. But let's get him to Mexico."

Garrett collected the sheets of paper and put them in his briefcase. He adjusted the frames of his glasses, and quickly patted his springy hair over his ears. "Do we, sir, really desire to send an ill man to a foreign country which is friendly to us? We can't, for one thing, guarantee what he'll stir up there."

"That's entirely up to the Mexicans. As long as he never enters Ireland or the U.K. or any E.E.C. country, I don't give a damn if he thinks he's Napoleon or runs naked through the streets. Mexican streets, that is."

"Beyond our security, sir, what about the man himself?"

"I'm not following you."

"Don't we have some moral obligation to him?"

"No, we don't. Is that clear enough?"

"He *has* helped us," Garrett said.

"Enough," the minister held up his hands. "Within the week I want him out of Ireland. See Ramirez again and finalize it. Do you have the other report yet?"

"No, sir. But I have this." He took out two typed pages stapled together and handed them across. The minister put on his glasses and began to read. "Grand," he murmured, turning the page. He read the second page and then looked up. "It's a start, at least. Well done."

"As you say, a start, but I don't think much will come of it."

"Do you have a confession from this—this—" he glanced at the page.

"Coughlin. Phillip Coughlin."

"Did he sign a confession?"

"He did," Garrett said, handing over a single typed page.

"Grand. How did you find him?"

"Simple procedure. We interrogated everyone at Mountjoy connected to the convoy. He started confessing at the first question."

The minister finished reading, took off his glasses and leaned back in the leather chair, swirling the whiskey around his glass. "Can I release this to the press?"

"I wouldn't, no, sir. As you can see, he's had no contact with the I.S.A. since 4 November. He seems to be a good man who made a tragic mistake out of some foolish notion he was serving his brother, one Michael Coughlin, an Official I.R.A. man killed in Belfast at Christmas '69. He's never had any political connections or motivations. I'd like to try and turn him so if he ever receives any communication from the I.S.A. he can relay the information to us."

"Very good. Dangle an accessory to murder in front of his face for insurance."

"Yes, sir."

"Now, what about the other report on the American?"

"I'm sending a man out to New York tomorrow to get information on O'Connor. N.Y.P.D. have no record of him. Neither do the F.B.I. My man will poke around and see if there's anything there."

"I want these bastards badly, Garrett. There's pressure, do you know that? All sorts of pressure. And I'm not just talking about the newspapers."

"I want them as much as you."

"Well," the minister said, taking a final sip, "that's what I want to hear. I asked you by today because from now on I want a personal report from you every day. Every day until these animals are brought to Dublin in a cage."

"Yes, sir."

"You've done marvelous work stepping into Murray's shoes. He was a one-man band over at Special Branch, I know. I know how difficult it is to replace so-called irreplaceable men. From what I see, you've done splendidly. But the honeymoon is over, Garrett. As of now. I'm going to be on you like a headmaster until we get satisfaction."

"Yes sir."

"Have you had breakfast? We do a good one here Sundays."

"Thank you, sir, but I should be home. Is there anything else?"

"No," the minister said, and walked with him to the door. He pointed at the briefcase. "Don't file any of that. Burn it."

"Yes, sir," Garrett said, and walked past him to the open door. The minister gave him a firm clap on the back.

The priest entered, following the two altar boys, and the congregation rose. Garrett had been deep in thought and got to his feet clumsily, standing beside Nuala. Next to her, Brendan and

Anne stood in the pew. Brendan looked exactly fifteen, sad and humiliated in his suit and tie, as if, Garrett thought, he were an American Indian forced to pose for a picture in the white man's clothes. Anne, on the other hand, had the vague air of a duchess giving the trophies at Wimbledon. At nine she was going through a stage of excessive piety and grandness.

It was a pity, he thought, that the Church had done away with Latin. "I enter the altar of God" wasn't a patch on *Introibo ad Altare Dei.* It took part of the mystery from the mass, and that was one of the remaining reasons he still attended. How horrified Nuala had been when he told her, just after Brendan's baptism, that he no longer believed and would not go to mass again. She had asked him to go for her sake, just to keep her company, he didn't have to believe, but just attend. It was then, the first few times going to mass and witnessing it without faith or guilt, that he began to see the timeless grace in the ritual, the special sounds, clothes, and light of a mysterious theater removed from a mundane world. He called himself one of the faithless faithful, just to see Nuala's pretty face reacting the way it did when she heard a dirty joke. Wanting to laugh, but compelled to show some sort of displeasure. Beyond doing his wife a favor, he went because the Church and its show brought him closer to his family. He didn't pray at mass, but contemplated Nuala and Anne and Brendan. He thought of them each, individually, and loved them one by one in quiet and peace. He also thought of his mother, his father, his brothers and sisters. There was the joy of somehow connecting his childhood to his children's. He remembered his father's way of telling them which Sunday of the year it was on their way to mass. "Today," his father would say, "is the day that many are cold, but few are frozen." Or, on Palm Sunday. "Slipperiest day of the year. Today Christ goes into Jerusalem on his ass." Telling the same old jokes to Brendan and Anne was, Garrett thought, a way of honoring his father.

The primal pull of the mass which drew him each week was something he had stopped resisting. The Church and its pomp, the Church and its flat words of hope and resurrection was something, the older he grew, the more he realized he could never escape. It was grafted firmly to the Irish identity. To break it away would be to break a large part of him away. It was easier to be faithless and faithful, easier to be part of a family than to be alone. There was a certainty about it all that rooted him. Just as he would kiss his wife every night before sleep, so he would be found here, every Sunday, at the eleven o'clock, at Mary, Star of the Sea.

The congregation sat as an old man began reading the epistle in an atrocious North Dublin accent. "The epistle of St. Paul to the Ephesians. I, the prisoner in the Lord, implore you to lead a life worthy of your vocation. Bear with one another charitably, in complete selflessness, gentleness and patience. Do all you can to preserve the unity of the spirit by the peace that binds you together. There is one body, one spirit, just as you were called into one and the same hope when you were called. There is one Lord, one faith, one baptism, and one God who is Father of all, through all and within all."

There was a tune running through Garrett's head, a piece of music that he'd had all morning. What was it? He concentrated and brought the words up. It was another verse of the song Farrell had quoted in the pages he had given him yesterday.

Come all you young rebels
And list while I sing
For the love of one's country
Is a terrible thing.

That was it. He would see him tonight and tell him it was Mexico for certain. Do I have a moral obligation to him? Yes. But I have orders, as well. And I'll follow them. But the man is ill. What of it? as the minister had said. And my lie about Coughlin. He'll never turn. Must think of a way of getting him away from the accessory to murder charge. The poor fool. When Kelly had said he might have something with a man at Mountjoy, Garrett had gone over and interrogated him personally, and listened to a man's life, listened again to one more pathetic fool who had thrown his honor away by succumbing to the historical Irish emotionalism and melancholy which was called patriotism. Looking at him after he had finished confessing, ashamed, but with a trace of stubbornness and pride in him, waiting to take his medicine, Garrett thought about himself, and that compassion in a policeman is a vice. "Do you really expect me to believe, Coughlin," Garrett had asked him, "that you acted solely because of love for your brother?"

"You can believe what you want."

"That you threw your lot in with terrorists?"

"Liam Cleary was no terrorist, and neither was Michael Coughlin."

"There are six innocent men dead. And a boy."

His face changed, falling slightly. "I had no idea it would come to that. God forgive me, I had no idea."

Garrett had been moved by the fool's horror at realizing the consequences of his simple act of misguided love. He had told him to take leave from his job, go to his sister's home in Cahirciveen and wait. Tell no one. He would pay for his crime by helping the State and not by serving time in prison. Garrett had then had a man watch him day and night, while he decided what to do with him. Was that more cruel? he wondered. He stood with the congregation while the priest read the gospel. Was it more cruel to leave him to himself? Justice was not a scale with weights and balances, as every policeman knows. Justice was a primitive phenomenon not yet understood, a painting on a cave wall with strange scrawls for a caption, still undeciphered.

The priest finished the gospel. "This is the word of the Lord." The congregation sat and the priest began his sermon. Garrett half listened. On the power of prayer. The old flannelmouth, he was capable of speaking for days. "Yes, we can pray for better times for ourselves and others, for those we love, yes we can pray for the relief of illness. But we all must remember that God did not guarantee us an easy life here on earth. Jesus demonstrated that to us by His crucifixion and agony on the cross." What in hell is he saying? All his brains are in his throat.

If I'm to be a hunter, then I'll hunt. Simple as that. "I want these bastards badly," the minister had said. That night, 4 November, when he had driven out with his aide, Des Kelly, to Kildare to take charge of the situation, seeing men he knew, colleagues, dead in that street, torn apart. The insanity. Speaking to the boy's mother, who could give him no real information, but demanding he listen. She had to tell her story, over and over, as if by telling it she could find a clue, a magic word, abracadabra, it never happened, little Francis is still walking across the street on his way home to tea. He'd hunt, yes, he'd put an end to it.

He followed his family to the altar rail. The priest fed them the host. "The body of Christ," to Nuala. "The body of Christ," to Anne. "The body of Christ," to Brendan. "The body of Christ," to Garrett. It meant nothing. He tasted the wafer, and part of it stuck to the roof of his mouth. Garrett made the sign of the cross and followed his family, walking in single file, back to the pew.

The house in Portmarnock was off the busy Malahide road, up a gravel driveway under trees where at the first bend a sentry box stood. The sentry, in plain clothes, came out, recognized Garrett and sent him on. Garrett thought he must improve that security point if he was to continue to use the house. He drove an eighth of a mile or so further into the grounds. The trees all around him were old and thick, covered in a strange kind of moss, something he had never seen in Ireland. The property was part of an old estate that the government had bought from a millionaire distiller, whose family all lived in England now. Raymond Murray had persuaded the minister to buy the land and build a house solely to protect and debrief informers. But there was something evil about the house, with its soundproof walls, bugged rooms and two-way mirrors. It could be used so easily for torture, and he knew Murray hadn't been above using it for that. He pulled the car into the circular driveway, the house standing under white floodlights in the November night. Two Irish Army soldiers waited with their self-loading rifles on the porch. It was a two-story white house, looking like a normal middle-class residence, except for the glare of the floodlights, and the shadows cast on the trees. The first time he'd seen it he had thought there was one other thing odd about the structure, but he couldn't quite figure out what it was. Not until he realized that there were no windows on the ground floor.

"Evening, sir," one of the soldiers greeted him, while the other checked his identification.

"Evening. Chilly tonight."

"There you go, sir," the soldier handed him back his card and pushed the bell next to the knobless door. It was opened and Garrett stepped inside. Sullivan closed the door behind him and followed him into the reception room where Garrett sat down on the couch and motioned Sullivan to sit in a chair across from him. "How is he?"

"Round the bend, sir. Keeps going on about the cat. And now he's taken to quoting the bible at me."

"Do you think, Sullivan, that he really is ill, or is he up to something?"

"I wouldn't be qualified to say, sir."

Garrett nodded, observing the big Kerryman. The file on him had said he was an adequate officer, which had been the pinnacle of praise from Murray. "Who is on the sentry box?"

"That would be Daley, sir."

"He didn't check me when I came through."

"I'll have a word with him," Sullivan said, taking out his notebook and pen.

"You'll do more than that. Replace him with someone who'll do the job."

"Yes, sir," Sullivan said, writing.

"We're going to move him out of here sometime this week to Dublin airport and put him on a plane. Set up the detail and give me a report by tomorrow afternoon."

"Yes, sir."

Garrett patted the hair at his ears. He hated the room he was in, its white Danish furniture, white carpet, white walls, and the neon lights that burned twenty-four hours a day. It was like being in a rack of test tubes in a laboratory. This place, Garrett thought, reflected its designer. Murray the bright, Murray the efficient, Murray the clean.

It had been a long day. Before he'd met the minister at nine he'd been at the office for three hours, going over reports, dictating a memo to Kelly concerning his mission to New York, and reading again the translated copy of Farrell's writing. The meeting with the minister had not gone the way he'd wanted. It was impossible for him to work with a man drinking whiskey at nine in the morning in a country club card room. At mass his thoughts had been scattered and useless, thinking of things that required no perception, contemplating ideas already fixed, lolling in the warm bath of nostalgia instead of facing the present. And after mass, the long lazy Sunday which he'd always hated was worse than ever. Nuala had taken Anne to a Sunday matinee and Brendan had gone to his room, to do his homework, he'd said. Garrett had done the dishes from the enormous Sunday dinner, and settled in the living room to stare at the English Sunday papers, reading the same sentence over and over, unable to make any sense of it, giving that up, turning the page and finding himself riveted like a moron to a cigarette advertisement. Fritz, the dachshund, lay at his feet, sleeping off his boredom. Brendan had come down and asked if it was all right to watch television. He had said yes, grateful for his company. The boy was at an age where he avoided his father's presence, and seemed faintly embarrassed whenever they were together. Instead of being happy just to be with his son, to cherish the moment with him, he'd destroyed it. Brendan was looking at a BBC program of professional wrestling from Wembley, watching the burlesque with a grin, totally absorbed. The wrestlers were an outrageously fat man with long silver hair, dressed in what looked like a girl's sundress, and a much smaller black man wearing a mask that covered his head from the neck up. "You know that's all fake, don't you?" Garrett had said.

"Yeah," his son said, still watching.

"Look at me when I'm speaking to you."

Brendan turned, his face blank and sullen. "Yes, sir."

"I should show you true wrestling. It's a beautiful sport when it's done correctly."

"Oh, Dad," Brendan said, and hooked his thumb toward the set. "It's only for a giggle. Everyone knows it's fake."

"What about that howling mob, do they think it's fake? It's a mockery."

"It's only for a giggle."

"I think taking amusement from something grotesque is immoral, Brendan."

Brendan said, "Oh, Dad," and shut off the set. "What's immoral about a bit of fun?" he said from the stairs.

What indeed? He cursed himself, taking out his boredom and anger on the boy. Later he made up to him, going to his room and apologizing, saying something about being very busy at the office of late, that he was sorry he'd inflicted his moodiness on him. Brendan nodded. Garrett had rubbed the boy's head as he was leaving, and Brendan had ducked slightly, his embarrassment as acute as pain.

"Anything else, sir?" Sullivan's broad face looking at him.

"Is he still asking for a priest?"

"He let up on that one last night. Haven't heard a peep out of him all day about it. I think the bible's pacified him."

"Were you in the service when this place was built?"

"I was. I carried out some of Mr. Murray's ideas for the house."

"Good. When Farrell is out of here, I want you to take charge of dismantling the bugs. And get rid of the two-way mirrors. We won't use this place again. I'll have to think of some other use for it."

"Yes, sir. But may I say, Mr. Murray worked—"

"Mr. Murray is dead, Sullivan."

"I'll get right on it as you say."

"You've done a fine job here. A first-rate job."

Sullivan nodded, and put away his notebook.

Garrett rose and said, "I'll see him now."

He followed the big man through the house toward the rear, down a white corridor lit with neon. They entered an anteroom where another guard sat in an easy chair, reading the magazine section of the *Observer*. He got to his feet and said, "Evening, Mr. Costello."

"Hello, Dan, will you open up for me?"

"Yes, sir," he said, and unlocked the white door.

Farrell was sitting across the room at the desk, his back to the door, writing. He was dressed in black slacks and a gray turtleneck sweater, hunched over the desk writing furiously, his bare feet stacked one on the other, the top foot clawing at the bottom.

"Leave me alone, Sully," he said without turning.

"A visitor, Peter," Sullivan said from the door, and closed it, leaving Garrett alone in the room with him. Farrell whipped around, and Garrett again could see why he was *le chat*. The way he had turned had been frighteningly quick, but there was nothing jerky about the movement, his whole body was just suddenly turned around. He had a thin face, with a long thin nose and a small mouth with delicate lips. His eyes, under thick black brows, were dark and shining, and even from across the room they were the first feature that caught Garrett's attention, and held him. Farrell stood and put his hands on his hips. "Shalom," he said.

"Hello, Peter," Garrett said and walked closer. He saw the bible open on the desk. "Been reading?"

"It's all rubbish. I've been havin' a go with Sully, though, ravin' on like Ian Paisley. Take this chair," Farrell said, lifting it away and placing it in the center of the room. He picked up the pages off the desk, put them in the drawer, and sat on the floor against the wall, his knees drawn up and his ankles crossed. He laid his palms on his knees and, except for his ankles scraping against one another slowly and rhythmically, he was dead calm, staring at

Garrett's face. As soon as he was seated Garrett said, "I got the word this morning, Peter. It's Mexico. And sometime this week."

"What day is it today?"

"Sunday."

"Sunday," he said, still staring. "That would be right. Sunday."

"How are you keeping?" Garrett asked, looking around. It was immaculate. A lamp, a chair, a desk, books on a shelf, and a white carpet.

"Not bad," Farrell said. "Tell me, with your influence, couldn't you send me to Israel?"

Garrett smiled. "Why do you persist in that kind of foolishness?"

"Why do I persist? Listen to himself. Why do I *persist*? You sound more like a Protestant than a bloody Jew."

"Tomorrow I'll be a Moslem, I suppose."

"Tomorrow you could be in heaven, Garrett, old man. Or the other place. What? Spot of tea? Cricket? Or would a matzo ball be more to your liking? Jesus, if me poor father could see me now. Bein' sent off to Mexico by a Protestant Jew." He laughed loudly, but stared, his eyes as bright as someone with fever. He began to sing, loudly, still staring and the top ankle beating time against the lower.

As I was mounted on the platform high
My agéd father was standing by
My agéd father did me deny
And the name he gave me was the croppy boy.

"I just wanted to let you know of the decision," Garrett said, getting up and starting to leave.

"Don't go," Farrell said softly, and when Garrett turned to him he was looking down at the carpet in the space between his legs. "Don't go just yet."

Garrett sat down. "What can I do for you?"

"I don't know a thing about Mexico." He looked up and wrapped his arms over his chest. "Not a thing. There's no French spoken there."

"Why do you want to go to France? Mexico is—"

"France is my home."

"Ireland's your home," Garrett said quickly, and it was out before he realized what he'd said.

Farrell laughed. "There's no one to make me welcome, though, is there? I never dreamed I'd be a traitor. I once loved this country. Truly loved it. I fought for it, for ideals that have come down, generation after generation, and I took them and fought for them. I've seen men die. I've killed men because of it. But I never thought I'd betray my country. I hate it. I hate it. I hate it. What has Ireland done for me? What has Ireland done for any of us? Except teach us the trade of traitor?"

"Words like traitor, Peter, are relative. You yourself wrote, questioning if you can be a traitor to thugs."

"I never did! I never called them thugs!"

"You're going to have enough money to live comfortably in Mexico. You could get help there—"

"What kind of help?" he shouted. "What kind of help?"

"Help for your headaches."

He relaxed, a child relieved that someone had believed his lie. "Ah, no. No help for me there, Garrett. Garrett," he looked up, his face innocent, questioning, "that's a right strange name for a Jew."

Garrett laughed, and Farrell joined him. "Well, you have a sense of humor anyway, Garrett. I lost mine somewhere. When you took my cat I didn't have a thing in the world left to amuse me. Mexico. I'll never live to see *that* bloody country. They'll get me before then. But I might have a trick left, hey, Garrett? A trick left to fool them."

"I'd say you have a lot of tricks left."

"All I need is one. What'd you think of my writing, anyway?"

"I thought it was quite good."

"You're lyin' now, Garrett," he grinned. "They don't teach French in Hebrew school."

Garrett smiled back. "I had it translated. Into *English*, Peter."

Farrell laughed. "But you enjoyed it, did you?"

"I just said I did."

"Well," he said, getting up and going to the desk, "it's lost its flavor by translating, I'd say." He took the sheets of paper from the drawer and resumed his seat on the floor. Looking up, with a wicked smile, "French is the language for writin' of fookin' and such like. Are you a married man? I'd say you were a married man. Kiddies?"

"Two. A boy and a girl."

"I never took the leap. I was always afraid the other girls would miss me too much."

"I understand they have girls in Mexico."

"Mexico. Death. Is there a difference?"

"I'd say a big one, Peter," he said, rising. "I'll see you tomorrow. Does your head still bother you?"

"It's all right." He waved the pages at him. "I'm writin' some more stuff for you."

"I'd be happy to read it."

"Grand," he said, springing up lightly to his feet. "Grand man, Garrett. I just want to say you're a grand man. Understand? I hold nothin' against you."

Garrett rapped on the door. When it was opened Farrell rattled the pages at him. "You'll get a laugh out of this."

Garrett drove up the Malahide road and stopped near the strand at a small store for a Coca-Cola. He was still stuffed from Nuala's Sunday feast, and thought something carbonated would help. He took the can of soda and walked across the road and sat on a bench, the wind blowing in his face freshly off the sea. Nearby was a kiosk selling ice cream and candy, surrounded by children and teenagers, talking loudly over the blare of a transistor radio. The younger children played rough chasing games, letting out the pent-up Sunday boredom of religion and family. Two girls walked away from the kiosk, unwrapping Popsicles and tossing the paper away without a look, adding to the piles of litter on the sidewalk and the road, scattering away in the wind.

It was probably around this time, he reckoned later, that Peter Farrell was opening his veins and dying. He was thinking of Farrell there on the bench near the children, deciding to move him out of the house and transport him to another government-owned house, much less severe, near Shannon. Getting him away from that place would help his state of mind, and he could be protected in the house near the airport just as efficiently. It was much too cruel to leave an ill man in a windowless cell. He also would see Ramirez at the Mexican embassy in the morning, and get specific assurances Farrell would find housing, and other English-speaking residents to assist him the first few weeks there. As soon as Farrell was gone he would have Sullivan begin work on dismantling the place. Perhaps even destroy the whole structure. No, that's stupid.

There must be other uses for it. Compassion in a policeman is a
vice, he told himself again; but I'm responsible for this man, not
just because he deserves it, because there's no one else. I can live
with my vice.

When he arrived home Nuala and the children were watching
television. Fritz ran to lean his long body against his leg. Nuala
looked up and said, "You have a message from a Mr. Sullivan,
Garrett."

"Yes?"

"He said you were to return to the white house immediately."

"Yes," he said absently, somehow knowing what had taken
place in the rooms at the back of that house. He turned for the
door. "Have something to eat before you go."

"I won't be long, love."

Sullivan let him in. His face looked heavier, as if the muscles
had sagged. "What is it, Sullivan?"

"He's cut his wrists, Mr. Costello."

"How long ago?"

"Not long after you left, I went in to give him a cup of tea
and found him."

"Let's see him."

Sullivan led him into the room. On the desk was a neat stack
of papers. There was a young man standing in the room, dressed
in a black suit, smoking a thin cigar. "This is Dr. Hogan, Mr.
Costello. I thought it best to call him when I couldn't reach you."
Hogan was another carryover from the reign of Murray. Garrett
had never met him, but had seen his name in the files on medical
checkups and death certificates.

"Is he dead?" Garrett asked.

"Quite dead. I haven't disturbed him because of your man's
advice. He used a razor blade and knew what he was doing."

"Will you make out the death certificate?"

"Certainly," he waved his cigar slightly.

"And ring a mortician and have him come at once. Sullivan,
show him the phone. Ring the minister when Dr.–Dr.–"

"Hogan," the young doctor said. "I know where the telephone
is."

"When Dr. Hogan is through, inform the minister of the death
and that I'm here taking charge. Now, where is he?"

"In the tub, sir."

When they were gone Garrett walked into the bathroom, just off the short hallway between the two rooms. Farrell lay floating in the tub. Wisps of steam still lingered above the surface of red water. His eyes were closed and his face was calm, as if he were sleeping. Garrett sat on the toilet and looked at the floor. There was a dense smell in the room, not unpleasant, but something lush and ripe. He looked at Farrell's face, the small mouth half opened, beads of sweat on the upper lip. Garrett touched Farrell's forehead lightly with a finger and rose. Next to the tub he saw a plump gray cigar ash. He turned out the lights and left the room.

Garrett had him buried on Tuesday after discovering there were no relatives who wished to collect the body. He persuaded a Franciscan priest, an old friend whom he had gone to university with, to say a few words. The only other mourners were Garrett and Sullivan, who was there at Garrett's order. The Franciscan spoke of redemption, and that no man was capable of judging his brother. He asked God's mercy on the soul of His child Peter, and then motioned for the three grave diggers to lower the casket which contained the body and the bible Sullivan had given him on Saturday.

At the office later that day, Garrett's secretary gave him the translated pages that Farrell had written the day he died.

Speaking beyond the grave, that's a luxury I can't deny myself. The plan, it's amazing, you know, I never really thought it but I have been planning it for weeks. Months? Years? It wasn't something that hit me on the head, it just came the day, today, or yesterday, when I thought it was Sunday. Yes, I think it must've been years. I'm off to Mexico with my cat.

Gudrun (how long ago?), when we were first together, anyway, used to drag me around to galleries and museums to look at pictures. She knew what she was doing, she had a bloody fortune hanging on the wall of her flat. She taught me a lot about it, and I even got to like some of the stuff you'd see hanging in Paris. That was something, Jesus, here I was Conor (or Peter, Judas? Judas Farrell, Conor Judas, rubbish) a kid from Dublin who thought art was a picture of Our Lady in three colors on a holy card sold by a tinker, me, understanding Picasso and Van Gogh (I liked his stuff) and Rousseau (I really liked his stuff, the mad little frog painting those tigers and jungles and other strange carry-on) where am I in all this? Gudrun. What I wanted to say was she took me to see an exhibition of Mark Rothko's stuff once. I thought it was the worst load of shite I'd ever clapped eyes on, those big stupid black things looked like he painted it with a broom, and I told her so, in the cafe on the Île that was our local, where you got the good beer in the cold mugs, and we were having a meal and I told her I thought Rothko was an eejit and his painting was junk and so on.

I know, she says, sipping her beer. Her mouth!

Then why waste a minute lookin' at it?

Because, she says, he killed himself recently.

That threw me. I'm a collector of suicides, says she. I enjoy studying their lives. Monroe, Sylvia Plath, and then she mentioned some Germans I've never heard of. Hemingway, she says, and your own Wolfe Tone.

He was no suicide! says I.

Don't get so excited.

And I was excited, Jesus, looking at her there, I see her face now, the way she looked. A collector of suicides. She'd make a hangman shiver, little Gudrun, and give him a hard-on at the same time. A collector. So now she's got me to mount on her wall. She told me how to do it. The best way. The vein, the blade, the hot water, end time. We'll see. Farewell, Gudrun, may we meet again. I have so much to tell you.

I bid you farewell too, Garrett. You've just left me. I have time now, Sully won't disturb me. You're not a bad man, Garrett, for a Jew. I've got nothing against Jews, mind you, I'm just a prejudiced man by nature. Race and color prejudiced. They're not bad folk, the Jews, even though the ones I've met I could count on my one hand. Better than the Arabs, I'd say, and I've met a fair amount of those buggers the last few years. Greasy Palestinians with their long stupid faces, afraid if they smile their arse will fall off. Fuck them, I hope the bloody Jews kill every last one of them.

So now I lay me down to sleep. I must go soon so Sully won't bother me. You can do what you want with the body. The body. My body. One request, now that I think of it. Put me in the ground. Don't burn me. I kept the one trick, Garrett, and Ireland

*is cheated of the death of Peter Farrell, loyal son and fighter for
her freedom. There'll be no tears for me and I give none to anyone.*

After taking a call from Kelly reporting in New York, Garrett
left the office at ten o'clock. Dublin was dark, wet, and seemed
very old. A cold night. There weren't many people out as he
walked along the sidewalks covered in a dirty film of wetness.
Why did the Danes, he wondered, the Vikings, ever decide to
live here? And the Romans, who never came, but named it
Hibernia, the land of wintry weather. Maybe the Vikings came
in the summer. Foolish man, your head is like a child's tonight.

He didn't want to face his family just yet and decided to wait
until the children were in bed before going home, and so he
walked to a pub just off Abbey Street called The Flowing Tide.
He was not a drinking man, but in Dublin there are no places to
go at night except public houses. The pub was a large crowded
room. He and Nuala had come once after the theatre with friends.
"Glass of lager, please," he told the barman.

He sat at the bar. The first cold sip of beer sent a chill through
him. Would a hot whiskey have been more appropriate? Probably.
But he disliked the taste of Irish. The room seemed very friendly
to him, a good warm place to get out of the cold and be with
people. He looked at the faces at the bar. There was life in their
expressions, happiness and contentment. There would be no tears
for Peter Farrell, he told himself, and there should be none. No
one was responsible for his death but himself, and his loss would
grieve no one. He had been a cruel man and would have met
his death violently if he hadn't done what he did. It was the best
thing, as the minister had said Sunday morning. It saved lives
probably. But I won't judge, Garrett thought. Justice is still
unknown.

He spent half an hour over his beer and then left The Flowing
Tide. Taking his time, he reached home at eleven-thirty. The
house was dark, except for a single light in the kitchen. Nuala's
signal to him that everyone was home and in bed.

CHAPTER 13

The Burren

The day is no more than an hour old and the huge stones, which seem to be growing like trees out of the fields, look purple in the new light. A cold wind blows across the flat limestone land where there is no vegetation to be seen, only rock. This place, called the Burren, stretches for miles across the western part of County Clare. It is an eerie place, because in its fields of stone there is little color, and the Burren must pick up all its character from the changing sky, which seems to be, after awhile, part of the land. The sky of western Ireland can change on a breeze from blue to moody gray to high rushing clouds black as rage, and then back to innocent sun once more, all in the space of half an hour. And so in turn the Burren changes its shape and its emotion. Although it may look lifeless, it is not. Botanists from all over the world come in the spring to search for the rare plants which grow in every available piece of soil and from the fissures of the limestone. Arctic plants grow side by side with plants found only in the tropics. No one knows why or how the seeds came to Clare. In the autumn and winter, when the naturalists have gone, the Burren lies brooding along with the sky, a place that seems too old, too full of secrets, to be interested in anything except its own strange self. Remote and cruel, it is a separate country within the pastoral land of Clare.

Not far from the village of Ballyvaughan, the Burren ends suddenly at a steep descent, called Gyre Hill, which runs down into a glen that is a pocket of green life by the sea. If you were to stand just at the edge of the stony, ominous land, and look west, into the glen, you would see cattle grazing in the cold morning air, motionless at this distance, spread out as if by design by a painter balancing his canvas. Gyre Hill's road corkscrews down and then descends in a straight line to an old country mansion sitting bulky and brown bricked, three storied, with smoke puffing from four of its twenty chimney pots. The north side of the valley is sheltered by three bald Burren mountains rolling in a range down to meet Galway Bay, where a thin strip of land curves like an arm into the sea, and just at the hand of the arm stands a lone tower.

The mansion, called Limeview, is the home of Robert Crenshaw, the last of the Clare Crenshaws. Robert is a wealthy man. He often reminds himself, always with a mild shock of pleasure, that he could spend five hundred pounds a day for twenty years and still be wealthy. Fifty-one years old, he is a private man who has spent most of his life in London but has now come home to Clare and lives at Limeview with his servants. His housekeeper, two maids, a cook, an old stablemaster, and a stableboy hired just yesterday.

His life in London had finally seemed purposeless to him. A man his age cannot live a life of idleness, of going to restaurants recommended by newspapers, the opera and ballet, and seeing friends as idle as himself, without a crisis occurring. Last May he had seen his life in just those terms, and had returned home to Ireland to make a new start. But the people he once hunted and socialized with in Clare were too sad and too silly to tolerate. Crenshaw saw then that the gentry of Ireland, the "West British," of which he was a part, had always been sad, silly people, but the nineteenth and early twentieth centuries had hidden their flaws. Now Ireland was becoming a modern state and time had run out on the Protestant Ascendancy. The women spent most of their time in Dublin and could be seen at the racetrack, or opening nights, or populating the new bars named Whispers, Feathers, Gatsby's. The men stayed on in the big houses, raising their hounds, writing checks for charities, having a go at the parlor maids, taking whiskey with lunch. The daughters were sent to England or the continent for education and the sons went into politics. Where once money and class kept life tuned like a clean quiet engine, now there was only money, and the machine, missing the grease of privilege, was stuttering and burning out. A final gasp before it seized and then the money would take them out of Ireland, away from the wreck for good.

Observe Robert Crenshaw as he has his breakfast in the dining room, near the fire and the window looking out on the blue and tame bay under cream clouds. A single place is laid at the end of the long table. Egg cup, plate, toast rack, coffee cup, and the book he is reading, *The Charterhouse of Parma*. You can't get a morning paper here until nine o'clock and so Crenshaw, who has the learned habit of reading while eating (like most people who live alone), reads fiction with his breakfast. Last week it had been a collection of short stories by Sean O'Faolain, which suited breakfast much more than the hard prose of Stendahl. It is difficult to concentrate. His privacy is about to be threatened. And there seems no way of getting around it. A letter had come three days ago from Frank Higgins, Chief of Staff of the Provisional I.R.A., requesting Limeview as venue for talks with the Irish Socialist Army. The I.R.A. will come tonight and the I.S.A. tomorrow morning. There is no way of refusing. It is not really a request, but an order.

He isn't in the mood to entertain Mr. Stendahl this morning, and so eats quickly and leaves the dining room to go to the library and feed his fish. It is a high-ceilinged room, lined in books from floor to ceiling with a mobile ladder on rods to reach the top shelves. The most striking feature of the room is the huge aquarium standing against the curtained window. He switches on the light and the water is alive with the floating fish and green plants. He checks the thermostat and then sprinkles the food on the surface. Three Spot Gourami swims greedily upwards and begins to feed. Crenshaw has named her Tricky from her Latin name, *Trichogaster Trichopertus*, and she is one of his favorites with her exquisite powder-blue color and the dark spots in a wavy pattern on her body, shimmering as she moves. Her long cat's whiskers undulate as she eats. Crenshaw wishes her good morning and speaks softly to her. He knows people would think him puerile, talking to fish, but he doesn't consider it strange. He had once thought people who addressed dogs in baby talk moronic, until he caught himself doing the same with his fish. If you loved something, why not express it? Fish were as noble as men.

Up swims his Penguin fish with his silver body striped black, the *Thayeria Obliqua*. Curious fellow, Crenshaw thinks, a genuine clown the way his tail is lower than his head. He goes to his desk, takes an index card from the drawer and types that observation. It will be good for the book. "The clown of the aquarium world."

Crenshaw has been engaged in writing a book about tropical fish since he'd come home last spring. The first few months of work had been wasted because he was writing a thoroughly technical book about breeding, identification, and disease. He had to throw all that out. It wasn't that the book was not expert in every way; it was that it was too technical, too expert, written for students of ichtyology. He had decided he didn't want to impress anyone, and, after all, the technical book was only aping his mother, trying to live up to her. Ten years of psychoanalysis should have rid him of that. Lady Crenshaw's book on plants of the Burren was considered a masterpiece of botanic research and classification. It was his mother's book, published fifty years ago, the year after he was born, that continued to draw naturalists to Limeview, and this library, and the wild Burren land. Crenshaw knows nothing of flowers except for aquarium plants. He had been deliberately stupid when his mother tried to teach him, and had instead studied everything possible about tropical fish, learning it all out of competition with his mother's expertise. It wasn't until years later that he realized he loved the fish, their colors, their lovely dreamy movements, for themselves and not because they were the object of a discipline conquered. He had thrown out the technical book, and begun a book for young people about the joy of maintaining an aquarium. It will be a more popular book, but he isn't writing it for money. He is writing it, he tells himself, to give something to people, to justify his life, and leave something behind.

Miss Harkin knocks at the open door and comes in, walking briskly, her clipboard in front of her, and takes a seat on the other side of the desk. She is an attractive woman of forty, who becomes better looking as the years go by. When she was younger, working in this house, her austere expression had made her look plain and pinched. Now she has grown into her looks, and appears efficient, intelligent, supremely confident. She started to work here at the age of nineteen as a maid, and became his mother's nurse and companion when Lady Crenshaw grew too ill to move without help. From this position Miss Harkin had realized her power and taken it, running the entire house. After his mother's death, there was no question that she would continue to rule Limeview. Crenshaw had been ready to offer her the job of manager of the house the afternoon of the funeral, but it was a *fait accompli*. She had come to him with a list of details that day, just as she is doing now. Crenshaw listens to her briefing him about food supplies, the faults of the two maids and the new stableboy, the price of feed for the animals, the painters coming next week. He wonders why she bothers. When he'd lived in London all those years she'd never consulted him.

"Yes, I agree, Miss Harkin. That is too much. I'm sure you'll find someone more reasonable. About the cash flow, as you so corporately put it—" he pauses, there is not a speck of humor in her face—"get in touch with Bill Mohan at the bank in town."

"I have, Mr. Crenshaw. He says you must take care of it."

"Good lord, did he really say that?"

"He did."

"That's inexcusable. He knows you're the manager here, that you handle—"

"Mr. Crenshaw," she interrupts politely. "It's because I'm a woman. Mr. Mohan, like every other man in County Clare, feels finance is a world understood solely by men."

Even though Miss Harkin is the daughter of a thatcher, and has never been further than Dublin, and there only once, she speaks and acts with the manner of a well-traveled aristocrat. She has had no education except for eight years of terrorization by the nuns, but her years with Lady Crenshaw have given her a way of speaking, a way of acting, and a way of looking at the world as if it were a stupid, foolish place controlled by peasants. "Have you ever been in touch with George Sawyer?" he asks.

"No," she says, writing down his name.

"His phone number and business address are in the directory in the hall. Sawyer and Son. They're in the City of London. I want you to ring him this morning in London. Mr. Sawyer and his firm have handled the Crenshaw estate and investments for years, so get on to him, tell him that I have directed you to have Mr. Sawyer inform Mr. Mohan that you are to be trusted with anything connected with Limeview and my account at the bank. Have him ring Bill Mohan about it today."

"Very good, sir."

He can see George smiling at the other end of the phone. "Some Irish fun," he will say to his colleagues. He wouldn't smile if he dealt with Miss Harkin in person.

"Now, we're going to have visitors tonight. Have three rooms ready. They should arrive after nine or so. Have some supper prepared."

"Yes, sir. Men or women or both?"

"Men," he says, and waits for her to look up. A flicker crosses her face, and he thinks he sees her eyes harden. "It won't be an orgy, Miss Harkin."

She looks down, blushing. "Three rooms, sir."

"And we'll have three more tomorrow morning arriving about ten. Two men and a woman. They'll be here all day. Have a lunch ready. Cigarettes, liquor, and the rest. Also have the lounge cleared, and put the long table in there."

"Yes, sir," she says, scribbling.

"Tell Anna May and the new girl—what's her name again?"

"Colette Breen."

"Yes, tell Colette and Anna May to leave this afternoon and return on Thursday morning."

She looks up from writing. "Yes," he says. "Limeview is to be used again. See to it that no tradesmen are due to arrive. Tim will be all right."

"The carpenter is coming tomorrow. I'll ring and cancel."

"Fine. I think that will be all."

Miss Harkin gets to her feet and says, "I believe your mother, God be good to her, would be very proud of you, Mr. Crenshaw. Very proud."

"It's for her I do it," he says, and looks away.

"Very proud, indeed." She is beaming when he looks up. "Now," she says, "what was wrong with the coffee this morning?"

"Coffee. Oh, yes, nothing. Nothing at all. I just didn't want any today."

"Can I get you a cup of tea?"

"That would be fine. I'll take it upstairs."

"The girl will bring it," Miss Harkin says, and leaves him.

Crenshaw was in the library working on the book after dinner when Miss Harkin came in and said, "One of our guests has arrived."

In the lounge a young man dressed in a green sweater and dark slacks was at the window looking out. "Welcome," Crenshaw said.

The young man turned. He was good looking with a sandy

military mustache and a piece of blond hair falling boyishly across his forehead.

"Mr. Crenshaw?" he asked.

"Yes," Crenshaw said, moving closer. What eyes, he thought. He had never seen eyes quite so green, so bright, so hard.

"Rúairí MacCurtain, Mr. Crenshaw. I'm sorry if I'm early."

"Oh, not at all, not at all. Frank said you might be early. Can I get you a drink?"

"Something soft. Is that Lady Crenshaw?" MacCurtain asked, looking past him at the portrait on the far wall.

"Why, yes, when she was young. Do you like John's work?"

"Who?"

"Augustus John, the portraitist."

"I have no interest in painting. My only interest is my work."

"Quite," Crenshaw said.

"She was a great lady, your mother. I feel privileged just to be in her house."

"It's my house now, Mr. MacCurtain."

"Of course. I meant no, no slight on you and your work for the Movement."

"I don't work for the Movement. I give you money and I let you use my house. Would you consider that work?"

"I would. Invaluable work. I'm sorry if I've offended you in any way."

"Nonsense. Now, for something to drink. I'll send Miss Harkin in."

Miss Harkin, who had learned to worship Republicanism from Lady Crenshaw, fed Rúairí in the dining room and treated him like a monsignor. Crenshaw watched the young man eat. He wondered if his mother, had she been alive, would have approved of the Provisional I.R.A. Lady Crenshaw had been involved in the struggle almost from the beginning when she organized a protest in Ennis the summer of 1916 against the executions of the leaders of the Dublin Rising. She became as well known as Countess Markievicz and other Anglo-Irish women who joined the Republican movement out of a sense of *noblesse oblige.*

Lady Crenshaw soon found she could maintain her style of life and support revolutionaries at the same time. There were precedents, a whole Irish tradition of rebel aristocrats from the Flight of the Earls to Lord Edward Fitzgerald to the hanging of

Sir Roger Casement in 1916. She discovered that revolution was much more satisfying than bridge or horses. It was nearly as interesting as botany. One met so many more interesting people in the Movement than one did among the naturalists.

The adulation the peasants, workers and intellectuals bestowed on any well-born person who joined their cause was something she had never known, and she worked hard to maintain their love. She had been jailed in both Dublin and London. She had contributed thousands of pounds to the I.R.A. during the War of Independence and during the Civil War she opened the doors of Limeview to the rebels to use as barracks and turned her grounds into a training field for them. Her name was known and revered by Republicans in Ireland, England, and the United States.

Just as with all of his mother's passions, Robert stayed clear of the Movement. It was her territory. No one could ever truly understand it the way she did. That suited Robert because he had no interest in politics. He had only one interest: to get away from his mother, Limeview, and Ireland, in that order, and live in London, anonymous and free.

In March 1967 Crenshaw was called home to see her. She told him quite frankly that she was dying, would, in fact, not live out the week, and asked that he do two things for her. One was to get married as soon as possible because he was no longer young and should have a companion for his old age. The second request was that he continue the Crenshaw tradition of supporting the forces of national liberation. She told him that George Sawyer in London gave a certain amount of money to a New York bank every six months, who then gave it to an organization there, who in turn gave it to the I.R.A. in Dublin. The circuitous route was deemed safest for the Crenshaws and Sawyer and Son. Robert was to continue that donation without fail. Also, if the Movement ever wanted to use Limeview they would have it at a moment's notice.

She did die within the week, and when the General Headquarters of the I.R.A. asked to be represented at her funeral, Crenshaw couldn't refuse. They fired shots over her grave and presented him with the tri-color that they had insisted be draped across her casket.

Crenshaw instructed Sawyer to continue the donations. Limeview had been used once since her death when the Provisionals had met with Protestant clergymen and Loyalist leaders in 1973 for two days. Crenshaw had been thrilled to think that a peace could be signed at his home, but nothing came of the meeting, except that one of the clergymen stole an antique letter opener from the foyer and one of the I.R.A. men drank too much and fell against the aquarium, giving himself a concussion and flooding the room.

This would be the last time, he told himself. He wanted to respect his mother, and would continue the donations, but allowing his home to be used again by thugs and louts was out of the question. This one, though, this MacCurtain, eating Miss Harkin's lamb and potatoes, he was no lout. But those eyes, they looked like they had seen everything and found nothing worthwhile. Rather have brainless gangsters here, like the last time, than cold ones like MacCurtain. The Provos had changed. After ten years they had become clever. It would not be pleasant to be on the wrong side of them.

When MacCurtain finished his meal, he asked if there was a blueprint of the house. Crenshaw said no. He then asked if he could have a tour of the house to check for security. Miss Harkin said she would gladly show him. Crenshaw excused himself and went outside down toward the stables and stopped under the elms. The night was cold, clear, and the wind blew cleanly off the Burren into the valley. A good night for a ride. The Burren was extraordinary on a clear night. As a boy he had been frightened of nearly everything; thunderstorms, faces on the street, strange dogs, life itself, but the Burren at night, which other people found terrifying, Crenshaw saw as a place of peace and safety. At night, with the stars and the moon above, the Burren lay white, and gray, and black. Shadows fled across the figures of the stone. It was a separate planet. Unsoilable, asking nothing and giving nothing. His alone.

He stood with his face to the wind, looking up Gyre Hill, seeing the faint form of the Burren peering over the rim of valley. Debating whether to take the stallion out or not. No, he should be here when they all arrive. Perhaps later, when they're all in bed? He turned back toward the stable. There was a light on in the boy's room.

The back door opened and the light fell out on the garden in a narrow line. MacCurtain came walking toward him. Blasted man. Security check, indeed. His mother would have had him horsewhipped for suggesting it. "May I ask what you're doing, Mr. Crenshaw?"

"You may not. What I do at my own home is my business, I believe."

MacCurtain took out a box of cigarettes and offered him one. "Thank you, no." A blue light sprang and turned yellow. Crenshaw looked at his eyes again as the match cupped toward his face.

"Mr. Crenshaw, I have the idea you don't like me. Is that true? Well, let me tell you, I don't care a fuck whether you do or not. I have to do my job, and not worry about your feelings."

"Oh, yes, your job, of course."

"I'm in a dangerous profession and I want to keep practicing it. There are precautions I must take."

"Quite. But isn't trust part of your profession?"

MacCurtain laughed and then looked over the valley. "No," he finally said. "Trust is not part of my profession. Who's in there?" he pointed with the red glow of his cigarette end toward the stable.

"The stablemaster and stableboy."

"I'll just have a look," he said and took a step.

"Mr. MacCurtain?"

He stopped and looked back.

"Mr. MacCurtain. Please don't. The old man has worked here nearly sixty years. He knows what is going on here. He won't bother us at all."

"And the boy?"

"He was hired yesterday. The old man will keep an eye on him."

"On your say so, Mr. Crenshaw, I'll let them be for now. But Commander Higgins will know the minute he arrives."

"Fine."

"Now, I'll ask you again," MacCurtain said, coming very close and speaking quietly, "what are you doing out here?"

"I came out for the air."

"Tell me," he said, in the same low tones, so close Crenshaw could feel his breath on his face, "are you frightened of me?"

"Yes. Yes, I am."

MacCurtain stepped back, and then walked past him toward the house, brushing his shoulder lightly. Crenshaw turned and watched him as he walked up the steps to the back door. When he opened it MacCurtain looked back toward the trees. He stood for a minute or more in the doorway, silent, unmoving.

When he had finally gone in the house and closed the door, Crenshaw walked quickly to the stable. He rapped on the door to Tim's room. The boy answered it, dressed in a sweatshirt and dungarees. Beyond him sat Tim, the stablemaster, working on a bridle in his lap. "Saddle Afton, George," Crenshaw told the boy.

"Now, sir?"

"Yes, now, damnit. Now, not next week."

The boy passed him and Crenshaw stepped into the room. "Are you all right, Bobby?" Tim asked.

"I'm fine. I just want to ride, is that so strange? To ride my own horse?"

"Not a'tall. You look like a drink is what you need. Where's that jug of mine?"

"I don't want a drink, Tim."

"Suit yourself. You'll want a jacket, though."

"Keep the boy away from the house."

"I already got me marching orders, Bobby."

"Good. Good." He looked about the room. What to say? "Goodnight, Tim."

He met George at the stable door, leading Afton who tossed his head, and pranced disgustedly. Without a word Crenshaw swung up and spurred the stallion away, down across the field and then up toward the Burren where high clouds sailed silently in the light of the moon. The Burren could be seen quite clearly, stretching away, each rock defined by the bright sky. Tim had been right, he could have used a jacket for the wind. The emptiness and the hard color of the place chilled him just looking at it.

Could a human being possess such vicious eyes? Of course he was human. "Are you frightened of me?" What a great excuse war is. It gives them license to indulge the baseness of the human character, instead of shunning it, controlling it. His breath on my face. "Are you frightened of me?" Even if I was, I should have lied.

Crenshaw turned Afton back and rode to a spot near the north wall of mountain to a place he had discovered as a child, a smooth flat stone, set just at the edge of the Burren on the lip of the valley. He dismounted and walked out to the place, and sat looking down at Limeview bathed in the fugitive moonlight. It had been a special thrill when he was a boy to come here and see the world without it seeing him. To be a secret observer, powerful and silent. It was his place. Noble and alone, seeing all, knowing all, saying nothing.

Crenshaw turned up the collar of his shirt and crossed his arms over his chest, putting his hands in his armpits for warmth. He saw a car's headlights flashing through the night and pulling up to the side of the house. That would be Higgins and the other one. Damn them. I'm such a fool, such a fool! Insulted, terrified in my own house. Giving comfort to people I loathe. I'm an accessory. And why? Because I believe in their cause? No. Because I still cannot overcome that ferocious woman, she still is commanding me from the grave, still telling me not to pick that shirt because it's vulgar, to have my hair neatly combed, to take sherry at six o'clock and never have whiskey before dinner, to support gangsters, butchers, and beasts because that is what is done. When I buried her I should have buried myself. I should have stayed in London, lived out my death, not made an attempt at coming home to her commands.

Crenshaw sat on the cold stone looking over the valley until the moon had set and the stars grew brighter in the depth of the night. He thought of his book, and battled with himself whether to continue it or not. Was it worth it? Would it be read? Would it help? He thought of traveling, of taking the manuscript with him to a place of heat and sea and sun, of working there and allowing Ireland to bury its dead without him for awhile. Fantasies of meeting new people. Attractive, civilized people. "Yes, I'm a writer. Away from home to finish my book. Cocktails at seven? Well, I usually have my evening dip then. Dinner at eight? Delighted." Pictures of perfectly prepared food served on a terrace overlooking a warm evening harbor, the lights of boats, the people sipping perfect wine, dressed in loose-fitting clothes, laughing. Love, and shaded rooms in the heat of the afternoon, where perfect bodies tanned except for the cream white of buttocks lay entwined, languorous, making the gentle and fierce moves to pleasure, oblivion, peace. And washing after in the pounding surf, watching a night approaching, stealing through the evening, walking under ripe trees, to a perfect bed and a perfect sleep.

Afton coughed behind him. Crenshaw was taking pastry and strong coffee in an outdoor restaurant, crossing his legs, dangling his sandal, waiting for someone who would come and laugh with him. The horse coughed once more, and Crenshaw stopped staring and looked around. The stallion was breathing heavily and shaking his body as if he were covered with flies. When Crenshaw petted his soft muzzle, the horse took a step toward him and leaned his great weight into him. There were only two lights on in Limeview. The rest of the valley was invisible.

In the stable Crenshaw unsaddled Afton while the mare looked on from her stall. He then rubbed the stallion down thoroughly, and when he was sure the horse was warm, went to work on him with the curry-combs. He heard someone walking outside and turned toward the door, holding the combs, waiting. Higgins came in at the far end, blinking at the bare bulb over Crenshaw's head. "Robert?"

"Yes. Here, Frank."

Higgins came forward, dressed in tweed slacks, a gray turtleneck, and a light leather jacket. An impressive looking man, with a barrel chest, thin waist, sharp intelligent features, and high, healthy color. Faint freckles on his hands and face. He leaned against the mare's stall, watching Crenshaw who had his back turned, currying his horse with long strokes.

"Jesus, you country gentlemen work harder than I thought."

Crenshaw said nothing.

"A bit late for a ride, Robert."

Crenshaw went around to the other side of Afton, and looked across the horse's back. "Did you have some food? A drink?"

"Your Miss Harkin took great care of us. She's a treasure."

"Good," Crenshaw said, combing.

"It's been quite awhile since I've been here, and I expected the master to receive me. You're living here the whole year 'round now, is that right?"

"That's right," Crenshaw said.

"Quite a change from Londontown, Robert. Do you miss it at all?"

"No."

"Good to hear. An Irishman's got to roam, I suppose, but he's never at home anywhere but Ireland."

Crenshaw threw a blanket over Afton and led him into his stall. He hung up the tack and the combs and turned back to Higgins who was still leaning comfortably, his hands in his jacket pockets. "This is the last time, Frank."

"Last time? Last time for what?"

"Limeview won't be available to you any longer."

"Ah, that's a shame. Why, Robert?"

"Why? Because I say so. It will not be available."

Higgins took one hand from his pocket and held it up. "Easy, boy. Easy, now. I was only askin'. Did Rúairí rattle you?"

"No."

"You must understand, Robert. Security has to be our number-one priority. If he—"

"I said no. No, he didn't disturb me."

"Grand. If he did I'll have a word with him. You've been too good for too long to us."

"Then if you believe that, Frank, don't ask for Limeview again."

"Certain circumstances may—"

"Under no circumstances."

"Well, Robert," Higgins turned around, facing away from him, and leaned both hands on the stall gate, looking at the mare as if he were considering buying her. "I don't know if I can agree to that. But I'll keep it in mind."

They heard footsteps coming toward the stable and both turned toward the open door. It was George, walking in sleepily, squinting, his long hair tangled from the pillow. "Mr. Crenshaw?"

"Yes, George, it's all right."

"Tim said I should just come and—"

"It's all right, boy. Go back to bed."

George turned, but Higgins called, "Come here, lad." When he was before him, Higgins turned to Crenshaw and said, "Well, will you introduce us, Robert?"

"This is Mr. Higgins, George."

George nodded. Higgins leaned back against the stall and looked him over. "Ever heard of me, lad?"

"No, sir."

"Then we're even. I've never heard of you, either."

George smiled, confused, and looked to Crenshaw.

"He's the stableboy, Frank. Hired just yesterday."

"Oh, I figured as much. I wasn't thinking he was your—your companion."

Crenshaw said to his smiling face, "You slimy bastard, you. One telephone call, just one, and I can put you in prison. You and that beast MacCurtain, all of you."

Higgins said calmly to George, "You don't consider Mr. Mac-Curtain a beast, now do you, boy?"

"Mr. MacCurtain? I only just started today, sir," he said, frightened, looking from one man to the other. "Just today, sir."

"Back to your room, George," Crenshaw said. "Tell Tim everything's fine here."

"Yes, sir," George said. "And goodnight to you."

Higgins and Crenshaw walked back to the house together, silent in the windy night. Under the soft sway of the elms, Higgins took him by the arm. "Now, I don't know what's gotten into you, Robert. But let's have a drink together so I can apologize."

"I don't want to drink with you."

"Just one. I want to say something."

In the lounge Crenshaw poured a Scotch for himself and handed Higgins a glass of Irish. Standing, Higgins lifted his glass. "I'm truly sorry, Robert. Sarcasm and needling is part of my nature these days. A soldier's humor is rough, I know. Taking the piss out of people is our favorite form of entertainment. It's no excuse, but I just wanted to say I'm sorry for my remark. I was trying to get a rise out of you for no good reason, just habit. Full apologies."

"Cheers," Crenshaw said, and took a sip.

"*Bás in Éirinn*," Higgins toasted, and took a long swallow.

They talked for awhile, Higgins inquiring after Crenshaw's health, as they sat in easy chairs near the fire. Miss Harkin came in, her dressing gown buttoned to the throat, "just to see how the fire was," and Higgins invited her to stay for a glass of "Liffey water," which she accepted. Higgins was charming, pouring out the drinks as if it were his home and Crenshaw and Miss Harkin his guests. If MacCurtain had been a monsignor to her, Higgins was the Archbishop. She listened respectfully to what he said, laughed at his jokes, and blushed at his flattery. She excused herself after one drink. Crenshaw, a man who didn't enjoy drinking, allowed his glass to be refilled. The Scotch was helping him. And the conversation, which was monopolized by Higgins, soothed him as well. When Crenshaw asked if he wanted music, Higgins said yes, anything he chose would be fine, and then questioned Crenshaw about the Schubert, but his curiosity seemed as measured as his flattery to Miss Harkin. From questions of music Higgins asked what Robert was doing to keep himself out of trouble these days, and Crenshaw told him about his book, not because he thought Higgins was sincerely interested, but because it was the first time he'd spoken of it to anyone, and it was a novelty, making the book seem somehow a living thing and not just a pile of typescript. It was the Scotch, he was sure, but it didn't matter. Crenshaw spoke out of loneliness. By opening his mouth and expressing his dream perhaps he could in some way put a final sense of order to his jumbled day.

Higgins said he would enjoy seeing the aquarium, when Crenshaw asked him. They would need a refill, however, for the long journey across the hall. Crenshaw spoke for a long time as they stood in the room, explaining the life that swam before them, until he realized that Higgins didn't really care, but was humoring him. He suggested they return to the lounge. Crenshaw brushed his shoulder against the doorjamb as they left the library. It had been a long time since dinner and he wasn't used to straight Scotch in this quantity.

He watched Higgins as he sat in the chair at the head of the table. "How long will the conference last, Frank? You said in your letter just one day."

"One day it will be. You'll be rid of us by late afternoon tomorrow."

"And as I said, never again."

"Yes, yes. Tell me, why do you drink Scotch instead of the Irish?"

"It tastes better."

"That's a good enough reason. You don't think much of Irish things, being to the bright lights of London, I suppose."

"It tastes better, Frank. And I don't say *sláinte* because it's not my language, if that's your next question."

He told himself it was the alcohol that sent those words out so quickly, and with anger. And damn lucky he had the Scotch for support. Why had he allowed himself to be charmed by Higgins? Taking an insult from him and accepting an apology that was as counterfeit and cold as a rich man's charity. To hell with him, anyway.

"But you're Irish underneath. You came home. You realize the need for *bás in Eírinn,* am I right, Robert?"

"I came home to *live* in Ireland. I'm not in love with death the way you and your whole stinking mob are. And don't give me any lectures about Ireland, if you please. You didn't invent this country. The I.R.A. won't dictate to me how I should feel, how I should live. Lady Crenshaw was Lady Crenshaw, Frank. Her belief was a hobby. Republicanism gave spice to her after-dinner chat."

"I don't care if you are her son. I will not hear that kind of shit about a great lady."

Crenshaw laughed, set his glass down, and leaned his hands on the table. "What would you do without heroes? You prefer them dead, too, don't you? Do you think you'll be a hero, Frank? Frank Higgins, loyal son, patriot, liberator. Or will you be remembered as a pit bull who doesn't have sense or feeling or anything but the instinct to inflict pain?"

Higgins whistled softly. "Now who's givin' who lectures?"

"Maybe you won't be remembered. That would be justice."

"You think I'm a dog, Robert? I'll tell you what I think of you. A silly queer. Another dumb Protestant Brit-loving rich man with his bloody horses and bloody fish and stableboys. Scared of your own shadow. A disgrace to your mother's memory and to the country she fought for. Go back to London. Call me a dog! I've had men crippled for thinking that, never mind saying it. What do you know, Mr. Robert Horse-Protestant Crenshaw, about justice? Ask the mothers on the Falls Road, ask the men of H-block, ask the poor Irish in London, in Dublin, about justice. Ask them what they think of the Provisional Irish Republican Army. 'Never use my house again, Frank.' Jesus, you couldn't pay me to use this place again. We'll do our business here tomorrow and then you won't see my heels for the dust. And after tomorrow you'd be advised to get some fire alarms for this place. It could go up like a paint factory when you aren't looking. It's been awhile since Clare's seen an Anglo's big house burning but by Jesus you might be the start of a trend." He took a drink and set the glass gently on the table. "I suppose we're clear now, Robert. I apologized and you wouldn't accept it. Fair enough. I just wish you'd told me you'd turned coward before we organized this meeting."

"I didn't turn coward. I turned brave."

"Yes, yes, well, enjoy your bravery. I have one more thing to say to you. If you ever make that one phone call you'll end up in a ditch with a big hole in your skull."

Crenshaw left his Scotch on the table. "You know where your room is?"

Higgins nodded.

"Then sleep well, Commander."

In his bed, Crenshaw lay a long time before trying to sleep. The Scotch had soured his stomach and left his brain with a will of its own which he soon gave in to. Memory washed him. When he was a child in this house he had always been frightened of the dark room and the huge house all around him settling and creaking in the night. The fear had come out of loneliness, because there had never been enough people to fill Limeview, and he had the feeling sometimes that ghosts would take him away to some room that was never used and no one would find him. Fear of something unknowable had been one of his first memories. Fear of lying alone in empty rooms, the only other presence being darkness, which made no sound, had no smell, but could be felt, touching him everywhere. He had lived through many nights since he was that boy alone in the big house, with only paid servants to care for him. He had gone nowhere, and nothing had changed, except now there was more of him for the darkness to touch. Not being aware of his exhaustion, sleep came, and Crenshaw's dreams were unknown to him when he woke.

Miss Harkin came into the room and opened the curtains. Crenshaw looked out on the gray sky. "It's past nine, Mr. Crenshaw," she said, avoiding the bed with her eyes as she picked up his clothes which he'd thrown at the chair last night. "Past nine, now."

"I'll take breakfast in the library," Crenshaw said, and rubbed his eyes. He felt surprisingly good. There was just a slight headache which was fading as he came up to full awakening. He showered quickly and dressed in brown corduroy slacks and a tan sweater. As he descended the staircase, Higgins, still in his leather jacket and tweed trousers, was passing from the lounge into the hall. Had he been to bed? Crenshaw wondered. Higgins looked up and waited until Crenshaw reached the hall. "Sleep well, Robert?"

"Yes, thank you."

"I managed an hour. I don't need much sleep. We must've both gotten too far into the old bottle last night."

"Why?"

"Well, I said some things to you I wish I hadn't."

"Yes?"

Higgins slowly smiled. "And I wager you regret some things you said."

"I don't like rows, Frank."

"It's a new day then." He turned and called into the lounge, "Kevin? Would you come out here?"

A young man with a full beard and horn-rimmed glasses stepped into the hall. "Mr. Robert Crenshaw," Higgins said, "Mr. Kevin Deasey."

"Good morning, Mr. Deasey."

"Good morning," he said. His face was composed, giving nothing. Higgins must run a tight ship, Crenshaw thought. Or did he pick people like MacCurtain and this Deasey especially for their gracelessness?

"Kevin here," Frank said, "is our propaganda chief."

"I see," Crenshaw said. "If you'll excuse me," he left them standing in the hall and went into the library. The room was cold. There was no fire. Where was that girl? Then he remembered they wouldn't be back until tomorrow. He set about making it himself. That was quite good, leaving them that way. He wouldn't be charmed by them, and he wouldn't be frightened by them. He'd have nothing to do with them. The fire set and lit, he tended his aquarium until Miss Harkin brought a tray with his breakfast. "The others will be here very soon, Mr. Crenshaw. Shall I call you when they arrive?"

"No. I won't be disturbed," he said and tasted the coffee. Rich, hot, strong, perfect. "Superb coffee, Miss Harkin."

"Thank you. Enjoy it, then," she said and left.

He ate his egg and toast, savored the marmalade, poured a fresh cup of coffee and set to work. It had been a difficult chapter but this morning he was flying through it. He didn't hear the bell, nor the voices in the hall, until Miss Harkin opened the door and said, "I'm sorry, Mr. Crenshaw. They insisted."

Crenshaw looked up as a white-haired man entered the room with a young dark-haired woman in a blue waterproof jacket behind him. Crenshaw got up quickly from his desk and hit the tray with his knee as he rose. The china and silverware and coffeepot flew over his desk and crashed to the floor. He bent to pick it up, hearing a short, barking laugh from the woman. They both knelt down to help him. Miss Harkin took control, telling them to leave it, and soon had it cleared up and out of the room.

"I'm Joseph Walsh," the white-haired man said. "And this is Deirdre O'Sullivan."

"Pleased to meet you," Crenshaw said.

"I'm sorry if we disturbed you. I wanted to see you and express my appreciation for your hospitality." Crenshaw listened to his cordial Ulster tone. Was he a Protestant? No, he wouldn't be, of course not, Crenshaw thought. Some Catholics from Ulster must have culture, too.

"Oh, it's quite all right," Crenshaw said, glancing at Deirdre who was looking around the room, at the books, the furniture, the carpet, and the aquarium. It was obvious she had never been in a room like this, and she didn't try to conceal her wonder. "I'm usually not this clumsy when I receive guests."

Deirdre turned to him, and laughed again. "I'm sorry," she said.

"Oh, no," Crenshaw said. "I'm beyond being embarrassed by girls laughing at me."

"I wasn't laughing at you. I am sorry."

She had the sound of Dublin in her voice. "Yew" for you, and the direct gaze of the Dubliner.

Walsh said, "I met you a long time ago, here at Limeview."

"Yes?"

"You were about fifteen then."

"My mother introduced me to so many people I got very lazy at remembering them."

A young man in a dark suit with dark blond hair was at the door. "Come in, John," Walsh said, "and meet Mr. Crenshaw. This is John Boland, a member of my staff."

"Pleased to meet you, Mr. Boland."

"You have a lovely home, Mr. Crenshaw."

"Thank you. Yes, well, I'm used to the old place by now." What are you doing? he asked himself. Being charmed, again. Others develop protection against it, but you can't turn away from it. He walked with them out to the hall. Walsh inquired about the Louis

Quatorze table, as his two young aides looked on. "Do you know furniture?" Crenshaw asked.

"I used to know a bit, but I've forgotten most of it. My eyes now and again can still tell what's beautiful and what's not."

They stood and Crenshaw talked about the table, the craftsmanship, the special oil made in America he used on it. He noticed Deirdre tracing her finger along the edge, and then peering into the polished pool of the tabletop, seeing her reflection. Her plain, open face softened by the gleam of wood.

MacCurtain opened the lounge door and said, "Whenever you're ready."

"Hello, Rúairí," Walsh said. "You look tip-top this morning."

MacCurtain left the door open and walked back into the room. Walsh winked at Deirdre and Boland. He smiled at Crenshaw. "I suppose we should begin," and they went into the lounge, Deirdre closing the door behind them. Crenshaw was left in the hall. He felt his smile hanging on his face, moronic, frozen.

Frank Higgins stood at the window watching as Deirdre, Joe Walsh and John Boland entered the room. Rúairí MacCurtain sat at the long table. It was polished and bare except for six crystal ashtrays and three wooden boxes of cigarettes. Near the table was a rolling bar. On the sideboard was an electric kettle and teacups.

Walsh walked over to Higgins as Deirdre and John Boland sat across from Rúairí, who was still, both hands on the table. Kevin Deasey was at the sideboard pouring tea for himself.

"Morning, Frank."

"Joe," Higgins nodded, not looking at him, but at John Boland sitting next to that little horror O'Sullivan. Walsh watched as Deasey held his teacup chest high, sipping delicately over his beard. "Who's your man there, Frank?"

"I was just about to ask you who that fellow at the table would be," Higgins answered, and saw Joe Walsh grin. It was an old technique. At an important meeting bring along as part of your delegation a stranger to the other side. It could throw them, get them thinking in the wrong direction, allow the armor to slip. Walsh was amused. It was nil to nil, he thought, before this started. The score's still tied, but now it's one to one. Higgins chatted with the old man, telling him who Deasey was and what a fine young officer he was. Walsh waited patiently for his turn to do the same for his man.

"Who handled the M-60 at Kildare?" Rúairí asked, staring at Deirdre.

"I forget." She took a cigarette and rolled it on the table. Picked it up and held it to her nose, sniffing, and then looking at Rúairí for the first time. He smiled, and lit the cigarette for her.

"Did you have any trouble with the belt feeding in?"

"Can't remember."

Still smiling, "The little one, the M-10, does it get hot on long bursts?"

Deirdre blew smoke at the ceiling, and seemed to be looking for an answer there. "That's a good question," she finally said. "A very good question. Does it get hot? I can't recall."

Rúairí looked at John Boland. "Do you have a name?"

"Yes," he answered quickly, and brought his hand up to his hair out of nervousness. He let it drop to the table.

"Is it John Boland? Formerly of Boland and Lafferty Limited? Experts in behind the back assassinations?"

Boland said nothing.

"Our intelligence had you pinned awhile ago. You're sloppy, you and your mate Lafferty. We were this close—" MacCurtain held up his thumb and forefinger, smiling—"this close to nailing the pair of you."

Deirdre turned to Boland. "This gentleman here is Rúairí Mac-Curtain, of MacCurtain Limited. Expert in child molesting, grave robbing and indecent exposure."

"The seeds that destroy an alliance, any alliance, Deirdre," Rúairí said, "are sown at the beginning."

"Then don't play, MacCurtain."

Rúairí nodded.

"Shall we begin?" Higgins asked when everyone was seated. "First I'd like to say that the Provisional I.R.A. is delighted to have the talent and determination of Republicans like yourselves, and the whole of your organization, back in the fold. There have been bitter years and many deaths separating us. But today can begin a new era for all of us, when we can concentrate our collective will against the enemy. I want to say that we come in good faith, that I have sounded out our entire movement, and everyone wants this alliance to succeed. Joe, do you have anything to say?"

"Let's get on with it. Let's hear the details."

"Fine. Kevin, will you start us off? Let's have an overview of our propaganda. See if you can agree with us, Joe. Kevin?"

"Our most vital issue is the blanket men of H-block. Our 'Smash H-block' campaign has been an enormous success, both here and in the States." Deasey continued to speak, directing the majority of his report to Higgins and MacCurtain, and only looking now and again across the table at the I.S.A. delegation. Deasey had become the propaganda chief only a week before, and had been informed of this meeting yesterday by MacCurtain. He had no idea what was happening. MacCurtain had told him to follow the chief of staff's lead at the meeting, and nothing more, and so he tried to stay away from the faces across from him. MacCurtain looked bored as Deasey spoke. But Higgins seemed enthralled by his report. Deasey glanced at the three I.S.A. leaders. Walsh was looking out the window. Young Boland was staring at him. Deirdre leaned back in her chair, smoking. The propaganda chief continued, looking over at Rúairí, and then quickly away. Dangerous man, that. MacCurtain was a games player, a natural intelligence officer who lived on intrigue. The alliance could be real or it could be phony. Deasey didn't know, and he didn't want to know. There had already been one lie in the meeting when it was only minutes old. The flowery opening about "sounding out the movement" was a lie. The only I.R.A. officers who even knew about the alliance were Higgins, MacCurtain, and himself. Deasey moved from the H-block campaign to the need for absolute coordination on the propaganda front. The I.R.A. line must come through simply, repeatedly, unfailingly. He stroked his beard as he spoke, and after awhile only looked at Higgins, his patron and protector.

Frank Higgins watched as Joe Walsh lit a cigarette. He's stronger than me, but he's only one man. Why do I have a sense of shame when I'm around him? Frank remembered being in the helicopter with him years ago, and the taunts of the British soldiers. How he had slipped away into himself, chained to the old man, and how Joe had remained calm, an officer, a leader. He'll never follow me, Higgins thought. He doesn't like me and he's stronger. He's only here because this is his last chance. Him and his utopian communist crew. Don't misjudge him though. Not again.

"And so," Deasey concluded after more than an hour, "it's in the best interest of the Movement that there be only one organ, *An Phoblacht*, our paper. We can, and we should, combine staffs. We all recognize the quality of the *Irish Patriot*, but it must cease to exist. I.R.A. propaganda must not be split."

"Thank you, Kevin," Higgins said.

Walsh asked, "When do you propose this death take place, Mr. Deasey?"

"Sorry?" Deasey adjusted his glasses.

"When do you propose the *Irish Patriot* stop publishing?"

"Immediately."

"That's impossible."

"In two months' time then," Higgins said.

"Impossible. As I said in Lucan at Halloween, the I.S.A. line will not emerge through to the public. We'll support H-block, we'll support any damn thing Mr. Deasey wants, but the *Irish Patriot* must continue. It'd be foolish to bury it. Two papers saying the same thing in different styles would seem to be much more effective."

Higgins turned to his intelligence officer. "Rúairí?"

"I have no objections. Let the rag run."

"What is this?" Deirdre leaned forward and crushed her cigarette in the ashtray. "What are you up to, MacCurtain? Do you want those shooters? If you do then I'd advise you to cut this shit."

"You want love as well as alliance?"

"Respect is what we want, you shifty-eyed fook."

Rúairí laughed.

"Deirdre," Walsh said.

"Come on, Higgins," Deirdre addressed him. "You're sweet as cream here, and this one—" she pointed at MacCurtain—"is coming on like poison. What's going on?"

Higgins looked at Walsh. "The *Irish Patriot* will continue to run indefinitely. But it *must* conform to our line."

"Of course," Walsh said.

"We don't consider the paper to be a rag. As of this moment it is not a rag. That right, I.O.?"

"Full apologies, Miss O'Sullivan," Rúairí said.

Walsh turned the meeting toward the logistics of aligning the two armies. He introduced John Boland as the I.S.A. liaison. Boland spoke at length, informing the I.R.A. that he would leave for Northern Ireland tomorrow and set up HQ in Derry. He would be available to the Provisionals for any questions in the weeks to come and he hoped that the courtesy would be reciprocal. Boland looked at Deasey and MacCurtain and Higgins as he spoke. It was his moment, and he seized it. His ambition, his intelligence, his gift for pleasing superiors, had finally come through for him. He'd come very far, very fast. In June he was one of many part-time party organizers, running youth committees, helping Joe Walsh with the newspaper. After Liam Cleary's death he had become an assassin, working with Lafferty, being blooded, learning the trade. Now, here at Limeview, he was part of the I.S.A. leadership.

"I'm impressed, John," Frank Higgins said when Boland finished. "We'll be able to work together very smoothly indeed." He checked his watch. "Shall we eat, and then come back for some detailed discussion about the weapons?"

"Fine," Walsh said, rising.

They followed the I.R.A. out of the room and down the hall to the dining room where Miss Harkin was offering Guinness, beer, sandwiches and soup. Walsh was wondering what the score was now. They must be careful with this lot. They must have something ready if things turned sour, and not give everything away today. "Where's Deirdre?" young Boland asked him.

"She'll turn up," Walsh said, looking over at Higgins, who was making Miss Harkin laugh.

Work was difficult when he tried to resume. He stared at his fish. The day was not beginning at all well. His convict cichlid was dashing about the tank, swooping to the bottom in a scatter of gravel and then shooting up, blindly rushing into the side glass. The other fish stayed out of his way, letting him be. Crenshaw thought he might isolate him for awhile. *Cichlasoma nigrofasciatum* was a very high-strung fish. Beautiful and rare, colored silver and yellow with his convict's stripes of black, coming all the way from Central America to have his nervous breakdown in the Burren.

It was near two o'clock when the meeting broke for lunch. He heard them open the door and walk down the hall, speaking in low voices. What were they talking about? They were carrying on like the United bloody Nations. The door to the library opened and he saw the young woman standing in jeans and a sweater, giving some shape to her thin figure which the waterproof jacket had hidden. He laid his book down and stood up. "Hello, come in, come in, Miss O'Hanlon."

She walked straight to the aquarium, and Crenshaw joined her, turning on the tank light. "It's O'Sullivan," she said, in a quiet voice, watching the fish.

"Oh, I *am* sorry. That's very rude of me. Your first name is—"

She smiled, turning to him quickly, "Deirdre," and then looked back at the fish.

"Deirdre," he said. "I am a bit better at first names. You call me Robert, Deirdre."

"What's wrong with that fellah?" she asked, pointing at the convict fish darting paranoically all over the tank.

"He's not very happy this morning. He's called a convict fish, do you see his stripes? He's like a thoroughbred horse, very skittish. The slightest disturbance in the water, the temperature, or the light sets him off."

"I had fish when I was a kid."

"Did you?"

"Oh," she said, "it was nothin' like this. I had goldfish," she grinned, almost embarrassed.

"Well, goldfish are quite nice."

"I always wanted a pet. I used to drag home every ratty kitten I found, or any old hound in the street, but my dad had asthma so the next morning they were gone. So it was fish for me."

"You're a Dubliner?"

"I am. North side. Oh, he's a pretty one, what do you call him?"

"Which one?"

"This one here, with the black spots."

"Yes, that's *molliensia sphenops*."

"Jesus," she said. "All that for a little fish?"

"Or she's known as a marbled molly."

"Much better."

Miss Harkin came in and said, "Your lunch is ready in the dining room, miss."

"Thank you." Still watching the fish.

"Would you like to eat here?" Crenshaw asked her.

"Yes." Looking at him. "If it's no bother."

"My dear girl," Crenshaw said. "It's my pleasure."

They sat near the fire with the tray of chicken sandwiches and tea on the floor between them. Deirdre had asked questions about the fish, their habits, their cost, their life expectancy. Suddenly she said, after Crenshaw told her about a shop in London that sold tropical fish and nothing else, "You're a Protestant, Robert?"

"Yes," he said.

"And rich?"

"Oh, filthy with it."

"And yet you support the Republican movement, too?"

Crenshaw bit a piece of sandwich and chewed. "Yes, I do, but not for much longer."

"Why is that?"

"I don't believe in it and I never have. I think the whole thing is evil."

"Evil? What're you talking about?"

"I'm not sure. I certainly don't want to insult you. I've supported the I.R.A. because of my mother and her wishes."

"A great patriot," Deirdre said respectfully.

"A great bitch as well," Crenshaw said. Deirdre was watching him closely, with the control a child uses when seeing a member of another race for the first time. Suspicious, fascinated. She looked very much like a child to Crenshaw, and not a woman at all. One of those little ones you see in Dublin begging aggressively, children without childhood, forced into intelligence and knowledge not by careful teaching, but by city streets and a world that never sees them. "Did you have," Crenshaw asked, "a—em—a difficult time growing up?"

"No," she said. "I had a good time. My dad drove a lorry for Guinness."

His theory shot, Crenshaw said, "I'm sorry for prying."

"Oh, hell," she laughed. "Pry away. I don't mind being pry-ed."

Just before she left to return to the lounge with the others, she asked about a picture on the wall. It was a line drawing with a sepia wash his mother had commissioned years ago depicting one of the plants of the Burren. Deirdre went closer and studied it.

She thanked him for the lunch and the talk and crossed the hall to the lounge. Crenshaw sat and observed the fire, burning low. He typed: "All that for a little fish?" on a note card and then got a hammer, a knife, and tape from the kitchen. He dismantled the frame around the line drawing and wrote, on the back of the thick paper with his Cross pen, "For lunch at Limeview, and for prying together," dated it, signed his name, rolled it up and taped the edges.

Miss Harkin was at the kitchen table with the accounts ledger and a cup of tea. Crenshaw laid the rolled drawing on the table. "Will you give that to Miss O'Sullivan before she leaves? Tell them I won't be here to see them off."

"Yes, Mr. Crenshaw."

"You won't forget about this?" he tapped the cylinder.

She looked at him squarely, insulted. "Of course I wouldn't forget."

He dressed in a bulky wool sweater, jodhpurs and his riding boots. He took a cap and gloves and had George, just coming in on Afton, saddle the mare with a horse blanket draped across the neck, and rode up into the Burren, walking her easily through the stony fields.

The afternoon meeting began by Joe Walsh saying, "Let's horsetrade, Frank."

"Grand. When can you deliver?"

"Before the year is out," Walsh said, turning to Deirdre and Boland sitting next to him at the long table. Deirdre nodded. "When can you open the door for us?" she asked.

"I think right away," Higgins answered. "Of course, we can't take your troops into the Army before January or so, and then we'll have to move them in carefully. We have a Christmas offensive organized and set to jump off. Bringing in new personnel at this stage could cripple it. After the new year, slowly and carefully, we can align."

"What sort of offensive?" Walsh asked.

"Bombings," Rúairí said. "Primarily against economic targets. We're going to light up the six counties for Christmas."

"Will our shipment be used in this offensive?" Walsh asked.

"It won't," Higgins said. "We're set for this job. Getting the shipment into the North will be a problem now, Joe. Our suggestion is we take delivery down here and move it in piece by piece."

"No," Walsh said, and lit a cigarette. "We'll deliver it to the North. John here will be up there working with Mr. Deasey to make the roads straight. And when it's delivered Deirdre and a team of our officers will work with your quartermaster."

"I don't know, Joe," Higgins said.

"We're not going to let you see the matériel until it's in the six counties. You understand, don't you? It's the only way we can play it."

Higgins said, "Yes. But do you realize how dangerous it is crossing the border these days? In the beginning we could move a whole division of men across playing pipes and bangin' drums and nobody was the wiser. Now the Brits hug that border. They check every lorry, every hay wagon, every thing that rolls."

"Then we won't use wheels," Walsh said, smiling.

"How then?" Rúairí asked. "Carrier pigeon?"

"John?" Walsh turned to him.

"By sea," Boland rose, unfolding a map of Ireland. He laid it flat on the table, and turned it facing Higgins, Deasey and Mac-Curtain. "We'll deliver the entire shipment here," he pointed to the northeast tip of the country, "to Ballycastle in Antrim."

Rúairí looked up. "It seems a good choice. Where is it now?"

"That's not important for you to know," Boland answered, and held Rúairí's eyes a moment before saying, "I hope your Christmas festivities won't affect Ballycastle."

"No. We'll keep it quiet there for you."

"By sea," Higgins said. "Excellent idea. When is the best time, John?"

"December twenty-sixth. Stephen's Day."

"Very good. I assume it will be agreeable if we have one of our men, an officer, of course, with your team for the voyage?"

"It's not agreeable, no," Walsh said.

"How will we communicate?"

"We will rendezvous with you in Ballycastle," Walsh said and pointed at the map. "Stephen's Day we'll meet at the Royal Port Hotel. From Stephen's Day on one of our people will be in the bar of the hotel waiting. Kevin and John can plot this more precisely later. Now there's a good quiet port here, on Rathlin Island. The matériel will stay there, on our vessel while we meet. We can get it to the mainland that day or the next."

"I see no problems," Higgins said.

"Make sure there are none, Frank."

Higgins looked up from the map to Walsh. His face was cold and suddenly angry. "You won't take my word, will you?"

"I'll take it for now. I don't want to give threats to you gentle-

men. But I will warn you. We are ready to move North and
will come up to either fight with you or against you. There must
be no tricks, no games, no break in communication." He looked
at each of them, in turn, before continuing. "We'll take you on if
we feel we're being waltzed about by you. And it won't be just
picking off strays like we did last summer. We'll go straight at
your center."

"That would be foolish, Joe," Higgins said.

"Perhaps more for you than us."

"Look," Rúairí said. "You said you wouldn't threaten, so don't.
If you think we made peace at Halloween because we were afraid
of you, then you're wrong. Dead wrong."

"We hurt you in Dublin. Imagine what we'd do to you in
Belfast."

Higgins touched Rúairí's arm. "Enough, now. No more threats.
We take your warning. And we agree to all your conditions. I
think we've made an excellent start. Kevin and John will work
together like hand in glove on all minor problems, I'm sure."

"But who's the hand?" Deirdre interrupted him, "and who's
the glove?"

Higgins looked at her, and then laughed. "God, you're a hard
girl. Hand in hand, how's that?"

"Better," she said, looking not at Higgins but at Rúairí Mac-
Curtain.

Higgins said, "Let's review the plan once more."

The meeting continued for another thirty minutes, and then
was adjourned by mutual consent. Boland and Deasey made ar-
rangements to meet in Derry and all shook hands. After Miss
Harkin presented Robert Crenshaw's gift, Deirdre left with Walsh
and Boland to return to Moher. She saw the chief looking intro-
spective, absentminded, and said to him, "What do you think?"

"It's a gamble," Walsh said. "They could be bluffing, but there's
no way to call them."

"I think it's on, Joe."

"We'll know soon enough."

They took the coast road south out of the Burren in the last
brief light. The fields of stone seemed to Joseph Walsh to be a
herd of still animals, wild, predatory, waiting. The low sky was
bringing the night down. An ashy end to the day. And the sun

out over the gray sea, drowning in clouds. On their right, miles out to sea, he saw the form of Inis Oirthin, the smallest of the Arans. He watched it sinking away until there was no light, no sea, no clouds.

Walsh shifted his weight from one side to the other and listened to Boland and Deirdre in the front seat. John was driving, talking about the meeting and the safe house he would use in Derry. Deirdre sat with the rolled drawing between her legs and both hands around it, trying to keep her cheery tone of voice under control. They should be pleased, Walsh thought. They had done very well indeed. How different I am from them. The difference of age. And I'm Ulster and they're Free State. Huge differences. Both Dubliners. That's why they're here, because of Dublin. The Dubliner sees the deprivation, the farce, the cruelty, the ugliness that the rural person does not. "John, when we get to Lisdoonvarna stop and get some cigarettes."

"And some whiskey?" Deirdre asked, turning. "We should have a drink to celebrate."

"No celebrating," Walsh said. "This isn't a football match."

"One drink, Joe."

"No," he said softly. "This is Gudrun's house we're going to. She's in charge and we won't come bearing gifts."

Boland said, "I thought it was the yank's place."

"The German's running the show there," Walsh told him. And then, to Deirdre, "Do you understand, Dee-Dee?"

"Yes, sir. No drink if it's not offered."

The rooms above the shops along the main street of Lisdoonvarna were full of light while the shopfronts were dark. At the south end of town Boland parked in front of a modern store. A girl in a long white apron was taking in wooden boxes of fruit and vegetables. Boland gave her a hand with a heavy crate of apples. "Thanks very much," she smiled when they were inside. It was a clean, well-lit place, selling foodstuffs, hardware, and behind the counter, spirits and wine. The radio was playing the hit from last summer by the Boomtown Rats, the Dublin punk band who had gone to England and were making it big. The girl turned up the volume before she asked Boland, "Yes?"

"Four packs of the Carroll's there."

Tell me why—

I don't like Mondays
Tell me why—
I don't like Mondays

"Anything else?" she asked, and then softly sang along.
"Three bags of crisps."

I don't like Mondays

Boland remembered Deirdre telling him about the song one
night last summer in Dublin. It concerned a California high school
girl who had opened up with an automatic weapon on a school
playground one Monday. When she was asked why, she replied,
"I don't like Mondays." Boland had laughed, sitting with Deirdre
in a chips shop on Parnell Street as the song boomed out of the
jukebox. Deirdre had said she saw nothing funny about it. If they
had written a short story about it instead of a pop song, would it
be funny? "It's just energy, Deirdre," he'd said. "Energy and
nothing else."
    "Anger," she'd said. "I hate the music, but I love the anger."
That night they'd met Lafferty in a back booth of the place and
Deirdre gave them their orders for the next day, twelve August,
when the three of them went to the home of Mrs. Crowley and
killed her sons.
    The girl placed the cigarettes and potato chips on the counter
and rang up the sale.
    "Nothing off for helping you with the apples?"
    "Ah, no," she said. "Wish I could," and gave him a flirty smile.
    In the car Boland passed the crisps around, and started off for
Moher. Walsh directed him up past the church when they were in
town and to the long low house on the hill. Boland parked next
to the garage, and then gave a hand to the chief, whose back had
stiffened up. Gudrun met them at the rear door. Boland had not
seen her since the night in Wicklow four months ago. The image
he'd kept of her was of a defiant, lonely face, bruised, her blouse
torn, erotic. Wicklow, in the back bedroom with Lafferty questioning her, suddenly backhanding her across the face, knocking
her off her chair, and telling him to get her up. Boland was new to
the game, shocked at Lafferty's pleasure in striking her, but followed
his order and decided to play as rough as his mentor. When he

grabbed her blouse it came away in his hands, ripping to show her throat. That had not been erotic. No. It was later, watching her with Burke on the porch, remembering her in the room, Lafferty's profanity, a cut on her knee and a raspberry of blood. Seeing her with the yank, bruised, insolent, that had been it. The sight of the unwilling victim had stirred and confused him. Now she was not defiant, but easy and hospitable. She was not erotic, but efficient and secure, dressed in corduroy jeans and a blue sweatshirt. She told them that Terrence and Martin had gone to check the yacht and were expected any minute. He was set to say something to her. An apology? Ridiculous. But she spared him by saying, "I haven't forgotten you. But I understand. All right, John?"

"Yes," Boland said, and nodded his thanks.

Cyril McGuffin was in the kitchen making dinner, all smiles and questions, cooking theatrically. He opened the oven and gave them all "a taste of things to come." Pot roast stewing in two pints of Guinness with potatoes, carrots, celery, onion and turnip. Everyone was happily surprised when McGuffin passed around small dishes of the stew. Gudrun opened a bottle of red wine and they stayed in the kitchen as Walsh briefed them about the meeting. Full alignment, the weapons would be delivered by sea to Northern Ireland before the year was out. Gudrun, Terry and McGuffin would run *Die Freiheit* up the coast.

Terry and Martin had gone to the yacht and from there had driven up to the Cliffs of Moher. There was only one other car parked in the gloomy late afternoon. Martin had come with Anne one brilliant September day when there had been two busloads of Americans on tour walking up along the cliffs. Today in the November damp and dark there was only one couple on the high ridge walking toward the tower. Terry stepped over the low stone wall. "Hey," Burke said. "Can't you read? You're not supposed to go out there."

"Come on, chickenshit."

Burke followed him out on to the table of rock and over to the edge. The cliff face fell straight down to the sea, three hundred feet or so, and to their left the wall of rock curved out to stare at the bleak Atlantic. Burke saw the sea breaking soundlessly below, and had the curious sensation of looking down on gulls wheeling above the water. He took a step back. O'Connor stood with the toes of his boots over the edge, looking down. "Do you ever feel like jumping when you're high like this?" he asked Burke.

"No. Come on, Terry."

"Some sight. The Cliffs of Moher. The Wall of Thomond."

"You're making me nervous, man. Come on."

O'Connor turned. "Nobody can *make* you nervous. You're either nervous or you're not."

"Yeah, I know. I taught you that. Nobody makes you feel anything. But you should come away. The wind gusts and you're gone."

"Should? You taught me that one, too. 'Should is not part of the vocabulary of a modern man.' Martin Burke, one-time laureate of Brooklyn."

Burke smiled. "Come on, kid. Listen to your teacher. You're scaring the hell out of me."

In the car they sat and smoked, looking out to the sea. Burke started the car but O'Connor said, "Let's stay awhile. That house is making me batty."

"Making you?"

"No," he smiled, and then sighed, "I'm just batty." The crash had finally come to him. He'd been high for months now, speeding on his life underground. But the weeks in Burke's house had brought him down. The waiting, and silence, again, like the waiting in Kinsale, had become a load to lift every morning and carry through his day.

Burke knew what he meant by "batty." He had learned a lot in the past month. Especially about silence. When O'Connor and Gudrun had been living at his house, with McGuffin staying over most nights, the silence the first few days had been nearly unbearable. McGuffin, the most garrulous man Burke had ever met, had taken to it surprisingly quickly, and seemed to enjoy it as much as an old soldier who sees proudly that his uniform still fits. For Burke the others' silence excluded him from his own house. They were all polite when he spoke to them, but none of them encouraged speech, or were afraid to let a conversation die. He soon found that the way to join them was to keep his mouth shut.

They ate all meals together, and sometimes watched television. Other than that, they would go to their rooms, and the house would feel as full and quiet as a monastery. After awhile Burke began to enjoy the silence. His hearing improved. Any footsteps outside came clearly to him. He could hear the slightest settling of the house. The fire burning in the grate was music in an accoustically perfect hall.

Gudrun had taken complete control of the house. She knew about safe houses; it had been her specialty in Europe, and that first night at Burke's she had organized them. They would shop for food and tobacco every two weeks. If you ran out of something, you did without. No beer or spirits in the house but wine every night at dinner, and at no other time. There is only one cook who has total control of the kitchen. The house is cleaned every day, the beds are made as soon as you're out of them, the dishes are washed and dried immediately after use, all weapons are cleaned daily, all doors and windows are left unlocked at all times. Unnecessary talk is counterproductive and threatens the integrity of the group.

"I'll be all right once we're moving," O'Connor said, wiping the condensation off the windshield.

"That's it, huh, keep moving?"

"That's it," Terry said. "Stand still and you rust."

"How long're you going to stay with it?"

"I'm gonna play it out, Marty. Keep it going as long as I can. I don't want it to ever stop."

"It will though," Burke said, and cracked the window to let the smoke out. "Everything does."

"What about you, teach?"

"I don't know. Not much longer. I'm like you now, I'm just playing in the band, but I'm going to get out. I don't want to die, or end up in an Irish jail."

"Oh, shit, Marty, who wants to die? Christ, I'm in this because I want to *live*. Don't you see that? You're alive now, man. Not like you told me you were before we brought the boat up. Juicing, mopin' around, sick of yourself. That's death."

"I lost my wife over this shit. You don't have a wife, do you?"

"No. But I've got me. I've got a direction, and I've got the means. I'm all set."

"You sound like some Baptist born-again asshole, Terry."

O'Connor laughed. "Praise the lord and pass the ammunition, brother Martin."

Burke was laughing with him. "You're hanging out with McGuffin too much."

"He's really a wild man, isn't he?"

"Yeah," Burke said, and started the car. "Don't get on his wrong side. Ever."

They drove off the ridge and took the road along the valley wall. The small green farms spread out below them to the beach at Moher. A rain storm could be seen blowing off the sea and into the valley, inching along, dropping lower and lower. "Look at that," O'Connor said, pointing.

"Yeah. Beautiful sight." A farmer walking two greyhounds on long leads coming towards them up the road. The hump-backed dogs trotted quickly, as if their feet were on coals. The farmer gave the nod. "You ever go greyhound racing, Marty?"

"Yeah. With McGuffin over in Limerick."

"Any fun?"

"It was all right. Ireland's perfect for greyhound racing."

"Why?"

"Well, you know about the 'little people.' It's easy to find the right sized jockeys."

They laughed again. The rain reached them, falling gently, bringing the night.

They were all in the dining room eating McGuffin's stew, listening to Walsh. McGuffin said, "Pardon me, Mr. Walsh, you know I'm a true patriot, and willing to put my life on the line runnin' that yawl up the coast into enemy waters, but I've got a woman to look after, and some jobs here that pay me pounds, not pats on the back."

"Certainly, Cyril," Walsh said, wiping his mouth, brushing his yellowing mustache with the cloth. "We'll give you an allowance for the woman."

The woman, Gudrun thought. Fat lot he cares for her, the poor frightened bird. He had deserted her for Burke's house, never phoned, only went to his own place now and again for fishing gear. And sex, probably. Gudrun had met her once, when Neena had hitch-hiked to Burke's one morning and McGuffin and Terrence were at the yacht. Burke had let her in and introduced her to Gudrun. How had he described her to Neena? Yes. "A visitor." As if she were a Martian with a German accent. The Englishwoman seemed terrified of something. Burke had made tea and talked with her in the kitchen while Gudrun had gone into one of the bedrooms off the hall. She could hear Neena weeping. And when McGuffin returned he'd embraced her, scolded her for coming, and drove her back to Ennistymon. Perhaps he really wanted security for her. More likely he wanted it for himself. Or was just raising the issue of money to stir things up so he could sit back later and watch the squabble he'd created. The Irish. Incomprehensible people, Gudrun thought.

"Now you're talking about 'an allowance'?" McGuffin asked. "That sounds like a shilling you give a child at the fair."

Deirdre said, "Are you in or out, Cyril?"

"In. I just want to have my rights."

"Your rights?" Deirdre laughed. "You have none. You're a soldier."

"No," Walsh said. "Cyril has a point. A legitimate point. We will take care of the woman. She'll receive checks for as long as you're on active service. It won't be much, mind you. Enough to keep her alive. And you will be paid."

"Grand," McGuffin said. "Could I ask how much?"

"Oh," Walsh replied. "I'd say a hundred pounds. Does that sound right, Deirdre?"

McGuffin went wild, leaping up, his face flushing as red as his hair. Gudrun had never seen anything like it. He must be playing, she thought. No one angers that quickly. She looked across at Terrence who winked at her. McGuffin stalked the room. Everyone stayed seated, watching the big man pacing, roaring, pointing at the window and the sea beyond, "I've fished those waters in every season for fifteen years. Take that fuckin' boat yourselves and see what happens. I'm qualified in four trades and no one pays me just to take a boat ride! One hundred pounds? Mother of Christ, Mr. Walsh, you pay that to the lad who drives the car on your fuckin' bank robberies." He glared at all of them, and stormed out of the room. They continued to sit, stunned, silent. Deirdre said, "He's out. We should ruin his knees for this."

"That won't be necessary," Walsh said, and looked at the faces around the table. "In a little while he won't need his knees." He looked calmly at Burke.

"He's just wild," Burke said softly.

"He's dangerous to us. He won't follow our discipline and he knows too much. A man after money has no belief. We must believe in each other and what we're doing. Isn't that right, Martin?"

Burke looked at the old man.

"Isn't that right, Martin?"

"Yes," he said.

This is the way McGuffin died. Walsh took Terry and John Boland into the front room and quickly plotted the operation. He then left the room to find the petulant McGuffin, soothe him, offer him two hundred pounds and return him to the fold. Walsh found him in the back driveway, his head stuck under the open hood of the Austin taxi. McGuffin was delighted with the new offer and slammed down the hood with a flourish. Would Cyril drive Terry and himself over to the yacht now? There were some things he wanted to get straightened out there. Certainly, McGuffin replied. We'll take the old taxi.

In the front room, after Walsh had gone, Boland handed Terry his .38 Cobra Special. "Cock it before you shoot it," he told him. "You've got five rounds but plan to fire only one. Understand? Hit him in the head."

"Right," O'Connor said and put on a green insulated sweatshirt with a zip front. He held the pistol and shifted it once, from his right hand to the left before putting it in his belt and zipping the sweatshirt over it. "Why me?"

"Why not you?" Boland said. "If you can't do it, say so now. Miss him out there and Joe'll do you and McGuffin."

"I can do it," Terry said, as Burke entered the room and sat in Anne's rocking chair next to the fire. Boland and Terry looked at him for a moment. Rocking, watching the fire, alone. "Do it now," Boland said, and Burke looked up quickly. "I'll be along behind you."

"Yeah," Terry said. "Let's get it over with."

McGuffin took the road south with Walsh sitting in the cane chair next to him and Terry in the rear. The old man chatted cordially with the victim, telling him that this was the first time since Kildare that he'd been comfortable in an automobile. "I could've used a chair like this on the back of that motorcycle, hey, Terry?"

"Right," Terry said, staring at the back of McGuffin's head.

Walsh then went on about the upcoming mission. They were

going to the boat to have a briefing there about the journey to the North. He thought it best to find out what McGuffin thought they'd need for the trip. They could take a detailed inventory while they spoke.

McGuffin drove down a curving hill and turned off the road onto a lane which wound its way through untended orchards up to the old derelict house. The taxi pulled off the lane into deep grass and McGuffin shut it down. "Let me take the torch," Walsh said, and McGuffin handed him the flashlight. They walked in single file through the orchard, Walsh leading with the light and Terry bringing up the rear. It was so dark they couldn't see each other from five feet away, and followed the flashlight cutting ahead. The wind ebbed and flowed, bringing a fine wetness off the water. A soft sour smell of fruit left to rot on the vine. They stepped on spongy pieces which had fallen into the deep grass. McGuffin was giving a list of items necessary for a successful voyage. Walsh stopped and McGuffin bumped into him. "Sorry, Chief."

"Where's the boat now, Cyril?" He heard Terry moving off to the right, sidestepping, circling. The flashlight shifting over the grass and finally resting on the trunk of a skinny tree, bending slightly with the wind.

"Just through this grove here and down the hill to the stream. Ah, it's custom-made for her. You can't see her from the sea, the road, or the lane. It's perfect. Come on, we're almost there."

Walsh took a few steps away from McGuffin and shut the light. "Terry?"

"Here," he answered, off to the left.

"What?" McGuffin began but went silent when the light was switched onto his face. He turned his head away. "Mother of Christ," he quietly said.

"Don't run, Cyril," Walsh said. "It will be easier here."

"I can't beg you. Can I just talk to you? You can listen to me, can't you? I was only blowin' off steam. Jesus, can't you see that?"

"Terry," Walsh ordered.

"I was Liam Cleary's friend, Joe. He talked about me the day he died. For Christ's sake! I was Liam's friend!"

"Terry," Walsh repeated.

O'Connor took one step, cocked the pistol and leveled it with both hands on the butt, a foot away from McGuffin's ear. The Irishman turned toward O'Connor at the metallic sound, and then turned back to the blinding light, closing his eyes as Terry fired. He fell away out of the light in a heap and O'Connor could still hear the shot as Walsh's light found Cyril's face in the long grass. The old man bent and took the face, white as flour in the cold light, by the chin and rolled it to the side. He didn't let his light linger for long on the place where the bullet had wrecked the skull. Just long enough to be convinced McGuffin was dead.

"Done," he said, rising, switching off the light.

They were silent in the darkness. Terry held the pistol in both hands in front of him, the barrel pointing down, before he put it in his belt. "Where is he?" he asked.

"Easy, lad. He'll be here." He paused, and then said, "It wasn't a bad death."

"For who? Him or me?"

"It wasn't sloppy. No panic. Quick."

There was silence. "Put the light on him again," Terry said out of the darkness.

"Why?"

"I want to see him. See if he's dead."

"He's dead."

"Put the light on him."

The flashlight came on and caught McGuffin's leg. "There," Walsh said.

"Okay," Terry said when the light was out. It wasn't a dream, or hallucination. The dead man lay between them. No panic, Terry thought. Quick.

A few minutes later they heard the sound of a trunk slamming and two men walking toward them. Walsh turned on the light and waved it.

It was Boland and Burke, both carrying shovels over their shoulders. "I couldn't keep him away," Boland said to Walsh.

"It'll be quicker with two of us," Burke said, standing in Terry's black slicker.

"Good," Walsh said. "Good man, Martin."

The digging was easy in the wet earth. The soil was sandy and came up smoothly, but still Boland and Burke worked for the better part of an hour digging a four-foot grave. When it was done, they dragged the body into the pit, folded the arms and covered him over.

It was late. Burke knew it was late. He lay on the old four poster with his shoes off, smoking cigarettes. For awhile he had heard voices across the hall in the living room. And then a car pulling away. Boland driving Joe to Dublin and then going to the North alone to set the stage. He thought of Neena, and decided he'd say he knew nothing. No, he'd tell her that Cyril had to go away and her best bet would be to go home to London. Probably never see her. Cyril. Dead. Digging his grave he hadn't thought about him. He was only aware of the work, of the other men around him in the darkness. Terry silent, invisible. Walsh holding the light. Boland working well, his long arms swinging in and up and back for more. Christ. They've blooded me. They've made me one of their own.

There's no question any more.

CHAPTER 14

Chivalry

As Garrett Costello walked up Molesworth Street on the afternoon of 4 December, one month to the day after the slaughter at Kildare, the sun was shining in the high winter sky and light rain was drifting down. He remembered what his mother would say when sun and rain were together: "The devil is fighting with his wife." It was strange, when he was a child that expression had seemed perfectly wise, and he had understood the saying more completely than the theory of gravity or the immaculate conception. Now, as an adult, the pure instinct of the child's perception was gone. It was a phrase he repeated in his mind when rain fell from sunny skies, nothing more. He might as well have repeated a phrase in a foreign language.

At the corner of Kildare Street, facing the rear of Leinster House, he walked up the three steps of Buswells Hotel, passed through the small lobby and walked into the bar. It was a handsome room of banquettes, comfortable chairs and small marble-topped tables stretching away from the bar. The soft green walls were decorated with white molding that would have been at home on a wedding cake. It was 3:35, five minutes past "the holy hour," the one hour of the day when licensed premises in Dublin are required to close. The young barman was counting pound notes at the cash register. "Could I have tea?" Garrett asked.

The barman looked around. "Tea, is it? I'll just inquire." He closed the register and opened the door behind the bar which led to the reception desk in the lobby. Garrett looked around the room. Down at the other end, at a table next to the mirror, were two men sitting in front of short glasses of straight whiskey. He recognized them both as journalists for the *Irish Times* who covered Leinster House. In the *Sunday Independent* last week he had read an article about alcoholism saying the two professions most susceptible to drink abuse were journalism and medicine. He could understand reporters having problems, in fact, he'd never met one who didn't drink ferociously, but doctors? One would think they'd know better. The barman came back in, closing the door. "I'm sorry, there's no tea. Mary, the girl who does it, is out today."

"Glass of lager," Garrett said. One of the best hotels in Dublin and no one can make a cup of tea except Mary. He wanted to ask him, when *he* was out, would anyone get a drink? This was what tourists called "Irish charm," Garrett thought, paying the barman and taking his glass to a table against the wall looking out at the lobby. Charm? Frustration was more like it.

The two newspapermen were laughing on the other side of the room. Perhaps it was foolish to pick Buswells to meet Jeffrey Norris. Jeffrey knew every reporter in town and there was always at least one member of the working press here. He doesn't know what I do, though, it will be all right. Garrett sipped the golden beer. I should have brought Des Kelly with me. I mustn't become a one-man band like Murray. To be efficient you must delegate, show your subordinates that you trust them. But Des was sleeping off his jet lag and, even if he were here, it would only make Norris suspicious.

Garrett had been waiting for him when the noon Aer Lingus flight arrived from New York. Kelly lived in Malahide, so Garrett had chosen the white house, just down the road, to talk with him. As he drove him from the airport he'd only asked questions about New York, and the young man responded enthusiastically, obviously in love with America. Short, well built from his hobby of weight lifting, with dark red hair cut short around his skull, as so many of the younger men wore it, Kelly was one of Garrett's prides. He had trained him himself, had taught him to think and not just be an automaton, the way Murray had preferred his officers. Kelly was going on about the plays he'd seen, how he'd tasted different cuisine every night, the subway, the cabs, how everything was so inexpensive and actually *worked*, from the telephones to the TV that went on twenty-four hours a day.

Sullivan had let them in and Garrett led Kelly to the reception room and sat across from him in a white Danish chair. "Now, Des, what do you have for me?" he asked, holding a legal pad and a pencil.

"Not much I'm afraid, Chief. I'll have my report typed and on your desk tomorrow."

"Good. But give me an oral report now, and then I'll let you go home and sleep New York off."

Des Kelly grinned, taking a notebook from his briefcase. "Well, like I said, there's not much. I saw his father in upper Manhattan. He says he hasn't heard anything from his son since he went to France nearly two years ago. I found out that O'Connor attended Fordham University and took a liberal arts degree there. It's a Jesuit school and they told me he was a good student and had no problems. He took a masters degree in filmmaking at Pratt Institute, quite a good school, I was led to believe. It's in Brooklyn. He was politically active there, but nothing unusual, it seems. Antiwar, youth protests and the like. Again, he was an excellent student. I found out he had worked in a students' pub near the school called—" he checked his notes and smiled—"yes, called 'Eric's,' and I went over to ask some questions. You should consider it fortunate to be looking at me now, Chief."

"Why?" Garrett asked, laying the legal pad in his lap.

"Well," Des Kelly said, still grinning, "I went to this place, Eric's, it was around eleven at night and when I walked in what was it but a colored bar. I was the only white man in the place. All these blokes in the wide-brimmed fedoras, you know, and double-breasted suits, jewelery and high-heeled shoes. These are the men I'm talkin' about. And the women, well, most of them were about half dressed. There was a fellow at the back of the place, sweat streamin' off him, with an electric guitar around his neck shoutin' about his baby leaving him and, oh, Chief, you should have seen it. Here I am standing at the bar asking the bartender my questions. I felt like a pigeon down a coal mine. They looked at me as if I were from the moon. No one had ever heard an Irishman before. The woman next to me at the bar asked was I from California. Seems her sister-in-law is from there and sounds just like me."

Garrett laughed.

"The owner finally came out and spoke to me. He called me 'Paddy,' do you believe it, Chief? When I convinced him I wasn't a New York policeman he bought me a drink and said that Eric's at one time had been a students' bar, but now it wasn't. He had no idea who O'Connor was. Then he said, 'Well, Paddy, these folks in here aren't students of Pratt, they students of life.' Then he bought me supper. Soul food, they call it. Quite good, actually."

"And the price was right," Garrett said.

"Wonderful man, he was. I had a marvelous night there. Did you know that blues singing is a whole social and cultural expression of—"

"Spare me your insights into Negro life, Des. What else about O'Connor?"

"Yes," Kelly said, looking at his notes. "Well, he was a fairly good motorcyclist and—"

"We know he can drive a motorcycle. Come on, Kelly. Work record, friends?" Garrett's pencil tapped the pad.

"Seems he didn't have many friends. He had only one job. At a place called Metromedia, a television station, working as a film editor. People remembered him as a good editor. A loner. I found out he'd made a short film for the educational channel in New York, the one that's funded by the government, about construction workers. Quite well received, he was considered talented. A nice fellow working there helped me. His mother was born in Limerick. And, oh yes, here's something interesting, he had made a proposal for another film to be about the F.A.L.N."

"And who are they when they're at home?" Garrett asked, writing.

"It's a Puerto Rican terrorist group."

"That's better," Garrett said. "What happened to the film?"

"It was never funded," Kelly looked at his notes. "They proposed to interview the terrorists and—"

"They?"

"Yes," Kelly said, back to his notes. "One Martin Burke. He also worked with O'Connor on the other film."

Garrett looked up. "What's the name?"

"Burke. Martin Burke."

Garrett remembered a young American woman in Herbert Park with a rambunctious sheepdog, a terrified woman in a crowded hallway, a conversation in a booklined study.

"Well, what about him?"

"Who is that? Burke?"

"Yes, Burke, damnit."

"I thought I was investigating O'Connor, Chief."

Garrett took a deep breath. "Is he an American?"

"I don't know. I suppose I should have followed through."

"Yes, you should have. But don't look like a condemned man there. Now, anything, anything at all more about Martin Burke?"

"No, sir."

"All right then. I'll drive you home and you get some sleep. Tomorrow have your full report ready. Ring New York tonight, talk to your son of Limerick at the state television place and ask him everything you can think of about this Burke."

"I'll ring him straight away."

"No. Sleep first. You've worked hard enough."

After he'd driven Kelly home Garrett had gone into town to the office and rung Jeffrey Norris. He said he wanted to ask a few questions, but Jeffrey had made some grand statement that he never discussed anything worthwhile on the telephone. He was on his way to town, could they meet for a drink?

The reporters, now joined by two others, were on their third round of whiskeys. Garrett's glass of lager was still half full. The creamy head had died into off-white dishwater when Jeffrey Norris, editor and publisher of the *Irish Review of Books*, made his entrance into the bar, sweeping his long brown hair back with one hand while his other hand clutched a battered leather case, ripped along one side where piles of manuscript strained to escape. Jeffrey was dressed in a safari jacket and green velvet trousers. A clear plastic belt around his waist which held a ring of dozens of large keys dangling near his crotch. "Garrett, Garrett," he said. "Am I very late?"

"As always, Jeffrey."

Jeffrey sat and put his case on the table. "If you're looking for work I can give you Liam de Paor's new one. Say yes, Garrett."

"No, Jeffrey."

"Will you have another one?" he asked, rising.

"No thanks."

Jeffrey ordered a vodka and lime and then went over to the reporters where he chatted for a minute. When he came back he said, "I'm sorry, Garrett. Bloody vultures all of them, always carrying on about the incompetence of the government and industry, do they ever mention the incompetence of journalists? Of course they don't. Drinking their papers' expense accounts, laying about in pubs, vultures and parasites, not one of them can write a proper sentence. Cheers, Garrett, and the hell with all of them," he took a long drink. "This is a bloody hell of a ridiculous town, Dublin, don't you think? It gets worse every minute, tearing down all those old buildings and putting up places that all look like prisons. The people don't give a tinker's curse about their environment, don't you think? Christ on the cross, did he put any vodka in this? One second, Garrett, I'll get a refill. You're sure you won't?"

Garrett watched him standing next to one of the wooden posts at the corner of the bar. He would have to ask Jeffrey in a subtle way, the man was such a gossip. When he was seated, Jeffrey asked, "Why won't you consider the de Paor book? I'll give you five quid more than I gave you for your last review. But only five."

"I don't have the time these days, Jeffrey."

"Don't have the time, you're as bad as the rest. What is life these days in Ireland? Are we so desperate to become like the yanks? All of us with ulcers, tearing down buildings, choking on traffic. Don't have the time, Jesus, that used to be our greatest natural resource, time. Nuclear power plants and bank robberies, do we have time for that? Plastic food and American morals. I don't know, Garrett. The world is going to hell on a handcart and everywhere the ceremony of innocence is drowned." He lifted his glass. "To Willie B., a man who fought modern life with style."

"He had the money to fight it," Garrett said.

"Cynical, are we? How I hate it. People think today that cynicism and intelligence are one and the same." He swept his hair off his forehead. "You know the yanks are making a new industry out of the bard of Sligo? Oh, they're rushing all over the whole of Ireland, looking for any pencil shaving he left behind. They've picked Joyce's carcass clean and now they're after Willie B. Bad luck to them," he toasted and drank.

"Perhaps they truly appreciate him."

"They bloody well should appreciate him. American poets have nothing to say, never did, either. Writing couplets about masturbation, are they insane? Ten more for the de Paor review."

"I can't, Jeffrey. Surely you can find someone else."

"Of course I can find someone else. Some Provo supporter who will love the opportunity to vomit all his half-baked Republicanism on my pages. You're the only sane person who knows politics I can think of. Except His Eminence, Admiral Cruise O'Brien, but people don't read his by-line anymore. I can't really blame them, though. What a weary writer he is, don't you think?"

"I've enjoyed what I've read of his."

"Oh, Garrett. He's always coming from Olympus to you. King Conor receiving the unwashed."

"Do you remember that young American woman at your party, Anne Burke?"

"Of course I remember her. What a question."

"Is she still in Dublin?"

"Let me buy you a beer. Yes? Grand. You can't fly on one wing there," Jeffrey said, going to the bar.

The room was filling. A young crowd in sweaters and denim had commandeered a corner of the room. One girl was shaking up a small bottle of lemonade with her thumb across the top and fizzing it into her glass of whiskey. She missed and squirted a long-haired boy holding a pint of ale. Laughter erupted. "There you are," Jeffrey said, settling in. "Those children shouldn't be allowed in here. Let them get paralyzed in their own places, I say. Cheers, Garrett."

"Is she still in Dublin?"

"Who would that be?"

"Anne Burke, the American."

"Oh, yes, yes she is, as a matter of fact. Here," he rummaged in his case and brought out the last issue of the *Irish Review of Books*. "Have you seen this?"

"An excellent issue."

"Of course. I don't need your say-so to know that. This is Anne's work."

"She's a photographer?"

"Quite a good one, don't you think?"

"Yes. Do you know where I could find her, Jeffrey?"

Jeffrey took a drink from his bright green glass. He smiled, "Are you interested in a portrait, or are there other motives?"

"No, I just want to see her."

"Ah, I never saw you in quite this light. Straight Garrett. Why can't we stick to Irishwomen? A bit of an accent on any piece of strange fluff and the Irishman drools."

"You have a filthy outlook on life," Garrett said, smiling. Jeffrey had given him his method. He had never even thought of it. Of course. She was attractive, after all.

"*I'm* filthy?"

"Is she married?"

"Fifteen more for the review. My last offer. It's outrageous."

"Is she married, divorced, separated?"

Jeffrey sat back and played absently with his ring of keys. "Her husband Martin is not at this time cohabiting with her. He's a writer. He reviewed the Joseph Heller novel last June, do you remember?"

"Oh yes," Garrett said, not remembering at all.

"They went down the country somewhere in August to live. Kerry? Mayo? Somewhere, in any event, and Anne was back alone in Dublin around the end of October. Shame really, they were quite a couple."

"In what way?"

"Oh, I don't know really," Jeffrey said, and took a sip, thinking, rattling his keys. "Talented, amusing, happy to be in Ireland. Good company. I don't know, really. They seemed to be in love."

"Do you have her address?"

"The marriage might still be on, Garrett. Be warned."

Garret smiled. "I just want to talk with her, Jeffrey. Can't men and women be friends?"

"No. Without exception. It's an impossibility. Let me see," he brought out an alligator address book. "She was staying with Maeve—oh, yes, she got herself a little flat in Ringsend. Here it is, 12 Irishtown Road."

Garrett copied it down in his notebook. "Is there a phone?"

"Do you want me to court the girl for you as well? No, there's no phone."

"It's completely platonic, Jeffrey."

"Rubbish. What if I sent you the book just to look over?"

"Fine," Garrett said, rising. "I'll look it over and tell you what I think."

"Where are you off to, man? I've only just arrived, for God's sake."

"I'll see you soon, Jeffrey. And thanks again."

A man and woman were rushing up the steps out of the rain when Garrett stepped from the lobby outside. They were young, their arms linked, laughing at the sudden downpour, at being together and reaching the warm light of Buswells before they were completely drenched. Garrett stood and waited to see if the rain would slacken. The day had turned dark and bitter. Two tall gardai at Leinster House gates stood sadly in their dark coats as the wind raced up Molesworth Street, scattering the rain against the Georgian houses and driving it in angled sheets across the street lamps. The devil's wife was gone and the devil played alone. Garrett ducked out and moved quickly around the corner to Kildare Street. Looking up he saw the dome of the Dail, stationary and fat in the rushing sky. He was getting closer to ending the sick game they were playing somewhere out there, beyond the Pale. What fortune to meet her, and now fitting her into the puzzle. He wouldn't be as lucky again so he would have to work that much harder. When he reached Stephen's Green the trees were blowing against the gray and black sky. He passed the Shelbourne, where the doorman was out in the street in his slicker whistling for a cab, while two well-dressed visitors waited on the steps, looking out on the wild day.

Mrs. Coogan was standing in the doorway, arms folded under her breasts, looking out at the rain with one of her teenage boys next to her. Anne, soaked from her hair to her shoes, struggled up the street with her disintegrating paper bags. Wouldn't think of sending the boy out to help, would she, the old slattern. When Anne reached the door Mrs. Coogan said, with no expression, "Good evening."

The boy grinned. Was he a cretin or just rotting with Irish mother love? Neither of them moved. "Will you get out of the way?" Anne said to her.

"Make way, Larry."

"I'm talking to you," Anne said, just as one of the bags broke and groceries spilled into the hall. The bottle of wine bounced and rolled away in the gloom. "Oh, fuck it," she said.

"That's fine language to be usin' around young ears, Mrs. Burke."

"And fuck you too, you stupid hag."

Mrs. Coogan grabbed her son by the arm and took him off down the hall where she closed her door just enough to let her look out on the American whore. Anne collected her groceries and walked up to her flat. She dumped everything on the table and laid a fire of turf briquettes. After turning on the tub taps, and sprinkling in essence of ivy, she stored the food and put the wine in the freezer compartment of the tiny refrigerator.

The one large room pleased her. It was an old house which was never looked after, but Anne had seen possibilities for the twenty pounds a week flat when she had first looked at it. She had fixed it up with a weekend of scrubbing away years of grime, and had put bright blankets over the ancient furniture, her photographs on the walls, borrowed books on shelves, and a large oil painting over the hearth of a mountain in Kerry she'd paid thirty-five pounds for. It was a good room, it was home for her, and she felt strong here. The one thing she really wanted, besides a good can opener (impossible to obtain in Dublin unless you were prepared to pay the earth), was a television set. But that would have to wait until she got on staff somewhere and could afford to move out.

I'll apologize to that goddamned bitch downstairs the next time I see her. Should I? She's incapable of any feeling. She looks at life the way people look at prizefights. Who's winning? Who's losing? Stupid woman. Yes, I'll apologize. I have to live here, it *was* rude, I said it just to shock her. Anne smiled, remembering Mrs. Coogan's eye staring out of the crack of her door. Maybe I should give her a word a month, just to keep her on her toes. The Word-a-Month-Club. Fuck this month, how about shit-heel for next month's selection? That's a good word. And for the month of January, to kick off the new year, how about cock-sucker? To warm her heart in February how about—I will apologize. Fine language for young ears? I bet that kid knows more than I do. I'll just say it quickly, get it over with, I'm sorry for my language, Mrs. Coogan, and turn away before she can give me her self-satisfied daughter-of-Mary look.

She sipped wine as she soaked. The soave was still warm, but it tasted good. Friday night. T.G.I.F. Good to be home and away from "the working-class blues," as Martin called them. For the past two weeks Anne had been working as a temporary typist at Trinity College. The money was horrible, but she had to take it to eat, pay the rent, and pay her mother back for loaning her a thousand dollars. Free-lancing in Dublin was fighting lions blind. Risky, if not thoroughly demented. She had tried to latch onto a staff at one of the dailies, or *Hibernia* or *Magill*, or the tourist magazine, but it was such an exclusive club. There had been work here and there, and she knew if she kept pushing, kept her head above water by taking typing jobs to eat and buy clothes that editors wanted to see you in, she'd get on staff somewhere eventually. She had faith in her talent. She would make it. Starting from scratch on a new life, alone, making it by herself, made her like herself much more than she ever had. And she hadn't been lonely for a moment since the day she'd moved out of Maeve's and taken this place. Well, maybe once or twice, like today, after work, in H. Williams, the supermarket.

She'd had a drink with Stephen Foley of the *Times* at Doheny & Nesbitt's. Stephen had made a polite pass at her after he'd led her away from the crush downstairs to the quiet upstairs lounge, sitting at a table looking down at rain falling into narrow Baggot Street. She had been flattered, and charmingly told him no. He had seemed very relieved she had refused, and they drank their drink, and parted better friends than before.

The loneliness came when she was in H. Williams, or "Haitch Williams," as the Irish pronounced it, the large store just a few steps from Nesbitt's, next to Burger Land, where kids loitered in the entrance waiting for the rain to pass. She bought pasta and wine, milk, eggs, and fruit. Stephen had probably just wanted to show her that he was virile. "I'll be soaked when I get home," she'd said, looking down on Baggot Street and the rain.

"Come home with me," Stephen had said, seriously. "I'll put you in a nice dry bed."

Stephen was dear, she thought, reading the label on a can of tomatoes. A good chum. It would be disastrous to go to bed with him. She noticed that the other customers in the store were mostly young women dressed in high heels and soft dresses, their hair done, shopping alone after work on a Friday night. It was the same in New York, she knew. All the supermarkets of the East Side and the West Side, filled with single women, shopping alone on Friday night. Going with him would have been just crazy. She didn't need anyone. Not true. She would have liked to have someone, someone she didn't have to talk to, just another person there, to be with quietly, to fill up the room.

Anne sat in front of the fire in her brown and white robe. Martin wasn't seeing another woman, she was sure of that. He was probably too drunk even to think about it, let alone get it up.

McGuffin's woman, that mouse, Neena, poor thing, did he share her? Wouldn't be surprised the way he treated her. No. Martin wasn't interested in another woman. He loves *me*, he just can't express it, he just has forgotten how to live. He'll come back. And when he does, there will be changes made. This is a good life, it was once a good life for both of us. He has to want to live with *me*.

There was a knock at the door. It was the gawky kid, Larry, looking away from her when he saw her in her robe. "There's a man here to see you, missus."

Anne walked past him. He's here. He's come back. The poor fool. Martin's come back. When she got to the first floor Mrs. Coogan was guarding the stairs. A tall man in a trench coat stood holding a cap. Springy thinning hair, and bright eyes behind wire-rimmed glasses. "Oh, hello," Anne said.

"Hello, Mrs. Burke."

Mrs. Coogan said, "I sent the boy up because I wasn't sure you were receivin' guests. You never know nowadays."

"Thank you, Mrs. Coogan. Come on up."

"You never know," Mrs. Coogan's voice followed them up the stairs.

"Is that the landlady?" Garrett asked when they were at her door.

"A neighbor. The self-appointed protector of public decency for Ringsend."

"What a terrible woman," he smiled, and Anne remembered his. name with relief. Garrett. Garrett Costello. He's married, isn't he? Isn't that what he said? No ring, but a lot of men don't wear them. Martin never did, he called it "jewelery," the damned fool.

"Come in," Anne said. "Here, let me take your coat, Garrett."

"Thank you," he said, looking around as Anne took his coat into the bathroom and hung it over the tub. Should she excuse herself and get dressed? The hell with it. Thank God the place is tidy. He was standing in front of the fire.

"Can I get you a glass of wine?"

"Yes, that would be fine."

"Sit down, Garrett," she said, bringing the wine in a half-pint glass. "Sorry about the glass."

"Oh, no. This is fine, Mrs. Burke."

"You know, you can call me Anne. I thought we settled that."

"I'm sorry. I called you that downstairs for the benefit of your neighbor. That's a very nice painting."

"Do you like it? I got it on Clare Street. You know the gallery next to Greene's bookstore? I've only had it two weeks but it seems like I've always had it. It's from Kerry. I've never been but I hear it's lovely."

"Oh, you should go. Kerry is beautiful. As beautiful as your painting."

He sipped the wine. He didn't like wine, and warm white wine was even less appealing. She sat across from him holding her glass. A beautiful woman. Her dark hair a glossy contrast to her bright, perfect complexion, and her neck white, a blush of color near the hollow of her throat. A quick smile showing a person who enjoyed herself. Long legs faintly outlined in the soft robe. Garrett noticed she was looking at him carefully, and they hadn't spoken for a beat or two. Was it his turn? "I thought I'd come 'round and see how you were getting on."

"I'm glad you did. I'm getting on splendidly. The last time I saw you I was really a mess."

"Oh, I wouldn't say that."

"Yes, a mess. Definitely a mess. You were very kind to me."

"It was nothing. Those brawls of Jeffrey's would make a statue overwrought."

"Am I a statue?"

"No," he smiled. "No, I'd say you were anything but a statue."

"Have you eaten?" she asked, getting up and going to the table. Garrett saw a flash of leg as she stood, as beautiful and sudden as a fish breaking the surface of a river. "It's only macaroni and cheese and tomatoes, but you're welcome. I live on the stuff. Where's that goddamned can opener? Hey, do you know where I can get a can opener, tin opener, I'm sorry, in this town that works and I don't have to pawn my shoes to afford?" She turned back to him. "You are staying, aren't you?" she asked, holding the can of tomatoes.

"Yes," he said. "Thank you."

After they had eaten at the table by the light of the utility candle Anne had placed between them, they sat with coffee near the fire. Over the meal he had asked her about photography and let her do most of the talking. She was a warm, interesting companion, he thought. So direct. Were all American women like that?

She flirted now and again, but it was all so aboveboard, she was so aware of her flirting and took such pleasure in it. Perhaps it wasn't flirting at all. If she had been unattractive he would have just considered her vivacious. She tossed two briquettes on the fire and rubbed her hands on her robe. Her skin picked up the tones of the moving light. "Did Jeffrey give you my address?" she asked.

"He did. I'm sorry if I've intruded on your privacy."

"Like I said. I'm glad you came. He's a sweet man. Crazy but sweet."

"I was asking about last month's cover portrait and we started talking about you."

"Here," she said, bringing the coffeepot. "Have some more."

"Thank you. It's delicious."

"Bewley's French Roast," she said, pouring. "I tried all of them but this is the real thing."

Garrett looked at her arm, flowing from her robe. The down of hair on her forearm. Her hand slender and the nails clipped short, perfectly manicured, no paint to spoil their pearly color. "Is your husband—are you—?"

She sat back. "We're living apart at the moment. God, doesn't that sound awful?" she laughed, and put on a broad English accent. "My husband and I are living apart at the moment. I don't know how else to say it. We just couldn't make it anymore and we decided to split up for awhile."

"I'm sorry."

"Why?"

The question threw him. "Pardon?"

"Why are you sorry, Garrett?"

"Well, I was flip, wasn't I? It just seems you're a woman who should have—have someone around who'll appreciate you."

"That's going a long way to say I need someone around to bong the gong."

"Pardon?" he said, the cup halfway to his mouth.

"Bong the gong. Humpety-jump. Seck shul intercourse."

"Yes. I guess it was a long way 'round."

"It's also sexist, Garrett. A woman alone needs a man around to relieve tension. Bullshit, don't you think?"

"Yes, I do. Half of what I say is bullshit, I sometimes think. I just open my mouth and out come old wives' tales, platitudes, and other assorted rubbish. It's good to talk with someone who doesn't accept that."

"That's sexist, too. Old wives' tales. Where are the old husbands?"

Garrett laughed. "Where is your old husband?"

"He's out in Clare. The town of Moher, do you know it?"

He nodded. Moher, by the sea. You could hide a battleship along that coast, never mind a yacht. Moher, a five-hour drive, four if you pushed it. "I guess I'm really a city kid," she was saying. "We were having problems anyway, but I thought if we'd been here in Dublin we would have made it. I felt so isolated out there, you know? It was just me and Martin and our problem, the three of us living together with nothing else."

"How long have you been apart?" Garrett asked.

"Since around the end of October. Why?"

"Just curious," Garrett said, and left it at that.

Anne looked at the fire, feeling suddenly frightened and violated. The silence hung between them. "What do you do for the government specifically?"

"I suppose you could call me a policeman, Anne," he said, placing his cup on the low table between them. "I'm sorry if I've deluded you."

"Why don't you just leave? Now."

"I want to help."

She turned from the fire and looked at him. "Leave, that would help. I don't like cops."

"Is Martin involved with Terrence O'Connor?"

"I'm not going to answer you. You bastard, you! Was it fun for you? Eat my food and have a good look at me before you get down to business, is that the way you operate? You sanctimonious asshole." She stood up. "Get out of here."

"I want to help you, Anne. And your husband."

"He doesn't need your help," she said, and sat down. "What is it, every American in Ireland is under suspicion? What about me, what're you going to do, arrest me? You're fishing, Costello. Fishing and I don't like it."

"I know Martin Burke was a friend of Terrence O'Connor. I know they worked together. They're both in Ireland now. Do you consider that fishing?"

"Martin hasn't seen or heard from him since he left the States two years ago. Martin's not a criminal. He's never done anything wrong."

Garrett stood up. "I'll just get my coat," he said and went to the bathroom. She was lying. Of course she was lying. He knew they were out there in Moher. He could wrap it all up by to-morrow. She was standing at the open door. "Anne, I am sorry. I should have been, what is it, up-front with you. I didn't want to upset you. I believe you. Of course your husband isn't involved. I'm sure of that. But I had to fish just a little. Thanks very much for the meal and—and everything. I'll see you again and we could perhaps—"

"Save it," she said, glaring at him.

"Well, thanks, and goodnight."

She closed the door softly behind him. He walked through the rain to his car and sat for awhile before starting it. Put a man on her? No, unnecessary. Leave her be. Get in touch with Kelly, set up a meeting with him straight away. Get on to the minister. Get in touch with the army. With the firepower the I.S.A. has we'll need them. Request Major John Mulligan, he's a good one, the one I worked with on the Herrema siege. Be there tomorrow before dawn and take them. Finish it. He started the car and drove off.

Maeve had just come back from walking Wellington and was stuffing her shoes with paper when the bell rang. She looked out the window. Anne was under the porch light dressed in jeans and a raincoat. Maeve buzzed her in. As she was coming up the stairs Maeve opened her door and called, "Where's your hat, girl?"

Anne came in, her hair hanging wet around her face. "Can I use your phone, Maeve?"

"You know where it is. Give me that coat. God, you're like a drowned rat."

Anne closed the bedroom door, sat on the bed in the darkness and dialed the operator. She gave the number in Moher and waited. The operator in Moher responding and then the phone ringing. She could see the telephone in Moher on the table in the hall. The plant on the shelf above. Four rings. Five. "Hello?"

"Martin?"

"Annie."

"Martin, oh, Jesus," she began to weep.

"What is it, honey? Are you all right? Annie?"

"I've just been questioned by a government man." She thought she heard a door slam. "Are you alone, Martin?"

"Who questioned you?"

"A policeman." She remembered the operator. "Is he there?"

"What kind of questions?"

Maeve opened the door. "Do you want coffee? Put on a light," she said switching it on.

Anne waved her away. "Sorry," Maeve said, and closed the door.

"Where are you, honey?"

"At Maeve's. This man was asking about you. About you and him. You know what I'm saying?"

"Yes. What did he want to know?"

"If you were involved. Is he there, Martin?"

There was silence.

"Tell me, goddamnit! Tell me, please."

"Yes," Martin said.

"Oh, no," she closed her eyes.

"What did you tell him?"

"Nothing," she said softly. "I didn't tell him anything. I told him—yes, I told him where you were, in Moher."

"Jesus."

"I didn't know. I didn't even know he was a cop until—"

"Anything else? Did you tell him anything else?"

"No. Nothing. Look, go to Shannon, go right now and—"

"Annie, easy now."

"Come here then, come to Dublin, we'll get a plane home tonight. Please, Martin, please come."

"I can't. Okay? I can't."

"Oh, baby, I'm begging you. There's no time. This isn't you, Martin. It's not you! We can be in New York tonight, can't you see?"

"Just keep cool, honey. Cool and easy if you see this guy again. Now, where can I reach you?"

"What?"

"Where can I reach you?"

"In New York. I'm getting out. What have you done to me?"

"I'm sorry, Annie. I love you."

"Yes. I don't know. Prove your love. I don't want you—hurt or —prove it to me, Martin. Please."

"I'll write. We better get off. Honey?"

"Yes."

"I miss you. Soon."

"Yes," she said. "Soon." And hung up.

There was a puddle around her shoes. Her hair was in her face. She shook her head and took a deep breath before calling Aer Lingus. There was a flight to Kennedy Airport leaving in three hours. Yes, there was space available. Yes, American Express cards were accepted.

Maeve helped her pack and drove her to the airport. Anne bought her ticket and had coffee with Maeve in the lounge. It was so easy. Just hop on the plane and leave it all behind. Maeve said, "I agreed, no questions. And I was good, too, wasn't I? But, Anne, just one. Will you ever come back?"

"Oh, Maeve," Anne said, and reached across to hug her. "You're so good. I'll never have a better friend than you."

Maeve's eyes filled. "Will you ever come back?"

"If Martin gets in touch with you—"

"Yes?"

"Nothing. Tell him—tell him nothing."

It was 2 A.M. local time when Anne walked into customs at the International Arrivals Building at J.F.K. The customs officer was a small wiry black man. He checked her passport, stamped it and handed it back. "Well," he smiled, "good morning and wel- come home."

Within ten minutes after Anne's call the house in Moher was cleared and empty. There was nothing to do except pick up their packed bags, turn out the lights and leave. Gudrun and Terry were dropped on the lane near the orchard where McGuffin was buried. They walked past his grave, down to the stream and within half an hour *Die Freiheit* was away. Martin drove Deirdre to Limerick Junction where she would catch the morning train to Dublin. He then drove on alone, at Deirdre's order, up to the village of Killy- gordon, County Donegal, near the Northern Ireland border, to a safe house. It was a room over a hardware store. He waited ten days. His bag packed, the car's tank full, silent, waiting, watching.

His one diversion had been to get quietly drunk on a bottle of whiskey bought in a pub and taken back to his room. When he was full of the whiskey, he took the Smith and Wesson that McGuffin had given him, walked to a pond on the edge of town, and threw the .38 in. The next morning when the woman of the house served him breakfast in the kitchen behind the store, he realized two things. The first was that he was through with drinking only to achieve oblivion. The second was that he wished he'd kept the pistol.

It had been a fiasco. A broad comedy, Garrett thought later. With elements of the Irish Army he had gone to Moher the next morning before dawn, received directions to Burke's house from the parish priest, and had moved in. To find no one. All the beds made. The floors swept. No laundry. Nothing. The priest had told him that the American had often been seen with Cyril McGuffin of Ennistymon. The second act of the farce ensued. They found the woman, Neena Middlemiss, alone, and brought her to the front room of Burke's house.

Garrett stood with his back to the window as the night grew darker toward morning. She looked pale, terrified, dressed in a man's sweater and a pair of slacks.

"Where is Burke?"

"I don't know."

"Are you English?"

"Yes."

"He's with O'Connor, isn't he?"

"I don't know anything."

"Where is Burke? Come on, woman."

"I don't know," Neena said, looking up. "That's the truth."

"Where's McGuffin?"

"I don't know."

"You don't know much of anything do you? Do you have any idea how much trouble you're in?"

"I've done nothing."

"And you know nothing, that it?"

"I don't know where they are, I'm telling you."

"Who?"

"Cyril or Martin. Cyril hasn't been home in weeks."

"What about Gudrun Böhm? Terrence O'Connor? Joseph Walsh? Deirdre O'Sullivan?"

"I don't know, I'm telling you. I don't know."

Hilarious, he thought, if you looked at it the right way. Bloody compassionate fool. I could have had them. I could have ended it. What were you thinking, you chivalrous idiot? That she wouldn't phone her husband, even if they are estranged? That she'd believe you, that you weren't really interested in her husband? Hilarious. What would Raymond Murray have done? He would have grilled that mechanic at Mountjoy like a steak. Taken Anne Burke and wrung her like a dishcloth. Jumped all over this Englishwoman with both feet. And had the whole lot of them in a cage for the minister to wheel through the streets of Dublin. Raymond would have had satisfaction. He would have done his job, and saved lives.

That afternoon, back in Dublin, he had requested a meeting with the minister and had offered his resignation, which was refused. The minister said he would take him off Anti-Terrorist duty. Perhaps the Special Crime Squad could use his talents.

He had wanted to capture them, but he hadn't been hungry enough. He had been inefficient, and stupid. Just to see them, Garrett thought, face to face, in custody. He asked the minister a few days later that, if and when the terrorists were brought in, he would like to sit in on the interrogations. The minister said he'd see what he could do.

In February Garrett would be granted his request, and see one of them, face to face, in a prison in Northern Ireland.

IV

CHAPTER 15

The Three-Card Trick

At the border Burke drove the Ford Escort onto the bridge behind a Toyota van. While a Royal Ulster Constabulary officer talked to the driver, a British soldier walked around the van twice, and then crawled into the back, taking his time, carefully investigating. The soldier, carrying an SLR, was dressed in high-laced boots and brown and green fatigues, the blotches of color on his uniform like a reptile in a jungle caught changing its camouflage. The fatigues were designed by British military experts to give the soldier maximum cover, both in the Northern Irish countryside as well as in the ruined cities of the province. The soldier wore a lightweight bullet-proof vest, and a beret with a band of plaid running around it, the sign of a Scottish regiment. He had his sleeves rolled up and Burke could see a tattoo on his forearm. A snake entwined on a sword.

"You're all right, Martin?" Deirdre asked.

He turned to her. She was smiling. The long wig, the same color as her own short hair, changed her appearance remarkably. It softened her face and showed the white curve of her shoulders partially bare with the soft sweater unbuttoned. She was wearing a dress and stockings. Deirdre had decided a young American wife would have long hair and wear a dress. Burke had no idea what she knew about American wives. He hoped it worked. If it didn't, they would probably be dead in the next few moments. Deirdre had her Ingram under the seat and had said she would pull it if questioned. She said she wasn't going to spend a minute in a British prison. Burke watched the soldier, now bending down to look under the van. If she used the gun, they'd be dead, he was sure of it. What was today's date? Tuesday, December 15, the day I die. Tuesday, December 15.

"You're all right, now? Easy does it?"

"Yeah," Burke said, as the RUC man walked back to them. Burke rolled the window down. "Morning, officer."

"Good morning. Could I see some identification?"

"Will a passport do?"

"That would do fine."

Burke handed him the small blue-backed passport. The RUC man opened it and closed it quickly. Handing it back, he looked past Burke at Deirdre. "This is your wife?"

"Yes."

"On holiday?"

"That's right."

"Enjoying yourselves?"

"Very much."

"That's good to hear. This van is going to be awhile, will you swing it out this way, there you go, enjoy yourselves now."

Burke drove off the bridge and into the town of Strabane, Northern Ireland. He lit a cigarette and blew the match out too quickly, lighting only one side. He puffed at it and then threw it out the window, reaching for another one. "It's always worse," Deirdre said, "once you know you're safe."

"Jesus," Burke said. "I'm a wreck."

Strabane was choked with traffic in the gray morning. In the shop windows were red and green Christmas decorations. They passed an auto parts store with a cardboard Santa Claus, life-sized, standing outside in the smoky day, his belly fat, gesturing, smiling maniacally. They waited for a light next to a brown brick building, half of it gone, the rest scorched black. Burke drove to a traffic circle and Deirdre directed him into the first spoke of the wheel down a narrow street and into a gravel parking lot. They parked and waited. Four soldiers in a spread diamond formation passed up the street next to them, walking slowly. All four held their weapons at waist height, and the man bringing up the rear point was walking backwards, checking rooftops.

"Bloody," Deirdre said. "He's late. Come on, let's have a look at the boot." Once the trunk was opened Deirdre said, a smile on her face, "Remember now, up here you're always being watched. Let's talk to each other." She gestured to the trunk. "We're a married couple on our way shopping."

John Boland walked across the parking lot in a dark suit. "Welcome to the United Kingdom," he said.

"You're late, John."

"You're early," he smiled. "Let's go. The Brits are really out this morning."

Burke drove out of Strabane, taking the A5 north. The sun was peeking halfheartedly through the thick clouds and it was raining easily again over the green farmland. A lorry packed with soldiers sitting in the rear passed them, tearing ahead. "They're bound for Derry, too," Deirdre said, turning to Boland in the back seat. "That's your reception committee, John."

"Any trouble at the border?"

"None. That American passport could get a sinner into heaven."

"Then you think you're still clean?" Boland asked Burke.

"I don't know. He didn't really look at me or the name."

"I'd say you were clean up here," Boland said. "The gardai and the RUC aren't on very good speaking terms. Never were, either. They like to keep their own secrets from each other." He laughed. "You're probably safer here than in the Republic."

Burke stopped at a two-pump station for petrol. A girl in jeans and a Rod Stewart T-shirt over a tight sweater filled the tank. Burke stood and watched her. "Cold today," she said. Ta-dee, in the Ulster accent. "The radio says snow later."

"How many miles to Derry?"

"Oh, you're almost there. I wouldn't know how many miles it is, but you're almost there."

Burke paid her. It was interesting. Even though the price of petrol was astonishing, still it was cheaper here than in the Republic. Nearly everything was cheaper.

Back on the road Boland began his report. He had been in the North since the day after the Limeview meeting nearly two and a half weeks ago, working in Strabane, Armagh, and Derry, trying to make a smooth path for the I.S.A. columns to move up and begin work with the Provos. "There's something wrong," he was saying. "Now that you're here, Dee-Dee, you can tell me whether or not I'm paranoid. You know MacCurtain's up here?"

"Yeah," she said. "I saw him in Dublin last month, after Joe and I went up from Clare to organize the meeting. He said he'd be North in awhile. Strange he didn't mention it at Limeview."

"Strange," Boland said. "That's the word for that hoor. I know he's here, and he knows I'm here, then why won't he see me? Deasey, the great bastard, he keeps denying MacCurtain's here."

"What's Deasey got to say otherwise?"

"With our bearded friend it's always, A.T.W. After the weapons. Every question I ask him he always says, 'Now, John, after the weapons are here we can discuss that.' He's given me nothing, Dee-Dee, nothing at all. No information, no intelligence, nothing. I feel like a poor relation every time I see him. When we were in Crossmaglen, he introduced me to an O/C down there and your man wouldn't take his bloody mask off."

"No," Deirdre said.

"Yes. Deasey said your man wasn't sure of me yet and so wanted to be masked."

"I'll talk to MacCurtain."

"If you can find him."

"I'll find him," she said.

"The thing is, we have to get Joe up here. Let him see the situation and make a decision. I'm ready to pack it in and let them come to us instead of me goin' around to them with my hat in my hand and my thumb up my arse. The great alliance we made was stitched together too fast, Dee-Dee, too fast and too sloppily. The whole thing's unraveling. The last time I talked to Joe I told him we should pull out, go back South and start over. He told me to stay, that the I.S.A. needed a presence in the North. That's me. A fucking presence. I feel like I'm on the wrong end of a three-card trick."

Burke swung out and passed a tractor driven by a boy. To his left, far away across the farms, he could see light snow drifting down on the hills. "What's Higgins say?" Deirdre asked.

"Fuck all, is what he says. He's another A.T.W. man. I've seen him exactly twice. Maybe it's that they don't trust me. Or they don't think I'm capable."

Deirdre turned. "Get that out of your head. You are an I.S.A. officer. You represent us up here. If these bastards want to play high and fookin' mighty, we can be even more grand than them. Keep working, John."

"Right," he said. "I'm glad you're here now."

"We won't let them play A.T.W. It was foolish of us to tell them when and where the stuff was arriving."

"That was one of their conditions."

"Yeah," Deirdre said. "But we should have fought it."

"When's it coming?" Burke asked. They both looked at him

and said nothing. "Forget it," Burke said. "Sorry I asked."

"It's coming December 26 to Ballycastle off the Antrim coast."

"Deirdre!" Boland said. "Are you mad? If the Brits ever get ahold of him he'd spill that in five minutes."

"Martin's one of us," Deirdre said.

"I don't care if he is. Some Sandhurst graduate sticks an electric rod up his backside and the weapons are gone."

"Ah, they won't get Martin. He'll wave his yank passport at them and they'll serve him tea. That right, Martin?"

"I hope so," Burke said. Snow began to fall with the rain, liquefying the instant it touched the windshield. Deirdre and Boland continued to talk. Burke glanced at the young man in the back seat. He had loosened his tie, and looked as exhausted as a man coming off a two-week bender. Smoking Deirdre's cigarettes, he would let one burn down to his fingers without puffing on it, and would then light a fresh one, and smoke it furiously. Deirdre encouraged him, filled him in on gossip from headquarters in Dublin. But Boland looked out the window, his face grim as the weather.

Ahead was the dark city of Derry, lying along the River Foyle, running solemnly in the pale day. "Ah, Derry," Boland said, without expression. "The town I love so well. Wish I was off to the boulevards of beautiful Belfast with you, but Derry needs me. Christ, I could use some company up here, Dee-Dee. When's Lafferty coming North?"

Deirdre laughed. "Never. Joe's keeping him these days near him like a guard dog. He's afraid to let him out of his sight. Can you imagine him up here? All these uniforms for him to have a go at? He'd be in the nick in a minute."

"I'd like to set Laff on Mr. Deasey. Have him singe that beard of his."

"Lafferty could fook up a nocturnal emission," Deirdre said.

Boland laughed. "I suppose so. But I could use his muscle. Do you see that garage on your right ahead, Martin?"

"Yeah."

"Drop me there. When will I see you, Dee-Dee?"

"Come Saturday. We'll have a few jars. I'll have it sorted out by then."

"That's another thing. None of them drink. At least not when I'm around."

"Higgins drinks," Deirdre said.

"He's the head cowboy," Boland said. "He does what he wants. But the rest don't touch it."

Burke pulled off the road near a wooden garage, the boards stripped of paint and one door missing. Inside they could see a man working by the glow of a portable light, changing tires on a Mini. Burke rolled his window down and could hear a radio coming from the garage. It was Aretha Franklin, her supple voice soaring through "A Rose in Spanish Harlem."

"Saturday," John Boland said, tightening his tie.

"Watch your back, John," Deirdre said. "And keep pushing."

Boland got out and slammed the door. He turned up the collar of his suit coat, put his hands in his pockets, and walked into the garage without looking back.

They took the A6 east to Feeny, jogged north a few miles to Dungiven, and then drove east again toward Belfast. They didn't speak. The silence was good company.

Like most journalists, or most modern people for that matter, Burke was a voyeur. He had practiced the vice for so long that it was done without awareness, and when he saw himself as a participant in the scenes he studied, it was a revelation, the same as a person hearing his voice tape recorded, or watching himself on motion picture film. The initial shock of seeing his life clearly had not been unpleasant. What was unpleasant was that he was not completely removed like the voyeur any longer. He continued to watch it dispassionately and couldn't take that first step of will and say No, but was compelled to let the players in the scene continue to play, feed him his lines, give him his cues, and wait to see how it all came out.

On their right Lough Neagh stretched away under the dark sky, and soon they lost sight of the water and were driving on through more colorless little towns fastened onto bleak December fields. Deirdre offered him a cigarette. The American turned. "Yeah," he said. "They're good for the chest, they told me in Clare."

He had changed in a month, she thought. First seeing him again on the deck of that boat, he had looked heavier, florid, and even in the dark she had seen his eyes looking like open wounds. Now that he was off the gargle, or rather not drinking like he was dying of thirst, he seemed in remarkable shape. *Déjà vu* came over her.

What was it? Liam driving. Terry driving, on their way to Kildare.
"Terry's a better driver than you," she said.

"So what?"

"So nothing. Just an observation."

"Ninety percent of the women in Ireland are better looking than
you," he smiled. "Just an observation."

"I thought you'd love me in my new hair and frock."

He looked over. "I do. You look great."

"I can't wait to get out of this gear. I forgot how uncomfortable
it all is."

"Yeah, that's what my wife always says."

"Do you miss her very much?"

"Yeah," Burke said, and flicked an ash out of the crack of the
window. "It's like grieving for someone. Something died."

They fell back to silence. Deirdre thought of Liam. The yank
had used the word grief, the most obscene word in the language
for the images it brought up. Black veils, the wake, keening
mourners, wailing, emptiness. Grief eats the soul, not at a gulp, but
piece by piece by piece. Liam had been more than a lover, he'd
been a teacher, a parent, a confidant. She had willed that night he
was murdered to have revenge. She had guaranteed herself that,
driving through Dublin streets with Burke. But now there was no
need for it. The horror was working with the people who had
killed him. Joe was right, of course, there had to be an alliance if
Liam's ideas were to be put into action. They couldn't continue
to play hide and seek in the Republic, they had to move up here to
the war and take part. Boland is worried. The three-card trick.
I'll straighten MacCurtain out, and quickly. Green-eyed fuck, he
mistakes arrogance for leadership.

Burke interrupted the silence. "Is that true what John said?
That they're not looking for me up here?"

"Probably true."

"How about you?"

"I'm wanted for murder up here. The guards and the RUC
don't have to exchange information about me."

When they were in Belfast, Burke dropped Deirdre at a terraced
house on Mountainview Parade just off the Crumlin Road. He then
drove to the other end of town to Botanic Avenue, near the university, to a bed and breakfast house. He felt the same sense of

excitement being in the city he'd had when he'd come up before as a reporter. Life was lived in Belfast, and not just passed through. It had always reminded him of home, of New York. And now, with the added bustle and excitement of the Christmas season, which looked real here, and not a farcical joke as in Strabane, Belfast could have been New York's Irish cousin. The faces on the street leapt out at you. There was a quickness to the step, an undefeated attitude that reflected from the ruin of the city's buildings and was transformed into something indomitable and beautiful in the city's people.

Burke parked the Escort under the trees on Botanic Avenue and went into the boardinghouse. It was a clean warm place, run by an elderly spinster, Miss O'Hagan, who showed him to his room looking out on a paved yard sheltered by trees still holding a few leaves against the winter. Burke, without unpacking it, placed his bag in the closet and tested the bed. He lay back and cupped his hands behind his head. He remembered what Boland had said, that the police and army up here probably weren't looking for him. Deirdre had known that, she must have. She probably hadn't told him to keep him on his toes. She was using him for cover. That was all right. If they don't know me here, then I can get out through England. Yes, a ferry to Liverpool, and a safe ride home.

He checked his watch. There was plenty of time before he'd meet Deirdre for dinner. He decided a walk and a glass of beer were in order. He knew a place, not far from here, a good pub on Great Victoria Street.

As he was going down the stairs an explosion, perhaps ten blocks away, thudded and shivered through the house. Miss O'Hagan was at the door. "Did ye hear that one?" she asked.

"Sounded close," Burke said.

"Aye," she said, with a smile. "Just close enough to sweep away the cobwebs."

Burke walked down Botanic Avenue. The snow was now just fine cold rain again. He looked back. Miss O'Hagan was still standing at her door, still quite amused at the bomb. Belfast had given the world new insights into the phrase, "a gallows sense of humor," Burke thought. It was a sick joke, wasn't it? Christ, you might as well laugh, said Belfast. Tears were futile. Laughter was life.

At quarter to eight Burke left Miss O'Hagan's, crossed the street

and entered the restaurant. The young woman at the door took his
trench coat, folded it over her arm, and led him to a table near
the window looking out on the street. "You've booked the table
for two, Mr. Burke?"

"My wife will be along any minute."

"Can I offer you an apéritif?"

"Yes, a sherry. Dry, please."

Burke looked out on narrow Botanic Avenue. It was cold and
wet. The street lights shining through the trees. He could have
been in Brooklyn Heights. The first time he'd come to Belfast he
was struck by the splendid setting of the city, ringed on three
sides by rounded mountains, and on the fourth side by the Belfast
Lough. Wherever you were in the city, you always could see either
the black and brown hills or the harbor leading out to the sea. The
waitress brought his sherry in a slim stemmed glass and two menus.

Burke studied the list of entrées. They wouldn't be poisoned.
Tasted his sherry. Very good, even if it was warm. Tio Pepe,
probably. He saw himself sitting in a restaurant, having a drink,
and felt wonderful. Burke fingered the shiny holly and red berries
in the vase in front of him. There's a way out, he told himself.
Through England. Rule Britannia. No one knows I'm here.

There was an expensively dressed couple across from him who
looked like they were left over from lunch, having dessert now,
holding hands, looking into each other's eyes. Across the room he
saw three clergymen working on thick steaks and a liter of red
wine. He recognized one of them, a large man with a full head of
white hair, thick black brows, and fierce gray eyes in deep sockets.
The Reverend Jeremy Davis, pastor of the York Presbyterian
Church in North Belfast and the Imperial Grand Master of the
Orange Order. Burke had interviewed him last summer in the
Orange Order offices on the Dublin Road, not far from the BBC.

The interview, which Burke taped in the Reverend's office as
his young secretary served them tea, had revealed very little until
the end. In his rich voice trained by years of Sunday shouting, the
Reverend began by telling Burke emphatically that the Catholic
population was *not* suffering from unemployment and bad housing,
they were *not* subject to discrimination (certainly not as disgrace-
fully as in America where the blacks have to walk on one side of
the street and the whites on the other), that all of that were lies
propagated by the news media which everyone knows is directed

from Moscow. He then went on to extol the wonders of the "Ulster Scot," and told Burke that thirteen American presidents had come from "Ulster Scot" stock. Just before he left, Burke asked him when he had received his calling to the ministry. The Reverend replied that he'd always felt it. When Burke pressed him, Jeremy Davis said that when he was five years old his mother had made him a child-sized clerical suit, and Jeremy had worn it around the house, at school, and at play.

The Reverend was speaking as he poured the wine. His colleagues nodded knowingly. The Reverend looked up, his eyes checking the room like he was counting heads in his congregation. Burke remembered a joke he'd heard in a Republican pub in Andersonstown. It seemed Jeremy Davis climbed into bed one night and his wife said, "My God, your feet are cold." And Reverend Davis replied, "Please call me Jeremy when we're alone."

He saw Deirdre getting out of a taxi. She hurried out of the chill toward the door, still in her dress but without her wig. When she came up Burke stood, and kissed her lightly on the cheek, smelling a trace of scent. "What was that for?" she asked when they were seated. "You're not jarred already, are you?"

"What's the perfume?"

"Do you like it? The stuff's so old I thought it lost its smell. Jesus, if Joe saw me now he'd think I'd gone over to the other side. What's that you're drinkin'?"

"Sherry. Pale fino."

"Sounds good to me."

They started with egg mayonnaise and then had the sea trout. Their conversation was about food, and wine, and other small talk they pursued to stay away from the reason they were in Belfast. Deirdre had not eaten in a place like this for months. The last time had been in the Royal Howth Hotel in April with Liam and Joe Walsh. There wouldn't be another meal like this for a long time and she was determined to enjoy herself. Although she had considered herself on active service from the night Liam had died in August, she looked at this meal as a final blow-out before going into the trenches.

Burke was going on about a restaurant in New York and hadn't noticed the tall, white-haired clergyman standing just behind him. He was flanked by two other ministers, younger, deferential, smooth fat faces. Prods, Deirdre thought immediately. She motioned with her eyes to Burke. The American turned.

"It is Mr. Burke, isn't it? I thought it was you. How are you keeping?"

Burke stood. "Fine, Reverend. It's good to see you."

"And is this your wife?"

"Yes. Deirdre, I'd like you to meet Reverend Jeremy Davis. Imperial Grand Master of the Orange Order." He watched her face. Just a smile, no other expression. Deirdre said, "Hi," and Burke instantly loved her for her coolness and the wit to use the Americanism.

"Mrs. Burke. Delighted. So you're back for more, Mr. Burke? You never sent that article you were doing to me like you promised."

Burke looked at him. Rude, vain bastard interrupting someone's meal without a thought. He won't introduce these two pricks next to him either. Probably will tell them later I was from the *New York Times*, or *Newsweek*. "It never ran, Reverend."

"A shame," Reverend Davis said. "I enjoyed our chat immensely. Will you be in Belfast long this time?"

"A few days. Sort of a working holiday."

"Call by and see me. I'd like to discuss the current situation with you." Sit-ee-ation. "We must tell the Americans the truth about Ulster."

"I agree. I'll give you a ring."

"Fine. Always a pleasure. The mint *gateau* is especially good for a sweet later. Mrs. Burke, delighted."

When they were gone Deirdre started to giggle. "People are watching, Dee-Dee," Burke said. "Always watching up here."

"Let 'em watch. Jesus, do you think those other two were body-guards?"

"Clones," Burke said, and she laughed. He told her about the interview and she laughed again. The muscadet had warmed them. Deirdre's plain face was glowing and Burke thought of Anne and her favorite pastime after a restaurant meal. He found himself very attracted to the Irishwoman across from him, sipping her coffee, her eyes bright and amused. "You know," Burke said, "I could probably sneak you past the landlady across the street."

"Then what would you do with me?"

"Make love to you," he said, lighting her cigarette. "Make you happy."

The waitress left the bill on a silver tray. Burke checked it and said, "Do you want a liqueur, or brandy?"

"No," Deirdre said. "How are you for money?"

"I've still got most of the five hundred Walsh gave me when he came to the house after the meeting."

"Keep a report on what you're spending. He's a bastard about money."

"You didn't respond to my offer."

She tapped her cigarette into the crystal ashtray. "Did you feel you had to?"

"No. I want to."

"Well, I'm flattered and—"

"It's not flattery, Deirdre."

"No, Martin. It wouldn't be good. This is enough."

"Okay," Burke said.

"I will have another coffee, though. Ask her to ring for a cab, too."

Outside they waited under a tree in the mist for the cab. "Are you warm enough?" Burke asked. "Here, take my coat."

"I'm fine," she said. "How long will you stay, Martin?"

"I don't know. Not past Christmas. I'll help you until then."

She nodded. "Sometimes I wish I could get out as easily."

"Really? But this is your life, isn't it? Dedication and all that?"

"Yeah," she said. "Yeah, but that doesn't mean I don't want to get out sometimes."

"Then do it, Dee-Dee."

"No. It *is* my life. There's too much death behind me now."

The cab came up Botanic and made a U-turn to pull in front of them. Deirdre turned and hugged him, holding him tightly, and said, "You're good, yank." She broke away. "Come at eleven tomorrow."

Burke waited until the cab was gone before walking across the street to the boardinghouse. Miss O'Hagan was in the parlor listening to a concert on her radio being broadcast from the Albert Hall in London. Burke just put his head in to say goodnight. The old woman nodded, smiled, and Burke went up the stairs to the sound of Beethoven's pastoral symphony. He undressed, turned on the space heater, and got into bed with his book, a collection of short stories by James Plunkett, and was soon lost in the soft, descriptive prose. He finished a story and noticed the room was stuffy. That was Ireland. You either rot with damp and cold or suffocate. He opened the window and got back in bed. The rain falling through the trees came murmuring in, and he could hear Miss O'Hagan's radio drifting up. He put his book on the table and turned out the light. There's too much death behind me, she had said, the sad little urchin in the grown-up clothes, standing in the rain. Did she mean Liam, and other comrades, or the people she had killed? And she wouldn't have me because she was afraid of comfort, she could dull her own edge just enough, and then it would have to be honed again. She's frightened of the humanity in her, that's her enemy. Any kind of warmth must be cut away.

Is she losing her faith? Or already lost it? What does the zealot do without faith?

He was just drifting off when sirens brought him up near consciousness. As the urgent noise faded, Burke fell back to sleep with sounds of rain in the trees and faint whispers of a symphony.

At eleven o'clock Burke parked the Escort in front of the house on Mountainview Parade. The new development looked fragile in the raw day. The white semi-detached houses were no more than a year old, and the cheap materials and quick construction techniques that created the neighborhood seemed no match for the blight of the Crumlin Road just up the hill, with its bombed-out buildings, bricked windows, torched shops, and cruising armored vehicles that only showed the driver's eyes through a slit in the metal. The whole area looked like a crop of white mushrooms blossomed overnight, ripe for destruction at the first storm. Kids played in the street, kicking a football from curb to curb. The cold drizzle fell straight down, and more clouds were massing on Wolf Hill and Black Mountain to the west. Burke nodded to two women talking in the doorway of the house next door. Both were smoking long cigarettes, and both eyed him carefully. After ten years of training, the women of Belfast see everything. Especially strange men in their neighborhood driving new cars with Republic of Ireland license plates.

Deirdre let him in. She was dressed in her uniform again. Faded jeans, a sweater, hiking boots. Last night was gone. The blade was sharp again. "I'm on the phone," she said, and went into the first room off the tiny foyer. The whole house smelled of paint, and there was no furniture or carpeting. In the kitchen at the back of the house Burke poured a cup of tea from the pot on the windowsill and then realized there was no place to set it, no chair to sit on. He wandered back to the small room where Deirdre sat crosslegged on the floor, the phone in her lap, a teacup without a saucer and a box of cigarettes on the bare floor next to her. Burke sat against the wall. He looked up and saw a long jagged crack running across the ceiling.

"Like I said, we only got here last night, I'm going over to the office in a minute," she paused, listening. "He's worried, yeah, they're playing with him. MacCurtain's here, he told me, but he won't see him." She sipped some tea, and lit a cigarette. Gestured with the pack to Burke. He shook his head. "I'll start laying down the law up here. I don't think any of John's worry has rubbed off but I don't know. I'll try and set up a meeting with MacCurtain. Yeah, John says Deasey's been no help at all." She paused. "But John's taking care of Derry, Joe. I don't want to step on his toes too much. We should give him a chance. Yeah. Yeah. Grand. No, he's fine. He's sittin' starin' at me right now. Yeah. You too." She hung up the phone. "So," she said to Burke. "How do you like our palace?"

"A little too crowded," Burke said. "I prefer the stark look."

"The price was right," she said. "And it's the right neighborhood for us."

"Catholic or Protestant?"

"Mixed. I've got one more call and then we'll go."

Burke took his cup back to the kitchen. Out the window over the sink he saw a barren garden and a high wooden fence. There was a bird feeder hanging from one wall, empty and damaged. A bird swooped down and sat on it, gingerly, twitching, suspicious. "Ready?" Deirdre asked from the door.

"Yeah," Burke said, and set his cup in the sink.

They drove over to the neighborhood south of the Falls Road. It was a place of tiny row houses set on narrow streets, with the Falls Road on one side and vast fields of razed buildings on the other. In the rabbit warren neighborhood there were no street lights, no traffic signals, no post office boxes, nothing in fact, that told you people still lived there. Most of the shops were gaping holes where timbers lay twisted and scorched among blown down walls. The pubs and shops that still existed had bricked windows and frames of chicken wire protecting the facade from Molotov cocktails. It was the worst slum of Western Europe. Sixty percent of the workers were unemployed. A family's average income worked out to thirty pounds a week. The people were Catholic and Republican. They had been that way for centuries, and had been poor just as long.

Burke parked the Escort and Deirdre told him to leave it running. They sat and waited a minute before a young fellow with long auburn hair in a denim jacket came out of the Irish Socialist Party headquarters across the street and walked over to them. He opened the driver's door and said, "I'll take her," and when Burke and Deirdre were out of the car the young fellow was in it and driving away. "Security," Deirdre said. "Leave a car on a street here and it'll blow up when you go to use it."

Burke followed her across the street to the headquarters. It was a two-storied concrete block structure, framed in chicken wire, set between two decrepit tenements. At the door Deirdre buzzed the intercom and as they waited a young woman came up the street with four small children. She was perhaps thirty with hands and face as red as tomatoes, in a formless housedress, a sweater against the chill, flopping in bath clogs along the December street. The children, dressed in shorts, were silent, their faces almost blue, and Burke saw one of them, a girl of ten or eleven, walking beside her mother with the tottering gait of an old woman. The boy next to her had a savage face, and when he opened his mouth his teeth were black with rot. "Is Mr. Maguire in?" the mother asked Deirdre.

"He should be."

"I must see him," she said.

The door was opened and they walked into the dark, concrete-floored hall. It was colder than the street. It felt like they were in a bunker far below ground. Sammy Maguire, a little portly man in an old suit and gray sweater, greeted them. The woman and her children hung back. "Deirdre, God it's good to see you. We thought Dublin had forgotten us up here."

"Never, Sammy. Do you know Martin Burke?"

"I do. The *Village Voice*, that right?"

"Hello, Sammy."

"Martin's just going to hang around today," Deirdre said. "Soak up all this great Northern atmosphere."

"Grand, grand. Soak is the word for today. At least the roof doesn't leak. You're welcome, Martin. Let me take care of this, Deirdre," he pointed at the woman and her children, "and I'll be right with you. It's warmer in the office."

As Burke followed Deirdre along the dim corridor he heard Sammy saying, "Ah, ye drank it up again, don't try and fool me. I can smell it off ye, now," and the woman's desperate, nearly hysterical denials. "Social work," Deirdre said over her shoulder and led him into a small office with a desk, a telephone, an electric heater with the bars glowing red. A portrait of James Connolly hung from one concrete wall, staring across the narrow room at a poster of a man's battered face, the lips split, the teeth broken, one eye slitted, the other torn at the corner. Under the picture the caption read, "British Fair Play." Over the desk hung another poster, this one picturing a squad of British soldiers patrolling in the countryside, and the caption read, "Get these terrorists out of Ireland."

"Here," Deirdre said, and set a box of newspapers on the desk, "our latest issue." She handed him one. "Educate yourself. I've got to meet with Sammy. It might be awhile."

"Sure," Burke said. "I'm free all day."

"There's the pool table down the hall," Deirdre said, and left him.

Burke sat behind the desk and picked up the newspaper. A teenage girl came in and set a cup of tea and a plate of chocolate biscuits before him on the desk.

"Thanks," Burke said. "That's great."

"Are you from New York?" she asked.

"Yes."

"Do you know Danny McCann?"

"McCann? No, I don't think so."

"It's my brother Danny. He's been out there two years now."

"Well, it's a big place."

She nodded, and left. Good for Danny McCann, Burke thought. The one who got away. His little sister still asking for him.

Burke read the *Irish Patriot*. Like every other radical sheet in the world, there were stories about Vietnam, Chile, Nicaragua, the C.I.A. There were pictures of a fund-raising rally where two I.S.P. members were shown with an electrocardiographic machine paid for by the people of the Falls and soon to be sent to a guerrilla army in Zimbabwe. The *Irish Patriot* was a cut above most of the left-wing papers Burke had read, probably due to Walsh, he thought, but it was still propaganda, and not news. British terror in Ireland. American imperialism. Support the cause. Which side are you on? If you're not part of the solution you're part of the problem. *Venceremos.* Organize. Learn. Support. Rise. Seize the time. Revolution. Counterrevolution. While Ireland holds these graves. Up the rebels. Up the Republic. England's distress is Ireland's opportunity.

On the editorial page Burke read a column about the blanket men of H-block, and a call to support these brave Republicans. The H-block convicts were all Provisionals, and this was the first time the *Irish Patriot* had accepted their cause. Burke looked through the rest of the paper, but there was nothing else about the Provos. There was none of the standard Provisional baiting, calling them "fascist renegades," "mindless adventurers," nothing else good or bad about them, except the one short column. Walsh is subtle, Burke thought. It would have been tempting to devote a whole issue to the suddenly blossomed alliance. But that was the Stalin method, and Walsh was not a Trotskyite for nothing.

Burke lit a cigarette. A newspaper junkie, he could spend hours over classified ads with pleasure. He heard people passing in the hall. Once or twice someone stuck his head into the office. The people working in the headquarters were young, by and large, with that omnipotent coolness all young intellectuals possess who have married their talents to a political theology. They were sure of themselves. They would argue theory for hours to convince you they were right. They had a handle on life.

He chewed a biscuit, and started on a past issue. There was a picture of Liam Cleary opening the new headquarters. A statement from him calling the new HQ the soundest they'd ever had. It was certainly sound, Burke thought. If a nuclear device was ever detonated in Belfast, the I.S.P. would emerge triumphant.

As a reporter, Burke had been to all the political party and para-military headquarters in Belfast. The bunker of The Republican Clubs, the new name for the Official I.R.A., not far from here on Cyprus Street. The Ulster Volunteer Force's headquarters on

the Shankill, called "The Eagle," where Burke interviewed four
of the Loyalist leaders who refused to give their names, refused
to be taped, questioned his credentials repeatedly, answered no
comment to half his questions, and stared sullenly, giving Burke
a good case of Belfast paranoia, which compelled him to look over
his shoulder for weeks after. The headquarters of the Ulster De-
fence Association on Newtownards Road in East Belfast, looking
like an old school building, where Burke interviewed Supreme
Commander Andy Tyrie, and was charmed by his intelligence and
wit, a young mafioso who would have fit in perfectly in the back
room of a restaurant in Bensonhurst, joking, cagy, hospitable, and
ultimately terrifying. The Provos' place on the Falls, where he
waited an hour and a half for an interview, only to be granted
five minutes from an assistant press officer. When Burke complained he was told, "File a favorable story or an unfavorable
story, we don't care. Who the hell are *you*, anyway? I was just
talkin' to CBS in New York, *Le Monde* is comin' up this afternoon. Who're *you*?" Except for the Provos (who eventually did
apologize and gave Burke time) all of the people Burke had interviewed were delighted to show off their headquarters. The war-
ring gangs of Northern Ireland wanted to tell the world that they
were serious. See how organized we are? See the size of our
building? We are bad men and our badness comes from our discipline, our newspaper, our leader, our sense of family. We are
not a gang of cornerboys and fools. Look at our building! We are
real. Our tribe is powerful, our tribe is rich, our tribe is unequaled
in its hatred of other tribes. We are fierce, we are strong, strong
as the stone of our headquarters.

Deirdre came in and sat across from him, propping her hiking
boots on the desk. "I'm goin' to Derry tonight," she said, "but
I'll be back tomorrow."

"You want the car?"

"No, I've got transport. Do you mind being alone?"

"I'll find something to do."

"Be out in front here at two o'clock tomorrow afternoon. Stay
in the car and wait for me."

"What's up?"

"His Honor, Rúairí MacCurtain, is coming here tomorrow and
then we'll take him over to Mountainview."

"You work fast, Dee-Dee."

"He just didn't trust Boland, I guess. Joe's coming North to-morrow to meet Higgins in Armagh. He'll be up here tomorrow night. We'll have it all nailed down by tomorrow."

"Well, maybe I'll take off then, catch a boat to Liverpool and not wait until Christmas."

"You can stay, yank. We could use you. I'm sure Joe goes along with me when I say you're welcome."

"I better go. I really don't belong here, Dee-Dee. Ireland's had enough of me."

"Or the other way around," she smiled and stood up.

"Yeah. I better get home."

"Tomorrow at two. Ask Sammy where you'll find the car," she said, and left the room.

Burke took out his address book and found Bill Fahy's number. If he was lucky he'd catch him at home. Burke dialed the number. Bill answered in his best "Front Page" style. "Fahy."

"What're you doing home when the whole world needs to be covered?"

"Who is this?"

"Your colleague and friend."

"Martin?"

"Yeah. How's it going, Bill?"

"It's going like it always goes. Fecking awful. Where are you?"

"Here in Belfast. What're you up to tonight?"

"Tonight. Let me look. Nothing. I've got to be in Lisburn this afternoon to take down the pearls of the Army, do you want to tag along? The press officer serves stupendous cocktails."

"No, I couldn't take the boredom," Burke said.

"You're getting very high and feckin' mighty. Who're you working for these days? Lord Beaverbrook?"

"Free-lance, Bill. You know me, type and pray."

"Type and starve, you mean. I'll be in the Europa at six."

"Great. See you."

At the end of the corridor Burke found Sammy Maguire in the low-ceilinged lounge talking to an old man while two teenagers shot eight ball at the pool table. Ché Guevara, his beret haloing his long hair, scowled from the wall. As Burke approached he heard the old man saying to Sammy, "An Englishman says to me the other night, 'Give me your name,' and I says, 'Then what am I to use?'"

Sammy laughed.

"What am I to use, Sammy?"

Sammy turned. "Yes, Martin, you'll be wantin' the car. Do you know the pub on the corner? Remember the boy who drove the car away? He'll be there and fetch it for you."

"Thanks, Sammy."

"Not a'tall, Martin. God bless."

The noon sun made the sky look lumpy and thick, the color of porridge, and the rain continued to fall. Burke walked into the pub at the end of the street. Like the headquarters, it was made of new cinderblocks covered with chicken wire. There were no windows and inside it was just a large, dark, damp room filled with men. Noon of a working day, and the pub was jammed. Some of the men looked like they'd been here awhile. The boy in the denim jacket got up from a table and told Burke, "Five minutes."

Burke ordered a glass of Macardle's ale, listening to the men at the bar talking about horse racing. He heard the toot of a car horn and finished his drink. The Ford was parked in front, the motor running. There was no sign of the boy on the empty street.

The guard came forward and frisked him. A female guard, there to frisk women, sat and stared at him. "There you go, sir," the guard said and Burke walked out of the shed, crossed the yard and entered the Europa. The hotel had been bombed seventeen times in ten years. No one confronted with that fact could ever complain about the body checks. The first time Burke had entered the Europa he'd been carrying a portable tape recorder. The guard had taken out the batteries and tapped each one on a hardwood table, concentrating on the sound. Then he had examined every cassette, holding them up to the light and then tapping them on the table. Burke had thought the man was a fanatic, until someone told him that the I.R.A. would, over a period of months, use hundreds of couriers, each one bringing in small particles of explosives, hiding them all over the hotel, until one man would go in and assemble an incendiary device.

Burke walked across the lobby toward the noise of the Whip 'n Saddle Bar. It was a large modern room, decorated in the bright colors you would see in a progressive kindergarten. He sat at the bar next to two hale Ulster businessmen in heavy tweed. They were talking about inflation rates in loud horrified tones. One of the Oriental barmaids stood before Burke. "Pint of Guinness, please," he ordered. She looked Vietnamese, but Burke had never asked her. She was tiny, exquisite, somehow perfectly compatible to the Whip 'n Saddle. He imagined her letters home to Hué or Haiphong. "Dear Mom, everything still the same. Papist continues to hate Prod and vice versa. British soldiers fall like the last leaves of autumn. I got a raise of two pounds. And Dermot McGee still pursues. Love to Daddy, cheerie bye." She set the pint in front of him and he handed her an English pound. The reason, he thought, she and her Oriental sister did not look out of place in the Whip 'n Saddle was because the unexpected, the contradictory, the downright insane, was Belfast's order and sense. Ulster was William Burroughs country. She handed him his change. "Excuse me," Burke said. "But are you Vietnamese?"

She looked shocked. "Certainly not. I'm Chinese. From Hong Kong."

One of the tweedy inflation fighters said, "G and t here, love, and another brandy and soda."

She smiled at Burke and went to make the drinks. Burke tasted the cream of his pint. His question was probably the same as asking an Englishman if he was Irish. Of course. Hong Kong, the British Crown Colony. Trained as a barmaid in an English club, she and her sister had gone all the way around the world to work in the British Crown Colony of Whip 'n Saddle.

There were trays of hot hors d'oeuvres at the end of the bar, being sampled by two men speaking Italian, tasting the miniature franks and clam rolls as if they were trying them only to tell friends back home about the abominable habits and tastes of the Northern Irish. Burke felt something sticking in his back. He turned and there was Bill Fahy's smiling face. He had changed. What was it? A beard, ginger and scraggly, on his terrier face. "Bang, you're dead," Bill said, his hand cocked like a gun.

"What's that all over your face, Billy?" Burke asked, slipping into the diminutive at the sight of him. He had the type of face that demanded the affectionate form.

The little man sat next to him. "Well, I finally decided that I needed it. You know how bullfighters all wear a little ponytail to set them apart, and painters affect the beret? I decided writers have beards as a sign of their *métier*. Like yourself. How are you, Martin? You look fit as a fecking horse there."

The barmaid was before him. "Good evening, Mr. Fahy. Large Jameson?"

"That's the one. How are you, Dottie? You look fit as a lovely pony there."

Dottie smiled, and poured two shots of whiskey in a glass and set it in front of him. "A Major Bill Shiels rang for you, Mr. Fahy. About an hour ago."

"Grand, Dottie. Thank you. Isn't she something?" Bill said as she walked away. He held up his drink. "Home," he toasted. It was Billy's standard toast. He was from Dublin, but his home, for the past eight years, was Belfast. He had started covering the troubles for an English tabloid, one of those London papers that has a nude pinup on page three and the highest-paid writer does the television page. Billy's reporting, even though it was butchered by rewrite hacks and had to exist under lurid headlines created by Fleet Street morons, was superb, day in and day out, and eventually one of the quality dailies snatched him away. Besides operating as a working journalist on the ground, the paper gave him space for a column once a fortnight and he was the stringer in the North for *Time*.

Burke had first met him here, at the Europa, introduced by an *Irish Times* reporter. They had chatted for awhile until one of the barmaids, who like everyone else in the hotel kept Billy up-to-date, told him that a radio bulletin had just come in. Six British soldiers had been killed by a bomb in the town of Lisnaskea, County Fermanagh. "Would you like to tag along?" Billy had asked, and Burke had gone with him. Billy was remarkable. Not only did he do his own work, but most of Burke's, explaining, moving him through Army press lines, telling him what questions to ask, and buying him drinks later in a village pub. Journalism was a major industry emerging from the troubles, and Fahy was one of the captains, yet he treated Burke as if he were V. S. Pritchett come over to see what was what.

They were on their third round. The pints were sliding into Burke, and the mental check on his drinking that he had used for the past month was forgotten. Billy, talking shop, was wonderful.

Burke suddenly understood why he was such an accomplished journalist. It was because Billy had no other interests. He was obsessive. His work was indistinguishable from his life. "So," he was saying, "you're back to write some more stirring prose, boo hoo, ain't it a shame, two days in the slums, a quote from Yeats and back to the warm fleshpots of Dublin. That it, you fecking horse?"

"I'm not that stale."

"Course you're not. War is what every reporter needs. It covers itself. If you know where to put in the commas and full stops, any half-wit comes off like Edward R. Murrow."

"You're sounding bitter, William."

"Ah, it's just that Belfast has changed."

"How so?"

"There's less *of* the flaming place. Did you hear about the fellah who was walking around the Falls one night and a man steps up and sticks a pistol in his ribs? He says, 'Are you Catholic or Protestant?' And your man says, 'I'm a Jew.' The gunman then says, 'Well, aren't I the luckiest bloody Arab in Ireland?' Dottie, my pony, will you set us up again. Jesus," he turned to Burke, "I've got to stop this drinkin' every night. Especially with yanks like you who don't pay. Now, put that money away. Don't get shirty with me, my lad."

Burke watched him as he talked to Dottie. The beard made him look older, and highlighted his eyes, which looked worn out. "Come on now," Billy said, "drink that one down like a good horse and we'll retire to my place for some food."

They drove to Billy's house on tree-lined Park Avenue, a quiet, clean Protestant neighborhood in North Belfast, set on a hill gently rising off the York Road. It was a small row house, and inside it looked like no one had lived there for months. Billy was in the kitchen frying pork chops, talking nonstop, while Burke drank red wine in the spotless living room, reading one of Billy's columns. They ate in front of the television set, until the nine o'clock BBC news was finished. Billy stuck a chunk of potato in his mouth and switched off the set. "Get off!" he said, chewing, gesturing with the fork. "And they call that news? Christ, *Pravda* is the voice of the free press compared to the Beeb."

"How do they get away with it?"

"England is England. And forever will be. Send us victorious, happy and glorious, long to reign o'er us, God save the Beeb. Here, pour more of that rotgut for me."

While Billy did the dishes, Burke took his whiskey, which his host had insisted he have, and walked out to the small front garden. Park Avenue was quiet and cold, the houses filled with bright lights which fell out on all the damp little gardens, across the freshly painted gates, and onto the shiny dark street. Burke lit a cigarette and leaned on the gate. A pattering of rain fell from the trees when the wind gusted. Billy had changed. He had never seen him drink this way, and his incessant, entertaining chatter had never been as cynical or sharp. There seemed to be something angry in him that had not been there before.

What would he think if I told him what I was doing? Would he laugh? Probably. Laugh, Belfast said. Laugh.

A woman bundled in a raincoat and a plastic kerchief was walking a collie up the sidewalk. "Evening," she said. "Bitter night."

"Yes," Burke said.

He watched her walk up the hill, and took a pull on the Irish. Why are you drinking? It tastes good, doesn't it? Deirdre at two tomorrow. And Heathrow Airport tomorrow night. New York the next day. Home. And Anne. Billy stood next to him, a long apron wrapped around his thin waist. He held a bottle in one hand and a glass in the other. "Here, Martin, have some more oats. Miserable night, don't you think?"

"Yeah."

"Come in out of it. If we must get drunk we should at least be dry."

"I like it out here," Burke said.

"It is nice, isn't it? But this old neighborhood depresses me. It's too quiet to live in by yourself. I should get married."

"You should," Burke said. "But could any woman keep the pace?"

Billy looked at him, his face softened by the darkness and the whiskey. "I'm thinking of quitting."

"Come on."

"I'm serious," Billy said. "Thinking of chucking the whole thing. I've an offer to go to London, you know. Cover Westminster, write analysis. I'm afraid I've grown sick of this place."

"When did this happen?"

"The offer? Oh, they've been pestering me for months."

"I meant your getting sick of Belfast."

"It must have been the Mountbatten killings," Billy said, pouring another drink, and then setting the bottle on the lawn. He leaned against the fence, and stared into the dark street. "Yes, I'm sure it was. I got the report over the radio and was down at Mullaghmore before anyone else. Just an RTE radio man and the Beeb man and me. I was excited, it was a real story that would write itself. And then it dawned on me. This old man, the boys, the old lady, blown to bloody blue hell, for what? Do you know why they were slaughtered, Martin? They were slaughtered for me. For my benefit. A gift, all wrapped up on a dull bank holiday. The Provos killed them for me. It shook me. Really. I asked myself what in God's name are you doin', Fahy? Do you care? Do you wish this thing would go on forever so you can continue to have good live copy that writes itself and gets you space twice a week? Jesus, I have to get out of this sewer. There's evil here, and I've been feeding on it for years. It's finally sickened me, the whole place. The feckin' Army. Bastards, incompetent, amoral eejits. Loving the war as much as me. Every Sandhurst mother's son of them dying to get up North and shoot Paddys. They love it. It's a sure way to get promoted quickly, you know. Come up and 'fight the war against terrorism.' Cruise around in armored vehicles, take a hop on a helicopter. Heigh-ho, off to the hounds. And the feckin' Provos, twisted, insane, feckin' gangsters, fighting now only because they're good at it. Don't have a clue about reasons anymore, just Brits out, Brits out, that's all they can think or say, and when the Brits go they'll find someone else to shoot or blow up. Sickening, the whole flaming thing, and here's me writing shite about 'political initiatives,' quoting demented, brain-damaged politicians, the 'leaders' of this province." He took a drink. "Sorry, Martin. I'm blabbering."

"What about the I.S.A.?"

"What about them? Fools, psychopaths, I don't know. They're as bad as the Provos. Well, not quite as bad. They've less power so they're better in that respect. Why?"

"No reason."

"Exactly," Billy Fahy said. "No reason. That sums it up. Now, my fine four-legged friend, I know you're dyin' to duck your head down and get a good graze of the old garden, but what do you say about returning to the stable?"

Later, Billy drove him to Botanic Avenue, and they made a tentative date for Friday evening. Burke took the stairs unsteadily and slowly undressed in his stuffy room. He opened the window and literally fell into bed. The room spun out and away from him. With the light on, the spinning slowed. Home on Friday. Billy won't miss me. No one will. Home, and another world. Safe, in the land of the free and the home of the brave. The sidewalks of New York. Home.

Joseph Walsh had come north from Dublin by car with Lafferty on the morning of Thursday 17 December, to the city of Dundalk, County Louth. Just a few miles north of Dundalk lies that masterpiece of gerrymandering, the border separating British territory from the Republic of Ireland. Dundalk is known as "El Paso" in Republican circles, because it is the largest border town in the South and is used as a haven for rest and recreation by guerrillas and as a jumping-off base for operations in the six counties. Since the border is not a natural one, but meanders across the countryside, and has miles of open fields and many farm roads crossing it, guerrillas can go North undetected, and slip back South at their leisure, where the British Army cannot go, and there is no extradition for political crimes. South Armagh, a few miles from Dundalk, is known by the British Army as "bandit country" and that is where Walsh was headed, to meet Frank Higgins, patch up the unraveling alliance, and then go on to Belfast to begin work with I.R.A. cells.

On the northern outskirts of Dundalk, Lafferty pulled off the road and into a weedy field, where a cluster of brightly colored caravans stood in the harsh December light. Lafferty stopped next to a long red trailer which had just been parked there the night before. Walsh got out of the car and went into the trailer as Lafferty drove off. Inside Walsh could see his breath puffing in front of him. He turned on a gas heater, and crawled into one of the bunks. Damp cold place, dark and lifeless. Jonah in the belly of the whale, he thought, pulling a cold blanket over him. If you won't sleep, he told himself, then rest. Just rest. I can sleep in Belfast. I'll sleep well tonight.

Near noon Lafferty returned. He had a bundle wrapped in brown paper which he set triumphantly on the table in the galley of the trailer.

"There's tea there, Lafferty," Walsh said, getting out of the bunk slowly. His back would never be any good. "Let's see what you've got and then we'll have some."

"Did you eat, Chief?"

"Yes," Walsh lied. Lafferty had become a mother hen lately, constantly questioning Walsh's health and well being. Was he warm enough? Would he like to go to the pictures? For a drink? Did he have clean clothes? Cigarettes? Matches? It was hard to believe, Walsh had thought, that this man, the coldest killer he'd ever known, could have developed such loving, maternal ways. But there you were. Mother Lafferty, makes your bed in the morning for you and puts a hole in your enemy at night. Walsh had given up trying to figure Lafferty.

"Here's your new duds," Lafferty said, tearing open the package and holding up an old shiny dark suit, a yellowing white shirt, and a flat cap, once a bright plaid but now faded and dark. Two high-topped black shoes, old and cracked, lay in the torn paper.

"Excellent," Walsh said. "Good work. Do you have the bike?"

"In the back of the car. Will you have a look?"

"Yes," Walsh said, and followed him out to the car.

Lafferty opened the back door and wheeled out a shiny new ten-speed. "Oh, Christ," Walsh said, looking at it, and then turned to Lafferty. "Are you truly as stupid as you seem, man? You get me old clothes and a brand-new bicycle?"

"It's a good comfortable bicycle, Chief," Lafferty said, looking defeated and sullen.

"Are you retarded? Do you want me arrested?" He looked at his watch. "There's still time. Now get me one that will suit my clothes. And quickly. I have to leave here at one o'clock sharp."

"Yes, sir. I was only thinkin' of your comfort."

"Please, Lafferty. Under no circumstances think. Now, get on with it."

Back in the trailer, Walsh had tea and brown bread. He settled into the bunk, and tried to rest once more. By the spring, he told himself, I'll be out of it. I can let Deirdre and Boland and Cosgrave carry out the operations on the ground, and then I can retire from it. Give leadership when it's needed, but stop all this running about.

I can die in peace, Jesus, what a blessing. But I must be ready for the next few months. This is the critical time. To move the I.R.A. toward our ideology. To begin the process of giving the fighter a voice and an intellect. It had started poorly. But Walsh was sure it was because of communication, and not mistrust. Higgins wanted to deal at the top, and not with Boland. Perhaps Boland had been too brash. Thank God for Deirdre. She and the American had only been North a few days and she was already beginning to sort it out. By tonight it will be stitched. By Sunday my troops will be in the field. By the new year they will be in action. By the spring I'll be out of it.

He was sleeping when Lafferty returned. Lying in his bunk like a rag doll, looking not at peace, but as if sleep had crept up and clubbed him. Let him be, Lafferty thought, tucking the blanket around the old man and taking a chair across from him, feeling that powerful emotion one has watching another sleep. Old Joe, he had barely known him before Liam's death. Joe must've seen something in me though, Lafferty thought. Giving me that good position in the war against the Provos last summer and autumn, entrusting Boland to me. And here Boland was now a leader. That suited Lafferty. He had never wanted to lead, but only to serve. Walsh had rewarded him as soon as he got back to Dublin after he was sprung in Kildare. He had told Lafferty he was now the personal guard for the chief of staff, and for the past month Lafferty had lived with the old man and taken care of him. In that short time Lafferty had grown to love Joseph Walsh. Even if he does insult me. It's only for my own good. Makes a better soldier of me. Some of the other lads gossiped that the real reason he was chosen as guard was because the chief wanted to keep an eye on him. Lafferty didn't believe that. It was because of my devotion and long service to the cause, that was the reason. Walsh had chosen *me* to be the protector. Lafferty would never forget that. He would do anything for the old man. He'd lay down his life without a thought. "I lay down my life for the Emerald Isle," that's what Bold Robert Emmett had said. I'll lay down my life for Joe Walsh. Ireland and Joseph Walsh were the same thing to Lafferty.

The old man stirred awkwardly. Lafferty checked his watch. Twenty to one. Better rouse him or he'll be all over me. Lafferty shook him gently. "There, Chief. Time now, Chief."

Walsh opened his eyes and looked up at Lafferty's pitted face. "What time is it?"

"Twenty to."

Walsh sat up, rubbed his face, and then stood. He began to undress. "Did you get the bike?"

"I did. The fookin' thing barely runs."

"Good," Walsh said and stepped into the old trousers.

"I want to go," Lafferty said.

"You have your orders."

"I want to go, Chief. He'll have someone there watchin' over him. Why can't you? You'll need me. I can look after you. Just until you get to Belfast."

Walsh buttoned the dirty shirt and tucked it in. He looked at his man. "No, Lafferty. Your job is here."

"Yes, sir. But would you take the old .45?" he asked, unbuttoning his jacket and taking out the pistol. "You could use it."

"No."

"If you'll pardon me, Chief," Lafferty said, a slight tone of desperation in his voice. "I'm your guard. I think I know best how to guard you. Please, either let me go with you or take the gun. Here, take the gun."

"Lafferty! For God's sake. How long have you been in this army? You have your orders, man."

"I'm only thinkin' of you," he said, tossing the pistol on the bunk, and quickly helping Walsh into the suit coat.

"There's nothing to worry about. A pistol would incriminate me if I'm lifted. One man on that road is never looked at. Two men and guaranteed the Brits bother you. Don't you see that?"

"Yes," Lafferty said, watching the old man lace up the high-topped shoes.

Outside, Walsh put on the cap and studied the old black bicycle. "Good work. Very good work indeed." Walsh mounted it and turned to Lafferty's sad resigned face. "Don't wait around here now," Walsh told him. "Report to Cosgrave the second you're in."

"Yes, sir. All the best, sir."

"Goodbye, Lafferty. Thank you."

"Goodbye, sir. Watch your back."

"Aye," Walsh said, and pedaled away slowly on the road going north.

It was a cold day, growing dark to the north and west. Walsh repeated a line in his head, "Ireland has her madness and her weather still," who was that? Elliot? No, Auden, yes, on the death of Yeats. He turned off the main highway and pedaled up the narrow two-laned road which would take him into Armagh. The fields were lush in the wet day and the light rain billowed out with the wind like a sheer curtain across the farms. There was no traffic. It was quiet, the only sound the clicking and clanking of the ancient bike under him. Three miles, he thought. Maybe four. Damn fool. Why didn't you sleep this morning? Why did you appease your insomnia once again? I wonder if the house on Mountainview Parade has a decent bed. Fool, simpleton, why didn't you sleep?

He had been up for two nights running, sleeping perhaps three hours out of the forty-eight. There had been meetings at the Wicklow farmhouse with ten I.S.A. officers, and interviews with his troops, numbering eighty-three men and eleven women. Then he had read the ninety-four files prepared by Boland before he had gone North. Finally, near dawn today, he had selected fifty troops to move up to Ulster, broken into ten columns, and had told the ten officers to prepare mobilization by Sunday at the latest. Some would move to Belfast under Deirdre's command, others to Derry to serve under John Boland, and still others to North Antrim to take delivery of the weapons arriving on December 26. One of the conditions of the Limeview settlement that Walsh had fought for and won was that the I.S.A. quartermaster and his unit were solely in charge of distribution. The Provisionals could have observers there, but it was the I.S.A.'s job to place the weapons in the hands of the new allied army. He hadn't informed Higgins of his plan to move his troops up so soon. If there was any trouble with the Provos, any new wrinkle to their three-card trick, any more hesitation or noncommunication, then the Provos would have to deal with an active service force of fifty troops on their own ground, not disorganized and scattered in the Republic.

After a final meeting, and phone calls to John Boland and Deirdre, Walsh had gone back to Dublin and tried unsuccessfully to sleep. Soon he was up and dressed and reviewing more files and reports, mostly concerned with requests to join the I.S.A., which had tripled since the raid at Kildare. Lafferty had picked him up at ten o'clock and driven him to Dundalk. He had napped uncomfortably on the drive up.

Walsh approached the border. It was defined by a jut of rusted metal that took away the left lane of the narrow road. A thousand yards now, he thought, maybe less, to Forkhill. The day had turned quite dark, and the rain fell heavier. Up ahead a soldier stepped from the trees onto the road, his green and brown camouflage fatigues making his body a blur against the dark green landscape. When Walsh approached he saw how young the soldier was, not yet twenty, his face pasty, and gray eyes staring. Walsh noted his beret. Flat, sand-colored, with a small pom-pom at the center. The Queen's Own Highlanders Regiment. The boy stepped to the center of the road, and pointed his SLR at Walsh's middle. "Where you goin', Dad?"

Walsh stopped the bike and straddled it. "Home."

"Where's home?" the soldier asked, and looked over Walsh's shoulder, and then at either side of the road.

"Just out of Forkhill. Another mile."

The soldier took a wide circle around Walsh, keeping his SLR trained on him, and said, "On your way then, Dad."

Walsh touched the brim of his cap and pedaled away. At the first bend another soldier, this one an Indian or Pakistani lad in the beret of the Q.O.H., stood at the side of the road, leveling his weapon and glaring at the old farmer on his broken-down bicycle. It was very quiet. There was the barely perceptible slipping sound of the rain in the trees, and the fragile call of two birds. To Walsh's left, beyond a stone bridge over a stagnant stream, rose up the hilly little village of Forkhill, with the chimneys puffing gray smoke into the gray and black sky. Two more soldiers came out of the bed of the stream and took positions on the bridge. One was a tall blond man who stood stock-still, looking and listening up the road where Walsh had just come from.

Across the bridge and in the village, Walsh parked the bike near the front door of Twomey's Public House. He looked up the empty street curving away higher into the town. Below, on the bridge, the two soldiers maintained their positions. Inside, the pub was dark and two middle-aged men, dressed nearly the same as Walsh, sat silently in front of pints, watching him as he passed. "Brandy," Walsh said to the woman behind the bar. She was very attractive. Tall and slim with silver-frosted hair.

She looked him over carefully. "All I have is Hennessy," she said flatly.

"I prefer Spanish brandy."

She leaned forward. "Right. That door to your left. Up the stairs, first door on your right. Knock before you go in."

Walsh nodded, and she turned away. He walked to the door and closed it behind him. The stairs led off to his left and a door stood facing him. Opening it, he looked out at a black Datsun parked in the gravel lot behind the pub. Walsh closed the door and mounted the stairs. A sharp stitch cut across his lower back, and he stopped, gripping the handrail tighter. The pain flared once more, then eased, and Walsh continued up. He knocked on the door. "It's open."

Walsh stepped into the room. It was dark, and he could see a bed to his left where a man sat pointing an Armalite rifle at him. In front of the curtained window was a gatelegged table, and behind it, facing him, sat Rúairí MacCurtain. "Welcome, Joe," he smiled.

Walsh held the doorknob in his hand. "Oh, Jesus," he sighed.

"Close it," MacCurtain said, "and take a seat."

Walsh tossed his cap on the table and sat across from MacCurtain. The young man's green eyes were staring, the beginning of a smile played at his mouth around the clipped mustache. He hooked his thumb toward the window behind him, "I was afraid those Highlanders would get you, Joe."

"I'm safe in saying that Higgins is not here?"

"Correct. We're your reception committee. Mr. Milo Shannon here—" Walsh glanced at him, young, shorthaired, with a broken nose, the flattened cheekbones and puffed eyes of a boxer—"and the two gents downstairs."

Walsh looked back at MacCurtain. "I'm going to reach in my jacket pocket for a cigarette and matches, Rúairí. Tell your man there."

"Go right ahead."

Walsh lit the cigarette and tossed the match on the floor.

"It's all over, Joe," MacCurtain said. "You know that, don't you?"

"Is this Higgins' order, Rúairí? Or are you free-lancing?"

"Oh, no. I'm a soldier. This is an operation ordered from GHQ by the chief of staff."

"The bastard," Walsh said, and blew smoke down his thin nose.

Rúairí turned and opened the curtains slightly. He looked out. Walsh flicked an ash to the floor. "Still there," MacCurtain said, and then turned to the old man across from him. "I'm sorry for the delay. We can't move until they do."

"I don't mind."

"You know, in a way, this is a compliment to you."

Walsh smiled. "Oh?"

"You're too good, too professional. We could never handle you, Joe. You're a natural leader, and you'd never play second fiddle, would you, now?"

"We had an agreement."

"Yes. But it's broken. We can't afford you. We want the weapons but a man like you is a risk to us. It's war, Walsh. We don't play."

"I can see that. You'll pay for this though, Rúairí. You're putting your entire organization in jeopardy by this. You'll have a two-front war to fight within a week. We'll take you on like a fire storm."

"No you won't," Rúairí said, turning to the curtain again. He spoke, looking out. "You have perhaps one hundred men? We have five hundred active service troops. And your one hundred have no experience up here. Without a general, say half of your troops come up. What the Brits don't lift the minute they arrive, we'll execute. Within a week, as you said, the I.S.A. will not exist. There," he turned away from the window, "now we can move. Milo?"

The young man cuffed Walsh's hands behind his back. They took him out of the room, down the stairs, and out the back door to the black Datsun. MacCurtain drove with Walsh sitting next to him and Milo in the back. The rain spattered the windshield and the wipers slowly swished, back and forth, as they drove across the stone bridge and turned north. Walsh felt completely at peace. Thank God for Deirdre, he thought. And thank God for not giving in to sleep the last few days. My house is in order. They won't need me. Walsh wasn't angry that the alliance had failed. It was a gamble that had to be risked. They had just lost this battle. But it would be a long war. He felt very tired, and would welcome what was coming. His corpse would serve a purpose. The I.S.A., and every politically intelligent Republican, would rally around his bones. His death would serve as a reminder that the Provisionals were murderers, not soldiers, a fascist gang and not a revolutionary army.

Rúairí turned off the road and up a lane past a grove of trees. Walsh could see three horses grazing ahead. A rounded-off mountain ridge sloped up from the field to the thick sky. Rúairí pulled off the lane and then reversed the car so it was pointing back down the lane toward the road. They led the old man across the field, the wet weeds and grass darkening their trousers. There was a weather-beaten shed off to their right, and they hurried Walsh into it. Inside, tools hung from the ceiling. There were empty fertilizer bags scattered on the damp earth floor. "On your knees, Joe," MacCurtain said.

Walsh didn't hear him. He was staring out the door at the mist blowing off the mountain and down over the green of Ulster. Milo hit him on the shoulder with the barrel of the Armalite and Walsh fell to his knees. He continued to look out. The last thing he saw was the Wessex helicopter, like a fat bulky insect, flitting over the ridge and dropping heavily to the field. Rúairí fired his .32 pistol six inches from the back of Walsh's head, and the sharp crack bounced back at them from the wooden walls. The body slumped forward, the head turned upwards, one dead eye staring.

Rúairí joined Milo at the door, looking out at the Wessex settling down and seven soldiers piling out, separating, bent over and running toward them. "Oh, mother," Milo said.

"Shut up," Rúairí ordered. "See the pilot, Milo? The pilot. Take him. Take the pilot."

Milo leaned his Armalite against the door and aimed. He squeezed off a round and they saw the soldiers dive out to the wet earth and the pilot of the Wessex disappear from the window.

Rúairí fired two shots in the direction of the soldiers and then chased Milo through the field toward the Datsun, their knees pumping high, racing across the mire and slop. A twanging sound whizzed past, and they heard shots cracking behind them in a wave.

Milo reached the car first, opened the driver's door and scooted across the seat. Rúairí jumped in and started it. "How close?" he asked the sweating face next to him.

"Oh, Jesus, they're almost on us."

Rúairí gunned the car away. Ten yards ahead he caught a pothole and the Datsun began to swing away from him. The back window shattered, and Milo ducked. Rúairí downshifted and brought it back on the lane. He checked his side mirror and saw that the Wessex was still stationary in the field. "You got him, Milo," Rúairí shouted. "You crippled them."

When they reached the road they turned north and drove at speed for a mile and a half to a T-junction where they abandoned the Datsun and took to the fields. Running first east for half a mile, and then cutting south for a half mile. They cleared a slight rise and ran down into a hollow to a farmhouse where chickens pecked suspiciously in the front yard. A woman in a plain print dress let them in and took their weapons. They went to a room at the back of the house, and collapsed into fireside chairs. MacCurtain looked over at Milo's lumpy face, streaming with sweat. "Good day, Milo," he said, gulping for air. "We got a traitor and a Brit. And we can talk about it."

Burke parked the Escort across the street from I.S.P. headquarters, shut the motor, and checked his watch. Ten to two. He looked out at the grim street through the windshield dotted and running with rain. His hangover was growing. A cold glass of lager would cure that, but he had decided to wait it out. One beer now and more than likely he would have another, and within an hour he'd be as soused as last night. You'll never learn. He lit a cigarette, thinking that he would try a beer later, before dinner, and see how it went. If he couldn't handle it, he'd put it down, for good. There was nothing but misery in drunkenness. One beer when I hit Liverpool, or should I wait until London?

Burke glanced back at his case lying on the seat. He had money, his passport, and a ticket for the five o'clock ferry to England purchased just moments ago in High Street. If he could catch a late flight out of Heathrow tonight, he'd be whistling Stars 'n Stripes Forever by dawn tomorrow.

His second cigarette was nearly finished when he saw Deirdre come out of the headquarters, pause, and put her hood over her head. She looked up the street and then ducked out, taking a skip and then running to cross the street ahead of a small van. Burke turned to toss his cigarette through the crack of the window when he heard the long, ringing rifle report, the sloppy skid of rubber on asphalt, and brakes grinding. He saw Deirdre in the street, her hood blown off her head, lying near the curb, face staring up at the cloudy sky. Her arms were splayed out, and one of her legs was bent under her. Burke saw a light twitching of her hiking boot and then she lay still, her mouth open.

Burke ran to her as two men raced over from the van, pointing up the street at a high narrow tenement. Burke bent down, and started to lift her. His only thought was to get her out of the rain. Somehow he reasoned that if she was out of the dirty street and comfortable she'd come around. "Leave her, mate," one of the men said, touching Burke's arm. He looked up at his face, sad, his teeth gritted. "Leave her. She's gone."

Burke held on for a moment more and then let her go. He stood, and his legs gave a little, and the man next to him grabbed his arm. "I'm all right," Burke said. "All right."

Sammy Maguire was at the door, shouting, "Go, Martin. Go. Get away. You don't want this trouble. Go."

Burke crossed the street and got in the car. He fumbled with the ignition key, shaking, and let out a low moan. He drove up to the Falls Road and an Army ambulance passed, sirens blaring insanely. He drove on, with no destination, stopping at lights, turning, moving on. Half an hour later he was on the busy Donegal Road, waiting for a light when a squad of soldiers, in the spread diamond formation, passed in front of him. The soldier on rear point seemed to look him over carefully before passing on. Burke was brought back to the street, and the car he was driving. Did soldiers always check out cars with Republic of Ireland plates? If the Army didn't pick him up, the murderers of Deirdre would find him. He pulled over and double-parked. There was a pub on the corner. Burke grabbed his case, told himself to walk slowly, and went up the crowded sidewalk.

The pub was half full, smelling of fried meat and beer. He stepped up to the zinc bar and ordered a glass of lager. The barman, dressed in a filthy sweater over an enormous paunch, and sporting a bright orange watch cap, set the foaming glass of beer before him. Burke gave him a five pound note and took a long swallow. Above the bar was a TV monitor, showing the street, the door of the pub, and the sidewalk outside in gray and white.

Burke asked, "Do you have a phone?"

"There in the back."

Burke took another swallow, burning his throat with the cold beer. He left his change on the bar and took his case with him to the telephone. He called Billy's number at home and let it ring ten times before hanging up. Back at the bar he finished his beer and ordered another, drinking this one slowly. When he lit a cigarette he noticed his hand had stopped quivering. The barman came over to chat, pressing his belly against the bar and moving his watch cap back on his head. "You've got a thirst on ye today. Looks like ye haven't tasted beer in a year's time."

"Do you have a phone directory?"

"I do." He went to the end of the bar and reached under for the book. Burke took it with him over to the phone, squinting in the weak light, until he found the Europa's number.

"Give me the bar," Burke told the receptionist.

"Whip 'n Saddle." A male voice.

"Is Mr. Bill Fahy there?"

"He is. Just on his way out. Mr. Fahy? Angela, run get Mr. Fahy for the phone. The girl's fetching him."

Billy came on. "Fahy."

"Billy, it's Martin."

"You scoundrel. Thought I was pissed last night, didn't you, you sly horse. Asking me about the I.S.A. How did you know?"

"What're you talking about?"

"Get away, Martin. You didn't know Joe Walsh is lying dead in Armagh this minute? I just heard the bulletin. I'm on my way down, do you want to tag along?"

Burke stared back at the bar. The barman was licking down a long cigar. He stuck it in his mouth and lit it, turning it slowly as the flame puffed up.

"Martin? Hello? You there?"

"Yeah," Burke said quietly. "Billy, can you do me a favor?"

"Sure, I'll pick you up right now. We'll be down there in no time."

"No. Can you rent a car for me? I need it right away."

"Certainly," Billy said. "What is it, Martin?" He waited for an answer. When there was none he went on, "If you're in, don't get in any deeper."

"I'll need it right away."

"Yes," Billy said. "I see. Meet me in half an hour on Little May Street just off Alfred Street. Do you know where that is?"

"Yes."

"I'll have a car for you. Don't worry about paying me. I'll lease it through the paper. Is there anything else you need? Money?"

"No."

"How about some advice?" Billy paused. "I can protect you. I can get you out. You can share your trouble with me."

"Thanks, Billy. All I need is a car."

When he left the pub he saw two RUC men near the double-parked Escort. One of them was taking down the license plate number while the other bent over to look under the axle.

Burke drove north to Antrim town in the new Fiat and then caught the A6 going west. At four o'clock he could see the rows of houses of Derry's neighborhoods approaching as the day died quickly in rain, sleet, and wind. He pulled off the road into the yard in front of the garage. The one door, moving in and out slightly in the wind, a fluttering flag at the end of the day. Inside, a light bulb cut a circle of white through the gloom. Burke walked into a smell of grease and rotted wood. A Morris Minor, its engine block hoisted by chain inches above the opened hood. "Freeze," a man said, dressed in oil-spotted coveralls, stepping out of the shadow. A long shotgun barrel poked in Burke's belly. "Against the wall. Hop it!"

Burke spread his legs out and his palms lay flat against the wood. "I'm looking for John Boland."

"What's that?"

"Boland. John Boland."

"Turn around."

Burke turned and faced him.

"You the yank then?"

"Yes."

"Wait here."

Burke rubbed his stomach and waited. The wind blowing steadily through the open door. He rubbed his hands together, and flexed them to remove the chill. Boland approached from the rear of the garage, dressed in coveralls, his hair moving back when he stepped nearer the door. "You're safe, Martin?"

"Yeah. You know what's going on?"

"I do. You shouldn't have come, you know. You could've been tailed."

"I—I just thought I'd let you know. What's next, John?"

"I'm going into Donegal in an hour. I suggest you clear out as well, yank."

"What about the shipment?"

"What about the shipment?" Boland laughed. "Fuck the bloody shipment. I'm going to save my life."

"O'Connor and the German, what about them, John? You can't leave them."

"I can and I will. They're nothing to me. They're nothing to the I.S.A.—"

"Nothing?"

"Yes, nothing. And the weapons are worthless now. I'm going south and take control of the Army. My first order is to go .to ground. And for a good long spell. The Provos can do what they want. It's over, Martin."

Burke lit a cigarette. "Let me get this right. You're bugging out, and those two are going to sail into Ballycastle, right into the open arms of the I.R.A. What do you think they'll do with O'Connor and the German?"

"Kill them. Martin, I'd love to stand here and discuss things with you, but I've got to move out. There's nothing to be done, don't you see? Nothing. We can't take them on. They'd chew us up like beef in a mincer. Our only hope was the alliance, and they broke it. They not only cut off our head, they tore out our heart. Liam Cleary, Joe Walsh, Deirdre O'Sullivan. Gone. I don't plan on adding the name of John Boland to that list of martyrs. I'm going south and will inform the Provisionals the I.S.A. are off active service. And I don't give a fuck what you think of me."

"When they arrive on the twenty-sixth, what's supposed to happen?"

"They meet at the bar of the Royal Port Hotel. From the twenty-sixth on, one of them is supposed to show up at the bar at half-twelve and wait half an hour. You're a fool, Martin. You're a dead man if you go."

"Right," Burke said, and walked out, leaving Boland standing, looking out the door until the Fiat drove off. He leaned against the Morris, bent his head, and shook it once or twice. "Happy Christmas, yank," he said to himself before going to the rear of the garage and turning out the light.

CHAPTER 16

Escape

O'Connor woke alone. He struggled out of the sleeping bag, coming awake tangled, uncomfortable, a moment of panic as he freed his legs and stood in the empty one-room cottage. The cold air hit him as soon as he moved and he threw on his heavy sweater, put on a pair of socks, and went toward the pail standing in the center of the room. On the dusty floorboards around the pail was a circle of wetness. Gudrun's bright orange sleeping bag was rolled and stored against the far wall. He hadn't heard her wash or leave the cottage. The splashed water, the tin pail exactly in the center of the room, was surrealistic. He could still be dreaming. O'Connor knelt down, dipped his hands in the pail, and brought the cold water to his face, shivering, bathing his neck. The candle on the windowsill half gone in its mess of cold wax on the broken saucer. Red coals died slowly in the fireplace. They had talked last night as the light rain drifted down on the thatched roof. He remembered her face across the empty room, as she sat against the wall, wrapped in the sleeping bag. She had taken a cigarette, something she rarely did, and smoked it down, talking first about her father, which was as rare as smoking for her, and then asking for another cigarette, going on about the need to keep thinking, keep being aware, always be ready to change your plan, always know there was an escape route. Just as a professional burglar will unlock the back door before beginning his work, so they must always be aware of a back door in their plans. O'Connor had listened, watching her lovely face in the shifting candlelight, hearing her throaty voice, wondering why she was so keyed up. It was probably because everything had worked so well. She had assumed leadership at Martin's house and everyone had fallen in behind her. The flight from Moher had been organized perfectly.

She had skippered them on this run up here, going far out to sea to skirt the Arans on the Atlantic side, rather than pass on the mainland side through the shipping lanes. And then on up here, off the coast of Connemara, to this little island, named Trippen Isle, which Deirdre had suggested because it had been abandoned last spring, and no one came near it anymore. That had been eighteen days ago, when they had come up the cliff, seeing the ghost village for the first time, the little thatched cottages clustered together, completely empty. There was nothing but a soft wind moaning, increasing the loneliness of the place, rattling through the swinging doors, filling the lifeless cottages. The islanders had even taken the locks and knobs from the doors. They had settled in to another time of silence and waiting, to move at the right time to make their schedule. They didn't want to arrive off the Antrim coast a day too soon, or a day too late. It had to be December 26, and Gudrun had plotted the journey north precisely.

Pushing the door open, he stepped outside to the morning, unzipping, relieving himself just next to the path, watching his thick stream smoking in the chilly morning. The wind was gentle, flowing straight from the east off Galway five miles away. There was a long ridge of dark cloud hiding the sun over the sea, and the mainland beyond. To the west, and straight above his head, the sky looked calm.

O'Connor laced up his boots, rolled his sleeping bag and stored it next to Gudrun's. He remembered last night again, when she had finally finished her long lecture about escape routes, and had looked over to the wet window, gleaming with the candlelight. Her profile moved him, as it would if she were a stranger he was seeing for the first time across a restaurant, or on a bus. O'Connor had gone over and embraced her. They had kissed easily, deeply, her hand at the back of his neck, massaging. O'Connor gently stripped the bag from her, shucked her jeans and panties, and kissed her belly, sticking his tongue in her navel, which made her half giggle, half groan, low in her throat, and opening her legs wide as he moved down, the warmth of her crotch coming to him with the clean full odor of low tide. Gudrun let her hands roam through his thick head of hair, saying his name once or twice, and then pulling so hard he had to wrench her hand away as she seemed to go away from him in a series of quivering sighs. Limp, deadweight, she'd gone to sleep in his arms. O'Connor had watched the candle burn low, the fire grow weak, before crossing the room to his sleeping bag.

He went to the tin pail again, and cupped some water to his mouth. Perhaps today they would go. What was the date? In his rucksack he found his watch under the M-10. The little window on the watch face at three o'clock said 23. December 23. O'Connor shook the self-winding watch three or four times and then strapped it on. Wearing it might be a good omen that they'd set sail for Ulster today. He hadn't worn it since they'd left Moher to keep it dry on the boat, and once they'd made Trippen, he'd kept it in the bag, winding it once a day, keeping it off his wrist because time watched when you were inactive was a chain. It was the watch his father had given him three nights before he'd gone to France. Why don't you write to him? O'Connor casti-gated himself. Because there's nothing to say. He touched the watch on his wrist, as if it were something fragile, like lace rather than glass and stainless steel. The face was a mottled gray and white, quite attractive, and he remembered the old man saying, embarrassed, as he always was when receiving or giving gifts, "It's only a Timex, Terry. If you'd given me more notice—"

"It's beautiful, Dad," O'Connor had cut him off, sitting at the kitchen table in Inwood, drinking Rheingold from bottles.

"Well, I'll give you a good feed anyway," the little man had said.

The "good feed" was in a coffee shop on Broadway run by a Greek family who seemed constantly engaged in verbal wars of Olympian proportions. The patrons in the restaurant were treated as interlopers to the contest, and were tolerated, it appeared, be-cause one couldn't deny another person food. The service was slow, the food sloppy and dull, but there was always plenty of it, and the general of the restaurant, a big broad lump of a man who headquartered near the cash register, knew O'Connor's father by name and railed at his battling sons to hurry up with "Mr. Oke-ner's" meal.

There was little to talk about. The old man was the loneliest being O'Connor had ever known. He had buried his wife when the boy was still an infant, and had raised him in silence and love by himself. A melancholy man to begin with, he had never over-come the death of his wife. After thirty-five years of running an elevator downtown in an apartment building on Fifth Avenue, he had the convict's gray pallor that confinement and living under light bulbs gives you. There was still a bit of County Monaghan in his voice, and still the rural Irishman's shyness and inhibition. Terry sensed his father's embarrassment, and talked of baseball, the old man's only passion. His father had been relieved, as Terry teased him for his loyalty to the pathetic Mets. He knew his father didn't want him to go. When he'd moved out to go to Pratt in Brooklyn, his father had asked him, "Sure, the Jesuits at Fordham can teach you about fil-um." And his father had said nothing one way or the other when Terry had told him he was off to France in three days' time. Why leave a good-paying job for one only promised in a letter? Why go to a foreign country where you will be alone, a stranger? He had known the pain of the immigrant, of being neither fish nor fowl, having no love for the country you left and none for the new land. Didn't Terry have a fine education that could see him through here? Why did he have to go? Of course his father never verbalized any of these questions. But they both knew the questions were there, over their meal of pot roast and potatoes, lemon meringue pie and coffee. The questions were all asked in his father's desperate talk of batting averages, the quality of John Stearn's arm, and whether the Italian kid in center was just a fee-nom or the real thing.

After the meal, with the General paid and much thanking of "Mr. Oke-ner," they had walked along the mad rushing river of Upper Broadway. O'Connor strolled with his father, and looked and listened. He might never come back to this neighborhood where he'd been born, gone to school, and grown up. Black teenage girls swinging along shrieking joyfully at a private joke, and Puerto Rican desperadoes in shirts the colors of carnivals, bopping by with boom boxes blaring Mongo Santamaria. Ancient Irish clock-punchers like O'Connor's old man, with gray faces as dull as their clothes, and stern expressions, hurrying home through what was once their neighborhood. Cabs flashing past a pimpmobile that would make Batman envious, and the unceasing padded boiler-room roar of Manhattan through it all.

At the subway entrance they stopped to say goodbye. "How long did you say you'd be gone, Terry?"

"I don't know, Dad. Depends on how long I can get work."

"Well, it's good you're goin' with a job waitin' over there. I know what it's like to cross an ocean and not have a friend or a job."

"Yeah."

"Will you get to Ireland?"

"I doubt it."

"It's just as well, I suppose. If you ever do, you could kiss the old place for me."

"I will. Thanks again for the watch."

"Ah, it's only a Timex. You take care of yourself, boy," he took O'Connor's hand in both of his. "Don't forget your faith. Send me a postcard of how you're gettin' on."

"Goodbye, Dad."

"Say a prayer for me."

As O'Connor was descending the stairs he heard his old man call, "Luck, Terry." And turned to see just his little head, delicately formed, his hair neatly combed, his face in mourning.

I will write, O'Connor resolved, putting the rucksack on his shoulder, and feeling the M-10's weight against his back. I'll write when we get to the North. He walked out and down past the cottages, seeing last night's rain trapped and glistening in the eaves of straw thatch, dripping off to the ground, one by one.

Gudrun woke and, once out of the sleeping bag, found her panties and jeans on the bare floor next to her. She slipped them on, found fresh socks, and put on her rubber and canvas yachting shoes. Out the window it was cold black. Dawn would break any minute. She stepped to the pail and splashed water on her face, watching Terrence sleeping heavily, feeling his warmth from halfway across the room. It was extraordinary, the heat the man had. If you just drew close to him, you could feel it, an aura of warmth around him, like someone with a severe sunburn. She remembered last night. His black and white hair in her crotch, his tongue darting, patient, controlled. It had been a long time since he'd done that. Men were such misers. He liked *soixante-neuf*, but she never had. It was impossible to concentrate. She felt cramps, low in her abdomen. Perhaps that's why she had come so soon last night.

Gudrun put on a sweater over her sweatshirt and walked out. The dawning sun had sent ribbons of gray light out around the horizon. This was a feeling of power she enjoyed, the only conscious person in the world. It was an accomplishment to beat Terrence. He fled from sleep like a schoolboy let out of class for summer. There had been that other day. Yes, the day before Kildare, when she'd been up before him.

The waves rolled lazily, pitching themselves up on the rocky beach like a final gasp of energy, too tired to bother, as Gudrun dragged the yellow dinghy to the water's edge. Gulls swept over the beach, and out on a table of rock, twenty yards from shore, small red and black birds seemed to be tap dancing, foraging in the new light. Rowing out, she was unconsciously, like all good sailors, checking the wind, the color of the water, the sky. *Die Freiheit* swung on its chain peacefully as she approached, and Gudrun rowed into the portside, shipped oars, slipped the knot off the gunwale, and secured the dinghy. She climbed on board and the dinghy bobbed out and behind as Gudrun hurried below decks, went to the head, and urinated. The only time, she had always joked, she had anything like "penis envy" was when she saw men just pulling it out anywhere, in a field, the side of the road, off a boat. She could urinate anywhere too, of course, but the squatting made you so vulnerable.

There was that time in the south of France with Conor, driving through the quiet, empty farmland after a long lunch in a provincial restaurant, when he had pulled over to the side of the road and pissed. She had been desperate to go, and seeing his stream made it worse. Conor had said, go ahead, there's no one around, and she had lifted up her skirt, her panties around her knees, and squatted down. To look up and see three nuns on bicycles cruising by in single file, each one staring. Conor had laughed. She had laughed too, and then Conor wanted to fuck her there at the side of the road, hoping, he said, the nuns would come back. He was serious, not joking any longer, and if she was true to herself, the idea had appealed to her as well. Conor. *Scheisskerl.*

She saw a spot of red on the lip of the bowl. Thank God. "Our little friend has arrived," as Irmgard, the family *Haustochter*, would say. Never explaining it, never being clear, it was all a dark mystery, something not quite shameful, but definitely something not to talk about. When she'd asked her mother, she was told to ask Irmgard. A lady of Mrs. Böhm's stature did not talk of such things with twelve-year-old girls, even if the youngster in question was her own daughter.

Gudrun inserted a tampon, the white string hanging like a trailing stern line in the blonde pubic curls. She remembered her mother's face, the cheekbones, nose and forehead as beautiful and cold as sculpture. Her wide mouth breaking into a smile. Her hair the color of white bordeaux, the eyes that could look right into you one moment and then be gone, empty, no one home. Irmgard had always said Gudrun was fortunate to favor her mother. And as a girl Gudrun would always say, yes, but not the eyes. I have my father's eyes. And she did, light brown, not the hard blue of her mother's eyes, not nearly as sad. She had spoken last night to Terrence about her father. Why? Pre-menstrual? Trying to find a link to him somehow? Speaking of escape.

Above deck she walked around the yawl, checking everything with her eyes, every line, every winch, every foot of deck. They would go today, on the tide this morning, a little early, but they could either lay up on an island off Donegal, or stay at sea until they were due. In the cockpit, on a shelf above the chart table, Gudrun turned on the radio, forgetting again, as she had almost every day since they'd arrived, that it was broken. She cursed. She didn't understand electronics, but Terrence had said he could fix it. He had spent nearly the whole first week at it, but without success. That frightened her. Sailing northern waters in winter without weather reports. She would just have to rely on the barometer, the portable wind gauge, her eyes and ears, and never stray too far from shore. She checked the chart. By leaving early they could, in the event of a blow, hug the coast all around Donegal Bay, instead of saving time by striking straight across the mouth from Benwee Head for a landfall at Malinbeg. Just looking at the chart made her realize that they were finally getting off this stony ghost isle, and would be under sail, bound for places she'd never seen. She clicked the radio on and off, gave it a rap with the flat of her hand, and cursed it again, but this time with a smile on her face. The hell with you, radio. I'd swim up there through a hurricane if I had to.

There was nothing to do above, so she went back below decks with a ring of line over her shoulder into the forward cabins and started resecuring the crates of weapons. If they hit heavy seas she didn't want a crate breaking loose and taking out a piece of the hull. She worked slowly, enjoying the labor. What did the Irish say? "God bless the work." Yes, she smiled to herself, God bless the work. It had always been a pleasure to work on *Die Freiheit*, the sense of life in the timbers made it feel like grooming a pet whale. The smells of pitch, the tar in the rope. Gudrun was joyful, alone on her property, working, ready to move.

Ireland had changed her. The raid at Kildare, especially her killing of the boy, made her distrust herself in action. If she ever again felt the way she had the first few hours after the raid, she could jeopardize the whole outfit. It had been the first time in twelve years that she'd ever been emotional after an operation. Perhaps she was getting shell-shocked. She didn't want to kill anyone. Especially unarmed men and eight-year-old boys. Perhaps British soldiers would be easier to waste.

She knotted the last line and went above. It was full morning, with the sun slipping in and out of clouds, and the sea beginning to swell a bit, running green into the shore. A cup of coffee and I'll go in, she told herself and went to heat the kettle. As she stirred in the instant granules, she thought that they should have brought more liquor with them. There had only been one bottle of Irish, and Terry finished that three days after they had arrived on Trippen. Liquor would be good to keep Terrence and herself on peaceful terms. The British Navy's famous daily grog ration to all hands had not been dispensed for charitable reasons, she knew. A shot or two of booze at the end of the day to look forward to might keep them out of each other's way. Men, never growing up, but what's worse, cherishing their childishness.

The coffee made, she carried it into the forward cabins, to check once again on the weapons.

Under sail they worked well together. There was no paranoid talk of the Special Branch closing in, no more talk of what they'd find in Ulster. Since August they had been diverted from their plan by betrayal, flight, and the Irish talent for intrigue. Now they were sailing with a fair wind, and were about to realize their goal.

One P.M. and off the bow was Slyne Head looking like two dark towers in the sun. Beyond were the smudges of twenty scattered islands. At four o'clock the wind turned colder as the late December night approached. The sun off the port side was lowering into a misty horizon as the world turned pink and purple. Frigid light shadowed across the deck and the long dark mass of Inishbofin lying ahead. Gudrun, working at the stern, heard a raucous barking and slapping somewhere, and looking up she saw Terrence standing, silent, pointing at a cluster of rocks near Inishbofin, where bull seals played in the sunset. The wind brought the sweet thick smell of turf smoke from the island as they stole past in the last long light of day.

The next morning a rogue gale blew up and Gudrun made for St. John's Point in Donegal Bay, a thin finger of land where they laid up off the lee shore to let it blow out. By dawn, Christmas Day, the storm was like an arm-weary heavyweight, still swinging, but without punch. A fair westerly finally replaced it and *Die Freiheit* caught it and was under sail. The sea threw up its spoils, and when they cleared Glen Head off the Donegal coast, they were sailing through hundreds of drowned sheep blown off the cliffs by the storm. The sheep floated, bobbing in the light swell, as innocent in death as they had been in life. When Terry caught Gudrun's eye, she looked away, back at the drowned herd.

They would make a landfall at Rathlin Island at around noon, December 26. They would meet their deadline.

CHAPTER 17

The Feast of Stephen

At one-thirty Burke folded his paper and got up from the table in the corner of the large barroom. There were only townspeople in the place, just as there had been for the past five days. A wide modern room, its business only picked up at one o'clock. He and the bartender had been alone from noon to one every day. Burke drank orange soda, and read the papers. Every day for an hour and a half, just in case they were early. He had seen no one who looked suspicious, no one man drinking by himself, no pair of men waiting around the hotel.

He gave the barman a short salute with his newspaper as he passed out to the lobby, happy to be away from the ersatz leather banquettes, the gaudy plastic Christmas tree, and the muzak which ran to lame steel guitar over a bolero beat.

Outside the hotel, across a narrow street, was a small park, and beyond that was the sea front. Rathlin Island's long white cliffs were shining four miles out in the winter sunlight and beyond, on the northern horizon, fourteen miles away across blue, white-capped water, was the gentle curve of Scotland. The Mull of Kintyre, reaching down from the mainland of Britain.

Christmas Eve. Thirty-fourth Street will be jammed with bundled people. The whole city will be rushing home and all the sidewalk Santa Clauses will be drunk, ringing their bells, calling Merry Christmas, Merry Christmas.

Burke walked off the porch and started up the hill along the sea front to his hotel. It was a clean Ulster town, seemingly unaffected by the troubles. Burke had been here a week, since the night of the seventeenth, and had been left alone by the town. He had told the proprietor of his hotel that he was a writer, up here for quiet to finish a book. The young fellow and his wife had tried, the first few days, to involve him in their life, but he had refused. Whatever was coming, Burke wanted to be alone and share it with no one.

Halfway up the hill was home. A beautiful old house, painted white with yellow trim, a delicate lattice-worked porch, and two bright globes at the entrance. Inside, off the hall, young Bradford, the proprietor, sat in the parlor with his wife having lunch before the wood fire. They invited him in to eat, but Burke declined and went up to his room off the hall lined with books. When he had checked in he had been given his choice of rooms. There were no other guests. Burke had chosen this one with a front view, and because just down the hall was a door leading to an outside set of stairs which descended to the alley next to the hotel where he could park the Fiat.

There was no lock on his door because, Mr. Bradford had told him, "students lost all the keys years ago so we've given up on locks and keys." Burke threw his trench coat on the bed and went to the table looking out on the short pier and long low Rathlin, L-shaped, gleaming in the fine afternoon. He started another letter to Anne, but couldn't find a second sentence. Out in the hall he grabbed a book, a life of Gladstone, and got into bed with it.

At eight o'clock Burke was in the dining room of the Royal Port Hotel. There was only one other party this Christmas Eve. A table across the room where three nuns, dressed in habits, were having dinner. He noticed one of them was older than the other two, and quite mad. She would fly into her soup with her spoon, splattering it on the table, on her habit. When one of her sisters cleaned her up she would stare at the hanging chandelier before attacking her bowl again. Tough duty for the two young ones, Burke thought. Babysitting for Mother Superior. Keeping her away from the convent during Holy Season.

He ate slowly. If only they had come today. The Provos must consider it safe. They're waiting until the twenty-sixth before they show. Boland has told them it's all theirs. I could have warned them. We all could get out alive. One more day. If they come tomorrow we'll make it. If they come on schedule—he wouldn't think about it—I'll just be there. I can't leave them.

Burke finished his wine and paid his bill. While he waited for change he looked over at the nun's table. The mad nun held her knife straight up in her fist, and still stared at the chandelier, while the other two sisters ate daintily, touching napkins to their lips after every bite.

He left the Royal Port, stepping out to the clear night. A group of girls, their faces bright in the cold air, passed, singing "God Rest Ye Merry Gentlemen." He lit a cigarette and listened as they went up the narrow street. Burke followed, hearing their giggles and young voices surging through the carol. Half a block from his hotel, he caught a glimpse of a man following him in the shiny glass storefront of the tobacconist. Burke turned. The man was in a hooded parka, twenty yards away, walking straight for him. Up the street the girls were just reaching the crest of the hill. The hotel's two globes shone white. Too far. Burke tossed his cigarette away and faced him.

The man stopped in front of him, pushed back the hood, and Burke looked into his face, remembering the widow's room that damp Dublin night in August. "Lafferty."

"Hello, Martin. Would you like to go for a drive with me? My car's just up here."

Burke followed him up past the hotel to a red Cortina. Lafferty opened the door for him and went around to the other side. The girls' voices continued to carry through the still night.

Lafferty unzipped his parka. There was a stench of tobacco smoke in the car. At Burke's feet was a wad of wax paper and two empty bottles of Harp lager. On the seat between them was a grease-spotted paper bag advertising a fish and chips parlor in Portrush. "How've you been keeping, yank?"

"What are you doing here, Lafferty?"

"Settling scores," he said, and drove out of Ballycastle toward Fair Head. There was a place to park just at the base of the cliff looking out on the sea, and the white lights of the village curving away. The dark coast of Scotland seemed to be hovering in a mist under a sky cold with stars. There was another car parked there, and when Lafferty swung in the headlights passed over it and they could see two heads separating quickly in the front seat. Lafferty shut the engine and turned out the lights. He looked over at the other car. "Lovers," he said. "I wouldn't mind a bit of that on a cold night. So, I expect you've been sort of lonely up here by yourself."

"I've done all right."

"I expect you have. John Boland told me you might be here. Did you hear about poor John?"

"No. What?"

"I blew his brains out last Saturday night. His body's in a ditch in Wicklow. Poor lad. Cigarette?"

Burke took it, not wanting it, but not wanting to refuse him either. Lafferty struck a match. "Why?" Burke asked.

"He was a traitor. He told me a few things before he departed. About you, and about this place. About Rúairí MacCurtain. Ever hear of that fellah?"

"No," Burke lied. The less Lafferty knew, the better, his instinct told him.

Lafferty turned away, the smoke flowing from his nostrils. His profile was blade sharp, from the cheap haircut to the tip of his scarred nose. "Rúairí's the boyo we want. He's the one who murdered Joe Walsh and Deirdre. Boland was going to let him get away with it. But not us, that right Martin?"

"I'm here to warn my friends, Lafferty. I have no scores to settle."

"Do you have a gun?"

"No."

"Christ," Lafferty said. "So you're going to warn them? What'll you do if the Provos start firin' a Lee-Enfield at you like they did Deirdre? Or take you out in a field for the Brits to find like they did Joe Walsh?" He slammed the steering wheel with his fist. "Bastards! What'll you do, yank?"

"I haven't seen anyone this past week."

He laughed. "You don't have the eyes for it. They're here all right."

"How long have you been here?"

"Three days. You never saw *me*, did you? They're here. Two of 'em. Over on a farm near Armoy with a big lorry to cart away that boatload that's comin'. Tom Strahan and Larry Canny, Belfast Provos, as tough as they come. The two lads who did Liam Cleary way back on the evening I met you. Remember that, Martin? With that headcase of a boy I was workin' with, the one who roughed you up. Remember?"

"I remember."

"Well, these two fellahs are waitin' for the boat. They don't think they have a care in the world since Boland told MacCurtain that we were through up here. But it's the last Christmas for those two. Tomorrow night they're finished. Are you interested?"

"No."

"Fair enough. I can handle it myself. I want to see you tomorrow night after the festivities. Is that all right? I'll come to your room."

"You know where I'm staying?"

"I'll come up the back way," he started the car and drove in silence to Ballycastle. Lafferty stopped two streets away from the hotel. "Are you going to mass tonight or tomorrow?" he asked.

"Why?"

"Because I'm goin' to midnight mass. I've got a jug we could dip into after mass, if you want."

"No thanks."

"Suit yourself," Lafferty said. "Christmas Eve midnight mass comes only once a year. I never miss it. Tomorrow night, Martin, I'll call on you."

Burke got out and watched the car driving away down Rathlin Road. He stood for awhile, looking blankly at a dark chemist shop, the shadows playing across a perfume display. Finally, he turned and walked through the back streets to the alley and up to his room. The hotel was quiet and dark.

The harsh calling of gulls and his room flooded with light when he woke. Christmas Day. Burke looked out the window. A boy dressed in his Sunday best was kicking a can along the street. His mother, dressed in a red wool coat and a wide red hat, took the boy by the arm and scolded him for scuffing his shoes.

He dressed, already exhausted. In the parlor, waiting for his breakfast, he looked down to see a cigarette in his hand. He didn't remember lighting it. A trace of a hangover. Too much wine with dinner last night. And those syrupy orange sodas in the bar during his daily vigil. He tossed the cigarette into the fire. "A happy Christmas, Mr. Thomas," young Bradford said, bringing his tray. "It's a fine morning again."

He was a big clumsy young man. Burke had never seen him when he wasn't smiling, seemingly a bit embarrassed about something. "I've saved some of Janey's cake for you, although it was a temptation to just gobble it all down myself." Burke looked up at his beaming face. "If you have no plans, Janey and I would love to have you join us for dinner."

"Thanks. But I have to keep working."

"Well, the offer's open. We'd hate to see you spend Christmas alone."

"Don't worry about me. I'll be fine, Mr. Bradford."

After breakfast Burke walked through the quiet village. A girl on a brand-new bicycle, in her church clothes, pedaling happily past. He walked over to the golf links and then down along the Margy River to the point where it meets the Carey River, and spent a long time watching the little rivers running together in the bright day. At noon he was back at the Royal Port. The doors to the bar were closed and locked. When he asked the receptionist, she told him that the bar was closed for Christmas. Burke bought three candy bars from her and a box of cigarettes.

Out to the small park across the road where he sat on a bench watching the entrance until one-thirty. Back in his room, he settled down to the archaic biographer's prose, and read all afternoon. At six o'clock Mr. Bradford brought him leftovers from their feast. Turkey, mashed potatoes and gravy, cranberries, peas, and plum pudding with hard sauce. He waited until the young man left him before flushing the meal down the toilet at the end of the hall. Back in his room he unwrapped a candy bar, and continued reading.

It was nearly eleven when the explosion boomed through the town. Burke went down to the porch of the hotel where Mr. Bradford and his wife stood in their robes. A lorry down the road was burning bright orange, the flames leaping incredibly high, and Burke could see people coming out of houses all up and down the street for a better look. The filthy smell of burning rubber came to them on the breeze. "Oh, God," Mrs. Bradford was saying, her arms wrapped around her, looking at the flames. "And on Christmas Day."

"I'll get dressed," Mr. Bradford said, "and see if anyone is injured."

Burke left the young woman and returned to his room. Lafferty was sitting at the table near the window in his parka. A half bottle of Bushmills lay on the bed. "Pretty, huh?" he said to Burke.

"Why? Why here?"

"Tom and Larry," Lafferty shook his head. "Poor lads. They'll be roastin' in that right now." He grinned. "Liam's avenged at least. Crack that jug there, Martin. I'm dry."

"Why here, Lafferty?"

"Bait," he said. "Bait for tomorrow."

Saturday, December 26, the Feast of St. Stephen, and Helen Mason, the daughter of the harbormaster of Rathlin Island, was walking to the post office when she saw the tall sail cutting through the mist in Church Bay. She held the letter in her hand, remembering what her father had always told her. If a vessel is sighted, drop everything and let him know. She ran back to the house, catching her father as he was just sitting down to a lunch of hot turkey sandwiches. "Good girl," he said when she told him. "Now run post that letter."

At one of the empty slips he waved a red towel, and they caught his message and brought the yawl expertly into port. She was a fine-looking craft. Mr. Mason loved all sailboats, but wooden ones were his favorite. The skipper was a young fellow, an American, shaking his hand on the pier as his blonde wife stayed on board, padlocking the doghouse door. "No need for that," Mr. Mason said.

"It's just habit for her," the American said.

"What brings you to Rathlin?"

"The birds," he said. "My wife's a nut about birds. We're due to see friends in Ballycastle, though. We won't be back until evening."

"Well," Mr. Mason said. "How're you going to cross?"

"We thought the dinghy."

Mr. Mason looked at the small yellow boat. "Oh no you're not. Take my launch there," he pointed at a long power boat. "I'll keep your beauty as collateral. I wouldn't let you cross in that wee thing. It's a good forty-five-minute crossing and these waters are like a woman. You never know what they're up to. Pardon me, missus."

"That's great. I can pay you for it. At least for the fuel."

"No, no. We'll look at your papers and settle on money when you return. The channel's marked now, and safety first, young man. This mist isn't too bad, but if it thickens, or the sea changes, you wait before you try and make it back. That's my house there. We'll be waitin' for you."

"Great. Thanks again."

He helped them into the launch with their three canvas bags, and gave a hand to the young woman. "You're coming from the South?" he asked her.

"That's right," she answered.

"Did you catch any of that storm?"

"Just the tail end," the American said.

Mr. Mason could see they were anxious to go. He told them how to run the launch, and that she faded to port under full power.

He waved them off into the light mist and returned to his lunch.

When they secured the harbormaster's boat and walked up off the pier into the village, four British soldiers were patrolling through the park. "I thought," O'Connor said to her, "they picked this town because it was safe."

"Something's wrong," Gudrun said. "It's gone wrong."

They walked into the Royal Port Hotel Bar and saw Burke behind a newspaper in the corner. There was a man and a woman at the bar. And at the far end, Lafferty drinking stout. A face like a bowl of frozen stew, Gudrun thought.

"Hello," Burke said, folding his paper as they sat across from him.

"Good news or bad?" Gudrun asked.

"The worst."

"Let me get a drink," Terry said. "Gudrun?"

"Bitter lemon."

"What're you drinking, Marty? Orange soda? Jesus, are you sick or something?"

Terry's smile, Burke thought. "I only start when my vigil is over. It's been a week of orange sodas."

Terry ordered a large Jameson's at the bar and the bitter lemon. While the barman poured, he exchanged nods with Lafferty. Back at the table he drank half the whiskey and said, "Go ahead, Marty."

Burke told them of the events of December 17, of John Boland's order to the I.S.A., his subsequent death at the hands of Lafferty, and the murder of the two Provos last night. "That's it," Gudrun said. "That's why the streets are full of soldiers. Why did he do it? Is he really as stupid as he looks?"

O'Connor had never seen her face this way. A wild expression. Fear. And rage. "Why?" she asked Burke once more.

"He wanted to draw more Provos here."

Gudrun shook her head quickly with disgust.

"Oh, right," Terry said. "He draws the Provos *and* the whole fucking British Army. What are we up to now?"

"There's a pub on Mary Street, further up into the town. Lafferty's reserved the back room for a meal where we can all talk."

"That sounds good," Terry said.

Burke nodded at Lafferty, and he zipped his parka and walked out. "Now, we should be careful going up there. One of us should wait a few minutes before leaving. We don't want a parade going up."

"Good," Gudrun said. "I'll wait. Leave me your paper."

Burke gave her directions to the pub and told her to wait five minutes. Terry drank off the last of the Irish, hitched his rucksack on his shoulder, and they walked out, Burke giving his daily salute to the barman.

The streets were busy with people. It was warmer than yesterday, still bright, but a trace of fog hung over the town, and out to sea the mist was just beginning to burn away. Walking up North Street O'Connor saw a new Suzuki parked across the road. "Let's check out that bike."

"Sure," Burke said. "We can wait for her here."

It was a monster of a bike. Too bad the owner was turning it into a junkwagon with saddlebags, mirrors, and pinstripes. The clean powerful lines were enough.

Burke looked down the street. There was no sign of her yet. Back up in the town he saw Lafferty near Quay Road, standing on the corner, smoking a cigarette. Beyond him, three blocks away, a squad of the King's Own Scottish Borderers were patrolling the street. Their regiment was one of the most experienced of the war. Normally their duty was patrolling the Falls Road of Belfast, but they'd been transported up via helicopter when the first report had come in about the burning lorry holding the two men. They had been on the streets of Ballycastle since a little after midnight. Two of them walked in the street next to the parked cars, and two walked along the sidewalk. Their Self-Loading Rifles were held low, and their eyes were constantly moving over every pedestrian, every car, every roof.

Terry bent down to see the guts of the bike. There were shouts up the street. A man shouting. Burke saw people running. There was Lafferty, his long arm held straight out and the .45 aimed across the street at a parked gray Rover. "MacCurtain!" Lafferty was screaming. "A rat to the cheese!" Burke and O'Connor saw two men sitting in the Rover. The driver had the flat smooth face of a boxer who leads with his nose. Lafferty shot three times, killing the driver through the windshield. The remaining people on the street got down on the pavement, and hugged entranceways to shops. Lafferty was walking across the street toward the Rover, his weapon still far out in front of him, when the Kosbies came down the street on a dead run, fanned out, two on each side. Lafferty fired a shot which hit the side door, and then was killed in a volley of shots from the soldiers as he continued to walk on. The soldiers quickly had MacCurtain out of the Rover lying spreadeagled in the middle of the street, face down. Burke saw him look up at Lafferty lying ten feet away. Blood oozing brightly on the gray pavement. One of the soldiers held his SLR in one hand, the barrel in MacCurtain's sandy hair, pushing his face to the street. He kicked at his legs with his boot, forcing them wider.

"Take care, Marty," O'Connor said.

Burke turned to him. He was walking away down the street. Burke followed and caught his arm. "Let me go, man. Either come with me or not."

"Halt! You there. Halt!"

O'Connor shrugged Burke's arm away and wheeled around, shedding the rucksack and holding up the M-10. He let go a burst, high over the soldiers, and then ran down into North Street. Burke took a step after him, and then turned back toward the soldiers, waving his arms, shouting.

The soldier who had been guarding MacCurtain had jumped out to the street when the M-10 opened up. Lying prone now, he took aim at the lone figure down the street. He couldn't make out what the man was saying. He was a good soldier, twenty-six, from Glasgow, doing his third tour in Ulster. The procedure, when shots were fired, was do two things: (a) find cover; and, (b) secure the area. This was guerrilla war. Friend and foe looked the same. The soldier had seen the man down the street with the other terrorist. It all happened quickly.

The soldier fired four rounds and all found their target. The man spun one way, and then the other, as the slugs caught either side of his chest. He fell back in the street. When the squad approached him he was lying face down, his hands clawing at the pavement.

A boot went under his shoulder and rolled him over on his back. Two rifles were trained on him. Martin had one more breath, and died.

Racing down to the pier, sheltered from the town by a slope of hedges, across the smooth flat stones, and arriving at the slip to find the launch gone. He looked out at the empty bay, the fog hovering. Nothing. On the road above the pier he saw flat brown berets bobbing along above the hedges, and heard the sound of boots falling heavily on the stones. There was a way out up through them to the road. He'd have to shoot through, and pray for a car to be passing. Terry whirled around again to the rolling sea, innocent in the sun. Gone. And then tossed the M-10 into the water. Turning back, he put his hands up high over his head as the soldiers moved out from the cover of the hedges and onto the open pier.

She slowed the launch coming across Church Bay and motored into the harbor. There was no one on shore. Watching the harbormaster's house, she secured the launch and left a twenty pound note fastened with a rubber band around the throttle. She took her bag up and walked down the pier to *Die Freiheit*. Within minutes she was motoring out. She hauled up the mainsail, and was away, going south to the tip of the island, around Rue Point, and then northeast into the North Channel.

The day was growing warmer, but the mist still lingered over the sea. Four miles out Gudrun anchored and began the long difficult job of bringing up the arms, crate by crate, and dumping them overboard. At the final splash, she sat on the gunwale and stared at the bubbles rushing up. Soon the sea covered the spot, rolling over into the same vast unchanging blue. She had lived with them since July, and had carried them from the busy harbor of Hamburg to the northern tip of Ireland. Gone now. Forever.

There was ten miles of sea to cross before a landfall. She hauled in the anchor, and set sail for Scotland. Father's house tonight, she told herself. The forty-five footer ran lightly in the foggy day.

EPILOGUE

The city cold and dark in a February morning. The sky low over the rooftops and in the streets the gaseous smell of coal smoke. Soot puffing up and feather floating down. A city like any other in the northern part of the British Isles in winter. Glasgow. Liverpool. Newcastle.

Belfast. Dirty and hard headed. Busy with itself. The weather omnipresent and miserable as guilt.

Garrett Costello had slept on the train up from Dublin. The night before he'd suffered all the petty tortures of insomnia. Falling asleep with no awareness of it approaching and then waking ten minutes later, depressed, exhausted. Lying next to the warmth of his wife's body for hours, concentrating on the sounds of the house settling and the now and again noise of the street. Until seven o'clock. The day announced in darkness by the rattle and clink of the milkman.

On the train to Belfast he dreamed. He was playing golf with Joseph Walsh. The old man's caddy was Peter Farrell who never spoke and hid his face when Garrett looked at him. He did this, Garrett knew, because he was dead. It was a silly dream, Garrett thought when he woke, and it hadn't bothered him. He had slept deeply for more than an hour, and that was a blessing.

Constable George Faulkner of the Royal Ulster Constabulary met him at the station and drove him to Crumlin Road Jail. Faulkner was a pleasant enough fellow, but Garrett put that down to his position in the public relations section of the RUC. George Faulkner would have been pleasant to Idi Amin if he was told to. The policeman from the Republic and the policeman from the British province of Northern Ireland both knew there was little cooperation between the two services. The Republic had asked for O'Connor to be extradited to stand trial for murder at Kildare, a

381

much more serious charge than the one he was convicted of in the North. But the request was refused. The American had been in custody seven weeks now, and Garrett was the first official from the Republic to see him. The RUC didn't share. He's our meat, Belfast said to Dublin, and after we've cooked him, you can have a piece.

They walked across the empty football pitch toward the stone walls of the prison wings. Faulkner said they'd had trouble with the yank. The Provo inmates, who made up the majority of the political prisoners, considered O'Connor an enemy. Rúairí MacCurtain was here, and had taken command of the Provo inmates. The I.S.A. prisoners didn't consider the American part of their struggle. And they were leaderless. They had to look after their own skins, and would not protect the new boy. O'Connor had been attacked in the prison laundry. A blade, made from a tin of soup, had been used on him. He was lucky, and received only a nasty cut. They'd had to isolate him after that. He now spent twenty-two hours of every day in his cell.

When O'Connor was brought into the interrogation room, and sat across the table, Garrett was struck by how much older he looked than thirty-one. It might have been the gray hair, cut close to his skull. There was a scar running in a half circle from his left eyebrow through the meat of the cheek and ending at the left nostril, split open and far from healed. His eyes seemed washed out. That was due to the heavy doses of tranquillizers "difficult prisoners" were forced to take daily. Terry sat straight, his hands on his knees, and stared. "Who are you?"

"Garrett Costello, Terry. Irish Special Branch."

"Oh, yeah. I've been waiting for you. I've been entertained by everybody else. The RUC, they spent a lot of time with me. The Army. A few Brits in plainclothes. They've kept me busy," he smiled.

Garrett began to question him, going through a list he and other officers had written in Dublin. They were mainly concerned with the relations between the Provisionals and the Irish Socialist Army. Terry said he knew nothing, but Garrett continued. There were questions about Gudrun Böhm. Terry responded that he knew nothing about her whereabouts. Garrett moved on to the subject of where and how they purchased the weapons that were used at Kildare and Ballycastle.

"You'll have to ask her about that," the American said. "Or Peter Farrell. Is he still singing for you guys?"

"Farrell is dead."

"No shit?" Terry said. It was hard to tell if he was interested or not. His eyes were dull and had no depth. "How'd he buy it?"

"Suicide," Garrett said.

"Yeah?"

Garrett put his notes down. "What're you going to do with your life?"

"My life? Are you serious? I've got twenty-one years to do." He laughed. "That's what I'm going to do."

"Do you feel any remorse?"

"For what?"

"For killing innocent people. For using a foreign country as a battlefield."

"Morality is a social invention."

"Is that supposed to be profound?"

"It's the truth, pal. Don't judge me. I don't judge you. Or the rest of the motherfuckers who've worked me over. I've got no remorse. I've got twenty-one years to do."

"Martin Burke—" Garrett began.

Life leapt in the American's face. Anger. "What about him?"

"You know he's dead?"

"I know he was murdered. That he wasn't armed. I know that, yeah."

Garrett said nothing. He watched the anger cool, and the scarred face grow dreamy again. Terry looked down at his hands. "Can you do me a favor?"

"What?"

"There's his wife. Marty's wife. Could you get in touch with her?"

"I already have. I've written to her about his death."

"You know her?"

"I did, yes."

"You must be one good cop, huh?"

"If I was you'd be in prison in the Republic. For murder."

The American's spacey smile, again. "Then we're both not so hot at what we do, right?"

"We're both failures. But my failure is worse than yours."

After O'Connor was led away, Faulkner asked if he wouldn't

mind waiting until the afternoon to interview MacCurtain. He could use the warden's facilities until the interview was organized. Garrett thanked him and said he'd like some air. Out on the football pitch, four prisoners were kicking a ball around as Garrett walked along the end line. They were having fun. Laughing. Excited as boys. When they noticed the tall man watching them they went quiet and cold, and took the ball up to the other end where they continued their game.

Ambrose Clancy was born in Brooklyn in 1948. His stories, journalism, and travel writing have been published on both sides of the Atlantic.